ELLERY QUEEN'S ELEVEN DEADLY SINS

STORIES FROM ELLERY QUEEN'S MYSTERY MAGAZINE

Edited by Eleanor Sullivan

The majority of stories in this anthology were collected from issues of *Ellery Queen's Mystery Magazine*, edited by Eleanor Sullivan.

URBANA FREE LIBRARY

WALKER AND COMPANY
NEW YORK

M STORIES
ELL
5-91 BT 2195

Copyright © 1991 by Davis Publications, Inc.

All rights reserved. No part of this book may be reproduced or transmitted in
any form or by any means, electronic or mechanical, including photocopying,
recording, or by any information storage and retrieval system, without
permission in writing from the Publisher.

All the characters and events portrayed in these stories are fictitious.

First published in the United States of America in 1991
by Walker Publishing Company, Inc.

Published simultaneously in Canada by Thomas Allen & Son
Canada, Limited, Markham, Ontario

Library of Congress Cataloging-in-Publication Data

Ellery Queen's eleven deadly sins / edited by Eleanor Sullivan.
p. cm. -- / (Stories from Ellery Queen's mystery magazine)
ISBN 0-8027-5779-0
1. Detective and mystery stories. I. Sullivan, Eleanor.
II. Ellery Queen's mystery magazine. III. Series: Stories from
Ellery Queen's mystery magazine.
PN6120.95.D45E434 1991
813'.087208--dc20   90-19406
                                                      CIP

Printed in the United States of America

2   4   6   8   10   9   7   5   3   1

ELLERY QUEEN'S ELEVEN DEADLY SINS

STORIES FROM ELLERY QUEEN'S MYSTERY MAGAZINE

Also edited by Eleanor Sullivan

Murder on Cue
Ellery Queen's Bad Scenes
Ellery Queen's More Murder on Cue

Acknowledgments

Grateful acknowledgment is hereby made for permission to include the following:

"The Case of Mr. Pelham" by Anthony Armstrong, copyright 1940 by Esquire, Inc., reprinted by permission of Brandt & Brandt Literary Agents, Inc.

"Doors" by William Bankier, copyright © 1982 by Davis Publications, Inc., reprinted by permission of Curtis Brown, Ltd.

"The Woman I Envied" by George Baxt, copyright © 1982 by George Baxt, reprinted by permission of the author.

"The Ehrengraf Riposte" by Lawrence Block, copyright © 1978 by Davis Publications, Inc., reprinted by permission of Knox Burger Associates, Inc.

"Telling" by Elizabeth Bowen, copyright 1928 by Elizabeth Bowen, reprinted by permission of Curtis Brown, Ltd.

"The Garden of Smoke" by Gilbert K. Chesterton, copyright 1920 by G. K. Chesterton, renewed 1948. Reprinted by kind permission of A. P. Watt, Ltd., on behalf of the executors of the estate of Miss D. E. Collins.

"Girls and Boys Together" by Julia DeHahn, copyright © 1980 by Davis Publications, Inc., reprinted by permission of the author.

"The Betrayers" by Stanley Ellin, copyright 1953, renewed © 1981 by Stanley Ellin, reprinted by permission of Curtis Brown, Ltd.

"Heaven Can Wait" by C. B. Gilford, copyright 1953 by C. B. Gilford, reprinted by permission of Scott Meredith Literary Agency, Inc.

"The Perfect Plan" by James Hilton, copyright 1946 by Alice Hilton and Security–First National Bank of Los Angeles, reprinted by permission of John Farquharson, Ltd.

"The Photographer and the Butcher" by James Holding, copyright © 1973 by Davis Publications, Inc., reprinted by permission of Scott Meredith Literary Agency, Inc.

"The Accused" by Ellery Queen, copyright 1953 by Ellery Queen, reprinted by permission of Scott Meredith Literary Agency, Inc.

"The Raspberry Patch" by Berton Roueché, copyright © 1968 by Berton Roueché; originally appeared in *The Evergreen Review*. Reprinted by permission of the author.

"The Case of the Three Bicyclists" by Georges Simenon, copyright 1932 by Georges Simenon, reprinted by permission of the author.

"The Kindest Man in the World" by Henry Slesar, copyright © 1979 by Davis Publications, Inc., reprinted by permission of the author.

"The Great American Novel" by R. L. Stevens, copyright © 1975 by Davis Publications, Inc., reprinted by permission of the author.

"The Boy Wonder of Real Estate" by James M. Ullman, copyright © 1963 by Davis Publications, Inc., reprinted by permission of the author.

"Just Enough to Cover a Thumbnail" by Cornell Woolrich, copyright 1940 by Popular Publications, Inc., reprinted by permission of Scott Meredith Literary Agency, Inc.

CONTENTS

INTRODUCTION

Webster's defines sin as an offense against God—a misdeed, a fault. Patristic (not biblical) literature defines the seven capital—or deadly—sins as pride, covetousness, lust, anger, gluttony, envy, and sloth. In this anthology, in the manner of the monks of the Dark Ages who often devised their own lists of sin, we will propose four more in addition to the seven. (The Dark Ages—a term coined by the proud Fifteenth and Sixteenth Century intellectuals, who called their own "enlightened" age the Renaissance!)

Adding the four was not at all easy, the original seven already being as convoluted as sin itself. For example, does the virtue of piety, carried to an extreme, become a form of pride? (In the Ellery Queen story "The Accused," beginning on page 55, the narrator says, "That was one of the things Ellery liked about this case. The villain was something like a saint and the young hero could have used a timely kick in the pants.") Would you classify the love of money that is the root of all evil under lust or covetousness? Is fatal inaction or unbenign neglect the result of sloth or anger? You see the dilemma.

The silliest, most puzzling misdeed, we think, is plagiarism. Is it sloth, covetousness, envy, or greed that motivates someone to pass off another's work as his or her own? It happens to be something of an occupational hazard in our line of work, and a mystifying one. Pride, along with gluttony and sloth (our associate editor's two personal favorites), although they have their serious consequences, are probably the funniest of the seven. A friend of ours guards against the first by keeping taped to his shaving mirror an unflattering photograph of himself he's captioned "Why should the spirit of man be proud?"

In an entertaining and edifying interview, "Fran Lebowitz on Sin," in the November 1986 *Vogue,* Ann Arensberg and the acumenical author enjoyed the following exchange:

AA: What sin would you add to [the seven deadly sins]?

FL: Litigiousness. And the coining of phrases by the general public—the invention of modern words. "Accessing." Things like that.

AA: Have you ever met a truly evil person?

FL: In fact, more than one.

AA: How did you know they were evil? Did you call them evil immediately?

FL: You mean to their face? Not a good way to behave with an evil person; not a good tactic, with an evil person, to call him evil.

Then we have covetousness, which can induce the evil of blackmail or theft or muder. ("The covetous man is always in want," Horace wrote a few decades B.C.) And lust, which leads to violence and shattered lives and sometimes murder. And anger, which plays out to hate and revenge. And envy, which reveals itself in malice and lack of mercy. (In Dante's *Inferno,* the eyelids of the envious are sewn together. "Such punishment," writes Leslie H. Farber, "would have suited Onasander, who wrote in A.D. 49 that 'envy is a pain of mind that successful men cause their neighbors.' ")

For a more complete coverage of the range of iniquity we see in the world today—and in the stories in this collection—we therefore offer these additional four:

8. *Abuse.* Of drugs, of course. And of power, freedom, natural resources, other human beings. Waste.

9. *Cowardice.* James Russell Lowell wrote: "The coward stands aside, doubting in his abject spirit, till his Lord is crucified." We would venture that fear in itself is normal and healthy, but when physical or emotional fear (of scorn, of loss, of reprisal, of truth) causes fatal inaction or aggression it is hardly a blow for the angels.

10. *Cynicism.* British film producer David Puttnam (*Chariots of Fire, The Mission, The Killing Fields, Local Hero*) in a *World of Ideas* interview with Bill Moyers said, "The thing I loathe more than anything has become fashionable, which is cynicism. I think cynicism is a desperately destructive thing within society. . . . The people who make films like *Rambo* regard their

audience as a kind of lumpen proletariat who, as long as they turn up in sufficient numbers and pay their money at the box office, are totally ill-considered. And you're creating a society which is a different society than the one I think (a) you want and (b) in the long run you can afford to have."

You understand we're not talking about healthy skepticism. A real cynic—self-absorbed, calculating, disdainful, hype-minded—is someone quite likely to presume you guilty of *anything* before you're proven guilty or innocent. A cynic is someone you would not want to serve on your jury—let alone spend much time with. (In fact, you don't want to spend much time with anyone consumed by any of the vices on this black little list. As James Hilton says in one of the star turns in this collection, "But for the mischance of working for Sir George, [Scarsdale] would probably never have murdered anyone.")

11. *Deceit.* "Knavery's plain face is never seen till used," Betty Paris quotes Iago in "Girl and Boys Together." Manipulators, hypocrites, plotters, traitors, the knaves of the world cause the darkest kinds of mischief and, like Iago, delight in encouraging sin in others. They are like the tempter of mankind himself—and you all know who we're talking about.

Speaking of whom brings us to the happier subject of the antidotes to sin and temptation—virtue and redemption.

Virtue has been the butt of many a good joke. "Virtue is insufficient temptation," said George Bernard Shaw. "What is usually taken for virtue in middle age," actor Michael Caine is quoted as saying, "is fatigue." But, as most sins are obsessions, so, like Lloyd C. Douglas's "magnificent obsession," are most virtues. And virtue, like sin, *is* its own reward. In the brilliant last chapter of her book about mass-murderer Ted Bundy, *The Stranger Beside Me,* Ann Rule wrote: "Ted has no conscience. . . . 'Conscience doth make cowards of us all,' but conscience is what gives us our humanity. . . . Whatever the drawbacks are to be blessed with a conscience, the rewards are essential to living in a world with other human beings."

It is in this spirit of light and darkness—and their rewards—that we present the sixtieth Ellery Queen anthology. We cannot, of course, specify which sins are contained in which stories—that would be giving too much away (another cardinal sin, at

least with mystery readers)—but it should add to your enjoyment to recognize the sin central to each story. Given the
complexities of mystery fiction and of human nature, though,
you'll find that many of the stories will reflect more than one
sin—as well as more than one countervailing virtue.

   "Good" reading!

E.S.

ELLERY QUEEN'S ELEVEN DEADLY SINS

STORIES FROM ELLERY QUEEN'S MYSTERY MAGAZINE

STANLEY ELLIN
THE BETRAYERS

Between them was a wall. And since it was only a flimsy, jerrybuilt partition, a sounding board between apartments, Robert came to know the girl that way.

At first she was the sound of footsteps, the small firm rap of high heels moving in a pattern of activity around her room. She must be very young, he thought idly, because at the time he was deep in *Green Mansions*, pursuing the lustrous Rima through a labyrinth of Amazonian jungle. Later he came to know her voice, light and breathless when she spoke, warm and gay when she raised it in chorus to some popular song dinning from her radio. She must be very lovely, he thought then, and after that found himself listening deliberately, and falling more and more in love with her as he listened.

Her name was Amy, and there was a husband, too, a man called Vince who had a flat, unpleasant voice, and a sullen way about him. Occasionally there were quarrels which the man invariably ended by slamming the door of their room and thundering down the stairs as loud as he could. Then she would cry, a smothered whimpering, and Robert, standing close to the wall between them, would feel as if a hand had been thrust inside his chest and was twisting his heart. He would think wildly of the few steps that would take him to her door, the few words that would let her know he was her friend, was willing to do something—anything—to help her. Perhaps, meeting face to face, she would recognize his love. Perhaps—

So the thoughts whirled around and around, but Robert only stood there, taut with helplessness.

And there was no one to confide in, which made it that much harder. The only acquaintances he numbered in the world were the other men in his office, and they would never have understood. He worked, prosaically enough, in the credit department of one of the city's largest department stores, and too many

1

years there had ground the men around him to a fine edge of
cynicism. The business of digging into people's records, of
searching for the tax difficulties, the clandestine affairs with
expensive women, the touch of larceny in every human being—
all that was bound to have an effect, they told Robert, and if he
stayed on the job much longer he'd find it out for himself.

What would they tell him now? A pretty girl next door?
Husband's away most of the time? Go on, make yourself at
home!

How could he make them understand that that wasn't what
he was looking for? That what he wanted was someone to meet
his love halfway, someone to put an end to the cold loneliness
that settled in him like a stone during the dark hours each
night.

So he said nothing about it to anyone, but stayed close to the
wall, drawing from it what he could. And knowing the girl as
he had come to, he was not surprised when he finally saw her.
The mail for all the apartments was left on a table in the
downstairs hallway, and as he walked down the stairs to go to
work that morning he saw her take a letter from the table and
start up the stairway toward him.

There was never any question in his mind that this was the
girl. She was small and fragile and dark-haired, and all the
loveliness he had imagined in her from the other side of the
wall was there in her face. She was wearing a loose robe, and as
she passed him on the stairway she pulled the robe closer to
her breast and slipped by almost as if she were afraid of him.
He realized with a start that he had been staring unashamedly,
and with his face red he turned down the stairs to the street.
But he walked the rest of his way in a haze of wonderment.

He saw her a few times after that, always under the same
conditions, but it took weeks before he mustered enough
courage to stop at the foot of the stairs and turn to watch her
retreating form above: the lovely fine line of ankle, the round-
ness of calf, the curve of body pressing against the robe. And
then as she reached the head of the stairs, as if aware he was
watching her, she looked down at him and their eyes met.

For a heart-stopping moment Robert tried to understand
what he read in her face, and then her husband's voice came

flat and belligerent from the room. "Amy," it said, "what's holdin' you up!"—and she was gone, and the moment with her.

When he saw the husband, he marveled that she had chosen someone like that. A small, dapper gamecock of a man, he was good-looking in a hard way, but with the skin drawn so tight over his face that the cheekbones jutted sharply and the lips were drawn into a thin, menacing line. He glanced at Robert up and down out of the corners of blank eyes as they passed, and in that instant Robert understood part of what he had seen in the girl's face. This man was as dangerous as some half-tamed animal that would snap at any hand laid on him, no matter what its intent. Just being near him you could smell danger, as surely the girl did her every waking hour.

The violence in the man exploded one night with force enough to waken Robert from a deep sleep. It was not the pitch of the voice, Robert realized, sitting up half-dazed in bed, because the words were almost inaudible through the wall; it was the vicious intensity that was so frightening.

He slipped out of bed and laid his ear against the wall. Standing like that, his eyes closed while he strained to follow the choppy phrases, he could picture the couple facing each other as vividly as if the wall had dissolved before him.

"So you know," the man said. "So what?"

"—getting out!" the girl said.

"And then tell everybody? Tell the whole world?"

"I won't!" The girl was crying now. "I swear I won't!"

"Think I'd take a chance?" the man said, and then his voice turned soft and derisive. "Ten thousand dollars," he said. "Where else could I get it? Digging ditches?"

"Better that way! This way—I'm getting out!"

His answer was not delivered in words. It came in the form of a blow so hard that when she reeled back and struck the wall, the impact stung Robert's face. "Vince!" she screamed, the sound high and quavering with terror. "Don't, Vince!"

Every nerve in Robert was alive now with her pain as the next blow was struck. His fingernails dug into the wall at the hard-breathing noises of scuffling behind it as she was pulled away.

"Ahh, no!" she cried out, and then there was the sound of a breath being drawn hoarsely and agonizingly into lungs no longer responsive to it, the thud of a flaccid weight striking the floor, and suddenly silence. A terrible silence.

As if the wall itself were her cold, dead flesh, Robert recoiled from it, then stood staring at it in horror. His thoughts twisted and turned on themselves insanely, but out of them loomed one larger and larger so that he had to face it and recognize it.

She had been murdered, and as surely as though he had been standing there beside her he was a witness to it! He had been so close that if the wall were not there he could have reached out his hand and touched her. Done something to help her. Instead, he had waited like a fool until it was too late.

But there was still something to be done, he told himself wildly. As long as this madman in the next room had no idea there was a witness, he could still be taken red-handed. A call to the police, and in five minutes—

But before he could take the first nerveless step, Robert heard the room next door stealthily come to life again. There was a sound of surreptitious motion, of things being shifted from their place, then, clearly defined, a lifeless weight being pulled along the floor, and the cautious creaking of a door opened wide. It was that last sound which struck Robert with a sick comprehension of what was happening.

The murderer was a monster, but he was no fool. If he could safely dispose of the body now during these silent hours of the night, he was, to all intents and purposes, a man who had committed no crime at all!

At his door, Robert stopped short. From the hallway came the deliberate thump of feet finding their way down the stairs with the weight dragging behind them. The man had killed once. He was reckless enough in this crisis to risk being seen with his victim. What would such a man do to anyone who confronted him at such a time?

Robert leaned back against his door, his eyes closed tight, a choking constriction in his throat as if the man's hands were already around it. He was a coward, there was no way around it. Faced with the need to show courage, he had discovered he was a rank coward, and he saw the girl's face before him now, not with fear in it, but contempt.

But—and the thought gave him a quick sense of triumph—he could still go to the police. He saw himself doing it, and the sense of triumph faded away. He had heard some noises, and from that had constructed a murder. The body? There would be none. The murderer? None. Only a man whose wife had left him because he had quarreled with her. The accuser? A young man who had wild dreams. A perfect fool. In short, Robert himself.

It was only when he heard the click of the door downstairs that he stepped out into the hallway and started down, step by careful step. Halfway down, he saw it, a handkerchief, small and crumpled and blotched with an ugly stain. He picked it up gingerly and, holding it up toward the dim light overhead, let it fall open. The stain was bright sticky red, almost obscuring in one corner the word *Amy* carefully embroidered there. Blood. *Her* blood. Wouldn't that be evidence enough for anyone?

Sure, he could hear the policeman answer him jeeringly, *evidence of a nosebleed, all right,* and he could feel the despair churn in him.

It was the noise of the car that roused him, and he flew down the rest of the stairs—but too late. As he pressed his face to the curtain of the front door, the car roared away from the curb, its taillights gleaming like malevolent eyes, its license plate impossible to read in the dark. If he had only been an instant quicker, he raged at himself, only had sense enough to understand that the killer must use a car for his purpose, he could easily have identified it. Now even that chance was gone. Every chance was gone.

He was in his room pacing the floor feverishly when within a half hour he heard the furtive sounds of the murderer's return. And why not? Robert thought. He's gotten rid of her, he's safe now, he can go on as if nothing at all has happened.

If I were only someone who could go into that room and beat the truth out of him, the thought boiled on, or someone with such wealth or position that I would be listened to—

But all that was as unreal and vaporous as his passion for the girl had been. What weapon of vengeance could he possibly have at his command, a nobody working in a—

Robert felt the sudden realization wash over him in a cold wave. His eyes narrowed on the wall as if, word by word, the idea were being written on it in a minute hand.

Everyone has a touch of larceny in him—wasn't that what the old hands in his department were always saying? Everyone was suspect. Certainly the man next door, with his bent for violence, his talk of ten thousand dollars come by in some unlikely way, must have black marks on his record that the authorities, blind as they might be, could recognize and act on. If someone skilled in investigation were to strip the man's past down, layer by layer, justice would have to be done. That was the weapon: the dark past itself, stored away in the man, waiting only to be ignited!

Slowly and thoughtfully, Robert slipped the girl's crumpled handkerchief into an envelope and sealed it.

Then, straining to remember the exact words, he wrote down on paper the last violent duologue between murderer and victim. Paper and envelope both went into a drawer of his dresser, and the first step had been taken.

But then, Robert asked himself, what did he know about the man? His name was Vince, and that was all. Hardly information which could serve as the starting point of a search through the dark corridors of someone's past. There must be something more than that, something to serve as a lead.

It took Robert the rest of a sleepless night to hit on the idea of the landlady. A stout and sleepy-eyed woman whose only interest in life seemed to lie in the prompt collection of her rent, she still must have some information about the man. She occupied the rear apartment on the ground floor, and as early in the morning as he dared Robert knocked on her door.

She looked more sleepy-eyed than ever as she pondered his question. "Them?" she said at last. "That's the Sniders. Nice people, all right." She blinked at Robert. "Not having any trouble with them, are you?"

"No. Not at all. But is that all you can tell me about them? I mean, don't you know where they're from, or anything like that?"

The landlady shrugged. "I'm sure it's none of my business," she said loftily. "All I know is they pay on the first of the month right on the dot, and they're nice, respectable people."

He turned away from her heavily, and as he did so saw the street door close behind the postman. It was as if a miracle had been passed for him. The landlady was gone, he was all alone with that little heap of mail on the table, and there staring up at him was an envelope neatly addressed to Mrs. Vincent Snider.

All the way to his office he kept that envelope hidden away in an inside pocket, and it was only when he was locked in the seclusion of his cubicle that he carefully slit it open and studied its contents. A single page with only a few lines on it, a noncommittal message about the family's well-being, and the signature: *Your sister, Celia.* Not much to go on. But wait—there was a return address on the stationery, an address in a small upstate town.

Robert hesitated only a moment, then thrust letter and envelope into his pocket, straightened his jacket, and walked into the office of his superior.

Mr. Sprague, in charge of the department and consequently the most ulcerated and cynical member of it, regarded him dourly. "Yes?" he said.

"I'm sorry, sir," said Robert, "but I'll need a few days off. You see, there's been a sudden death."

Mr. Sprague sighed at this pebble cast into the smooth pool of his department's routine, but his face fell into the proper sympathetic lines.

"Somebody close?"

"Very close," said Robert.

The walk from the railroad station to the house was a short one. The house itself had a severe and forbidding air about it, as did the young woman who opened the door in answer to Robert's knock.

"Yes," she said, "my sister's name is Amy Snider. Her married name, that is. I'm Celia Thompson."

"What I'm looking for," Robert said, "is some information about her. About your sister."

The woman looked stricken. "Something's happened to her?"

"In a way," Robert said. He cleared his throat hard. "You see, she's disappeared from her apartment, and I'm looking into it. Now, if you—"

"You're from the police?"

"I'm acting for them," Robert said, and prayed that his ambiguity would serve in place of identification. The prayer was answered. The woman gestured him into the house, and sat down facing him in the bare and uninviting living room.

"I knew," the woman said, "I knew something would happen," and she rocked piteously from side to side in her chair.

Robert reached forward and touched her hand gently. "How did you know?"

"How? What else could you expect when you drive a child out of her home and slam the door in her face! When you throw her out into the world not even knowing how to take care of herself!"

Robert withdrew his hand abruptly. "You did that?"

"My father did it. *Her* father."

"But why?"

"If you knew him," the woman said. "A man who thinks anything pretty is sinful. A man who's so scared of hellfire and brimstone that he's kept us in it all our lives!

"When she started to get so pretty, and the boys pestering her all the time, he turned against her just like that. And when she had her trouble with that man, he threw her out of the house, bag and baggage. And if he knew I was writing letters to her," the woman said fearfully, "he'd throw me out, too. I can't even say her name in front of him, the way he is."

"Look," Robert said eagerly, "that man she had trouble with. Was that the one she married? Vincent Snider?"

"I don't know," the woman said vaguely. "I just don't know. Nobody knows except Amy and my father, the way it was kept such a secret. I didn't even know she was married until all of a sudden she wrote me a letter about it from the city."

"But if your father knows, I can talk to him about it."

"No! You can't! If he even knew I told you as much as I did—"

"But I can't let it go at that," Robert pleaded. "I have to find out about this man, and then maybe we can straighten everything out."

"All right," the woman said wearily, "there is somebody. But not my father—you've got to keep away from him for my sake. There's this teacher over at the high school, this Miss Benson. She's the one to see. And she liked Amy; she's the one Amy mails my letters to, so my father won't know. Maybe she'll tell you, even if she won't tell anybody else. I'll write you a note to her, and you go see her."

At the door he thanked her, and she regarded him with a hard, straight look. "You have to be pretty to get yourself in trouble," she said, "so it's something that'll never bother me. But you find Amy, and you make sure she's all right."

"Yes," Robert said. "I'll try."

At the school he was told that Miss Benson was the typewriting teacher, that she had classes until three, and that if he wished to speak to her alone he would have to wait until then. So for hours he fretfully walked the few main streets of the town, oblivious of the curious glances of passersby, and thinking of Amy. These were the streets she had known. These shop windows had mirrored her image. And, he thought with a sharp jealousy, not always alone. There had been boys. Attracted to her, as boys would be, but careless of her, never realizing the prize they had. But if he had known her then, if he could have been one of them—

At three o'clock he waited outside the school building until it had emptied and then went in eagerly. Miss Benson was a small woman, grey-haired and fluttering, almost lost among the grim ranks of hooded typewriters in the room. After Robert had explained himself and she had read Celia Thompson's note, she seemed ready to burst into tears. "It's wrong of her!" she said. "It's dreadfully wrong of her to send you to me. She must have known that."

"But why is it wrong?"

"Why?" Because she knows I don't want to talk about it to anyone. She knows what it would cost me if I did, that's why!"

"Look," Robert said patiently, "I'm not trying to find out what happened. I'm only trying to find out about this man Amy had trouble with, what his name is, where he comes from, where I can get more information about him."

"No," Miss Benson quavered, "I'm sorry."

"Sorry," Robert said angrily. "A girl disappears, this man may be at the bottom of it, and all you can do is say you're sorry!"

Miss Benson's jaw went slack. "You mean that he—that he *did* something to her?"

"Yes," Robert said, "he did," and had to quickly catch her arm as she swayed unsteadily, apparently on the verge of fainting.

"I should have known," she said lifelessly. "I should have known when it happened that it might come to this. But at the time—"

At the time the girl had been one of her students. A good student—not brilliant, mind you, but a nice girl always trying to do her best. And well brought up, too—not like so many of the young snips you get nowadays.

That very afternoon when it all happened, the girl herself had told Miss Benson she was going to the principal's office after school hours to get her program straightened out. Certainly if she meant to do anything wicked she wouldn't have mentioned that, would she? Wasn't that all the evidence anyone needed?

"Evidence?" Robert said in bewilderment.

Yes, evidence. There had been that screaming in the principal's office, and Miss Benson had been the only one left in the whole school. She had run to the office, flung open the door, and that was how she found them. The girl sobbing hysterically, her dress torn halfway down, Mr. Price standing behind her, glaring at the open door, at the incredulous Miss Benson.

"Mr. Price?" Robert said. He had the sense of swimming numbly through some gelatinous depths, unable to see anything clearly.

Mr. Price, the principal, of course. He stood glaring at her, his face ashen. Then the girl had fled through the door and Mr. Price had taken one step after her, but had stopped short. He had pulled Miss Benson into the office and closed the door, and then he had talked to her.

The long and the short of what he told her was that the girl was a wanton. She had waltzed into his office, threatened him with blackmail, and when he had put her into her place she had artfully acted out her little scene. But he would be merciful, very merciful. Rather than call in the authorities and blacken the name of the school and of her decent, respectable father, he would simply expel her and advise her father to get her out of town promptly.

And Mr. Price had remarked meaningfully that it was a lucky thing indeed that Miss Benson had walked in just in time to be his witness. Although if Miss Benson failed him as a witness it could be highly unlucky for her.

"And he meant it," Miss Benson said bitterly. "It's his family runs the town and everything in it. If I said anything of what I really thought, if I dared open my mouth, I'd never get another job anywhere. But I should have talked up, I know I should have, especially after what happened next."

She had managed to get back to her room at the far end of the corridor, although she had no idea where she got the strength. And as soon as she had entered the room, she saw the girl there, lying on the floor beneath the bulletin board from which usually hung the sharp cutting scissors. But the scissors were in the girl's clenched fist as she lay there, and blood over everything. All that blood over everything.

"She was like that," Miss Benson said dully. "If you reprimanded her for even the littlest thing she looked like she wanted to sink through the floor, to die on the spot. And after what she went through, it must have been the first thing in her head: just to get rid of herself. It was a mercy of God that she didn't succeed then and there."

It was Miss Benson who got the doctor, a discreet man who asked no questions, and it was she who tended the girl after her father had barred his door to her.

"And when she could get around," Miss Benson said, "I placed her with this office over at the county seat. She wasn't graduated, of course, or really expert, but I gave her a letter explaining she had been in some trouble and needed a helping hand, and they gave her a job."

Miss Benson dug her fingers into her forehead. "If I had only talked up when I should have. I should have known he'd never feel safe, that he'd hound her and hound her until he—"

"But he isn't the one!" Robert said hoarsely. "He isn't the right man at all!"

She looked at him wonderingly. "But you said—"

"No," Robert ssaid helplessly. "I'm looking for someone else. A different man altogether."

She shrank back. "You've been trying to fool me."

"I swear I haven't."

"But it doesn't matter," she whispered. "If you say a word about this, nobody'll believe you. I'll tell them you were lying, you made the whole thing up."

"You won't have to," Robert said. "All you have to do is tell me where you sent her for that job. If you do that you can forget everything else."

She hesitated, studying his face with bright, frightened eyes. "All right," she said at last. "All right."

He was about to go when she placed her hand anxiously on his arm. "Please," she said. "You don't think unkindly of me because of all this, do you?"

"No," Robert said, "I don't have the right to."

The bus trip which filled the remainder of the day was a wearing one, the hotel bed that night was no great improvement over the bus seat, and Mr. Pardee of Grace, Grace, & Pardee seemed to Robert the hardest of all to take. He was a cheery man, too loud and florid to be properly contained by his small office.

He studied Robert's business card with interest. "Credit research, eh?" he said admiringly. "Wonderful how you fellas track 'em down wherever they are. Sort of a Northwest Mounted Police just working to keep business healthy, that's what it comes to, doesn't it? And anything I can do to help—"

Yes, he remembered the girl very well.

"Just about the prettiest little thing we ever had around here," he said pensively. "Didn't know much about her job, of course, but you got your money's worth just watching her walk around the office."

Robert managed to keep his teeth clenched. "Was there any man she seemed interested in? Someone around the office, maybe, who wouldn't be working here anymore? Or even someone outside you could tell me about?"

Mr. Pardee studied the ceiling with narrowed eyes. "No," he said, "nobody I can think of. Must have been plenty of men after her, but you'd never get anything out of her about it. Not with the way she was so secretive and all. Matter of fact, her being that way was one of the things that made all the trouble."

"Trouble?"

"Oh, nothing serious. Somebody was picking the petty cash box every so often, and what with all the rest of the office being so friendly except her it looked like she might be the one. And then that letter she brought saying she had already been in some trouble—well, we just had to let her go.

"Later on," continued Mr. Pardee pleasantly, "when we found out it wasn't her after all, it was too late. We didn't know where to get in touch with her." He snapped his fingers loudly. "Gone, just like that."

Robert drew a deep breath to steady himself. "But there must be somebody in the office who knew her," he pleaded. "Maybe some girl she talked to."

"Oh, that," said Mr. Pardee. "Well, as I said, she wasn't friendly, but now and then she did have her head together with Jenny Rizzo over at the switchboard. If you want to talk to Jenny go right ahead. Anything I can do to help—"

But it was Jenny Rizzo who helped him. A plain girl dressed in defiant bad taste, she studied him with impersonal interest and told him coolly that she had nothing to say about Amy. The kid had taken enough kicking around. It was about time they let her alone.

"I'm not interested in her," Robert said. "I'm trying to find out about the man she married. Someone named Vincent Snider. Did you know about him?"

From the stricken look on her face, Robert realized exultantly that she did.

"Him!" she said. "So she went and married him anyhow!"

"What about it?"

"What about it? I told her a hundred times he was no good. I told her, Just stay away from him."

"Why?"

"Because I know his kind! Sharp stuff hanging around with money in his pocket, you never knew where it came from! The

kind of guy's always pulling fast deals, but he's too smart to get
caught!"

"How well did you know him?"

"How well? I knew him from the time he was a kid around
my neighborhood here. Look." Jenny dug into a desk drawer
deep-laden with personal possessions. She came out with a
handful of snapshots, which she thrust at Robert. "We even used
to double-date together, Vince and Amy, and me and my
boyfriend. Plenty of times I told her right in front of Vince that
he was no good, but he gave her such a line she wouldn't even
listen. She was like a baby that way—anybody was nice to her,
she'd go overboard."

They were not good photographs, but there were Vince and
Amy clearly recognizable.

"Could I have one of these?" Robert asked, his voice elabo-
rately casual.

Jenny shrugged. "Go ahead and help yourself," she said, and
Robert did.

"Then what happened?" he said. "I mean, to Vince and Amy?"

"You got me there. After she got fired, they both took off. She
said something about Vince getting a job downstate a ways, in
Sutton, and that was the last I saw of them. I could just see him
working at anything honest, but the way she said it she must
have believed him. Anyhow, I never heard from her after that."

"Could you remember exactly when you saw her last? That
time she told you they were going to Sutton?"

Jenny could and did.

She might have remembered more, but Robert was out of the
door by then, leaving her gaping after him, her mouth wide
open in surprise.

The trip to Sutton was barely an hour by bus, but it took
another hour before Robert was seated at a large table with the
Sutton newspaper files laid out before him. The town's newspaper was a large and respectable one, its files orderly and well
kept. And two days after the date Jenny Rizzo had given him
there was the news Robert had hoped to find. Headline news
emblazoned all across the top of the first page.

Ten thousand dollars stolen, the news report said. A daring

lone bandit had walked into the Sutton Bank and Trust, had bearded the manager without a soul around knowing it, and had calmly walked out with a small valise containing ten thousand dollars in currency. The police were on the trail. An arrest was expected momentarily.

Robert traced through later dates with his hands shaking. The police had given up in their efforts. No arrest was ever made.

Robert had carefully scissored the photograph so that Vince now stood alone in the picture. The bank manager irritably looked at the picture, and then swallowed hard.

"It's him!" he told Robert incredulously. "That's the man! I'd know him anywhere. If I can get my hands on him—"

"There's something you'll have to do first," said Robert.

"I'm not making any deals," the manager protested. "I want him, and I want every penny of the money he's got left."

"I'm not talking about deals," Robert said. "All you have to do is put down on paper that you positively identify this man as the one who robbed the bank. If you do that, the police'll have him for you tomorrow."

"That's all?" the man said suspiciously.

"That's all," Robert said.

He sat again in the familiar room—the papers, the evidence, arranged before him. His one remaining fear had been that in his absence the murderer had somehow taken alarm and fled. He had not breathed easy until the first small, surreptitious noises from next door made clear that things were as he had left them.

Now he carefully studied all the notes he had painstakingly prepared, all the reports of conversations held. It was all here, enough to see justice done, but it was more than that, he told himself bitterly. It was the portrait of a girl who, step by step, had been driven through a pattern of betrayal.

Every man she had dealt with had been an agent of betrayal. Father, school principal, employer, and finally her husband, each was guilty in his turn. Jenny Rizzo's words rang loud in Robert's ears. "Anybody was nice to her she'd go overboard." If he had spoken, if he had moved, he could have been the one.

When she turned at the top of the stairs to look at him, she might have been waiting for him to speak or move. Now it was too late, and there was no way of letting her know what these papers meant, what he had done for her.

The police were everything Robert had expected until they read the bank manager's statement. Then they read and reread the statement, they looked at the photograph, and they courteously passed Robert from hand to hand until finally there was a door marked *Lieutenant Kyserling*, and behind it a slender, soft-spoken man.

It was a long story—Robert had not realized until then how long it was or how many details there were to explain—but he told it from start to finish without interruption. At its conclusion, Kyserling took the papers, the handkerchief, and the photograph, and pored over them. Then he looked at Robert curiously.

"It's all here," he said. "The only thing you left out is why you did it—why you went to all this trouble. What's your stake in this?"

It wasn't easy to have your most private dream exposed to a complete stranger. Robert choked on the words. "It's because of her. The way I felt about her."

"Oh." Kyserling nodded understandingly. "Making time with her?"

"No," Robert said angrily. "We never even spoke to each other!"

Kyserling tapped his fingers gently on the papers before him.

"Well," he said, "it's none of my business, anyhow. But you've done a pretty job for us. Very pretty. Matter of fact, yesterday we turned up the body in a car parked a few blocks away from your place. The car was stolen a month ago. There wasn't a stitch of identification on the clothing or anything—all we got is a body with a big wound in it. This business could have stayed up in the air for a hundred years if it wasn't for you walking in with a perfect case made out from A to Z."

"I'm glad," Robert said. "That's the way I wanted it."

"Yeah," Kyserling said. "Any time you want a job on the force you just come and see me."

Then he was gone from the office for a long while, and when he returned it was in the company of a big, stolid plainclothesman who smiled grimly.

"We're going to wrap it up now," Kyserling told Robert, and gestured at the man.

They went softly up the stairs of the house and stood to the side of the door while Kyserling laid his ear against it for some assurance of sound. Then he briskly nodded to the plainclothesman and rapped hard.

"Open up!" he called. "It's the police."

There was an ear-ringing silence, and Robert's mouth went dry as he saw Kyserling and the plainclothesman slip the chill blue steel of revolvers from their shoulder holsters.

"I got no use for these cute little games," growled Kyserling, and suddenly raised his foot and smashed the heel of his shoe hard against the lock of the door. The door burst open. Robert cowered back against the balustrade of the staircase—

And then he saw her.

She stood in the middle of the room facing him wildly, the same look on her face, he knew in that fantastic moment, that she must have worn each time she came face to face with a betrayer exposed. Then she took one backward step, and suddenly whirled toward the window.

"Ahh, no!" she cried, as Robert had heard her cry it out once before, and then was gone through the window in a sheet of broken glass. Her voice rose in a single despairing shriek and then was suddenly and mercifully silent.

Robert stood there, the salt of sweat suddenly in his eyes, the salt of blood on his lips. It was an infinity of distance to the window, but he finally got there, and had to thrust Kyserling aside to look down.

She lay crumpled on the sidewalk, and the thick black hair in loose disorder around her face shrouded her from the eyes of the curious.

The plainclothesman was gone, but Kyserling was still there watching Robert with sympathetic eyes.

"I thought he'd killed her," Robert whispered. "I could swear he had killed her!"

"It was his body we found," said Kyserling. "She was the one who did it."

"But why didn't you tell me?" Robert begged. "Why didn't you let me know!"

Kyserling looked at him wisely. "Yeah?" he said. "And then what? You tip her off so that she gets away—then we really got troubles."

There could be no answer to that. None at all.

"She just cracked up," Kyserling said reasonably. "Holed up here like she was, not knowing which way to turn, nobody she could trust. It was in the cards. You had nothing to do with it."

He went downstairs then, and Robert was alone in her room. He looked around it slowly, at all the things that were left of her, and then very deliberately picked up a chair, held it high over his head, and with all his strength smashed it against the wall.

WILLIAM BANKIER

DOORS

Joe Conroy stood at the foot of the stairway and called up into the darkness. "Aren't you coming down for coffee?"

"I'm not going with you this morning." His wife's voice was muffled behind the bedroom door. "I can't go back there."

"The magistrate brings in his decision today. It won't look good if you aren't there."

"Then it won't look good."

Conroy stared at a threadbare patch in the carpet. The quotation for having new broadloom installed was among the sheaf of bills stacked beside the breadbox. The estimate was three times what he could afford. With inflation, it would be fifteen percent higher next year. These were the good times.

He walked upstairs, went to the door of his wife's bedroom, and put his lips close to the panel. "Clara, don't leave me to do this alone."

"I want to sleep. Then I have to go and get the kids, Rebecca can't keep them any longer."

"Are you bringing them home?"

"I'll have to take taxis. I'll need money. Leave the checkbook on the kitchen table."

"Clara, are you bringing Lenny and Mark *home?*"

The telephone rang. Conroy listened to his wife answering on the extension. It sounded as if Chuck Hutchison was coming around to pick him up in the car. Clara confirmed this when she hung up. "He's on his way."

The closed door confronting Conroy seemed to extend to infinity in every direction. It had a personality—the door was smug and without sympathy. Sleeping in separate rooms was a bad thing. He had never enjoyed being down the hall in the small back room. But Clara slept so lightly, and a few years ago he had begun tossing and turning—or so she said. All he had was her word for it, but why else would she punch him awake in the middle of the night, bringing him out of what he thought was deep sleep? The drawn face, hollow eyes glaring at him, half-lit by the bedside lamp. "Can't you lie still?" she had hissed at him, keeping her voice down, reminding him of the two young boys in the next room.

He lay back, heart pounding, furious, yet sorry for her at the same time. She was not happy. And to Conroy's way of thinking, that was Conroy's fault.

He gave up on achieving his wife's companionship for this final day in court and went downstairs to wait for Hutchison. He put on his boots, then his raincoat, buttoned it in front of the long oak mirror in the living room, turning his head to inspect his haircut. He had dead hair. The short grey strands refused to comb flat as they had done in the past. Following a football game, he used to shower and comb it wet to emerge from the dressing room bruised and clean and gleaming.

The girls would be there, the guys would gather them up. Then came drinking and dancing and singing and once in a while a glorious punchup in the parking lot. "If you can't win the game, win the fight." Who had given Conroy that piece of advice? He remembered who it was. His father, bent over a table covered with papers, eyes focusing with difficulty through thick glasses on young Joe poised to say goodbye with his schoolbooks under one arm and his football helmet crooked in the other.

"Can you come to the game, Dad?"

"No time for games, son. An accountant's work is never done. My clients are a bunch of crooks. If I don't hide their swindles, we'll all go to jail."

A car pulled up outside the house. Conroy went to the window and recognized Chuck Hutchison's ancient sedan. With its pattern of patches where he had hammered out dents and applied undercoat, the vehicle looked camouflaged like a World War II staff car. Conroy went to the foot of the stairs. "I'm off, Clara!"

Silence.

Clara Conroy listened to her husband's movements downstairs, terminated by the slam of the front door. She sat up, punching two pillows into a support for her head and shoulders, then switched on the bedside lamp so she could see to dial the telephone.

"Rebecca, it's me. He's just left."

Rebecca's voice was half-obscured by the shrill clamor of children taking each other on. "Are you packed?"

"Mostly. I should be there by noon."

"Soup and a sandwich. You've been warned."

"Can we get away as soon as we've eaten? I want to be gone before Joe gets home."

"I'm with you. It's the car, though. The muffler people promised me for two o'clock but I'll believe that when it happens."

"I'm nervous about what Joe may do."

"Don't worry. By the time he finds out you're gone we'll be a long way down the road."

Clara put down the telephone. She looked at the mosaic of snapshots in small individual frames on the wall beside the bed. Joe in skates on the rink he had built in the back yard. Lenny in his sea-cadet uniform. Mark in the mortarboard the nursery school put on him when he graduated. Herself crouching on the front steps with the boys on either side, possessive arms drawing them close.

The answer would have been for her never to have married Joe in the first place. She liked older men and had pursued this one with her customary tenacity. Then almost from day one of the marriage, she had sensed her mistake. He was an authoritarian who disapproved of most of the activities that gave her pleasure. It was like having a second father.

On the way downtown to the courthouse, Joe asked Chuck how he thought the verdict was going to go. Chuck seemed to chew the question along with his quid of gum. His hat brim almost covered his eyes, which meant he had to hold his chin up at an aggressive angle. "The magistrate will let us off," he said. "What else can he do?"

"He can put us in jail."

"You're kidding. With jails crowded the way they are and the media full of campaigns to reduce the prison population, he won't even suspend us."

"You think not?"

"They haven't got enough guards as it is. They can't recruit decent candidates to train for the prison service. Not with the conditions we have to work under and the lousy pay. So he's going to suspend two experienced guards? Never."

"I wish I had your confidence."

The car stopped at a traffic light. Hutchison took the gum from his mouth. "You can have it," he said, pressing the gum onto Conroy's forehead.

It was a typically outrageous, disgusting, hilarious Hutchison act. Conroy could laugh or be sick or bring his elbow sharply against the side of his companion's head, stunning him, perhaps killing him. He experienced all these inclinations. In the end, as the car pulled away, he did nothing but sat there, solemn and silent, being driven to court by his fellow-accused in a rattletrap tumbril of a car with a gob of wet chewing gum stuck to his forehead.

The magistrate had what seemed to be a bottomless stack of papers to turn over. He wore thick glasses and from time to time he glanced up and frowned. He was an elderly man and seemed to be, in Conroy's opinion, the embodiment of disapproval. After a few false starts, including a critical comment to the reporters on the press bench and a request for fresh water in his carafe, he began his summing-up.

"We have been collecting testimony this week," he began, "to discover if there is sufficient evidence in the case of Denzil Stone to justify binding over the two accused for trial by jury." The magistrate turned a page and cleared his throat. "Denzil Stone died in his prison cell sometime between the hours of eight P.M. and four A.M. on the night of March fifteenth, last. The medical examiner has testified that he died as a result of internal injuries brought about by—"

Conroy remembered well the night of March fifteenth. He was on duty in E wing. Stone had been causing trouble all day. His behavior was so extreme Conroy could only believe the man was deliberately trying to be provocative. All right, maybe he was a mental case. But crazy people, too, in Conroy's opinion, had their reasons for doing what they did. And sometimes the reason was evil.

"I'm going to look in on Number Eleven," he had said, listening to the noise from the far end of the corridor.

"I'll come with you." Hutchison finished his coffee and placed the empty mug on the window ledge.

"He really gets on my nerves."

"That's his game. And he's good at it."

Conroy unlocked a steel door and the two guards passed through into a corridor and walked quickly past a single row of cells to the room where Denzil Stone was isolated. Again a key, the turning lock, the swinging heavy door, and there was Stone, naked to the waist, sweating, his face flushed. The wreckage of his bed littered the floor of the cell.

"Now you've got noplace to sleep, dummy," Hutchison said, aiming a kick at the shredded mattress.

Conroy closed the door behind him and confronted the prisoner. Stone was far from the first manic case they'd been put in charge of. He and Chuck were trained guards—they could cope up to a point. After that, there were doctors, restraints, sedatives. But this man was something else.

He was triumphant, that was it. He believed he couldn't lose. He was an inflated, spoiled baby. The prematurely bald head, the pursed wet lips, the glazed eyes—and, tonight, the almost naked body—persuaded Conroy that here was infantile unreason. But it went beyond that. Stone was intelligent, articulate— he was goading Conroy for some reason, enjoyed needling him. "You stink, man. Look at your shirt. Why don't you use a deodorant, pig?"

Hutchison said, "Do we call in the medical officer?"

"I don't think he's crazy," Conroy said.

"I don't think he is, either. Last time the doc didn't like being called down here for nothing."

"Clear this up," Conroy said to the prisoner. "Get it together so you can sleep on it."

"Can't I sleep with you?" Stone asked in a sing-song voice. "You're so big and strong and I'm so afraid."

Conroy looked at Hutchison, who absorbed whatever he saw in Conroy's face and then glanced away. Conroy stumbled over the broken frame of the bed and had to catch himself against the painted brickwork.

"How many drinks have you had?" Stone crowed. "Is it true you're a lush?" The prisoner laughed. He blew his nose on his fingers and snapped them in Conroy's direction.

Conroy grabbed Stone by the wrist and used the prisoner's arm to wipe the stuff from his tunic. Stone put his other arm around Conroy's neck. "Kiss, kiss," he said.

Conroy hit Stone in the stomach, driving him against the wall. The head went down, then came back up, grinning at him, encouraging him to go on. Conroy moved closer and punched again. Stone's bloodied face beamed in ecstasy.

The magistrate was still recapitulating the case. "Mr. Stone was in prison for damaging a door handle. His wife had gone to stay with her parents that night because the deceased was in a state of high excitement. During the late evening Mr. Stone went to the house of his in-laws and tried to gain entry. They had locked the doors and, probably wisely, refused to open up. In his efforts to gain entry, Mr. Stone broke the handle from the front door and caused further damage by kicking against the panel. Shortly thereafter, the police arrived and he was taken into custody."

Conroy looked across the room at Stone's widow, who was seated beside her mother. The women could have been sisters. Both were youthful, long hair professionally styled, confident faces, demanding mouths. He had never seen Stone's wife until this week, but Conroy felt he had always known her. The magistrate was concluding: "I do not find, therefore, that there is sufficient evidence to warrant a jury trial in this case."

The reaction around the courtroom included chatter from the press bench and a cry of disappointment from Stone's family. "However, I think it would be unsuitable for the two officers involved to resume their duties at this time. I recommend that they be suspended until further notice. This hearing is closed."

Conroy leaned close to Hutchison. "You know what that means."

"Yeah. We have to start looking for a job outside the prison service. Some hope."

"I'm sorry, Chuck."

"You did what you had to do."

Stone's widow was resisting the efforts of friends to lead her from the courtroom. Her eyes told the guards that if she had a sharp knife and they were alone she would carve them into small pieces.

"Only somebody who's worked in a prison," Hutchison concluded, "would understand."

Conroy arrived home at three in the afternoon, having stopped off with Hutchison for a couple of drinks. It took him a few minutes to absorb the implications of the empty rooms, the missing clothes. When he understood, he left the house and headed for Rebecca's place two blocks away, alternating between a fast walk and a trot.

Rebecca's car was in the driveway, the trunk open, baggage inside. The front door of the house stood open. As he came up the walk, somebody slammed the door and he heard the bolt slide home.

Conroy moved onto the lawn where he could see in through the front window. The boys were there, looking out at him, Mark's expression one of sly embarrassment, Lenny frowning, tight-lipped, dominated by an obsession he might never understand to see things done correctly.

Clara appeared suddenly between the boys, bending to them, seizing a son in either arm and drawing them to her. He could read her lips: "Go away!" Then she felt she had to turn to the boys and smile reassuringly, and when she looked back through the window a trace of the smile remained.

Conroy saw his family behind the glass as nothing real—as a snapshot in a frame. He strode back to the door and grasped the brass handle. He shook it, but nothing moved. The door was ignoring him as if he didn't exist. His urge to penetrate it was overwhelming.

Conroy twisted the handle. It snapped, came away in his fist, and he flung it onto the lawn. As he began putting his boot to the panel, seeing it splinter, hearing the screams inside, he knew Clara would be on the telephone to the police, but there was nothing he could do about it now.

GILBERT K. CHESTERTON

THE GARDEN OF SMOKE

The end of London looked very like the end of the world: and the last lamppost of the suburbs like a lonely star in space. It also resembled the end of the world in another respect: that it was a long time coming.

The girl, Catharine Crawford, was a good walker; she had the fine figure of the mountaineer; there almost went with her a wind from the hills through all the grey labyrinth of London. For she came from the high villages of Westmoreland and seemed to carry the quiet colors of them in her light-brown hair, her open features, irregular yet the reverse of plain, the framework of two grave and very beautiful grey eyes. But the mountaineer began to feel the labyrinth of London suburbs interminable and intolerable, swiftly as she walked. She knew little of the details of her destination, save the address of the house and the fact that she was going there as a companion to a Mrs. Mowbray, or rather to *the* Mrs. Mowbray—a famous lady novelist and fashionable poet, married, it was said, to some matter-of-fact medical man reduced to the permanent status of Mrs. Mowbray's husband. And when she found the house eventually, it was at the end of the very last line of houses, where the suburban gardens faded into the open fields.

The whole heavens were full of the hues of evening, though still as luminous as noon, as if in a land of endless sunset. It settled down in a shower of gold amid the twinkling leaves of the thin trees of the gardens, most of which had low fences and hedges and lay almost as open to the yellow sky as the fields beyond. The air was so still that occasional voices, talking or laughing on distant lawns, could be heard like clear bells. One voice, more recurrent than the rest, seemed to be whistling and singing the old sailors' song of "Spanish Ladies." It drew nearer and nearer, and when she turned into the last garden gate at the corner the singer was the first figure she encountered. He

27

stood in a garden red with very gorgeous ranks of standard roses, and against a background of the golden sky and a white cottage, with touches of rather fanciful color—the sort of cottage that is not built for cottagers.

He was a lean, not ungraceful man in grey, with a limp straw hat pulled forward above his dark face and black beard, out of which projected an almost blacker cigar, which he removed when he saw the lady.

"Good evening," he said politely, "I think you must be Miss Crawford. Mrs. Mowbray asked me to tell you that she would be out here in a minute or two, if you cared to look around the garden first. I hope you don't mind my smoking. I do it to kill the insects, you know, on the roses. Need I say that this is the one and only origin of all smoking? Too little credit, perhaps, is given to the self-sacrifice of my sex, from the club-men in smoking-rooms to the navvies on scaffoldings, all steadily and firmly smoking, on the mere chance that a rose may be growing somewhere in the neighborhood. Handicapped, like most of my comrades, with a strong natural dislike of tobacco, I yet contrive to conquer it and—"

He broke off, because the grey eyes regarding him were a little blank and even bleak. He spoke with gravity and even gloom; and she was conscious of humor, but was not sure that it was good humor. Indeed she felt, at first sight, something faintly sinister about him; his face was aquiline and his figure feline, almost as in the fabulous griffin—a creature molded of the eagle and the lion, or perhaps the leopard. She was not sure that she approved of fabulous animals.

"Are you Dr. Mowbray?" she asked, rather stiffly.

"No such luck," he replied. "I haven't got such beautiful roses, or such a beautiful—household, shall we say. But Mowbray is about the garden somewhere, spraying the roses with some low scientific instrument called a syringe. He's a great gardener, but you won't find him spraying with the same perpetual, uncomplaining patience as you'll find me smoking."

With these words he turned on his heel and hallooed his friend's name across the garden in a style which, along with the echo of his song, somehow suggested a ship's captain—which was indeed his trade. A stooping figure disengaged itself from a distant rosebush and came forward apologetically.

Dr. Mowbray also had a loose straw hat and a beard, but there the resemblance ended. His beard was fair and he was burly and big of shoulder. His face was good-humored and would have been good-looking but that his blue and smiling eyes were a little wide apart—which rather increased the pleasant candor of his expression. By comparison, the more deep-sunken eyes on either side of the dark captain's beak seemed to be too close together.

"I was explaining to Miss Crawford," said the latter gentleman, "the superiority of my way of curing your roses of any of their little maladies. In scientific circles, the cigar has wholly superceded the syringe."

"Your cigars look as if they'd kill the roses," replied the doctor. "Why are you always smoking your very strongest cigars here?"

"On the contrary, I am smoking my mildest," answered the captain grimly. "I've got another sort here, if anybody wants them."

He turned back the lapel of his square jacket and showed some dangerous-looking sticks of twisted leaf in his upper waistcoat pocket. As he did so, they noticed also that he had a broad leather belt round his waist, to which was buckled a big crooked knife in a leather sheath.

As he spoke, the french windows of the house opened abruptly and a man in black came out and passed them, going out at the garden gate. He was walking rapidly, as if irritable, and putting on his hat and gloves as he went. Before he put on his hat, he showed a head half-bald and bumpy, with a semicircle of red hair, and before he put on his gloves he tore a small piece of paper into yet smaller pieces and tossed them away among the roses by the road.

"Oh, one of Marion's friends from the Theosophical or Ethical Society, I think," said the doctor. "His name's Miall, a tradesman in the town—a chemist or something."

"He doesn't seem in the best or most ethical of tempers," observed the captain. "I thought you nature-worshipers were always serene. Well, he's released our hostess, at any rate, and here she comes."

Marion Mowbray really looked like an artist, which an artist is not supposed to do. This did not come from her clinging green draperies and halo of Pre-Raphaelite brown hair, which need only have made her look like an esthete. But in her face there was a true intensity; her keen eyes were full of distances— that is, of desires, but of desires too large to be sensuous. If such a soul was wasted by a flame, it seemed one of purely spiritual ambition. A moment after she had given her hand to the guest, with very graceful apologies, she stretched it out toward the flowers with a gesture that was quite natural, yet so decisive as to be almost dramatic.

"I simply must have some more of these roses in the house," she said, "and I've lost my scissors. I know it sounds silly, but when the fit comes over me I feel I must tear them off with my hands. Don't you love roses, Miss Crawford? I simply can't do without them sometimes."

The captain's hand had gone to his hip, and the queer crooked knife was naked in the sun, a shining but ugly shape. In a few flashes, he had hacked and lopped away a long spray or two of blossom and handed them to her with a bow.

"Oh, thank you," she said rather faintly and one could fancy, somehow, a tragic irony behind the masquerade. The next moment she recovered herself, and laughed a little. "It's absurd, I know, but I do so hate ugly things, and living in the London suburbs, though only on the edge of them. Do you know, Miss Crawford, the next-door neighbor walks about his garden in a top hat? Positively in a top hat! I see it passing just above that laurel hedge about sunset—when he's come back from the city, I suppose. Think of the laurel that we poor poets are supposed to worship," and she laughed more naturally, "and then think of my feelings, looking up and seeing it wreathed round a top hat."

And, indeed, before the party entered the house to prepare for the evening meal, Catharine had actually seen the offending headdress appear above the hedge, a shadow of respectability in the sunshine of that romantic plot of roses.

At dinner they were served by a man in black like a butler, and Catharine felt an unmeaning embarrassment in the mere fact. A man-servant seemed out of place in that artistic toy cottage and there was nothing notable about the man addressed as Parker except that he seemed especially so—a tall man with a wooden face and dark flat hair. He would have been proper enough if the doctor had lived in Harley Street, but he was too big for the suburbs.

Nor was he the only incongruous element, nor the principal one. The captain, whose name seemed to be Fonblanque, still puzzled her and did not altogether please her. Her northern Puritanism found something obscurely rowdy about his attitude. It would be hardly adequate to say he acted as if he were at home—it would be truer to say he acted as if he were abroad in a cafe or tavern in some foreign port. Mrs. Mowbray was a vegetarian, and though her husband lived the simple life in a rather simpler fashion he was sufficiently sophisticated to drink water. But Captain Fonblanque had a great flagon of rum all to himself and did not disguise his relish—the meal ended in smoke of the most reeking description. And throughout, the captain continued to fence with his hostess and with the stranger with the same flippancies that had fallen from him in the garden.

"It's my childlike innocence that makes me drink and smoke," he explained. "I can enjoy a cigar as I could a sugarstick—but you jaded, dissipated vegetarians look down on such sugarsticks." His irony was partly provocative, whether of her hosts or herself, and Catharine was conscious of something slightly Mephistophelean about his blue-black beard and ivory-yellow face amid the fumes that hung round his head.

In passing out, the ladies paused accidentally at the open french windows, and Catharine looked out upon the darkening lawn. She was surprised to see that clouds had already come up out of the colored west, and the twilight was troubled with rain. There was a silence and then Catharine said, rather suddenly:

"That neighbor of yours must be very fond of his garden. Almost as fond of the roses as you are, Mrs. Mowbray."

"Why, what do you mean?" asked that lady, turning back.

"He's still standing among his flowers in the pouring rain," said Catharine, staring, "and will soon be standing in the pitch dark, too. I can still see his black hat in the dusk."

"Who knows?" said the lady poet softly. "Perhaps a sense of beauty has really stirred him in a strange, sudden way. If seeds under black earth can grow into those glorious roses, what will souls even under black hats grow into at last? Don't you like the smell of the damp earth, and that deep noise of all the roses drinking?"

"All the roses are teetotalers, anyhow," remarked Catharine, smiling.

Her hostess smiled also. "I'm afraid Captain Fonblanque shocked you a little; he's rather eccentric, wearing that crooked Eastern dagger just because he's traveled in the East, and drinking rum, of all ridiculous things, just to show he's a sailor. But he's an old friend, you know."

"Yes, he reminds me of a pirate in a play," said Catharine, laughing. "He might be stalking round this house looking for hidden treasure of gold and silver."

Mrs. Mowbray seemed to start a little, and then stared out into the dark in silence. At last she said, in a changed voice:

"It is strange that you should say that."

"And why?" inquired her companion in some wonder.

"Because there is a hidden treasure in this house," said Mrs. Mowbray, "and such a thief might well steal it. It's not exactly gold or silver, but it's almost as valuable, I believe, even in money. I don't know why I tell you this, but at least you can see I don't distrust you. Let's go into the other room." And she rather abruptly led the way in that direction.

Catharine Crawford was a woman whose conscious mind was full of practicality, but her unconscious mind had its own poetry, which was all on the note of purity. She loved white light and clear waters, boulders washed smooth in rivers, and the sweeping curves of wind. It was perhaps the poetry that Wordsworth, at his finest, found in the lakes of her own land, and in principle it could repose in the artistic austerity of Marion Mowbray's home. But whether the stage was filled too much by the almost fantastic figure of the piratical Fonblanque, or whether the summer heat, with its hint of storm, obscured such clarity, she felt an oppression. Even the rose garden seemed more like a chamber curtained with red and green than an open place. Her own chamber was curtained in sufficiently cool and soothing colors, yet she fell asleep later than usual, and then heavily.

She woke with a start from some tangled dream of which she recalled no trace. With senses sharpened by darkness, she was vividly conscious of a strange smell. It was vaporous and heavy, not unpleasant to the nostrils, yet somehow all the more unpleasant to the nerves. It was not the smell of any tobacco she knew and yet she connected it with those sinister black cigars to which the captain's brown finger had pointed. She thought half consciously that he might be still smoking in the garden and that those dark and dreadful weeds might well be smoked in the dark. But it was only half consciously that she thought or moved at all. She remembered half rising from her bed—and then remembered nothing but more dreams, which left a little more recollection in their track. They were but a medley of the smoking and the strange smell and the scents of the rose garden, but they seemed to make up a mystery as well as a medley. Sometimes the roses were themselves a sort of purple smoke. Sometimes they glowed from purple to fiery crimson, like the butts of a giant's cigars. And that garden of smoke was haunted with the word "Bluebeard" on her mind and almost in her mouth.

Morning was so much of a relief as to be almost a surprise. The rooms were full of the white light that she loved, and which might well be the light of a primeval wonder. As she passed the half-open door of the doctor's scientific study or consulting room, she paused by a window and saw the silver daybreak brightening over the garden. She was idly counting the birds that began to dart by the house when she heard the shock of a falling chair, followed by a voice crying out and cursing again. The voice was strained and unnatural, but after the first few syllables she recognized it as that of the doctor. "It's gone!" he was saying. "The stuff's gone, I tell you!"

The reply was inaudible, but she already suspected that it

came from the servant, Parker, whose voice was as baffling as
his face. The doctor answered again in an unabated agitation:

"The drug, you devil or dunce or whatever you are! The drug
I told you to keep an eye on!"

This time she heard the dull tones of the other, who seemed
to be saying, "There's very little of it gone, sir."

"Why has *any* of it gone?" cried Doctor Mowbray. "Where's
my wife?"

Probably hearing the rustle of a skirt outside, he flung the
door open and came face to face with Catharine, falling back
before her in consternation. The room into which she now
looked in bewilderment was neat and even severe except for
the fallen chair still lying on its back on the carpet. It was fitted
with bookcases and contained a rack of bottles and phials, like
those in a chemist's shop, the colors of which looked like jewels
in the brilliant early daylight. One glittering green bottle bore a
large label of POISON, but the present problem seemed to
revolve around a glass vessel, rather like a decanter, which
stood on the table more than half-full of a dust or powder of a
rich, reddish brown.

Against this strict scientific background the tall servant
looked more important and appropriate. In fact, she was soon
conscious that he was something more intimate than a servant
who waited at table. He had at least the air of a doctor's
assistant—and indeed, in comparison with his distracted employer, might also at that moment have been the attendant in a
private asylum.

"It's the cursed plague breaking out again," said the doctor
hastily. "Go and see if my wife is in the dining room." He pulled
himself together as Parker left the room and picked up the
chair, offering it to the girl with a gesture. "Well, I suppose you
ought to have been told. Anyhow, you'll have to be told now."

There was another silence, and then he said: "My wife is a
poet, you know—a creative artist and all that. And all enlightened people know that a genius can't be judged quite by
common rules of conduct. A genius lives by a recurrent need
for a sort of inspiration."

"What do you mean?" asked Catharine almost impatiently, for
the preamble of excuses was a strain on her nerves.

"There's a kind of opium in that bottle," he said abruptly, "a very rare kind. She smokes it occasionally, that's all. I wish Parker would hurry up and find her."

"I can find her, I think," said Catharine, relieved by the chance of doing something, and not a little relieved, also, to get out of the scientific room. "I think I saw her going down the garden path."

When she went out into the rose garden, it was full of the freshness of the sunrise, and all her smoke nightmares were rolled away from it. The roof of her green-and-crimson room seemed to have been lifted off like a lid. She went down many winding paths without seeing any living thing but the birds hopping here and there. Then she came to the corner of one turning, and stood still.

In the middle of the sunny path, a few yards from one of the birds, lay something crumpled like a great green rag. But it was really the rich green dress of Marion Mowbray, and beyond it was her fallen face, colorless against its halo of hair, and one arm thrust out in a piteous stiffness toward the roses, as she had stretched it when Catharine saw her for the first time. Catharine gave a little cry, and the birds flashed away into a tree. Then she bent over the fallen figure and knew, in a blast of all the trumpets of terror, why the face was colorless, and why the arm was stiff.

An hour afterward, still in that world of rigid unreality that remains long after a shock, she was but automatically, though efficiently, helping in the hundred minute and aching utilities of a house of mourning. How she had told them she hardly knew, but there was no need to tell much. Mowbray the doctor soon had bad news for Mowbray the husband, when he had been but a few moments silent and busy over the body of his wife. Then he turned away, and Catharine almost feared he would fall.

A problem confronted him still, however, even as a doctor, when he had so grimly solved his problem as a husband. His medical assistant, whom he had always had reason to trust, still emphatically asserted that the amount of the drug missing was insufficient to kill a kitten. He came down and stood with the little group on the lawn where the dead woman had been moved to a sofa to be examined in the best light. He repeated his assertion in the face of the examination, his wooden face knotted with obstinacy.

"If he is right," said Captain Fonblanque, "she must have got it from somewhere else, that's all. Did any strange people come here lately?" He had been pacing up and down the lawn, when he stopped with an arrested gesture. "Didn't you say that theosophist was also a chemist?" he asked. "He may be as theosophical or ethical as he likes, but he didn't come here on a theosophical errand. No, by gad, nor an ethical one."

It was agreed that this question should be followed up first. Parker was despatched to the High Street of the neighboring suburb, and about half an hour afterward the black-clad figure of Mr. Miall came back into the garden, much less swiftly than he had gone out of it. He removed his hat out of respect for the presence of death, and his face under the ring of red hair was whiter than the dead.

But though pale, he also was firm; and that upon a point that brought the inquiry once more to a standstill. He admitted that he had once supplied that peculiar brand of opium, and he did not attempt to dissipate the cloud of responsibility that rested on him so far. But he vehemently denied that he had supplied it yesterday, or even lately, or indeed for long past.

"She must have got some more somehow," cried the doctor, in dogmatic and even despotic tones, "and where could she have got it but from you?"

"And where could I have got it from anybody?" demanded the tradesman equally hotly. "You seem to think it's sold like shag. I tell you there's no more of it in England—a chemist can't get it even for desperate cases. I gave her the last I had months ago, more shame to me; and when she wanted more yesterday, I told her I not only wouldn't but couldn't. There are the scraps of the note she sent me, still lying where I tore it up in a temper."

The doctor seemed to regard the hitch in the inquiry with a sort of harassed fury. He browbeat the pale chemist even more than he had browbeaten his servant about his first and smaller discovery. His desire at the moment, so concrete as to be comic in such a scene, seemed to be the desire to hang a chemist.

The figures in the little group on the lawn had fallen into such angry attitudes that one could almost fancy they would strike each other even in the presence of the dead when an interruption came, as soft as the note of the bird but as unexpected as a thunderbolt. A voice from several yards away said mildly but more or less loudly: "Permit me to offer my assistance."

They all looked around and saw the next-door neighbor's top hat, above a large, loose, heavy-lidded face, leaning over the low fringe of laurels.

"I'm sure I can be of some little help," he said. And the next moment he had calmly taken a high stride over the low hedge and was walking across the lawn toward them. He was a large, heavily walking man in a loose frock-coat; his clean-shaven face was at once heavy and cadaverous. He spoke in a soft and even sentimental tone, which contrasted with his impudence and, as it soon appeared, with his trade.

"What do you want here?" asked Dr. Mowbray sharply, when he had recovered from sheer astonishment.

"It is you who want something—sympathy," said the strange gentleman. "Sympathy and also light. I think I can offer both. Poor lady, I have watched her for many months."

"If you've been watching over the wall," said the captain, frowning, "we should like to know why. There are suspicious facts here, and you seem to have behaved in a suspicious manner."

"Suspicion rather than sympathy," said the stranger with a sigh, "is perhaps the defect in my duties. But my sorrow for this poor lady is perfectly sincere. Do you suspect me of being mixed up in her trouble?"

"Who are you?" asked the angry doctor.

"My name is Traill," said the man in the top hat. "I have some official title, but it was never used except at Scotland Yard. We needn't use it among neighbors."

"You are a detective, in fact?" observed the captain. But he received no reply, for the new investigator was already examining the corpse, quite respectfully but with a professional absence of apology. After a few moments he rose again, and looked at them under the large drooping eyelids which were his most prominent features, and said simply:

"It is satisfactory to let people go, Dr. Mowbray; and your druggist and your assistant can certainly go. It was not the fault of either of them that the unhappy lady died."

"Do you mean it was a suicide?" asked the other.

"I mean it was a murder," said Mr. Traill. "But I have a very sufficient reason for saying she was not killed by the druggist."

"And why not?"

"Because she was not killed by the drug," said the man from next door.

"What?" exclaimed the captain, with a slight start. "How else could she have been killed?"

"She was killed with a short and sharp instrument, the point of which was prepared in a particular manner for the purpose," said Traill in the level tones of a lecturer. "There was apparently a struggle but probably a short, or even a slight one. Poor lady, just look at this"—and he lifted one of the dead hands quite gently and pointed to what appeared to be a prick or puncture on the wrist.

"A hypodermic needle, perhaps," said the doctor in a low voice. "She generally took a drug by smoking it, but she might have used a hypodermic syringe and needle, after all."

The detective shook his head. "If she injected it herself, she would make a clean perforation. This is more a scratch than a prick—and you can see it has torn the lace on her sleeve a little."

"But how can it have killed her," Catharine was compelled to ask, "if it was only a scratching on the wrist?"

"Ah," said Mr. Traill; and then, after a short silence, "I think," he said, "that when we find the dagger, we shall find it a poisoned dagger. Is that plain enough, Captain Fonblanque?"

The next moment he seemed to droop again with his rather morbid and almost maudlin tone of compassion. "Poor lady," he repeated. "She was so fond of roses, wasn't she? Strew on her roses, roses, as the poet says. I really feel somehow that it might give a sort of rest to her, even now."

He looked around the garden with his heavy, half-closed eyes, and addressed Fonblanque more sympathetically. "It was on a happier occasion, Captain, that you last cut flowers for her, but I can't help wishing it could be done again now."

Half unconsciously, the captain's hand went to where the hilt of his knife had hung, then his hand dropped, as if in abrupt recollection. But as the flap of his jacket shifted for an instant, they saw that the leather sheath was empty and the knife was gone.

"Such a very sad story, such a terrible story," murmured the man in the top hat distantly, as if he were talking of a novel. "Of course it is a silly fancy about the flowers. It is not such things as that that are our duties to the dead."

The others seemed still a little bewildered, but Catharine was looking at the captain as if she had been turned to stone by a basilisk.

Indeed that moment had been for her the beginning of a monstrous interregnum of imagination, which might well be said to be full of monsters. Something of such mythology had hung about the garden since her first fancy about a man like a griffin. It lasted for many days and nights, during which the detective seemed to hover over the house like a vampire. But the vampire was not the most awful of the monsters.

She hardly defined to herself what she thought, or rather refused to think. But she was conscious of other unknown emotions coming to the surface and co-existing, somehow, with that sunken thought that was their contrary.

For some time past, the first unfriendly feelings about the captain had rather faded from her mind; even in that short space he had improved on acquaintance, and his sensible conduct in the crisis was a relief from the wild grief and anger of the husband, however natural these might be. Moreover, the very explosion of the opium secret, in accounting for the cloud upon the house, had cleared away another suspicion she had half entertained about the wife and the piratical guest. This she was now disposed to dismiss, so far at least as he was concerned; and she had lately had an additional reason for doing so. The eyes of Fonblanque had been following her about, in a manner in which so humorless and therefore modest a lady was

not likely to be mistaken; and she was surprised to find in
herself a corresponding recoil from the idea of this comedy of
sentiment turning suddenly to a tragedy of suspicion.

For the next few nights she again slept uneasily; and, as is
often the case with a crushed or suppressed thought, the doubt
raged and ruled in her dreams. What might be called the
Bluebeard motif ran through even wilder scenes of strange
lands, full of fantastic cities and giant vegetation, through all of
which passed a solitary figure with a blue beard and a red knife.
It was as if this sailor not only had a wife, but a murdered wife,
in every port. And there recurred again and again, like a distant
but distinct voice speaking, the accents of the detective: "If
only we could find the dagger, we should find it a poisoned
dagger."

Yet nothing could have seemed more cool and casual than
the moment, on the following morning, when she did find it.
She had come down from the upper rooms and gone through
the french windows into the garden once more; she was about
to pass down the paths among the rosebushes, when she looked
round and saw the captain leaning on the garden gate. There
was nothing unusual in his idle and somewhat languid attitude,
but her eye was fixed, and as if it were frozen, on the one bright
spot where the sun again shone and shifted on the crooked
blade. He was somewhat sullenly hacking with it at the wooden
fence, but stopped when their eyes met.

"So you've found it again?" was all that she could say.

"Yes, I've found it," he replied rather gloomily, and then after
a pause, "I've also found several other things, including how I
lost it."

"Do you mean," asked Catharine unsteadily, "that you've
found out about—about Mrs. Mowbray?"

"It wouldn't be correct to say I've found it out," he answered.
"Our depressing neighbor with the top hat and the eyelids has
found it out, and he's upstairs now, finding more out. But if you
mean do I know how Marion was murdered, yes, I do; and I
rather wish I didn't."

After a minute or two of objectless chipping on the fence, he
struck the point of his knife into the wood and faced her
abruptly.

"Look here," he said, "I should like to explain myself a little. When we first knew each other, I suppose I was very flippant. I admired your gravity and great goodness so much that I had to attack it; can you understand that? But I was not entirely flippant—no, nor entirely wrong. Think again of all the silly things that annoyed you, and of whether they have turned out so very silly? Are not rum and tobacco really more childlike and innocent than some things, my friend? Has any low sailors' tavern seen a worse tragedy than you have seen here? Mine are vulgar tastes—or if you like, vulgar vices. But there is one thing to be said for our appetites: that they are appetites. Pleasure may be only satisfaction, but it can be satisfied. We drink because we are thirsty, but not because we want to be thirsty. I tell you that these artists thirst for thirst. They want infinity, and they get it, poor souls. It may be bad to be drunk, but you can't be infinitely drunk; you fall down. A more horrible thing happens to them—they rise and rise, forever. Isn't it better to fall under the table and snore than to rise through the seven heavens on the smoke of opium?"

She answered at last, with an appearance of thought and hesitation.

"There may be something in what you say; but it doesn't account for all the nonsensical things you said." She smiled a little and added, "You said you only smoked for the good of the roses, you know. You'll hardly pretend there was any solemn truth behind that."

He started, and then stepped forward, leaving the knife standing and quivering in the fence.

"Yes, by gad, there was!" he cried. "It may seem the maddest thing of all, but it's true. Death and hell would not be in this house today if they had only trusted my trick of smoking the roses."

Catharine continued to look at him wildly; but his own gaze did not falter or show a shade of doubt, and he went slowly back to the fence and plucked his knife out of it. There was a long silence in the garden before either of them spoke again.

"Do you think," he asked in a low voice, "that Marion is really dead?"

"Dead!" repeated Catharine. "Of course she's dead."

He seemed to nod in brooding acquiescence, staring at his knife, then he added: "Do you think her ghost walks?"

"What do you mean? Do you think so?" demanded his companion.

"No," he said, "but that drug of hers is still disappearing."

She could only repeat, with a pale face: "Still disappearing?"

"In fact, it's nearly disappeared," remarked the captain. "You can come upstairs and see, if you like." He stopped and gazed at her a moment very seriously. "I know you are brave," he said. "Would you really like to see the end of this nightmare?"

"It would be a much worse nightmare if I didn't," she answered. The captain, with a gesture at once negligent and resolved, tossed his knife among the rosebushes and turned toward the house.

She looked at him with a last flicker of suspicion. "Why are you leaving your dagger in the garden?" she asked abruptly.

"The garden is full of daggers," said the captain as he went upstairs. Mounting the staircase with a catlike swiftness, he was some way ahead of the girl, in spite of her own mountaineering ease of movement. She had time to reflect that the greys and greens of the dados and decorative curtains had never seemed to her so dreary and even inhuman. And when she reached the landing and the door of the doctor's study, she met the captain again, face to face. For he stood now, with his face as pale as her own, and not any longer as leading her, but rather as barring her way.

"What is the matter?" she cried—and then, by a wild intuition, "Is somebody else dead?"

In the silence they heard within the heavy and yet soft movements of the strange investigator. Fonblanque spoke again with a new impulsiveness:

"Catharine, I think you know how I feel about you; but what I am trying to say now is not about myself. It may seem a queer thing for a man like me to say, but somehow I think you will understand. Before you go inside, remember the things outside. I don't mean my things, but yours. I mean the empty sky and all the good grey virtues and the things that are clean and strong like the wind. Believe me, they are real, after all; more real than the cloud on this accursed house."

"Yes, I think I understand you," she said. "And now let me pass."

Apart from the detective's presence, there were but two differences in the doctor's study as compared with the time she stood in it last; and though they bulked very unequally to the eye, they seemed almost equal in a deadly significance. On a sofa under the window, covered with a sheet, lay something that could only be a corpse; but the very bulk of it, and the way in which the folds of the sheet fell, showed her that it was not the corpse she had already seen. For herself, she had hardly need to glance at it; she knew almost before she looked that it was not the wife, but the husband. And on the table stood the glass vessel of the opium and the other green bottle labeled POISON. But the opium vessel was quite empty.

The detective came forward with a mildness amounting to embarrassment.

"You are naturally prejudiced against me, my dear," he said. "You feel I am a morbid person. I think you sometimes feel I was probably a murderer. Well, I think you were right; not about the murder, but about the morbidity. I can't help being interested in tragedies that are my trade; and you're quite wrong if you think my sentiment's all hypocritical."

Catharine didn't doubt his good nature. But the unanswered riddle still rode her imagination.

"But I thought you said," she protested, "that Mrs. Mowbray was not killed by the drug."

"She was not killed by the drug. She was killed *for* the drug. Did you notice anything odd about Dr. Mowbray when you were last in this room?"

"He was naturally agitated," said the girl doubtfully.

"No, unnaturally agitated," replied Traill; "more agitated than a man so sturdy would have been even by the revelation of another's weakness. It was his own weakness that rattled him like a storm that morning. He was indeed angry that the drug was stolen by his wife—for the simple reason that he wanted all that was left for himself. I have rather an ear for distant conversation, Miss Crawford, and I once heard you talking at the window about a pirate and a treasure. Can't you picture two pirates stealing the same treasure bit by bit, till one of them killed the other in rage at seeing it vanish? That is what happened in this house; and perhaps we had better call it madness, and then pity it. The drug had become that unhappy man's life, and that a horribly unhappy life. He had long resolved that when he had really emptied this bottle," and Traill touched the receptacle of opium, "he would at once turn to this"—and he laid his lean hand on the green bottle of poison.

Catharine's face was still puzzled.

"You mean her husband killed her, and then killed himself?" she said, in her simple way. "But how did he kill her, if not with the drug? Indeed, how did he kill her at all?"

"He stabbed her," replied Traill. "He stabbed her in a strange fashion, when she was far away at the other end of the garden."

"But he was not there!" cried Catharine. "He was up in this room."

"He was not there when he stabbed her," answered the detective.

"I told Miss Crawford," said the captain in a low voice, "that the garden was full of daggers."

"Yes, of green daggers that grow on trees," continued Traill. "You may say if you like that she was killed by a wild creature, tied to the earth but armed."

His morbid fancy in putting things moved in her again her vague feeling of a garden of green mythological monsters.

"He was committing the crime at the moment when you first came into that garden," said Traill. "The crime that he committed with his own hands. You stood in the sunshine and watched him commit it.

"I have told you the deed was done for the drug, but not by the drug. I tell you now that it was done with a syringe, but not a hypodermic syringe. It was being done with that ordinary garden implement he was holding in his hand when you saw him first. But the stuff with which he drenched the green rose trees came out of this green bottle."

"He poisoned the roses?" asked Catharine, almost mechanically.

"Yes," said the captain, "he poisoned the roses. And the thorns."

The girl gazed at him distractedly. Then she said, "And the knife . . .?"

"That is soon said," answered Traill. "The presence of the knife had nothing to do with it. The absence of the knife had a great deal. The murderer stole it and hid it, partly perhaps with some idea that its loss would look black against the captain, whom I did in fact suspect, as I think you did. But there was a much more practical reason; the same that had made him steal and hide his wife's scissors. You heard his wife say she always wanted to tear off the roses with her fingers. If there was no instrument to hand, he knew that one fine morning she would. And one fine morning she did."

Catharine left the room without looking again at what lay in the light of the window under the sheet. She had no desire but to leave the room, and leave the house, and above all leave the garden behind her. And when she went out into the road, she automatically turned her back on the fringe of fanciful cottages and set her face toward the open fields and the distant woods of England. And she was already snapping bracken and startling birds with her step before she became conscious of anything incongruous in the fact that Fonblanque was still strolling in her company.

And, as the tales go, it was like the end of the world in that it was the beginning of a better one.

DANIEL WEBSTER

THE FATAL SECRET

An aged man, without an enemy in the world, in his own house and in his own bed, is made the victim of a butcherly murder for mere pay.

Deep sleep has fallen on the destined victim and on all beneath his roof. A healthful old man, to whom sleep is sweet, the first sound slumbers of the night hold him in their soft but strong embrace. The assassin enters, through the window already prepared, into an unoccupied apartment. With noiseless foot he paces the lonely hall, half lighted by the moon. He winds up the ascent of the stairs and reaches the door of the chamber. Of this, he moves the lock, by soft and continued pressure, till it turns on its hinges without noise—and he enters, and beholds his victim before him.

The room is uncommonly open to the admission of light. The face of the innocent sleeper is turned from the murderer, and the beams of the moon, resting on the grey locks of his aged temple, show him where to strike.

The fatal blow is given—and the victim passes, without a struggle or a motion, from the repose of sleep to the repose of death!

It is the assassin's purpose to make sure work and he yet plies the dagger, though it is obvious that life has been destroyed by the blow of the bludgeon. He even raises the aged arm, that he may not fail in his aim at the heart, and replaces it again over the wounds of the poniard. To finish the picture, he explores the wrist for the pulse. He feels for it, and ascertains that it beats no longer.

It is accomplished. The deed is done. He retreats, retraces his steps to the window, passes out through it as he came in, and escapes. He has done the murder—no eye has seen him, no ear has heard him. The *secret* is his own, and it is safe.

Ah, gentlemen, that was a dreadful mistake. Such a secret can

47

be safe nowhere. The whole creation of God has neither nook nor corner where the guilty can bestow it and say it is safe, not to speak of that eye which glances through all disguises and beholds everything.

True it is, generally speaking, that "murder will out." True it is that Providence hath so ordained, and doth so govern things, that those who break the great law of heaven by shedding man's blood seldom succeed in avoiding discovery. Especially in a case exciting so much attention as this, discovery must come.

A thousand eyes turn at once to explore every man, every thing, every circumstance connected with the time and place; a thousand ears catch every whisper; a thousand excited minds intensely dwell on the scene, shedding all their light, and ready to kindle the slightest circumstance into a blaze of discovery.

Meantime, the guilty soul cannot keep its own secret. It is false to itself; or rather it feels an irresistible impulse of conscience to be true to itself. It labors under its guilty possession and knows not what to do with it. The human heart was not made for the residence of such an inhabitant. It finds itself preyed on by a torment which it dares not acknowledge to God or man. A vulture is devouring it, and it can ask no sympathy or assistance either from heaven or earth.

The secret the murderer possesses soon comes to possess him; and, like the evil spirits of which we read, it overcomes him and leads him withersoever it will. He feels it beating at his heart, rising to his throat, and demanding disclosure. He thinks the whole world sees it in his face, reads it in his eyes, and almost hears its workings in the very silence of his thoughts. It has become his master. It betrays discretion, it breaks down his courage, it conquers his prudence.

When suspicions from without begin to embarrass him, and the net of circumstance to entangle him, the fatal secret struggles with still greater violence to burst forth. It must be confessed, *it will be* confessed, there is no refuge from confession but suicide, and suicide is confession.

BERTON ROUECHÉ

THE RASPBERRY PATCH

The telephone rang and I heard Mrs. Logan answer it at her desk.

"It's for you, Mr. Jeffries," she said.

I finished with my depositor and put the sign under my grille and closed my cash drawer and walked over to the telephone, and it was Mother.

"Yes," I said. "What is it, Mother?"

But I couldn't hear her. All I could hear was a babel of voices and then a lot of laughing. "For heaven sakes," I said. "You've got the TV on. Turn it down."

The laughter ended with a gulp.

"I don't know what you're talking about," Mother said.

"Well," I said. "What is it?"

"Edward—"

"Yes?"

"I meant to tell you at lunch, but you left in such a rush."

"Tell me what?"

"You don't have to shout at me, Edward."

"All right, Mother," I said, "but Mrs. Logan wants to use her desk. What is it?"

"I'm trying to tell you, Edward," she said. "I want you to stop at the drugstore on your way home and get me some Empirin. I've got one of my headaches. I've had it ever since breakfast."

"Empirin?" I said. "What's the matter with aspirin? you've got aspirin. I put the bottle on your table this morning."

"I can't take aspirin any more," she said. "It doesn't agree with my bloat medicine. If you ever listened to me, you'd know that."

"All right," I said. "Okay. But I've got to go now."

"And, Edward—" she said.

"Mother," I said, "it's after two. It's almost closing time."

"I want you to be sure and get the large bottle."

49

"All right," I said, and hung up.

I took a deep breath and held it as long as I could. That's an exercise I learned at a yoga class I went to before Mother had her second stroke. It always seems to help. Then I took a Gelusil tablet and went back to my cage. I could already feel the tension subsiding. Yoga breathing and Gelusil—they really work. I don't know what I'd do without them. But I wasn't very proud of myself. I'd come pretty close to actually losing my temper. I suppose, in a way, it was partly Mother's fault, but that isn't any excuse. That's the way Mother is. She just doesn't understand about business. It was the same when Father was alive. Mother has always been a world unto herself.

Frank Palmer and I left the bank together. It was twenty past four and we were almost the last to leave. I don't know what Frank's trouble was, but mine was my drawer. I thought I'd never get it proved. There wasn't anything really wrong, I just couldn't seem to concentrate. We came out of the passage and into the heat of the street, and Frank stopped and lit a cigarette.

"Well," I said.

"Wait a minute," Frank said. "I'm meeting Martha for a drink at the Domino. How about joining us?"

"I'd like to," I said, and I meant it. I was flattered. Frank is at least ten years younger than me. And I've always liked Martha Palmer. But then I thought of Mother. "I'd like to, Frank, but I guess I'd better not. I really ought to get home."

"It isn't that late," he said. "Besides, it's Friday."

"All right," I said. It wasn't really late. Mother likes to eat early, but I could still get home in time to have dinner ready by six. "But I've got to stop at the drugstore first and get some medicine for Mother."

"Okay," he said. "How *is* your mother, Ed?"

"Oh, she's fine," I said. "She's coming along fine. She still spends most of her time in her chair, but she's beginning to get around pretty well with a cane."

"She sounds like a wonderful woman," he said.

"She is," I said. "She really is."

The Domino was dark and cool, and Martha was already there. She waved to us from a booth across from the bar. She looked pretty and smiling, and it made me feel good to see her.

"Why, Ed," she said, "this is great." She looked at Frank. "And you—I hope you realize how late you are."

"I had nothing to do with it." He slid into the seat beside her. "A beautiful girl tried to pick me up. I almost didn't get away."

"I don't blame her." Martha leaned over and kissed him on the cheek. "And now order me something long and cold and delicious. I've never been so thirsty."

"One beer," Frank said. "What about you, Ed?"

"A beer sounds fine," I said.

We all had beer. The beer was cold and it tasted good, but after a few swallows I didn't really enjoy it. I liked sitting in the cool and the dark with the jukebox playing and having a drink at the end of the week with my friends, but I didn't feel right. I had a kind of empty feeling and I couldn't seem to get relaxed. But I made myself finish my beer. I sat back with my glass and listened to Frank laughing about a funny twenty that turned up in the Star Lanes deposit and watched Martha smiling and listening to every word he said, and tried to look calm and comfortable. And then I couldn't stand it any longer.

"Well," I said. I put down my glass and tried to smile. "I'm afraid I've got to go."

"Go?" Martha said.

"Why, we only just got here," Frank said.

"I know," I said, "and I wish I could stay. But Mother's alone and—"

I walked back to the bank and around to the parking lot in back and got my car and drove home along the river road. The clock in the big Esso station under the bridge said twenty-five past five. The Domino had been a mistake, but I wasn't really late. I touched my pocket to make sure the bottle of Empirin was still there, and turned into our street and down the block to our house.

There was a car parked in the driveway of the old Hamilton house next door. It was a red Volkswagen, and I remembered that I'd seen it there at noon. And all of the windows in the house were open. The Hamilton house had been vacant for over a year, but it looked as if somebody had finally taken it. I drove on past and up our drive and put the car in the garage, got out, closed the doors, and went in the kitchen door. I could hear the TV talking in the living room. I went through the dining room and across the hall.

"I'm home," I said.

Mother was sitting erect with her hands on the arms of her chair.

"Edward," she said, "where in the world have you been? It's almost six o'clock."

"I've got your Empirin," I said. I got the package out of my pocket and put it with the other things on her table. "That's a hundred tablets. It's the largest size they had."

Mother unwrapped the bottle, looked at the label, and put it back on the table. "Well," she said, "aren't you even going to kiss me?"

I bent down and touched her cheek.

"You've been drinking," she said.

"I had a beer with one of the fellows at the bank," I said. "He asked me to."

"I see," she said. "And I suppose you have to do everything you're asked?"

I didn't say anything. I was looking out the window at the backyard next door. Old Mr. Hamilton had been a gardener and most of the yard was garden and most of the garden was a raspberry patch. A girl in a jersey and tight blue jeans was standing there in the tangle of canes. She looked very pretty in her tight blue pants against the pale-green leaves and the bright red berries. And young. She looked even younger than Martha Palmer. She looked about twenty-five. She said something to somebody in the house and laughed. I turned away. "I'd better go and change," I said. "Do you want me to get you anything first?"

"You could fill my water glass," she said. "I might want to take an Empirin."

"How is your headache?" I said.

"I think it's coming back," she said.

I took the glass out to the kitchen and filled it from the cooler

in the refrigerator and brought it back and put it on the table.
"I'm going up now," I said. "Okay?"

She nodded. I went up to my room and took off my coat and
tie and rolled up my shirtsleeves and went into the bathroom
and washed, and came back down again.

I looked in the living room. "I'm going to start dinner," I said.
"And I thought I'd make some iced tea. I thought that might
taste good."

"If that's what you want," she said. "But be sure and make it
strong enough."

I went out to the kitchen and got the rest of last night's roast
out of the refrigerator and sliced off four or five slices. Then I
got out a package of frozen green beans and a package of frozen
potatoes. I set the table in the dining room and came back and
put the kettle on to boil.

"Edward!"

I went back and across the hall to the living room.

"There isn't a breath of air in here," Mother said. "It's even
worse than it was this afternoon. I think I'll have to have the
fan."

"I don't think you should," I said. "You know what Dr.
Tillinghast said about drafts."

"I know what he said," she countered. "But he didn't intend
for me to suffocate. This room is stifling and I want the fan. It's
up in the storeroom closet."

"All right," I said.

I went back up the stairs. The storeroom was under the eaves
and it was really stifling. I opened the window to let in some
air. The girl next door was still in the raspberry patch. Only
now she wasn't just standing there. She had a dish or a bowl or
something and she was picking raspberries. I stood at the
window and watched her. She was younger than Martha Palmer,
and prettier, too. I heard a screen door slam. A man in a T-shirt
came out of the house and across the yard and down the garden
path. That would be her husband, but he wasn't much more
than a boy. The girl was squatting down between the canes.
The boy came up behind her and gave her a pat on her tight
blue bottom. She looked up and smiled, and pushed a raspberry
into his mouth.

I moved away from the window and opened the closet door. It was dark in there and even hotter than the room. I waited a minute until I could see. The closet was full of Father's things—his fishing rods, his waders, his shotgun, his golf clubs in their big leather bag. The fan was on the shelf. I reached it down and my hand touched something else. It was a box of shotgun shells. I shook it. There were shells inside.

I put down the fan. My heart was beating hard, and I felt heavy and out of breath. It was all I could do to breathe. I put out my hand and picked up Father's shotgun and broke it open, holding it up to the light. It was a double-barreled shotgun and both barrels looked dark and linty. But a little dirt wouldn't make much difference.

I loaded the gun, backed out of the closet, and knelt down at the open window. They were still down there picking raspberries. I sighted on the boy and squeezed the trigger the way Father always said. There was hardly any noise. I hardly heard a thing. But the boy sat down and fell back in the canes. I squeezed the other trigger. The girl stood up and took a step and fell across the boy.

I pulled back the gun and closed the window. I stood there for a moment. Then I took a deep breath and held it as long as I could. Then I stood the gun back in the closet and closed the door and picked up the fan and went out of the room and down the hall.

Mother was standing at the foot of the stairs.

"Edward," she said, and she had the strangest look on her face. She didn't look like Mother. She looked almost frightened. "What was that noise? What happened?"

"I was up in the storeroom," I said. "You said you wanted your fan."

ELLERY QUEEN

THE ACCUSED

Wrightsville is a New England industrial town famous for nothing, set down in the center of an agricultural county of no particular distinction. It was founded by a man named Jezreel Wright in 1701, and after 250-odd years its population is just past 10,000. Parts of it are crooked and narrow, other parts glare with neon signs, and a great deal of it is downright dingy. In other words, Wrightsville is a very ordinary American town.

But to Ellery it is Shangri-La.

Pressed to explain why he runs off to Wrightsville at the drop of a hat, Ellery will say that he sort of likes cobblestoned, grimy Low Village, and the Square (which is round), and Twin Hill Cemetery, and The Hot Spot on Route 16, and the smoky burgundy of the Mahoganies to the north; that he finds Band Concert Night behind the Our Boys Memorial relaxing in direct ratio to the amount of noise and buttered popcorn produced; that the sight of the farmers' starched families coming with stiff pleasure into town on Saturday afternoons positively stimulates him. And so forth.

But if Ellery were to tell the entire truth, he would have to include the fact that Wrightsville has been wonderfully good to him in the matter of interesting crimes.

On the latest occasion, he dropped off the Atlantic Stater at Wrightsville Station under the delusion that he would pass a bangup week at Bill York's Lodge on Bald Mountain, skimming down the second-rate ski slopes like a bird and sitting at tall fires afterward, soaking up contentment and hot toddies with the sportsmen of the town. He got no closer to the Lodge than the Hollis Hotel on the Square.

Ed Hotchkiss gave him the bad news as he dumped his skis into Ed's taxi outside the station and turned to pump the large Hotchkiss hand. There wasn't enough snow on old Baldy this winter, Ed mourned, to make a passable fight for Bill York's six youngsters. But as long as Mr. Queen was in town, there *was* that darned business of Ed's second cousin Mamie and Mamie's boy Delbert.

When Ellery had checked into the Hollis, washed up, and come down to the lobby to buy a Wrightsville *Record* at Grover Doodle's cigar stand, he was already half committed to look into the case of young Delbert Hood, who was out on bail awaiting trial for a crime Ed Hotchkiss and his cousin Mamie were sure the boy hadn't had a thing in the world to do with.

Certain elements of the affair encouraged Ellery's interest. For one thing, the victim of the crime seemed the villain of the piece. For another, Officer Jeep Jorking, one of Chief Dakin's bright young men, was in Wrightsville General Hospital, his left side immured in a cast from the hip down. For a third, everybody in town except Ed Hotchkiss and Mamie Hood Wheeler was convinced that Delbert had done it.

This last by itself was almost enough for Ellery—and by the time he had eavesdropped among some Wrightsville ladies of his acquaintance, busy at their organizational luncheons at the Hollis and Upham House, and had chewed the fat with Chief Dakin at police headquarters and with sundry others, Ellery was ready to go the whole hog.

The background of the case, according to the ladies, was as follows:

Wrightsville had awakened one morning to learn that Anson K. Wheeler was marrying the widow Hood. This was tantamount to a revolution, for Anse Wheeler was Hill Drive and Mamie Hood was Low Village.

It was not as if Mamie Hood were young and beautiful. She was forty-six if she was a day. Her features were definitely on the plain side, and one of the ladies reported that Tessie Lupin, popular operator of the Lower Main Beauty Shop, had never given Mamie Hood so much as a facial, and didn't her complexion look it! As for Mamie's figure, it was spready around the top and the middle and, when you got right down to it, so to speak, around the bottom, too. She didn't know what a decent foundation garment *was*, apparently.

And there was Anse Wheeler, from one of the old families.

The Wheeler mansion on Hill Drive was a showplace. The Wheelers were proud of their name, careful with their money, and properly set in their ways. Anse still drove the Pierce-Arrow which had belonged to his father. They had never streamlined their plumbing. Old Mrs. Wheeler, who wore boned chokers and a gold chest-watch to the day of her death, nevertheless had always insisted on putting up her own pickles. And even though Anson K. Wheeler owned the big farm-machinery plant over in the Valley near the airport—employing hundreds of people—he conducted his business the way his father had before him, along the most conservative lines, with 1910 bookkeeping methods and Anse personally picking up his plant payroll at the bank every Friday morning.

Anse had been First Selectman twice. He was president of the Wrightsville Historical Society. He was senior vestryman of St. Paul's-in-the-Dingle, with a cold rebuke for those so prone to Low Church lapses as to fail to call the rector "Father" Chich-ering. His grandfather, General Murdock Wheeler, had been Wrightsville's last surviving veteran of the G.A.R. His first cousin, Uriah Scott ("U.S.") Wheeler, was principal of Gunnery School over in Fyfield and one of Wright County's leading intellectuals.

Anson Wheeler had never married because of his mother. His devotion to ailing Mrs. Wheeler had been a beautiful thing, and when she died at the age of eighty-nine he was like a fish out of water.

That was when *she* got in *her* licks, of course, with her imitation-lady's voice and sugary ways. Anse Wheeler, just about the best catch in town—and Mamie Hood, *his house-keeper,* caught him!

Mamie Hood was not only his housekeeper—a domestic, really—she had a grown child to boot. Delbert had his father's bad blood. There'd always been something queer about Alf Hood, with his radical ideas and his shifty ways. Alf had sent himself throuugh Merrimac U. by stoking furnaces, waiting on table, and even more menial jobs than that—you always felt he'd do anything to make a dollar. When he opened his law office on State Street, he might have got along if he'd played his cards right. Louise Glannis was wild about him and wanted to elope. The Glannises and their set would have accepted him in time to keep the town from talking, and he could have made something of himself. What did the fool do? Jilted Louise and married Mamie Broadbeck of Lower Whistling Street! After that, of course, he was through. He never got a single Hill or High Village client—the Glannises saw to that.

So high-and-mighty Alf wound up tramping the streets looking for work. But it was 1931, in the Depression, and Charlie Brady was soon picking him up under the influence. Finally Brady caught him in the act of breaking into Logan's Market at three in the morning. He was trying to steal some groceries. Charlie took him around to the old jailhouse on Plum Street and the next morning they found him with both wrists slashed. Mamie gave birth to Delbert the week after the funeral.

Delbert was his father all over again. Mamie hired out for day work, so the boy grew up a typical Low Village street loafer, with no respect for property, and as uppity as Alf ever was. He actually nursed a *grudge* against Wrightsville. Swore he'd "get even" for what they'd "done" to his father!

A boy like that was bound to get into trouble. The Korean War ought to have straightened him out, but he came back in less than a year with a chest wound. By this time, Mamie was the Wheelers' housekeeper and all Delbert did was sit around the Wheeler kitchen making sarcastic remarks about the Hill families. For Mamie's sake, Anson Wheeler took him into the plant. Delbert lasted just three weeks. One lunch hour Anse caught him giving a speech to a large group of working people, ranting about what fools they were to stand for some of the conditions at the plant. Naturally, Anse had to fire him.

How Anson Wheeler could have married Mamie Hood after *that* was the only real mystery in the case—according to the ladies. Anse had asked for it and he got it—two cracks on the skull and the theft of fifteen thousand of his dollars, and the sooner that horrible boy was sent up to the State Penitentiary where he belonged the easier they'd all breathe nights.

"I'll take you up the Hill to see Mamie and Del," said Ed Hotchkiss eagerly.

"Wait, Ed," said Ellery. "Who's Del's lawyer?"

"Mort Danzig. He's got his office over his old man's stationery store near the Bijou, on Lower Main."

"I'll walk over to Mort's while you get your cousin Mamie to bring Delbert there. I'd rather talk to them in friendly territory."

"Who says it's friendly?" And, muttering, Ed drove his taxi off at twice the legal speed limit.

"I just don't know, Mr. Queen," said Ben Danzig's balding son worriedly in his plain office above the clatter of Lower Main. "There's an awfully strong circumstantial case against him. And if *I* can't make up my mind about his guilt or innocence—I've begged Mamie to get a different lawyer, but she's latched onto me."

"Who's sitting in the case, Mort?"

"Judge Peter Preston. Of the Hill Prestons," Mort Danzig added grimly. "If the judge hadn't been sick on and off this winter and the calendar crowded, I'd never have been able to delay the trial this long."

"What's your defense?"

Danzig shrugged. "No positive identification. Failure of the money to be found. Negative stuff. What else can I do? The boy's got no alibi—he says he was tramping the woods, alone, around Granjon Falls. He tried to escape afterward, he's responsible for poor Jeep Jorking's being laid up in the hospital, and there's that blamed handkerchief." The young lawyer stared at Ellery hopefully. "Do *you* think Del Hood is innocent?"

"I don't know yet," said Ellery. "Del did me a good turn once when he was bellhopping at the Hollis, and I remember him as a smart, nice kid. Mort, who went bail for him?"

"Anson Wheeler."

"Wheeler?"

"Well, the boy's ma is Anse's wife now, isn't she? You know the cockeyed code these old Hill families live by."

"But—then why did Wheeler press the charge?"

"That," said Morton F. Danzig drily, "is another section of said code. *I* don't pretend to understand it.—Oh, come in!"

Mamie Hood Wheeler was a plump, sturdy woman who looked like any year's All-American Mother, dressed up for the annual ceremony. She wore a modish hat and a Persian lamb coat that shrieked of newness and Boston. There was nothing

Boston could do for her hands, however—they were worked out, in ruins, and beyond repair. From the state of her eyes, she had been crying since September, and this was January.

If she'd stop crying, Ellery thought, she'd be an attractive woman. What were those women talking about?

"Now, now, Mrs. Wheeler," he said, taking her hands. "I can't promise anything."

"I know you'll get my Del off," she sobbed. She had a soft, surprisingly cultivated voice. "Thank you, thank you, Mr. Queen!"

"Mom." The tall boy with her was embarrassed. He was lean and burnt-out looking, with a slow, unhappy smile. "Hello, Mr. Queen. What do you want to bother with me for?"

"Del," said Ellery, looking him in the eye, "did you hold up your stepfather on the Ridge Road last September twenty-first and rob him of his payroll?"

"No, sir. But I don't expect you to believe me."

"No reason why you should," Ellery said cheerfully. "Tell me this, Del—how do you explain that handkerchief?"

"It was planted. I hadn't worn it for weeks—I thought I'd lost it."

"But he didn't mention it to anybody," said Mort Danzig. "Just to make it harder."

"I'm being framed, Mr. Danzig!"

"And this, Del," said Ellery. "Why, when Officer Jorking arrested you, did you try to run for it?"

"Because I went chicken. I knew they'd all hang it on me. It wasn't only the handkerchief. There were all those fights I'd had with old Anse."

"Del," said his mother, "don't speak about your—about Mr. Wheeler that way. He thinks he's doing the right thing. What we've got to do is convince him—and everybody—that you had nothing to do with it."

"What do you want me to do, Mom," cried the tall boy, "kiss his foot for trying to send me to prison? He's had it in for me from the day he caught me explaining to some of his plant workers what suckers they are. I should have cleared out then!"

"You've been out on bail for months," remarked Ellery. "Why haven't you cleared out while you've had the chance?"

The boy flushed. "I'm not that big a rat, with him putting up the bail. Besides, my mother still has to live in this one-horse town. The only thing I'm sorry about is that I lost my head when Jorking tried to pull me in."

"And you're still living in your stepfather's house, Del?"

"It's my mother's house now, too, isn't it?" Delbert said defiantly. "She's got some rights as his wife."

"Del," moaned Mamie.

"But isn't it awkward, Del? For you as well as for Mr. Wheeler?"

"We just ignore each other."

"Seems to me," said Ellery, "your stepfather's been awfully decent about several phases of this affair."

"All right!" shouted Delbert Hood. "I'll give him my Purple Heart!"

That was one of the things Ellery liked about this case. The villain was something of a saint and the young hero could have used a timely kick in the pants.

"Well, Delbert, there's only one way to get you out of this hole. If you're innocent, somebody else is guilty. Take your mom home and stay there with her. You'll hear from me."

Ellery crossed the Square to the Wrightsville National Bank and asked to see its president, Wolfert Van Horn.

Old Wolf hadn't changed. He merely looked older, scratchier, and more wolfish. He eyed Ellery's hand as if it were diseased and sat back to click his dentures carnivorously.

"You'll get no cooperation from me, Queen," said Wrightsville's leading banker in his knifelike voice. "That boy's guilty and Anse Wheeler is one of my bank's best customers. Would you like to open an account?"

"Now, Wolfert," said Ellery soothingly, "all I'm trying to do is pick up the facts of a business that happened almost five months ago. Tell me how Anson Wheeler's regular payroll day happened to be changed after so many years."

"Nothing to tell," said Wolfert Van Horn. "Tellers always made up Anse's payroll late Thursday afternoon, and first thing Friday morning Anse would pick it up at the bank here on his way to the plant. One Friday morning, middle of last September, a man with a handkerchief over his face tried to hold him up on the Ridge Road. Anse got away by stepping on the gas. So the next week—"

"Time," murmured Ellery. "As a result of the near holdup, Mr. Wheeler called a council of war that same evening at his home. Who were present at that meeting—in his study, I believe?"

"Anse Wheeler, Mamie, Chief Dakin, me, and my head cashier, Olin Keckley."

"Not Delbert Hood, then."

"He wasn't in the study, no. But he was in the living room reading, and the transom over the door between was wide open. He couldn't have helped but hear the whole thing."

"Delbert was still in the living room when the conference broke up and you left?"

"He was," said Wolfert, "and I'm going to say so on the witness stand under oath."

"At this meeting, it was decided that, unless the masked man were picked up beforehand, the next week Keckley would make up the Wheeler payroll on Wednesday instead of Thursday, and on Wednesday evening he, Keckley, would secretly take the payroll to your home. Mr. Wheeler was to pick it up at your house Thursday morning on his way to the plant. And all this was to be kept top-secret among those present. Is that right, Wolfert?"

"I know what you're after," grinned Van Horn, "but it wasn't *my* handkerchief that's Exhibit Number One in this case."

"Tell me—whose suggestion was it that the payroll day be advanced from Friday to Thursday?"

Wolfert started. "What difference does that make?" he demanded suspiciously. "I don't remember, anyhow!"

"Could we have Olin Keckley in here?"

Van Horn's head cashier was a gaunt grey man with a tic and a cringing look. In the days when John F. Wright had owned the bank, Ellery recalled, Keckley had been a pleasant fellow with a forthright eye.

"The suggestion about changing the day?" the cashier repeated, glancing quickly at Wolfert Van Horn. The banker looked bland. "Why, I'm sure I don't remember, Mr. Queen." Wolfert frowned. "Unless," Keckley hurried on, "unless it was me. Yes, I think—in fact, I'm sure it was me made the suggestion."

"Why, Olin, I think it was," said his employer.

"Clever of you, Mr. Keckley." Chief Dakin had told Ellery the suggestion had originated with Wolfert Van Horn. "And the following Wednesday night you dropped off the Wheeler payroll at Mr. Van Horn's house as planned?"

"Yes, sir."

"The payroll was in the customary canvas bag?"

"Well, no, sir. We figured that since the whole idea was to fool the robber, we ought to wrap the payroll in paper, like an ordinary package. In case," Keckley said earnestly, "the robber was watching the bank, or something like that."

"What kind of paper?"

"Plain brown wrapping paper."

"Sealed?"

"With scotch tape—yes, sir."

"I take it, Mr. Keckley, you didn't discuss the new plan with anyone at all?"

"No, sir! I didn't even let the other tellers see me make up the Wheeler payroll that Wednesday afternoon."

"And I suppose you didn't give any information away, Wolfert," said Ellery when the cashier, perspiring, had left. "I know, I know—don't bother. What time that Thursday morning did Anson Wheeler pick up the payroll at your house?"

"Quarter past seven."

"That early?" Ellery sat up. "And he was going directly to the Ridge Road, to his plant?"

"The plant's workday starts at eight o'clock."

"While the Wrightsville National Bank," murmured Ellery, "doesn't open its doors till nine-thirty."

He rose suddenly. "Be seeing you, Wolfert!"

Ellery had Ed Hotchkiss drive him up to Hill Valley. At the point where Shingle Street ends and Route 478A turns east to Twin Hill-in-the-Beeches, the Ridge Road begins, bearing north around the heavily forested hills above Wrightsville and then due west into the Valley.

Ed slowed his taxi down. "This is where the dirty work was

done, Mr. Queen. Nothing here but the road and woods, y'see—"

"We'll nose around the scene of the foul deed in due course, Edward. First let's talk to Anse Wheeler."

The Wheeler Company occupied a long low building of blackened brick not far from Wrightsville Airport. It was as ugly a factory as the old machine shop in Low Village, which was Ellery's standard frame of reference. Inside, the building was poorly lighted and even more poorly ventilated, the floors sagged alarmingly under the weight of the heavy machinery, generations of dirt crusted the walls, and the workmen labored in silence. Ellery, who had begun to like Anson Wheeler, decided to dislike him all over again.

He found the owner in a bare, chilly office of scarified golden oak. Wheeler was a tense-looking man of middle age and height, with eyes as pale as his cheeks. His high-pitched voice had a chronic note of resentment in it, almost a whine.

"I know, I know what you're here for, Mr. Queen," he said bitterly. "Van Horn's already phoned me. Well, I consider myself a fair man. I won't have you think I'm persecuting him. But I tell you the boy did it. If I weren't convinced, do you think I'd press this case? I'm—I'm very fond of Mrs. Wheeler, but she's got to see Delbert as he really is. A troublemaker, a thief! It's not the money, Mr. Queen. It's—*him.*"

"But suppose, Mr. Wheeler, you found out that Del didn't do it?"

"I'd be a very happy man," said Anse Wheeler with a groan. Then his thin lips tightened. "But he did."

"That first time—the unsuccessful attempt. Did you get a good look at the masked man before you got away?"

"Well, he was sort of tall and thin. There was a silk-looking handkerchief over his face. I was too excited to notice anything else. But later, looking back, I realized it must have been Delbert."

"He was pointing a gun, I believe?"

"Yes. But the boy has a gun. He brought one back with him from Korea."

"He made no attempt to fire after you as you stepped on the gas?"

"I don't know. They didn't find any bullet holes in the car. I almost ran him down. He jumped into a bush."

"You understand, of course, Mr. Wheeler, that it might have been anybody tall and thin—"

"You think I'm pinning it on him!" cried Anson Wheeler. "Well, how about that handkerchief? The next Thursday?"

"Tell me about it, Mr. Wheeler," said Ellery sympathetically.

"I picked up my payroll at Wolfert's house early that morning and took the Ridge Road as usual." Wheeler's high voice climbed higher. "There, at almost the same spot as the Friday morning before, was a tree across the road. I came on it so unexpectedly around the bend, all I could think to do was jam on my brakes, grab the package of money, and try to run for it. He—he hit me. As I got out of my car."

"Del hit you, Mr. Wheeler?" murmured Ellery.

"I didn't actually see him, no. My back was to him. But wait! The whack on my head dazed me only for a second or two—he must have missed where he was aiming. I tried to fight him." Wheeler's pale eyes flashed fire suddenly. "He's a strong boy and he's been in the Army—oh, he knew how to get me! He crooked his arm around my throat from behind, and I was helpless. I reached up and tried to claw at his face. I felt something silky in my fingers and then he hit me on the back of the head again. Next thing I knew Officer Jorking was reviving me. The money was gone, but I'd held onto the handkerchief. *It was Delbert's!*"

"You're positive," said Ellery, "it was his?"

"Had his initials on it! I'd given him that silk pocket handkerchief when I married his mother. I outfitted that boy from head to foot!"

Ellery left Anson K. Wheeler in his grimy office, tight face bloodless and long fingers feeling the back of his head.

Officer Jorking lay in the men's ward at Wrightsville General Hospital munching disgustedly at a winter apple. His left leg and thigh were buried to the hip in a bulky cast, and he was lying in a maze of traction apparatus.

"I feel like some screwball's invention," said the young policeman out of a deep gloom. "And stuck in this contraption

since last September! If they don't give that kid ten years, Mr.
Queen, I'll personally break his neck."

"Tough all around, Jeep," mourned Ellery, sitting down beside
the hospital bed. "How did it happen?"

Young Jorking spat out an apple pip. "The Ridge Road's part
of my beat—I cover the whole district north of town. When
Mr. Wheeler was almost held up that first time, Chief Dakin
ordered me to keep my eye on him without letting on. So when
Wheeler picked up his payroll that morning at Van Horn's on
North Hill Drive, I was tailing him in my prowl-car.

"He turned into Ridge Road, me staying far enough back so I
won't make Wheeler suspicious. I didn't come around the bend
of the road till it was all over—that's how the kid got away from
me. Wheeler was stretched out cold, blood streaming from his
head, and a skinny tall figure was just diving into the woods to
the east of the road."

"To the east?"

"Yes, sir. I fired a couple of shots in his direction, but I didn't
hit anything, and by the time I'd pulled up where he'd gone for
cover there wasn't a sign of him. So I reported to headquarters
on my two-way radio and took care of Mr. Wheeler. He wasn't
dead, wasn't even hurt bad.

"The first thing I spotted was that silk handkerchief in his
hand, with the initials *DH*. Every buck in town knew that
handkerchief—it was the first silk one young Del'd ever owned,
and he kept showing it off—so I knew right away who it had
been."

"How did he break your hip?" asked Ellery.

"I broke it going after him." The young officer spat out
another pip. "Del walked into the house quite a while after I
got Mr. Wheeler home. The kid was sort of scratched up and
his clothes were full of bits of twig and thorn. He said he'd been
tramping through the woods. I told him what happened,
showed him his hanky, and said I'd have to pull him in. Darned
if he didn't take off—jumped clean through a window! I chased
him along the edge of that ravine behind the Wheeler house,
and that's how I came to bust my hip. Tripped over a root and
fell smack into the ravine. It's a wonder I didn't break my back.

"It was Del packed me out of there. Seems he saw me tumble

in and decided to turn Boy Scout." Young Jorking scowled at his mummified left foot and flung the apple core at it. "Ah, it's a crazy mixed-up kind of case, Mr. Queen. I wish I didn't have to testify."

So then Ellery went over to police headquarters and sat down in Chief Dakin's swivel chair near the picture of J. Edgar Hoover and he said, "Mind if I mull over this for a while?"

"Mull away," grunted Dakin. The Chief stood at his window studying State Street.

Finally Ellery said, "My muller seems out of order. Did you *consider* any other possibilities, Dakin?"

"Like fury," said the Chief of Police, not unkindly. "But who would you have me pin it on? The only others who knew about that switch in payroll days were Wheeler himself, Mamie, Wolfert Van Horn, and Olin Keckley.

"Wolf Van Horn might have done it, sure, if there were a million or two involved. But I can't see him risking the pen at his age for a measly fifteen thousand—not with all the money he's got. Keckley? A man like Olin might help himself from the till under certain circumstances, but armed robbery? masks? hitting folks over the head? jumping into bushes?" The Chief shook his head. "Not Olin. He'd faint dead away first."

"Then one of them must have babbled."

"Could be. Only they all say they didn't."

"Damn." Ellery gnawed on a knuckle. "About the payroll, Dakin. You never found any part of it?"

"Nary a dime."

"Where'd you look?"

"We searched the Wheeler house and grounds, and just about every other place in and out of town where young Del's known to hang around. He's got it hid somewhere, of course. Probably hid it right after the holdup."

"Did you search the woods?"

"Near the scene, on the theory that the robber might have dropped it when Jorking chased him, or hid it as part of a plan? Yep," said Chief Dakin, "we searched those woods east of the road with a fine-tooth comb, Mr. Queen."

"Only east of the road?"

Dakin stared. "That's the direction the robber took when he lit out."

"But why not west, too? He might have doubled back across the road somewhere out of Jeep's view."

Dakin shook his head. "You're wasting your time, Mr. Queen. Supposing you even found the money. That'd be fine for Anse Wheeler, but how would it help get young Del off?"

"It's a loose end," said Ellery irritably. "You never know how a loose end ties in, Dakin. And, anyway, I've covered everything else. Come on, you're going to search with me . . ."

They found the stolen Wheeler payroll in the woods not fifty yards west of the Ridge Road, on a due line from the spot where Anson Wheeler had been held up the preceding September.

Chief Dakin was chagrined. "I feel like a dummy."

"Needn't," said Ellery, intent, on his knees. "Last fall these woods were in full foliage, and to have found anything like this would have constituted an act of God. In January, with the trees stripped bare and the ground clear, it's a different boiler of bass."

The package of money had been buried in a shallow pit at the base of a tree. But rains and winds had torn away the thin covering of dirt and leaf mold, and both men had spotted the package bulging soddenly out of the earth at the same time.

Nature had been unkind to Anson Wheeler's payroll. The brown paper in which it was wrapped had disintegrated under the action of soil and elements. Small animals and birds had evidently gnawed at the rotting, mildewed, moldy bills. Insects had contributed to the wreckage. Most of the paper money was in unrecognizable, fused lumps and shreds.

"If there's two thousand dollars in salvage left," muttered Wrightsville's Chief of Police, "Anse is in luck. Only there ain't."

"It was that awfully hot Indian summer and this mild winter," murmured Ellery. "Most of the damage was done before the ground hardened." He got to his feet. "Fortunately."

"For who?"

"For Del Hood. This mass of corruption is going to keep young Delbert out of jail."

"What!"

"Up to now I've only hoped the boy was innocent. Now I know it."

Chief Dakin stared at him. Then, bewilderedly, he squatted to examine the remains of the payroll, as if he had missed a clue buried in it somewhere.

"But I don't see—"

"Later, Dakin. Right now we'd better gather this filth up. It's evidence."

When everyone was arranged to Ellery's satisfaction, he looked about him and said, "This one has the beautiful merit of simplicity.

"Look. Robber assaults Mr. Wheeler on the Ridge Road, snatches the payroll in its paper wrappings, and shortly thereafter buries the package in a shallow pit in the woods not fifty yards from the scene of the robbery. This is last September I'm talking about.

"Now, a robber who buries his loot immediately after he's stolen it either intends it as a temporary cache—till the first hue-and-cry blows over—or as a long-term hiding place, till the case is practically forgotten, say, or till he's served a prison term.

"Did our robber mean that hole in the woods to be the hiding place of his loot for a short time or a long time?

"For a short time," said Ellery, answering himself, "obviously. No robber in his right mind would take fifteen thousand dollars in paper money, wrapped in paper wrappings, and bury it for any length of time. If he had the sense he was born with, he'd know what he'd find when he came back—what, in fact, Chief Dakin and I did find—a soggy, eaten-up, chewed-away, disintegrated wad of valueless pulp. For a long-time burial, he'd have provided himself with a weather-resistant container of some sort—of metal, or at least of heavy wood.

"Our robber, then, had no long-term view in mind. By burying the payroll in its perishable paper wrappings—in a shallow hole—he tells us that he intended it to lie there for a very short time. Perhaps only for hours—or, at the most, days.

"But as it turns out, he left it there for almost five months—until, as you see, it was practically destroyed. I ask the reasonable question—why, after planning to retrieve it in a short time, did he leave it there to rot? Certainly at some period in the past five months it must have been perfectly safe for him to dig it up. In fact, he would have been safe any time after the first few days. Nobody's been shadowed in this case—not even Del, out on bail. And the spot is a lonely one, well off the road in the woods. So again I ask—why didn't the robber come back for his loot? To spend it, or to transfer it to another hiding place, or to repackage it if for no other reason?"

Ellery grinned without much humor. He said simply: "If he didn't come back for the payroll when there was every reason for him to do so, and with no risk, then logically it can only have been because he *couldn't* come back. And that's why I've had you wheeled into this private room," Ellery said, turning to the young policeman trussed up in the hospital bed, "so you could face the man you've victimized and the woman you've crucified and the boy you've tried to throw to the dogs, Jeep— yes, and the honest cop who trained you and trusted you and who's looking at you now and really seeing you, I'm sure, for the first time.

"You're the only one involved, Jorking, who physically couldn't get back to that cache in the woods.

"You learned about the change in the payroll day through Chief Dakin, who assigned you to the job of tailing Mr. Wheeler in your prowl-car. But you didn't tail Mr. Wheeler in your prowl-car that morning, Jorking—you were already on your selected site, as you had been the week before, lurking behind your ambush, your police car hidden off the road.

"You assaulted Mr. Wheeler from behind and you saw to it that Del's silk handkerchief—it was easy enough for you to get it once you decided to frame him—remained in Mr. Wheeler's grip. If he hadn't ripped the handkerchief off your face, you would have left it in or near his hand.

"And while he was still unconscious, you darted into the woods to the west and hastily buried the package of money— because you were playing two roles at the moment and time was precious just then—intending to come back for the money later in the day, or the next day, when the coast would be clear. But after taking Mr. Wheeler back to his home and solemnly arresting Delbert for the crime you had committed, the boy bolted, you had to chase him, you accidentally broke your hip, and they rushed you to the hospital where you've been immobilized ever since. You're not only a thief, Jeep, you're a disgrace to an undervalued profession, and I'm going to hang around Wrightsville long enough to see you immobilized in the clink."

When Ellery turned from the frozen man in the bed, he realized that he was—in a queer sense—quite alone. Chief Dakin was facing the wall. Mamie Hood Wheeler sat crying joyfully in a sphere of her own. And above her, Anse Wheeler, so pale with excitement that he was sky-blue, thumped Del Hood repeatedly on the back, and Del Hood, with a wild friendliness, was giving his stepfather thump for thump.

So Ellery went away, quietly.

JULIA DEHAHN

GIRLS AND BOYS
TOGETHER

In the world of high fashion and modeling, things are seldom what they seem.

That sleek brunette running toward the Dutch airliner in the *Sunday Times* magazine section (full page) last week was going nowhere but home to West 24th Street for some fish stew and aoli with her husband when the shooting session ended that day. And the lightly tanned, very young blonde with the crackly voice, the thick eyebrows, and the long braid down her back in the current peek-a-boo bathing-suit commercials worked them in between her final exams at Sarah Lawrence. I know because they're both my models.

I'm Midge Gibson, owner of the Gibson Model Agency here in New York. If you're not in the rag or cosmetics business it's possible you haven't heard of me, but if you are you know I'm the tough-but-heart-of-gold ex-model from Ohio—father a fire chief—who made it big as a cover girl in the Forties and early Fifties.

Unlike most top models in those days, I saved my money and used it to start the agency when my modeling assignments dwindled to a barely living wage. I've always had a good head for business and modeling is the business I know best—I sure didn't know how to keep a marriage together.

For a few years the agency went nowhere—I still have nightmares about that mean period—but then, in 1963, the phone and the cash register started ringing and I knew exactly what to do when they did.

Three years later I moved the agency from a small office in Murray Hill to the penthouse we occupy now in the Fifties just west of Fifth Avenue.

Betty Paris, another ex-model and my best friend, joined me

73

as associate in 1970 after her husband died. With Betty, Phyllis Freeman, the receptionist, a live-in couple, Billy and Blanche Bartee, who cook, clean, chauffeur, take care of the two cats, Baby and Shah, and tell us all when we're getting out of hand, the agency runs as smoothly as any I know.

Smoothly, that is, until this past November. That's when Nadine Nicholson signed with us. We keep a maximum stable of ten top models under exclusive contract. Barrie Abrams moved to Spain when her second three-year contract ran out in September and Betty and I interviewed for weeks before deciding on Nadine as her successor.

No doubt it happens to everyone hiring in any business: no matter how good you think you are at judging character and professionalism, once in a while you pick a lemon.

I remember the guys at the Stage Door Canteen calling hand grenades lemons. That's the kind of lemon Nadine was.

Yes, was. Billy Bartee found Nadine floating face-down in the indoor swimming pool she was so fond of here early one morning last week.

Her first few weeks with the agency I didn't notice anything off about her. She kept to herself, came and went discreetly between jobs. She took advantage of the pool from the beginning, but for exercise and relaxation, I think, not as an excuse to make friendly. New models are often shy with the others, or they believe in keeping their distance at first, or they're too preoccupied between appointments to divide their attention. I was too preoccupied myself to pay much attention. But as Christmas approached I observed a number of incidents that disturbed me.

Incident. Phyllis Freeman crying at the switchboard. Phyllis is as attractive as most models in the business, but she has two children and wants more fast, refuses to give more than minimum time to her appearance, and flinches when she sees a camera. She could make a fortune on her voice. One day when Howard Reese phoned, he took notice of it and offered her a voice-over in one of his commercials, but she said no. She's very calm and competent, a jewel. When I found her crying, I immediately thought of her children and asked if something had happened at home.

Shock at that idea put things in perspective. She blew her nose. "It's nothing, Midge, really." The board lit up with a beep and she reached to answer it.

"Come by and see me before you leave," I told her. She frowned and nodded her head.

I had to crank it out of her. She'd been told she was a stupid hick for having—according to Nadine—bungled a phone message. "Impossible," I said.

"That I bungled a message?" Phyllis said. "Believe me, it's possible. Sometimes it's like a zoo out there. I could easily transpose some numbers or mishear a message or a name. No one's ever accused me of it, but everybody's so understanding around here."

Incident. Jeannie Carmichael, the college girl in the bathing-suit commercials. She was bent over her art-history books in the lounge one afternoon when I was in the adjoining kitchen planning the Christmas party with Blanche. Leila Moth was working on a piece of embroidery and Nadine was sitting at the edge of the pool at the far end of the lounge when I'd passed through. Blanche and I were at the kitchen table, she making a shopping list, me doing some fast addition, when I heard Nadine.

"Sarah Lawrence." She sounded amused. "Who's she?"

"It's a school, dummy."

"Are you a freshperson?" Nadine asked.

Blanche and I looked at each other.

What? I thought. *What?* Who was asking for it here? Jeannie, who was the new girl before Nadine, or Nadine?

Incident. Another exchange, this one between Nadine and Charlene Bush.

If I have a favorite among the girls, it's Charlene. She's a stunning, impeccably educated black woman from Camden. She and Ursual Kruger are the tallest of our models—Charlene is five eleven and Ursula is six one. Charlene is so unfashionably top-heavy we hesitated about signing her. But what a mistake if we hadn't! The presence, intelligence, and beauty of that girl— she's one of a kind. And she'll last.

This day my office door was open as Nadine passed Charlene in the reception area on her way out. "There's a message for you at the desk, Butch," she said.

"Thanks," Charlene said. "The name's Bush."

"Oh. As in bush league?"

"No, as in beat the bushes long enough and you'll find out."

Incident. Billy Bartee. "No big problem, Midge, but that new girl has some wrong ideas about how things work around here. About meals and how often her dressing room gets cleaned up after her. I keep having to set her straight about the use of the car, too."

I told him I'd explained all that to her before she'd signed up, as I had to all the girls.

"I know," Billy said. "What I'm saying is she needs a little reminding—from you."

Incident. Getting into her coat to go home one evening, Phyllis hesitated, then said, "I don't want you to think I have it in for Nadine, Midge, but you should know she takes more than passing interest in the phone messages I leave on the counter. It makes me nervous. There's information there that's none of her business. Should I change the system or what?"

Incident. Betty knocked on my door the Monday morning before Christmas and asked if I had a few minutes. She'd gone to the theater the night before with Barney Silverman, the fashion photographer, and he'd told her our new model had beautiful, delicate coloring, a faultless sense of pose—and the nastiest mouth of any model he's worked with in years. He'd spent the first few weeks in December on a store catalogue featuring Nadine and June Nesbitt from the Carroll Agency and Nadine was so snide with the other girl, Barney didn't relish the idea of working with her again.

Incident. The eve before Christmas Eve. Every year I hold open house for anyone special who's ever been connected with the agency, and their guests. Blanche and Billy, with some impromptu help from all of us, do the decorating and cooking and serving—except for the bar, which is usually tended by husbands and boy friends, but this year my son (and only child) Dave, a junior at Yale, and Betty's twin sons, who are in high school in New York, took over. When they leaned too heavily—

or too lightly—on the liquor or the ice or the seltzer bottle, no one hesitated to make the adjustments. There was good music on the stereo and snow falling past the windows. Everyone was flushed, brushed, and polished. There was happy talk, laughter, and presents. Hugs and kisses.

Enter the cause of the incident—Mario Bonilla, Ramona's brother, an intern at St. Luke's. Ramona earns most of her phenomenal income advertising eye products. Her thickly lashed dark eyes speak volumes about her origins and hint promisingly of the future. Mario's do the same.

He hung his coat on one of the hired racks in the foyer and went straight to Angel Ciccone, Ramona's close friend here at the agency. Angel, who's taller than Mario and our lithest girl—she's studying to be a dancer—and Mario were planning to marry when he was able to pull his full weight financially. He didn't trust the money Angel was making or what it would do to their marriage if they were both dependent on it.

I was talking with Dolly River, the first model I ever signed. Her white-blonde hair is still shoulder-length, her jewelry as dramatic as ever. She and her husband Jules, a television producer, live on the Coast now, but they usually spend the holidays in New York.

"Oh, my," she said, sighting on Mario. "What a specimen. He ought to be in pictures. Is he, by any chance?"

"You're way off. He's on his way to becoming a doctor," I told her. "That girl on his arm is Angel Ciccone, one of my girls. The one in the pink taffeta suit talking to them, moving to the music, is his sister Ramona, also one of my girls."

"You've always had wonderful taste."

"In women, anyway," I agreed.

"*That's* a new face." Dolly was eyeing Nadine, off in a corner allowing Jules to retie the delicate bow at the shoulder of her deep-violet camisole-top gown. "Or should I say a new shoulder. Is it one of yours?"

"Yes."

"She looks a little predatory to me. Is she?"

"I don't know." My voice came back wistful.

Dolly picked up on it. She laughed and squeezed my elbow before drifting off toward the corner. "I didn't mean that seriously. I was just pretending to be threatened by a pretty young face. I do it all the time now."

Before Dolly reached Jules, Nadine had drifted away from him through the crowd, getting to know people and to be known.

I did some drifting of my own, before settling down in my office for a quiet drink with Charlene and her husband, John, Betty, and Barney Silverman. We were discussing how the day is coming when top models will earn as much as star athletes—whatever the traffic will bear—when I saw Blanche at the door giving me the high sign for a private word. I excused myself and joined her in the kitchen.

"We've lost two guests," she said. "They didn't stop to say goodbye or Merry Christmas."

"Who?"

"First, Angel—in a rush, dragging her coat after her—then, a couple of minutes ago, Mario, looking crazy."

"Where's Ramona?"

"Out there"—she directed her head toward the lounge—"drinking too much, looking daggers at Nicholson."

"Was Nadine coming on with Mario?"

"She's coming on with every man in the room. That little old bow on her shoulder sure does need a lot of retying." She shook her head. "All these boy scouts and not one of them can tie a decent knot."

"It's pretty obvious if it's a number."

"It's a number all right, and it's pretty obvious. She's a pretty obvious lady. To women."

"But not to men—"

Barney Silverman, all stunning white hair and black tuxedo, was at the swinging door, his chesterfield over his arm. "I'm sorry if this is private but I don't want to leave without thanking you. I have an early day tomorrow. It was another wonderful party, girls."

We exchanged kisses, Blanche and Barney, Barney and me.

He stepped into the kitchen and the door flapped shut behind him. He looked from me to Blanche. "You got a problem?"

I gave him a shrug maybe.

"You think somebody here is obvious to women but not to men?" Blanche gave him her poker face. "If that somebody's who I think she is, you might be interested to know I find her obvious, obsessed, obtuse, and obnoxious. In a word—objectionable."

"My, my," Blanche said.

"Yes." Barney looked from her to me. "Trouble in paradise," he said. "This is serious."

Dave and I spent the three-day holiday catching up with each other, talking late, sleeping late. We saw a play and had supper out afterward one night but the rest of the time he spent with his friends. He confessed he was smitten with Jeannie, which surprised me not at all, and brought the conversation around to her at the drop of a hat, a pine needle, an icicle from the roof, a hint from me, anything.

The second day back, Betty and I sat down over tea and toast and discussed Nadine. "I don't like what I'm seeing," I told her. "I've looked over her references and the notes we took when we interviewed her, and I don't understand. We've turned down dozens of girls with the character she's exhibiting. Why did we sign her? She seemed different in the interviews. She had a good professional reputation."

"You've answered your own question," Betty said. "And let's not kid ourselves. There was always something calculating about her, but she was obviously capable of making us a lot of money. And there was all that competition from the other agencies, remember? We were lucky to get her."

"So we thought. Did she manufacture that competition, do you think?"

"She may have exaggerated it, but she didn't manufacture it."

"She calls both the cats Mouser."

"I know, that's her idea of humor. She's got a thing about disparaging people's names and what they do." She inspected a cold piece of toast and took a bite. "What are the positive things about her? Maybe if we concentrate on her good qualities."

"She's not lazy."

"She's not unamibitious," Betty agreed.

"Money in the bank for us."

Betty nodded. "Go on."

"She's professional."

"If you call being catty professional."

Baby was sleeping innocently on the chair in the corner. Cats are so maligned. "She works hard," I said desperately.

"You said that."

"She's prompt."

"She'd better be."

"She has guts."

"She'd better have."

"Her sex appeal is exceptional."

"Aye."

"We've never broken a contract with anyone. What do you think would happen if we broke this one with her?"

"With a good substantial bonus?"

"Yes, of course."

"She'd sue us for breach of contract, with no substantial cause, and she'd be right. Even if she didn't, it would dirty our reputation."

"She could use," I ventured, "what's called counseling. Do we dare suggest it? At our expense?"

"I hate playing God," Betty said. "Unless I'm asked, of course."

I started slamming the china back onto the tray. "I hate having the problem. She's so tricky, Betty. Why didn't we see it? We've been around."

" 'Knavery's plain face is never seen till used.' "

"What?"

"Nothing. A little Shakespeare."

"Oh, good. Just what I need right now."

Incident (Observed). After looking through Leila Moth's portfolio with great friendly interest, Nadine asked her how one goes about camouflaging a very short neck.

Incident (Reported by Blanche). Nadine encountered Leila, who gains weight easily, snacking on applesauce in the kitchen and told her the amount she'd consumed represented 230 calories. Leila called her a name and Nadine said she'd only mentioned it for her own good.

Incident (Reported by Charlene). Nadine asked Ramona if the reason she never smiled at the cameras or anyone was because she had bad teeth or something.

Incident (Observed). A group of the girls relaxing in the lounge, Nadine, her legs crossed, the foot of the crossed leg circling slowly over and over, staring unblinkingly at Charlene's generously endowed figure as if it were seriously flawed.

Incident (Reported by Phillis). Ursula, who separated from her husband after the holidays, showed up puffy-eyed one morning. "A sleepless night?" Nadine asked her.

For a short while the girls launched a counteroffensive, attacking her maliciousness and narcissism, aping her posture and gestures and tone of voice, kissing themselves in the mirror and mocking each other airily. "My deah, have you evah considered corn-rowing yoah hayah?" Leila asked Charlene. "You-ah are-ah ah natural."

"Speaking of *natural,*" Charlene said, "come the next revival of *Cat on a Hot Tin Roof,* you are a shoo-in for the role of one of the no-neck monsters."

Leila slithered past her and sang. "Ah'm the cream in mah cawfee—"

"I'm the top!" Charlene belted—her voice ranges from strong contralto to hearty soprano— "I'm the Colosseum—"

"Ah go to mah *haid,*" Leila started stormily, "lak the bubbles in a—" she hesitated "—blah blah blah blah. What are the words?" And she and Charlene broke into laughter.

But it was all too clear Nadine loved the attention, so they went back to pretending indifference.

And then she was killed.

I didn't see her at all the day before. It was a ratrace kind of day, practically everybody paying the piper for having had the holidays. Most of the girls' schedules were so full they weren't stopping by for a breather between appointments. I was up to my ears in bookkeeping, trying to keep this year's accounts up to date and starting to prepare last year's taxes.

Midafternoon I went into the kitchen, made myself a cup of tea, and brought one out to Phyllis. "Is anyone around?" I asked her.

"Jeannie and Ramona."

"Any others due in?"

"Only Ursula later that I know of."

I wandered with my tea to the lounge, where Jeannie sat absently stroking Baby, who was nestled in the chair beside her, as she read the Italian *Vogue* that had come in the morning's mail. "Mama mia," she said, ogling a gown that managed to be both baroque and bare.

"Where's Ramona?"

"In her dressing room, I think."

I wandered back to the kitchen, finishing the tea and thinking about Ramona—and Angel and Mario. Something was wrong there and had been since Christmas. Whatever had happened at the party almost certainly had something to do with it.

I had no inkling of Nadine's private life aside from the fact that she spent a disconcerting amount of time sleeping over— far more than any other girl ever had. The dressing rooms all have daybeds and the girls are welcome to sleep over any time and as often as they want. But they seldom take advantage of it unless there's a blackout or they have a very late or early flight to or from Kennedy. Even during the transit strike it didn't turn into a dormitory.

Rinsing the cup and saucer and putting them in the dishwasher, I thought how neither Angel nor Ramona had joined in the other girls' counteroffensive on Nadine. Before the holidays, her push-pull overtures and withdrawals had thrown them both off balance. They were streetwise, both of them, but they were family-oriented and we were all one big happy family, weren't we? When Nadine followed one too many truces with yet another insult, the hostility was complete. They refused to respond to anything but the contempt. With stony silence. But what bothered me more than that was that since Christmas Ramona and Angel were distant with each other.

I knocked on Ramona's door.

"Who is it?"

"Midge."

"Come in."

She was at the dressing table, polishing her long nails a porcelain-pale shade of pink. "Hi," she said, no smile. "Make yourself at home."

"I was taking a breather," I said. "Jeannie said you were here."

It was very quiet. She acknowledged the unusualness of it with a toss of her head. "It's like the eye of a hurricane."

"I never complain when business is good." She didn't look at me. "Are you tired?" I asked her.

"Very."

"It doesn't show physically."

"I can't afford to let it, can I?"

She placed the brush in the bottle and observed her wet nails. They were perfect, a work of art. "When I get old I can always be a manicurist." Old, according to her, was about 35. The statement itself was a barb about how I lecture the girls about saving their money and thinking about the future. When Ramona did discuss her future, it was usually to imply that her opportunities were limited. Which cut no ice with me.

"Why not open your own beauty salon?"

She gave me a look.

"Is something bothering you, Ramona? Is there anything I can help you with?"

"No."

Which is what I deserved for asking two questions at the same time.

Billy was doing his nightly—or I should say early-morning—cleaning when he found her floating face-down in the swimming pool, her once-beautiful back hideously bruised, one of the light aluminum poolside chairs drifting not far away from her. He checked the premises—there were only he and Blanche—then he phoned me and the police; in that order, within seconds of each other.

When I arrived half an hour later, the police were in charge and Nadine was now face-down on the tile floor by the side of the pool, purple and wet in her favorite print bikini. I went to the office and cried. Where is all the oxygen in the atmosphere when you really need it? I knew I had to pull myself together fast. There's all too much reality in the fantasy world where I work but never more so than at that moment.

Plainclothes Sergeant Joseph McCool from Manhattan's special homicide task force was a big, soft-looking man with a soft, whispery voice I imagined could be quite lethal. It would be a mistake to think he was soft inside.

He interrogated the three of us about our actions and observations of the previous twenty-four hours, Billy in his work clothes, Blanche in her terrycloth robe—both of them dry-eyed and cautious—and me in I don't remember what, saying I hardly knew what.

I described how my day had gone until I had left, just after seven, leaving no one there but Ramona, Blanche, and Billy. I'd gone home to my apartment on Central Park West, stopping only at a drugstore near my apartment for some things.

"How did you spend the evening?" Sergeant McCool asked the Bartees.

"We had dinner here, went to a nine o'clock movie at the Little Carnegie, came back, had a beer and watched the eleven o'clock news, then went to bed," Blanche told him.

"We go to bed after the news most nights," Billy said. "Then I get up around three to clean up for the morning."

"Do you set the alarm?"

"I don't need to."

"Meaning what? Your wife wakes you up? You're an insomniac? You have a biological alarm clock?"

"That last, I guess. I just wake up in time to do what I have to do. I don't care much about sleep."

"How about the lights when you went to bed?"

"They were all on dim. We leave them on dim when we go to bed—and when we go out and no one's in the lounge or the kitchen. The girls are free to come and go at any hour and so the lights are always on."

"Was there anyone in the pool when you went to bed?"

Billy looked sick. "I don't know. I didn't hear anyone."

"Miss Bonilla was here when Miss Gibson left," the sergeant said. "Was she still here when you left for the movies?"

"She may have been in her dressing room," Blanche said. "I didn't see her."

"Was anyone else here between the time Miss Gibson left and you went to the movies?"

"I didn't see or hear anyone," Blanche said. Billy shook his head in agreement.

"How about when you got back?"

"They all could have been in their dressing rooms asleep for all we'd know," Blanche said. "All the doors were shut and it was quiet."

"Is that usual?"

"The *most* usual?"

Sergeant McCool turned back to me. "Don't you keep a log? Don't they have to sign in and out, at least after hours?" I shook my head. "I'd like to speak to you alone," he said.

I led the way to my office and he shut the door behind us. As he did, the phone rang. I reached for it but he restrained my hand and took the call. "Yeah," he said, then listened. "Nope. Nope. No comment. And have a pity. It's dead of night for non-hounds." He had been watching me and when he hung up he said, "You need a drink." He went to the bar and poured a good belt of bourbon into an old-fashioned glass. I had to hold the glass with both hands to drink from it.

"Have one yourself," I told him.

He shook his head. "Never on duty. Plenty enough off. Drink up."

The phone rang again and he talked into it while I drank. "The press again," he said, hanging up. "You're going to get a lot of publicity. I'll have Chaney and Donalson spell each other at the switchboard for the next day or two. There's more than one way a murderer returns to the scene of a crime. There are newsmen downstairs. I'll talk to them on my way out, but in your own best interests I advise you not to comment to them."

"Happy to oblige," I told him. "But today is a workday. How do the girls come and go without harassment?"

"My boys will help," he said.

His boys! Jeannie and others have voiced their disapproval at my calling them my girls and I agree with them in principle but so far haven't found a workable alternative. I wondered how the sergeant's men liked being called his boys.

He asked me how the agency operated, who the salaried

personnel were, facts about the girls. He wanted them all here sometime during the day—he'd do his best to time his interrogations around their appointments.

"I'll do what I can," I promised, "but one is on vacation visiting her family in Australia and three are on jobs out of the country. One of them, Charlene Bush, is due back from Rome sometime tomorrow."

He looked through me, thinking.

"You'll like her. She's a strapping girl."

He smiled. "I like you."

"That's nice."

"I like you, but I don't like what's happened here."

"Do you think I do?"

"No, I don't think you do. I hope you can help us get to the heart of it fast."

"I'll try," I said.

"The faster the better. The longer it takes to solve a case, the less likely we will. It goes downhill as the clues get cold. We depend on confusion shock. That's why we put in long hours at the beginning of a case." There was movement in the foyer outside the closed door. "Excuse me for a minute," he said, and went out.

They were removing the body. I didn't want to see that. I waited and drank more of the bourbon. When it was gone, I went for another, and was half into it when he returned.

"They've closed off the lounge and the pool. The dressing rooms are being checked out now, but they should be okay for your girls by the time they come. Walk me to the door."

As I did, he stopped and peered at the framed photographs on the walls of Gibson models past and present. "Shh," he said, shaking his head, "they're all so gorgeous." At the door he added, "*She* was gorgeous. I *like* this place. What happened here?"

"I don't know," I said, thankful for the whiskey. "She was only with the agency for a few months and I was beginning not to like her—she was one of those people who enjoy making trouble just for the hell of it. But she didn't deserve this. I'll help you any way I can, I promise."

"I believe you will," he said. "But if you have any idea of the homicide statistics in this city, you'll know we don't have much time to spend on this one, no matter how big the headlines get. Let's help each other in that time all we can."

He put on his hat. "I'll see you in a little while."

I pulled a blanket and pillow down from the closet shelf and arranged them on the sofa, then finished the drink and brought the empty glass to the kitchen. As I swung in the door, Billy was facing me, his face hard and tense. Blanche was standing apart from him, facing the long counter below the cupboards, crying, her arms folded in front of her. I went and put my arm around her.

"It must have been terrible for you both."

"Tell her, Billy," Blanche said, sniffing. "Tell her, damn it."

"Damn it yourself, woman. If you're so eager to make it public, tell her yourself."

Blanche's damp eyes blazed. She swiped at them with an honest-to-God handkerchief from her bathrobe pocket and said, "She came on to him, Midge. All the time. Whenever she came in for a swim or something. She used this place like no one ever has, you know that—it was like wherever she lived she didn't want to go to. She came on to him and finally one night last week when he came on back to her she put him down so bad he—he came in and told me about it. He's been in a bad temper ever since."

I looked at him. He stared into space, his eyes bloodshot and his jaw like stone.

"How do you tell the police that kind of action and expect them not to collar him for that?" Blanche asked, gesturing with her head toward the pool. "Billy can be mean when he's hurt, Midge, and so can I, but if he was going to murder anyone he'd have murdered me and a couple of other people a long time ago. She was a serious aggravation to *both* of us, but *no way* was she worth murdering."

I was up a little after seven. Detective Chaney, an amiable young man in a brown-tweed jacket and grey slacks, was at the switchboard reading a textbook on criminal justice. I told him I'd be making some calls. But I wasn't early enough—he'd already taken calls from Betty and Angel, both of whom had heard about Nadine on the radio and were trying to reach me. I made a cup of instant coffee for us both and went back to my office and sat down with the phone.

Betty arrived around eight, Sergeant McCool just before nine. He talked with the forensic men, who left shortly after, and spent all morning and part of the afternoon interviewing the girls as they checked in. They all seemed in a state of shock. I thought of his phrase—confusion shock.

What had almost surely happened, he told Betty and me after he'd talked with them all, was that someone had flung the chair at Nadine from behind and she'd fallen into the pool and drowned. The chair did have fingerprints on it, but nothing clear. It had happened sometime before midnight. If it could be determined when Nadine had last eaten, they'd have a closer idea. No one, including Blanche, had been able to help him there.

In trying to reach Nadine's family from the information she'd given me, he'd learned there was not only no address at that address but no family by the name of Nicholson in that city. But from her social-security number, which was genuine, he'd traced her family to a small town in Pennsylvania. It had once been a family of seven girls, but only three of the daughters were still at home. The father had taken off some years ago and the mother was a patient in the nursing home where one of the daughters worked. One of the other girls was still in high school and the other was a waitress, twenty-five years old. Her name was Carol and she was making arrangements to take a bus to New York to see about disposal of the body and answer some questions.

"We've gotten complacent," Betty told me, rising. "Excuse me a minute. I want to go and check out some records in my office."

"It happens to everyone," McCool said as she left. He was perched on the corner of my desk.

"I have to know," I said. "From what you know so far, do you suspect anyone?"

"I suspect everyone."

I stared at him. For the first time I realized there was no reason for him to suspect me less than anyone else.

"The girl was pretty much of a disruption around here. Who needed that?" he said.

"That could have been solved by something a good deal short of murder. Do you think I'm capable of murder?"

"Not a planned murder, no. Not that you're not smart enough. You're very smart." He gave me his disarming smile. "I really *like* you."

"I'm beginning to think you're a bit of a psychopath yourself."

"Just because I like you?"

I was flustered and I think he loved it.

"How can you like someone you think is capable of murder?" I said.

"You're the one who keeps calling it murder. It could have been accidental."

"Even if whoever hit her with that chair didn't mean to kill her, he or she left her to drown."

"And you wouldn't be capable of that."

"No!"

"Okay, I disqualify you as a suspect."

"Can you tell me who you *don't* disqualify?"

"I told you. Everyone else." He got up and went for his raincoat on a chair. "Except possibly the least likely suspect."

"Who's that?"

"The receptionist—the Freeman girl. Nice person. Nice disposition. Besides, she was playing cards with her husband and another couple at home in New Jersey last night." He walked out into the foyer. In a few minutes he was back. "Chaney says the sister is on the way. We'll pick her up at the Port Authority around five. I'd like to bring her here after we've been to the morgue and I've had a talk with her."

I'd canceled a theater date and had been hoping to go home. "I'll be here," I said. "There's food and a bed for her here if she wants it."

He smiled. "See you," he said.

The sister was attractive but worn down, older than her years. Like Nadine, she colored her hair red, but it was a harsher shade

and an inch of dark roots showed. Her skin wasn't properly
cared for, either, but her teeth couldn't have been lovelier. She
wore a frayed cloth coat over a blue sweater and black skirt.

Betty and I told her how sorry we were.

"Yes. Well." She said it without resentment, but not without
sorrow.

Sergeant McCool directed her to an easy chair and pulled a
straight-backed chair closer for himself. Betty was on the sofa, I
was behind the desk.

"Carol's been telling me about Nadine's formative years,"
McCool told us, "and after I left here today I looked into her
life apart from the agency these past few months and over the
last year or two. There hasn't been much aside from her work."

I was astonished. "What about men?"

"As far as I can see, she had no trouble getting men interested
in her, but when they asked her out or home or wherever, she
backed off."

"That can make a man very angry," Betty said.

"I know. We've got a list of some possibly angry men. They're
being checked out. Something else I discovered is that she's got
a bad name with several of your clients, who say, one, they've
never before encountered such meanness in one of your girls,
and two—and very curious—they hadn't encountered it in *her*
until after she'd signed with you."

The enforced, cruel honesty of murder. I looked at Carol. She
was digging in her handbag. I pushed the cigarette box and
ashtray toward her and the sergeant went for his lighter. "What
was she like at home?" I asked her, then realized I was probably
out of line. I flashed McCool a look.

"Be my guest." He smiled.

"She was unpredictable. She could be nice, but she could be
brutal. I don't think there was anyone in the family who didn't
take a sock at her at least once. She played on our weaknesses,
like—went after our boy friends, made fun of what we did, our
looks, our friends, the way we liked to spend our time.

"My mother couldn't do anything with her. Punishment
didn't bother her. The only one who had any control over her
was Janice. She was the oldest. But she left home when she was
eighteen."

"To do what?" McCool asked her.

"She went to Alaska. With her boy friend."

"Where did Nadine place in the family?"

"She was second oldest."

"Did she take over the responsibilities when Janice left?"

"Take over? She took off. Three weeks later she packed her stuff and went to Los Angeles."

"Did she come to New York from Los Angeles?"

"As far as I know. She wasn't always in touch."

"Is it possible anyone she grew up with could have done this?"

"I can't imagine anyone in town then or now I'd have suspicions about. She made a lot of people mad, especially the family, but it didn't last. We were all too busy with ourselves to take much notice."

She took a deep drag on her cigarette and stared with curiosity at the glamorous faces on the wall, one after another.

Carol did sleep over and had one of Blanche's best breakfasts, then she and I settled some practical matters. I arranged for the body to be shipped home and interred in the cemetery where her grandparents were buried. Carol said she had no idea what Nadine would have wanted, but that she would like it that way. There was no will. Since Nadine had lived in New York, the estate would have to be probated in New York State, so I put Carol in touch with a good lawyer.

Before she left she told me she wanted to make something clear: she didn't know who had failed whom in their family, but Nadine had always sent money home when she had it. It was seldom accompanied by so much as a note, but they had often received money from her, and never as much or more often than in the past year.

"This business of her belittling the activities of the others," McCool said. "Didn't she have any special interests of her own?" He'd pulled a chair up close to my desk. It was after eight that evening.

"Swimming is the only one I knew of."

"That's it?"

I was very tired. "Don't you ever sleep, Sergeant?"

"Sure. Sure I do." He stood and moved the chair back to its original position. "There's never enough time. That's what really bugs me about murder. None of us has enough time as it is and then some hothead comes along and kills off what we do have."

He took his notebook from his jacket pocket. "Do you have another minute?"

"Of course."

"I don't believe everything your girls are telling me—that they didn't like the deceased but they didn't hate her." He flipped some pages. "One of the ringleaders in that cute little campaign against her." He stopped and looked at his notes. "Jean Carmichael. Part-time college student. She was here the day of the murder. When asked if she had taken a chair to Miss Nicholson, perhaps in self-defense, she said, very college-girl cool, 'It could have happened that way, officer, but it didn't.' " He looked at me. "I started the interview by telling her I recognized her from a bathing-suit commercial. She told me I'm very observant."

He licked a finger and turned the page. "Ursula Kruger. Recently separated from her husband. No children." He looked up at me. "Yet. She thinks she may be going to have a baby."

"Oh, Lord."

"She's waiting for the results of a test. She wasn't here at all that day. She went to her husband's club to talk with him but he wasn't there, so she walked around, bought some groceries, and went home. Husband's club is on West Forty-fourth, home is on East Sixty-third between Third and Second. Doctor's name is Mills."

"You mentioned Jeannie Carmichael before. Did she say where she was that night?"

"Yeah. At Elaine's." He flicked another page. "Ramona Bonilla. Unmarried. Was here during the day, then went shopping—the department stores were open late—then she went home. Lives alone in a one-bedroom apartment on East Seventy-ninth Street.

"Angel Ciccone: Had a dance class that evening—hadn't come here during the day. After class she had coffee with some friends and then went straight home. Lives with her parents and a younger brother and sister in an apartment in SoHo. Easy to corroborate."

"Her father's a policeman."

"Yeah, I know." He flicked again. "Getting information from all of these was like getting blood out of a stone, especially the last two. But then we come to Leila Moth. She's a reglar Chatty Cathy, isn't she? Except for the hard facts. She was at home that night, she says—on West Sixty-fifth Street—with a friend, whose name she was reluctant to give me. I'm holding.

"I made the mistake of telling her what we'd found out about Miss Nicholson's family background. That got me this, quote: 'One of seven girls! *That's* why her mean side didn't emerge until she'd signed with Midge. I'm one of six girls myself, and when I came here I had a terrible time suppressing all my old behavior with my sisters.' "

He slapped the book shut. "Dime-store psycholgy from Leila Moth. What kind of name is that, anyway? What kind of a place is this—one crazy name after another. And I have a gut feeling your porter and his wife aren't telling me the whole truth and nothing but the truth, either. Talking to them has been a waste of time."

Oy, did he need sleep.

"You seem to be convinced that whoever did it is connected with the agency," I said.

"That's right."

"Why?"

"Because it happened here. It's possible it was an intruder or someone she knew from the outside, but there's no evidence to suggest it."

I moaned and rubbed my forehead, studying the blotter on my desk and trying to remember something that might help. He moaned, too. I looked at him. He was looking down at the rug. Shah, the Persian, was pacing back and forth at his feet, rubbing herself against his dark pant legs, purring.

Betty and I decided to stay over again rather than try to field the reporters still outside. We changed into our robes and had a catchall supper in the kitchen, bringing a plate and a glass of milk to Donalson, who had taken over from Chaney until midnight. Blanche and Billy had eaten earlier and were keeping to themselves in their room. I hated it but hadn't decided if anything could be done about it.

Over coffee, as Betty fitted a cigarette into her cigarette holder, I told her that Ursula might be pregnant. "Oh, no," she said.

"She told Sergeant McCool she wasn't here the night before last. But Phyllis told me that afternoon she was due in."

"Did you tell McCool that?"

"No. I'd rather talk with Ursula first."

"Right." She exhaled smoke. "Why do people get murdered?"

"Someone hates them. Someone loves them to the point of obsession. Someone's jealous of them or has something to gain by their death—money, peace of mind. Someone thinks he or she will be in less pain if that person's not around."

"How about accidental death and the person who caused it hasn't the courage to admit he or she was responsible?"

"And let the victim drown? No wonder he or she hasn't the courage."

"That's the inescapable fact of it, isn't it?" Betty said.

I looked at the wall clock. It wasn't quite nine. "I'd like to phone Ursula."

"You look exhausted, Midge. Why not wait until tomorrow?"

"I'm not sure I'll be able to sleep until I've talked with her."

"And if you learn something you don't want to learn, will you be able to sleep then?"

Just then the outside door opened and we heard someone enter and shut the door. We looked at each other. Then we heard Charlene's voice, and Donalson's. A few minutes later she came to the kitchen, set her bags down in the corner, hugged us both, pulled out a chair, and sat between us at the third side of the table.

"Was it a good trip?" Betty asked her, getting up and going to the cabinet for a dish.

"Wonderful. No food for me, please, Betty. But I'd love a cup of coffee." Betty replaced the dish and took out a cup and saucer. "Has it been awful here?"

I nodded. "When did you hear about it?"

"A few hours after it happened. News travels fast in this business. Poor Billy, finding her like that."

The front door opened and closed again. Another exchange—this time only a brief greeting—between Donalson and a woman whose voice I couldn't make out, but it was obviously someone Donalson knew. Light footsteps, then Ursula opened the swing door, her face radiant.

"I hoped you'd be here," she said. "May I join you?"

We made room while Betty served up more coffee and Charlene answered Ursula's questions about what was new in Rome. "What about you, Ursula?" she asked, her face turning serious.

"That's what I came here to tell Midge," Ursula said. "I have good news and bad news." We waited. "The bad news first. I may be pregnant. I'll know tomorrow. The good news is that Karl and I are getting back together. I reached him at the office today and we got together and talked. He wants us together whether there's a baby coming or not, and so do I. But I think you should know now that if there is a baby we want it. I'll have to bow out of our contract."

Happy Clause Number 7, the girls call it.

Ursula drank coffee. "If you'd seen me the last few days, you'd have seen a totally different person. What a mess. I knew about the baby but I couldn't reach Karl. I was planning to come in the day before yesterday but when the job I was on was over it was late and I figured no one would be here but Billy and Blanche, whose ear I'd already talked off about my problem, or maybe Nadine, whose ear I didn't want." She put down her cup. "I'm sorry."

Just then the outer door opened and closed again. Betty rolled her eyes at me. "Are you expecting anyone?" Charlene asked us.

"It could be Sergeant McCool back," I said and started for the door—encountering Ramona on the way.

"Ramona!" Charlene said. "I was just about to ask if you were here. I have something for you. Not from me—from an admirer." She rummaged through the lighter of her two bags and brought out a small gift-wrapped box. "Here."

Ramona reached out for it. "Open it," Charlene prodded. "I

don't know what it is. I've been dying to see." Ramona studied
the handsome wrapping and then started to undo it with her
beautiful nails. Two of which had been repaired since the day
before yesterday. By the overhead light I could see the thin
ridges buttressing the real nails with the false ones. I felt panic
and looked away.

And back again as I heard the others murmur in admiration.
In her delicate fingers, Ramona held an exquisite ring, its
diamonds and rubies forming a star. She opened the envelope
and extracted the card, which, astonishingly, she read aloud to
us. "We are star-crossed. Giorgio."

We all knew who Giorgio was, and that he was married. The
silence that followed was made up of many things—amazement,
embarrassment, sentiment, concern. "Some food, Ramona?"
Betty asked at last.

"It's a beautiful, beautiful ring," Ursula said. "Give it here, will
you? For just the tiniest moment," she promised.

What followed was a first. Except for the Christmas party, I
don't serve liquor to the girls. But somehow it seemed necessary to have a nightcap in my office and suggest they all stay
over rather than go home.

Eventually, as I should have foreseen, the conversation turned
to Nadine. And I've been to enough Irish wakes to recognize
the tone. The consensus, especially after I told them she'd been
financially generous with her family, was that she'd been just a
poor, mixed-up kid, another very human mortal, after all.

"You give her too much credit," Ramona said, placing her
glass carefully down on the center of a tooled-leather coaster
on the coffee table.

I waited. Not long.

"You do give her too much credit—no doubt because she's
dead. But if one of us had died, it wouldn't have mattered to
her."

"You can't know that, Ramona," Betty said.

"Okay, maybe not. But she ruined the relationship between
my brother and Angel. And between me and Angel. And me and
Mario. They were both friendlier to me when they were going

together than either of them ever had been before. I realize that now."

"That would have passed," said Betty.

"No." Ramona looked at me and my heart stopped. "You know how temperamental I can be, Midge. I'm very moody. In school I had a lot of fights. I was given detention all the time."

Detention. Dear God.

"I moved away from home because I couldn't get along with my family. I haven't been able to keep a roommate—or a man." She rubbed at her mended nails. "We had a big loud quarrel here that night, she and I—"

Help! Stop!

"We were alone. Billy and Blanche had gone out—"

"When did Nadine come in?"

"I don't know. I was here—you know, you and I talked. Phyllis had told me Ursula was coming by. I was suffering— Mario and Angel's difficulties were a new part of that." She looked at Ursula. "I knew you were suffering, too, and, I don't know, I just wanted to talk to you, that's all. We're like sisters here. Or we were. You hadn't told Phyllis how late you might be, so I took a nap. When I got up, I went looking for you. No one was around but Nadine, as usual, floating around the pool, trying to drown that *espantoso* loneliness of hers.

"She said she hadn't seen you. When I turned to leave she asked me how my baby brother was and if he ever spoke of her. I didn't answer and started back to my room with the intention of going home, but she was out of the pool like a snake and asked me what I was doing here.

"I told her my business was none of hers and kept walking. She grabbed my shoulder—to detain me, to quarrel—and I can't explain what her touch did to me. I grabbed a chair nearby and hit her with it with all my might. She fell into the pool and I threw the chair in after her and ran. I didn't know I'd done so much damage, that she was unconscious and would drown, but my mind was white hot—I didn't care.

"I still don't care, really. I'm not one of your more civilized girls, Midge," she said, her eyes enormous and black. "I'm always depressed—I have a lot of resentment. Is that luck or what?"

"She's not a killer," I told McCool. She had made it easy for me by confessing and I still didn't know what I would have done if she hadn't.

"Spontaneous violence," he said. "It's the most common cause of homicide in New York."

"Will she go to prison?"

He stroked his broad forehead. "I don't know. I really *don't* know."

"I've discovered a new vocation. Reading up on the law."

"Oh, God, good. Do it. Everybody do it."

We were standing in the foyer, he and Betty and I. "Can you see to it that she gets help?" I asked.

"Yes," he said. He held out his hand. "I make good on *my* promises, too." We shook. "And get a logbook," he said, opening the door. "I don't have to spell it out for you how it could have helped us here."

"Are you married, Sergeant?" Betty asked him—not for herself, I knew. My friend who hates playing God unless she's asked.

"I used to be," he said.

" 'I used to be,' " I repeated when he'd left. "Nice wedding ring he's got there. Either he's protecting himself with it or he's a widower."

"Probably both," said Betty, a very unusual gleam in her eye.

LAWRENCE BLOCK
THE EHRENGRAF RIPOSTE

Martin Ehrengraf placed his hands on the top of his exceedingly cluttered desk and looked across its top. He was seated, while the man at whom he gazed was standing, and indeed looked incapable of remaining still, let alone seating himself on a chair. He was a large man, tall and quite stout, balding, florid of face, with a hawk's-bill nose and a jutting chin. His hair, combed straight back, was a rich and glossy dark-brown; his bushy eyebrows were salted with grey. His suit, while of a particular shade of blue that Ehrengraf would never have chosen for himself, was well tailored and expensive. It was logical to assume that the man within the suit was abundantly supplied with money, an assumption the little lawyer liked to be able to make about all his prospective clients.

Now he said, "Won't you take a seat, Mr. Crowe? You'll be more comfortable."

"I'd rather stand," Abel Crowe said. "I'm too much on edge to sit still."

"Hmmm. There's something I've learned in my practice, Mr. Crowe, and that's the great advantage in acting *as if.* When I'm to defend a client who gives every indication of guilt, I act *as if* he were indeed innocent. And you know, Mr. Crowe, it's astonishing how often the client does in fact *prove* to be innocent, often to his own surprise."

Martin Ehrengraf flashed a smile that showed on his lips without altering the expression in his eyes. "All of which is all-important to me, since I collect a fee only if my client is judged to be innocent. Otherwise I go unpaid. Acting *as if,* Mr. Crowe, is uncannily helpful, and you might help us both by sitting in that chair and acting as if you were at peace with the world."

Ehrengraf paused, and when Crowe had seated himself he said, "You say you've been charged with murder. But homicide is not usually a bailable offense, so how does it happen that you are here in my office instead of locked in a cell?"

"I haven't been charged with murder."

"But you said—"

"I said I wanted you to defend me against a homicide charge. But I haven't been charged yet."

"I see. Whom have you killed? No, let me amend that. Whom are you supposed to have killed?"

"No one."

"Oh?"

Abel Crowe thrust his head forward. "I'll be charged with the murder of Terence Reginald Mayhew," he said, pronouncing the name with a full measure of loathing. "But I haven't been charged yet because the rancid scut's not dead yet because I haven't killed him yet."

"Mr. Mayhew is alive."

"Yes."

"But you intend to kill him."

Crowe chose his words carefully. "I expect to be charged with his murder," he said at length.

"And you want to arrange your defense in advance."

"Yes."

"You show commendable foresight," Ehrengraf said admiringly. He got to his feet and stepped out from behind his desk. He was a muted symphony of brown. His jacket was a brown Harris tweed in a herringbone weave, his slacks were cocoa flannel, his shirt a buttery tan silk, his tie a perfect match for the slacks with a below-the-knot design of fleur-de-lis in silver thread. Ehrengraf hadn't been quite certain about the tie when he bought it but had since decided it was quite all right. On his small feet he wore highly polished seamless tan loafers, unadorned with braids or tassels.

"Foresight," he repeated. "An unusual quality in a client, Mr. Crowe, and I can only wish that I met with it more frequently." He put the tips of his fingers together and narrowed his eyes. "Just what is it you wish from me?"

"Your efforts on my behalf, of course."

"Indeed. Why do you want to kill Mr. Mayhew?"

"Because he's driving me crazy."

"How?"

"He's playing tricks on me."

"Tricks? What sort of tricks?"

"Childish tricks," Abel Crowe said, and averted his eyes. "He makes phone calls. He orders things. Last week he called different florists and sent out hundreds of orders of flowers to different women all over the city. He's managed to get hold of my credit-card numbers and placed all these orders in my name and billed them to me. I was able to stop some of the orders, but by the time I got wind of what he'd done, most of them had already gone out."

"Surely you won't have to pay."

"It may be easier to pay than to go through the process of avoiding payment. I don't know. But that's just one example. Another time ambulances and limousines kept coming to my house. One after the other. And taxicabs, and I don't know what else. These vehicles kept arriving from various sources and I kept having to send them away."

"I see."

"And he fills out coupons and orders things C.O.D. for me. I have to cancel the orders and return the products. He's had me join book clubs and record clubs, he's subscribed me to every sort of magazine, he's put me on every sort of mailing list. Did you know, for example, that there's an outfit called the International Society for the Preservation of Wild Mustangs and Burros?"

"It so happens I'm a member."

"Well, I'm sure it's a worthwhile organization," Crowe said, "but the point is I'm not interested in wild mustangs and burros, or even tame ones, but Mayhew made me a member and pledged a hundred dollars on my behalf, or maybe it was a thousand dollars, I can't remember."

"The exact amount isn't important at the moment, Mr. Crowe."

"He's driving me crazy!"

"So it would seem. But to kill a man because of some practical jokes—"

"There's no end to them. He started doing this almost two years ago. At first it was completely maddening because I had no idea what was happening or who was doing this to me. From time to time he'll slack off and I'll think he's had his fun and has decided to leave me alone. Then he'll start up again."

"Have you spoken to him?"

"I can't. He laughs like the lunatic he is and hangs up on me."

"Have you confronted him?"

"I can't. He lives in an apartment downtown on Chippewa Street. He doesn't let visitors in and never seems to leave the place."

"And you've tried the police?"

"They can't seem to do anything. He just lies to them, denies all responsibility, tells them it must be someone else. A very nice policeman told me the only sensible thing I can do is wait him out. He'll get tired, he assured me, the man's madness will run its course. He'll decide he's had his revenge."

"And you tried to do that?"

"For a while. When it didn't work, I engaged a private detective. He obtained evidence of Mayhew's activities, evidence that will stand up in court. But my attorney convinced me not to press charges."

"Why, for heaven's sake?"

"The man's a cripple."

"Your attorney?"

"Certainly not. Mayhew's a cripple, he's confined to a wheelchair. I suppose that's why he never leaves his squalid little apartment. But my attorney said I could only charge him with malicious mischief, which is not the most serious crime in the book and which sounds rather less serious than it is because it has the connotation of a child's impish prank—"

"Yes."

"—and there we'd be in court, myself a large man in good physical condition and Mayhew a sniveling cripple in a wheelchair, and he'd get everyone's sympathy and undoubtedly be exonerated of all charges while I'd come off as a bully and a laughingstock. I couldn't make charges stand up in criminal court, and if I sued him I'd probably lose. And even if I won that, what could I get? The man doesn't have anything to start with."

Ehrengraf nodded thoughtfully. "He blames you for crippling him?"

"I don't know. I had never even heard of him before he started tormenting me, but who knows what a madman might think? He doesn't seem to want anything from me. I've called him up, asked him what he wanted, and he only laughs and hangs up on me."

"And so you've decided to kill him."

"I haven't said that."

Ehrengraf sighed. "We're not in court, Mr. Crowe, so that sort of technicality's not important between us. You've implied you intend to kill him."

"Perhaps."

"At any rate, that's the inference I've drawn. I can certainly understand your feelings, but isn't the remedy you propose an extreme one? The cure seems worse than the disease. To expose yourself to a murder trial—"

"But your clients rarely go to trial."

"Oh?"

Crowe hazarded a smile. It looked out of place on his large red face, and after a moment it withdrew. "I'm familiar with your methods, Mr. Ehrengraf," he said. "Your clients rarely go to trial. You hardly ever show up in a courtroom. You take a case and then something curious happens. The evidence changes, or new evidence is discovered, or someone else confesses, or the murder turns out to be an accident, after all, or—well, *something* always happens."

"Truth will out," Ehrengraf said.

"Truth or fiction, something happens. Now here I am, plagued by a maniac, and I've engaged you to undertake my defense whenever it should become necessary, and it seems to me that by so doing I may bring things to the point where it *won't* become necessary."

Ehrengraf looked at him. A man who would select a suit of that particular shade, he thought, was either color blind or capable of anything.

"Of course I don't know what might happen," Abel Crowe went on. "Just as hypothesis, Terence Mayhew might die. Of course, if that happened I wouldn't have any reason to murder him, and so I wouldn't come to trial. But that's just an example. It's certainly not my business to tell you your business, is it?"

"Certainly not," said Martin Ehrengraf.

While Terence Reginald Mayhew's four-room apartment on Chippewa Street was scarcely luxurious, it was by no means the squalid pesthole Ehrengraf had been led to expect. The block, to be sure, was not far removed from slum status. The building itself had certainly seen better days. But the Mayhew apartment itself, occupying the fourth-floor front and looking northward over a group of two-story frame houses, was cozy and comfortable.

The little lawyer followed Mayhew's wheelchair down a short hallway and into a book-lined study. A log of wax and compressed sawdust burned in the fireplace. A clock ticked on the mantel. Mayhew turned his wheelchair around, eyed his visitor from head to toe, and made a brisk clucking sound with his tongue. "So you're his lawyer," he said. "Not the poor boob who called me a couple of months ago, though. That one kept coming up with threats and I couldn't help laughing at him. He must have turned pruple. When you laugh in a man's face after he's made legal threats, he generally turns purple. That's been my experience. What's your name again?"

"Ehrengraf. Martin H. Ehrengraf."

"What's the H. stand for?"

"Harrod."

"Like the king in the bible?"

"Like the London department store." Ehrengraf's middle name was not Harrod, or Herod either, for that matter. He simply found untruths useful now and then, particularly in response to impertinence.

"Martin Harrod Ehrengraf," said Terence Reginald Mayhew. "Well, you're quite the dandy, aren't you? Sorry the place isn't spiffier but the cleaning woman only comes in once a week and she's not due until the day after tomorrow. Not that she's any great shakes with a dustcloth. Lazy slattern, in my opinion. You want to sit down?"

"No."

"Probably scared to crease your pants."

Ehrengraf was wearing a navy suit, a pale-blue-velvet vest, a blue shirt, a navy knit tie, and a pair of cordovan loafers. Mayhew was wearing a disgraceful terrycloth robe and tatty bedroom slippers. He had a scrawny body, a volleyball-shaped head, big guileless blue eyes, and red straw for hair. He was not so much ugly as bizarre; he looked like a cartoonist's invention. Ehrengraf couldn't guess how old he was—thirty? forty? fifty?—but it didn't matter. The man was years from dying of old age.

"Well, aren't you going to threaten me?"

"No," Ehrengraf said.

"No threats? No hints of bodily harm? No pending lawsuits? No criminal prosecution?"

"Nothing of the sort."

"Well, you're an improvement on your predecessor," Mayhew said. "That's something. Why'd you come here, then? Not to see how the rich folks live. You slumming?"

"No."

"Because it may be a rundown neighborhood, but it's a good apartment. They'd get me out if they could. Rent control—I've been here for ages and my rent's a pittance. Never find anything like this for what I can afford to pay. I get checks every month, you see. Disability. Small trust fund. Doesn't add up to much, but I get by. Have the cleaning woman in once a week, pay the rent, eat decent food. Watch the TV, read my books and magazines, play my chess games by mail. Neighborhood's gone down but I don't *live* in the neighborhood. I live in the apartment. All I get of the neighborhood is seeing it from my window, and if it's not fancy that's all right with me. I'm a cripple, I'm confined to these four rooms, so I don't care what the neighborhood's like. If I was blind I wouldn't care what color the walls were painted, would I? The more they take away from you, why, the less vulnerable you are."

That last was an interesting thought and Ehrengraf might have pursued it, but he had other things to pursue. "My client," he said. "Abel Crowe."

"That warthog."

"You dislike him?"

"Stupid question, Mr. Lawyer. Of course I dislike him. I

wouldn't keep putting the wind up him if I thought the world of him, would I now?"

"You blame him for—"

"For me being a cripple? He didn't do that to me. God did." The volleyball head bounced against the back of the wheelchair, the wide slash of mouth opened, and a cackle of laughter spilled out. "God did it! I was born this way, you chowderhead. Abel Crowe had nothing to do with it."

"Then—"

"I just hate the man," Mayhew said. "Who needs a reason? I saw a preacher on Sunday-morning television; he stared right into the camera every minute with those great big eyes, said no one has cause to hate his fellow man. At first it made me want to retch, but I thought about it, and I'll be an anthropoid ape if he's not right. No one has cause to hate his fellow man because no one *needs* cause to hate his fellow man. It's natural. And it comes natural for me to hate Abel Crowe."

"Have you ever met him?"

"I don't have to meet him."

"You just—"

"I just hate him," Mayhew said, grinning fiercely, "and I *love* hating him, and I have heaps of *fun* hating him, and all I have to do is pick up that phone and make him pay and pay and pay for it."

"Pay for what?"

"For everything. For being Abel Crowe. For the outstanding war debt. For the loaves and the fishes." The head bounced back and the insane laugh was repeated. "For Tippecanoe and Tyler, too. For Tippecanee and Tyler Three."

"You don't have very much money," Ehrengraf said. "A disability pension, a small income."

"I have enough. I don't eat much and I don't eat fancy. You probably spend more on clothes than I spend on everything put together."

Ehrengraf didn't doubt that for a moment. "My client might supplement that income of yours," he said thoughtfully.

"You think I'm a blackmailer?"

"I think you might profit by circumstances, Mr. Mayhew."

"Fie on it, sir. I'd have no truck with blackmail. The Mayhews have been whitemailers for generations."

The conversation continued, but not for long. It became quite clear to the diminutive attorney that his was a limited arsenal. He could neither threaten nor bribe to any purpose. Any number of things might happen to Mayhew, some of them fatal, but such action seemed wildly disproportionate. This housebound wretch, this malevolent cripple, had simply not done enough to warrant such a response. When a child thumbed his nose at you, you were not supposed to dash its brains out against the curb. An action ought to bring about a suitable reaction. A thrust should be countered by an appropriate riposte.

But how was one to deal with a nasty madman? A helpless, pathetic madman?

Ehrengraf, who was fond of poetry, sought his memory for an illuminating phrase. Thoughts of madmen recalled Christopher Smart, an Eighteenth Century Londoner who was periodically confined to Bedlam where he wrote a long poem that was largely comprehensible only to himself and God.

Quoting Smart, Ehrengraf said, " 'Let Ross, house of Ross, rejoice with Obadiah, and the rankle-dankle fish with hands.' "

Terence Reginald Mayhew nodded. "Now that," he said, "is the first sensible thing you've said since you walked in here."

A dozen days later, while Martin Ehrengraf was enjoying a sonnet of Thomas Hood's, his telephone rang. He took it up, said hello, and heard himself called an unconscionable swine.

"Ah," he said. "Mr. Mayhew."

"You are a man with no heart. I'm a poor housebound cripple, Mr. Ehrengraf—"

"Indeed."

"—and you've taken my life away. Do you have any idea what I went through to make this phone call?"

"I have a fair idea."

"Do you have any idea what I've been going through?"

"A fair idea of that as well," Ehrengraf said. "Here's a pretty coincidence. Just as you called, I was reading this poem of Thomas Hood's—do you know him?"

"I don't know what you're talking about."

"A sonnet called *Silence*. I'll just read you the sestet—

'But in green ruins, in the desolate walls,
Of antique palaces, where Man hath been,
Though the dun fox or wild hyena calls,
And owls that flit continually between,
Shriek to the echo, and the low winds moan—
There the true silence is, self-conscious and alone.'

"Don't you think that's marvelously evocative of what you've
been going through, Mr. Mayhew?"

"You're a terrible man."

"Indeed. And you should never forget it."

"I won't."

"It could all happen again. In fact, it could happen over and
over."

"What do I have to do?"

"You have to leave my client strictly alone."

"I was having so much fun."

"Don't whine, Mr. Mayhew. You can't play your nasty little
tricks on Mr. Crowe. But there's a whole world of other victims
out there just waiting for your attentions."

"You mean—"

"I'm sure I've said nothing that wouldn't have occurred to
you in good time, sir. On the other hand, you never know what
some other victim might do. He might even find his way to my
office, and you know full well what the consequences of that
would be. Indeed, you know that you *can't* know. So perhaps
what you ought to do is grow up, Mr. Mayhew, and wrap the
tattered scraps of your life around your wretched body, and
make the best of it."

"I don't—"

"Think of Thomas Hood, sir. Think of the true silence."

"I can't—"

"Think of Ross, house of Ross, and the rankle-dankle fish with
hands."

"I'm not—"

"And think of Mr. Crowe while you're at it. I suggest you call him, sir. Apologize to him. Assure him that his troubles are over."

"I don't want to call him."

"Make the call," Ehrengraf said, his voice smooth as steel. "Or your troubles, Mr. Mayhew, are just beginning."

"The most remarkable thing," Abel Crowe said. "I had a call from that troll Mayhew. At first I didn't believe it was he. I didn't recognize his voice. He sounded so frightened, so unsure of himself."

"Indeed."

"He assured me I'd have no further trouble from him. No more limousines or taxis, no more flowers, none of his idiotic little pranks. He apologized profusely for all the trouble he'd caused me in the past and assured me it would never happen again. It's hard to know whether to take the word of a madman, but I think he meant what he said."

"I'm certain he did."

They were once again in Martin Ehrengraf's office, and as usual the lawyer's desk was as cluttered as his person was immaculate. He was wearing the navy suit again, as it happened, but he had left the light-blue vest at home. His tie bore a half-inch diagonal stripe of royal-blue flanked by two narrower stripes, one of gold and the other of a rather bright green, all on a navy field. Crowe was wearing a three-piece suit, expensive and beautifully tailored but in a rather morose shade of brown. Ehrengraf had decided charitably to regard the man as color blind and let it go at that.

"What did you do, Ehrengraf?"

The little lawyer looked off into the middle distance. "I suppose I can tell you," he said after a moment's reflection. "I took his life away from him."

"That's what I thought you would do. Take his life, I mean. But he was certainly alive when I spoke to him."

"You misunderstand me. Mr. Crowe, your antagonist was a housebound cripple who had adjusted to his mean little life of isolation. He had an income sufficient to his meager needs. And I went around his house shutting things down."

"I don't understand."

"I speak metaphorically, of course. Well, there's no reason I can't tell you what I did in plain English. First of all, I went to the post office. I filled out a change-of-address card, signed it in his name, and filed it. From that moment on, all his mail was efficiently forwarded to the General Delivery window in Greeley, Colorado, where it's to be held until called for, which may take rather a long time."

"Good heavens."

"I notified the electric company that Mr. Mayhew had vacated the premises and ordered them to cut off service forthwith. I told the telephone company the same thing, so when he picked up the phone to complain about the lights being out I'm afraid he had a hard time getting a dial tone. I sent a notarized letter to the landlord—over Mr. Mayhew's signature, of course—announcing that he was moving and demanding that his lease be canceled. I got in touch with his cleaning woman and informed her that her services would no longer be required. I could go on, Mr. Crowe, but I believe you get the idea. I took his life away and shut it down and he didn't like it."

"Good grief."

"His only remaining contact with the world was what he saw through his windows, and that was nothing attractive. Nevertheless, I was going to have his windows painted black from the outside—I was in the process of making final arrangements. A chap was going to suspend a scaffold as if to wash the windows but he would have painted them instead. I saw it as a neat coup de grace, but Mayhew made that last touch unnecessary by throwing in the sponge. That's a mixed metaphor, from coup de grace to throwing in the sponge, but I hope you'll pardon it."

"You did to him what he'd done to me. Hoist him on his own petard."

"Let's say I hoisted him on a similar petard. He plagued you by introducing an infinity of unwanted elements into your life. But I reduced his life to the four rooms he lived in and even threatened his ability to retain those very rooms—that drove the lesson home to him in a way I doubt he'll ever forget."

"Simple and brilliant," Crowe said. "I wish I'd thought of it."

"I'm glad you didn't."

"Why?"

"Because you'd have saved yourself fifty thousand dollars."

Crowe gaped. "Fifty thousand—"

"Dollars. My fee."

"But that's an outrage. All you did was write some letters and make some phone calls."

"All I did, sir, was everything you asked me to do. I saved you from answering to a murder charge."

"I wouldn't have murdered him."

"Nonsense," Ehrengraf snapped. "You *tried* to murder him. You thought engaging me would have precisely that effect. Had I wrung the wretch's neck you'd pay my fee without a whimper, but because I accomplished the desired result with style and grace instead of brute force you resist paying me. It would be an immense act of folly, Mr. Crowe, if you were to do anything other than pay my fee in full at once."

"You don't think the amount is out of line?"

"I don't keep my fees in a line, Mr. Crowe." Ehrengraf's hand went to the knot of his tie. It was the official tie of the Caedmon Society of Oxford University. Ehrengraf had not attended Oxford and did not belong to the Caedmon Society any more than he belonged to the International Society for the Preservation of Wild Mustangs and Burros, but it was a tie he habitually wore on celebratory occasions. "I set my fees according to an intuitive process," he went on, "and they are never negotiable. Fifty thousand dollars, sir. Not a penny more, not a penny less. Ah, Mr. Crowe, Mr. Crowe—do you know why Mayhew chose to torment you?"

"I suppose he feels I've harmed him."

"And have you?"

"No, but—"

"Supposition is blunder's handmaiden, Mr. Crowe. Mayhew made your life miserable because he hated you. I don't know why he hated you. I don't believe Mayhew himself knows why he hated you. I think he selected you at random. He needed someone to hate and you were convenient. Ah, Mr. Crowe—" Ehrengraf smiled with his lips "—consider how much damage was done to you by an insane cripple with no reason to do you harm. And then consider, sir, how much more harm could be done you by someone infinitely more ruthless and resourceful than Terence Reginald Mayhew, someone who is neither a lunatic nor a cripple, someone who is supplied with fifty thousand excellent reasons to wish you ill."

Crowe stared. "That's a threat," he said slowly.

"I fear you've confused a threat and a caution, Mr. Crowe, though I warrant the distinction's a thin one. Are you fond of poetry, sir?"

"No."

"I'm not surprised. It's no criticism, sir. Some people have poetry in their souls and others do not. It's predetermined, I suspect, like color blindness. I could recommend Thomas Hood, sir, or Christopher Smart, but would you read them? Or profit by them? Fifty thousand dollars, Mr. Crowe, and a check will do nicely."

"I'm not afraid of you."

"Certainly not."

"And I won't be intimidated."

"Indeed, you won't," Ehrengraf agreed. "But do you recall our initial interview, Mr. Crowe? I submit that you would do well to act *as if*—as if you were afraid of me, as if you *were* intimidated."

Abel Crowe sat quite still for several seconds. A variety of expressions played over his generally unexpressive face. At length he drew a checkbook from the breast pocket of his morosely brown jacket and uncapped a silver fountain pen.

"Payable to?"

"Martin H. Ehrengraf."

The pen scratched away. Then, idly, "What's the H. stand for?"

"Herod."

"The store in England?"

"The king," said Ehrengraf. "The king in the Bible."

GEORGE BAXT

THE WOMAN I ENVIED

I'd have left my husband except I loved our apartment. I suppose that sounds like a facetious statement, but it happens to be quite honest. We married almost forty years ago, when falling in love and marrying was less expensive. Abner was considered a genius and I was looked upon as an oddity. I had read Marx and Engels when others were reading Tiffany Thayer and Edna Ferber. We were both twenty years of age and we married in haste because there was a war hanging over our heads like the sword of Damocles. My best friend offered us her studio for a honeymoon, then Abner went off to war—the European theater (theater, what a tame appellation for that bloody arena!)—leaving behind a pregnant bride, Rebecca Berger, aged twenty. Another kind friend gave me a job as a clerk in his bookstore on the Upper West Side of my beloved New York City. I had no idea at the time, and this is the truth, that it was a Communist front. I just thought it was intellectually advanced and I met a lot of interesting people, some of whom went on to literary and theatrical fame, some to notoriety, and most to oblivion. I wish I had joined the oblivions, but it's too late now.

My baby was born on Christmas Eve and that made me feel biblical, so I called him Aaron Moses. I went back to work almost immediately, except this time as the editor at a small publishing house that specialized in what would some years in the future be referred to as inflammatory and anti-American. Actually, some of what we published was quite good and about a dozen of the books are today represented on the back lists of other houses. Of course, they're no longer radical. They're minor classics.

When the war was over and Abner came home to our vast barn of an apartment on Riverside Drive where the rent was delightfully modest, we were, like too many other wartime couples, strangers. He took pride in our son, who was now three years old and resented this peculiar older man's intrusion, but he didn't quite relish living off his wife, who was now earning a healthy salary. There was also a live-in housekeeper, Natasha Brown, a lovely black lady whose mother had named her after Rudolph Valentino's second wife, Natasha Rambova. I thought that was rather cute. Abner said it was degrading, and once he said it I knew we were going to be in trouble.

My name was becoming an important one in literary circles. Rebecca Walsh Berger. I had found, nursed, and published an impressive list of young writers. No need to inscribe them here. You can buy my autobiography when it comes off the presses next autumn. Anyway, my life, my triumphs, and my tragedies are not what this story is all about. What I'm doing now is laying the groundwork so you'll understand the horror I shall eventually unveil.

In time, because I worked very hard at it, Abner and I grew comfortable together. It wasn't the youthful passion of our courting days, but what there was was serviceable. I introduced Abner to a film producer who was negotiating the rights to a novel by one of my writers—Jack Dresden's remarkable *Bloody Castanets,* about Franco and the Spanish Civil War, which of course was never filmed because the Franco government protested vehemently—and they took to each other immediately. Norman Lubin, the producer, took Abner to Hollywood, where they traded their lofty beliefs and ideals for a series of innocent, inane comedies that made Mr. Lubin a millionaire and provided Abner with a steady income. He wasn't a good enough businessman to demand a percentage, but then not being good enough was always Abner's shortcoming. Still, he began to earn the respect of the film industry, which was not yet reeling from the shattering competition the television industry would soon offer.

And since he was spending most of his time on the West Coast and I spent most of my time on the East Coast, we both took lovers.

But by the time our son Aaron went off to private school, Natasha had left me and I was alone. No son, no housekeeper, no husband, no lover. There was plenty to occupy my mind,

however. There was something called the House UnAmerican
Activities Committee, for instance. The witch hunt found Abner
and me among the victims. Abner's innocuous films were
somehow branded Communistic. (Watching them occasionally
on late-night television, I'm still astonished at how lamebrained
those scripts were.) And while loathsome gossip columnists
were pillorying Abner on the West Coast, I was being assailed
in the East as the Red Queen. My company bravely stood by me
and ignored the hundreds of anonymous phone calls and hate
letters directed at me. But when poor Abner was sent to jail for
refusing to name names, the jig, as they sometimes say, was up.
Actually, I would have dug in my heels and continued resisting,
but then Aaron was brutally beaten by some of his classmates
because his mother and father were "dirty Commie reds."

I removed him from school. I visited Abner in jail. I couldn't
kiss him hello or goodbye because there was a glass barrier
between us, but then there had always been barriers between
us. I sublet our gorgeous apartment to a dimwitted young
woman who was earning a fortune writing books about her
funny, funny life as a schoolteacher. (You might remember
Rachel Goddard. She was stabbed to death by one of her
students after he learned how to read.)

I took Aaron to England, and after a few months of hardship I
set up a television producing company. In five years I was a
millionaire. Aaron was my associate producer, the youngest in
the business. After serving a year and a day in jail, poor Abner
got a job managing a luncheonette in Queens. He couldn't get a
passport to join us in London.

I held onto the Riverside Drive apartment and when the
building went cooperative I bought it for what would be
considered a steal today. In a letter from my then tenant, Miss
Goddard, I learned that the apartment next door had been
bought by a psychiatrist, Daniel Ostrer. Well, it was certainly
big enough to be divided into offices and residence, but why
did I feel uneasy as I read and reread Rachel Goddard's letter
about Doctor Ostrer? I didn't know the man, let alone what he
looked like. I did know from Rachel that he was in his early
forties, that his wife was a quiet woman named Ethel, and that

they had a teenaged daughter named Rosalie who was very polite when encountered in the hallway or the elevator. Rachel also let me know that a laundry room had been installed in the basement.

Abner now had his passport but no inclination to join me in London. Instead he went to Hollywood again. At about the same time, Aaron decided it was time to fly the nest and he, too, took wing for Hollywood, where you all know he became a multi-millionaire television producer (due in part to his lack of any taste). In London, my world slowly disintegrated. My lawyers robbed me of almost all my millions (without even knowing the numbers of the Swiss accounts) and the type of television I was producing fell out of favor. It was time to go home. All the witch hunters were dead. And so was my tenant, Miss Goddard.

When I returned to New York, I wasn't exactly poverty-stricken. I still owned residual interests in my television series and there were the dozens of paintings I had bought in Europe in addition to my strongbox filled with jewelry. And in no time Dame Fortune once again favored me through a new East Coast film company, the owner of which, Dominic D'Amigo, persuaded me to join as a full partner once we began our affair. It didn't bother me that I then became known as The Queen of Pornography.

But then, right after I redid the apartment from top to bottom, Dominic was found at the wheel of his car in a parking lot in Canarsie with four bullets in his head. And right after I took possession of the film company, Abner came home from Hollywood to die.

"It's terminal," he told me, "and I'm frightened."

I put my arms around him and kissed him on the lips. Oh, his hair was white and there was a pink tonsure that was a bit shiny when the sun hit it and his face was wrinkled and his skin was the color of a baked potato and his hands trembled and he hadn't done anything of note professionally in years, but I knew I'd take care of him. I didn't realize he might go into years of remission, which he did, and become such a painful thorn in my side.

And I was tired. Very tired.

One day as I left the apartment, locked the door behind me, and crossed to the elevator, the door to the adjoining apartment opened and out stepped a very pretty woman with two children, a boy and a girl. I guessed the woman to be in her early thirties and the boy and the girl about six or seven years old, possibly twins. The elevator came and I held the door open while the woman attended to the four locks on her door. I only had one lock because I'd long ago assumed a devil-may-care attitude toward the percentages in being robbed or mugged on the street.

"Oh, thank you so much," she said in a velvet voice as she herded the youngsters into the elevator. The children smiled politely, but there was something weird about them. They were too perfectly behaved. They didn't chatter or misbehave the way most kids that age do. He was a perfect little gentleman and she was a perfect little lady—and the mother, now that I got a closer look at her, was perfection. Not a hair out of place and just a trace of makeup on her face, because with that glorious skin who needed artificial embellishments? Her suit was exquisite and magnificently tailored. I introduced myself.

She smiled and said almost shyly, "I'm Rosalie Appleby. This is my son Nicholas and this is my daughter Evangeline." Nicholas smiled and Evangeline hung her head. With a name like that, I didn't blame her. "You've been back from England quite a while now, haven't you?"

I told her yes and asked if she knew what had become of the doctor who had had her apartment.

"That was my father, Doctor Ostrer. He was a psychoanalyst. He and Mother went to live in Florida after his breakdown, so my husband, the children, and I moved in. Daddy gave the place to us." I felt there was something she wanted to ask me, but we had arrived at the lobby.

She let me precede her family out of the elevator. The doorman, who was an Iranian student, held the door open for us and we walked out into a blaze of sunshine.

"Going shopping?" I asked her.

"Just to the supermarket," she said. Dressed to the nines just to go to the supermarket? "Are you going to your office?"

"Yes, I am."

"I wish I was going to an office." Had her voice trembled then? I'm not sure. It was so many months ago. I only remember being preoccupied with why the doorman had suddenly held the door open for us when usually I had to struggle with it on my own while he concentrated on his comic book. Then I remembered. It was only seven weeks until Christmas.

"I've never had a job," Rosalie Appleby said wistfully.

"You *have* a job," I told her. "You're a mother. You're raising two perfectly lovely children." I tried not to sound like Betty Furness giving a consumer report, but I wasn't succeeding. What I was saying I was saying halfheartedly. She obviously felt trapped. *Felt* trapped, hell, she *was* trapped. Of all the strange times and places for me to have a sudden and much-needed flash of self-awareness—at that moment I realized what a lucky woman I had been. Despite the trials, the tribulations, the vicissitudes, and mental tortures I had endured, I understood now that I had lived one hell of an exciting life. And that I would like nothing better than to change places with her!

I said it out loud. "I wish I was going to the supermarket with my children. I wish I was a young married woman with a loving husband. Oh, dear Mrs. Appleby, count your blessings."

"You're so sweet," she said. "I hope we get to know each other better." Then she took the children each by a hand and they went marching off to the supermarket while I flagged a cab and directed him to my world of carnal sin.

That night when I got home, Abner told me Rosalie Appleby had invited us over for a drink. He was stretched out on the couch in the living room, reading a murder mystery and looking very healthy. It was a bit after seven.

"Too late now, isn't it?" I asked.

"No," said Abner. "She said she puts the kids to bed at seven."

"Seven! Surely not in this day and age. Only pioneer families put their children to bed at seven."

"Please, Rebecca." His voice was suddenly weak, and belonged to a martyr. "She said seven. It's after that now. If you're interested in a drink with the Applebys, go ring their bell and join them."

"What about you?"

"I'm not up to it."

"Aren't you feeling well?"

"How do you think a dying man feels?"

"I don't know. I've never been a dying man." I went to the bedroom and changed into a superb new pants suit. When I returned to the living room, Abner was sitting up watching a game show on television. "Change your mind and come with me," I said. "I'd like your opinion of Rosalie Appleby and her children." I told him about my morning encounter.

"No, thanks," he said. "I'd rather watch TV. Are we eating in or out?"

"I'll let you know when I get back."

Rosalie Appleby greeted me like a long lost friend. Victor Appleby was a knockout. He was easily ten or fifteen years older than his wife. Had she married a father figure? He was a stockbroker who jogged five miles every morning before going to work. His hair was chestnut brown and fell in seductive waves around his ears like Prince Valiant. His eyes—magnificent eyes—were Paul Newman-blue and sparkling. His trim moustache married his goatee and he looked as distinguished as a presidential candidate. He was well over six feet, and I could see through his smoking jacket and body-hugging trousers that here was a physical specimen to set any maiden's heart aflutter. Or the heart of a next-door neighbor pushing sixty, albeit reluctantly.

And *she* envied me?

I forget what we talked about. All I know is that when I finally got back to my own apartment Abner was on the verge of succumbing to starvation. I threw together a meal of hamburger and salad but had little appetite for it. I had fed my full on Victor Appleby . . .

I saw a lot of the Applebys. Rosalie and I did our laundry together in the basement room most Saturdays. The children remained proper and boring. I had a feeling that they were perplexed not only by adults but by childhood. They never played games. All they did was read books—but I mean very impressive books for their age: Freud and Jung and Norman Mailer. When I asked Rosalie about it, she explained, "They've been precocious since birth." Some explanation.

I often had them in for dinner or brunch or drinks and Victor was most sympathetic to Abner's condition. His father and a younger brother had both succumbed to terminal illnesses. Once, when we were alone in the kitchen, he kissed me lightly on the cheek. I said something stupid like "Thank you, kind sir," but he wasn't blind. He could see my face ablaze with not-too-restrained passion.

Then one day he invited me to lunch. We met at a quiet Italian restaurant in the East Thirties, chosen by him, I'm sure, because it was discreet and we weren't likely to run into mutual acquaintances, such as my husband (who wouldn't have given a damn) or his wife (who would have). After our first martini, he got down to cases. Living with Rosalie, it seems, was like living with a time bomb. She was suicidal and had repressed their children. (I wasn't blind.) I was saving Rosalie's life, Victor said.

"Me? What have I done?"

"You told her you envy her. Rosalie has never been envied. She's like her mother, who always thought every other woman in the world had a better life than she did. She would have traded places with most of her husband's woman patients. Rosalie's the same. Envy, envy, envy! If I hear that word again—"

I reached across the table and took his hand. He reacted warmly. His skin was pure velvet and my mouth went dry. "I'm glad I've helped Rosalie," I managed to say.

Very softly, he said, "Rebecca." For the first time I liked the sound of my name.

Then he mentioned a hotel on East Fortieth Street that rented rooms by the hour, no questions asked. Lunch was cancelled. We found a more fulfilling sustenance elsewhere.

That afternoon with Victor changed everything. Though I continued to act my role of envying Rosalie, I secretly despised her. Victor and I were stealing hours together wherever and whenever possible. He rented a car and kept it in a garage near our apartment building and we soon knew dozens of motels outside of the city—across the George Washington Bridge in New Jersey, over the Henry Hudson Bridge in Connecticut. If

Abner suspected anything, he couldn't care less. If Rosalie suspected anything, she had missed her vocation as an actress.

One Saturday morning, wheeling my soiled laundry from the apartment into the hall, I was astonished to see Rosalie waiting for the elevator, dressed as though she'd been invited to a coronation.

"Hi," I said. "No laundry this morning?"

"No," she answered. "I have an appointment in New Jersey. I've rented a car." That sent a prickle of guilt and apprehension up my spine. "Victor's in Chicago," she added. "The children are with my in-laws."

I almost blurted, "I know Victor's in Chicago—he begged me to meet him there."

The elevator arrived and the descent seemed forever.

"You certainly look terrific," I told her. "Where in New Jersey are you heading?"

"Hackensack."

Hackensack! "Why Hackensack?" I said.

"I want to purchase something there."

"Something they only sell in Hackensack?" I wasn't trying to be funny. There was something too weird and other-worldly about our conversation. She didn't reply to my question. We had arrived at the lobby and she was hurrying out. I continued down to the basement.

That night Abner looked all too healthy and I told him so.

"I'm getting this new treatment," he explained.

"What new treatment?"

"It was discovered in the mountains of Peru by a missionary for the Seventh Day Adventists. In those parts, they live to be over a hundred." I winced and hoped he didn't notice. "It's a culture from goat cheese and llama blood."

"Illegal, I'm sure."

"Well, don't I look better?"

"Yes," I agreed glumly.

Then we heard the shot. It could have been automobile backfire, but there was no use kidding ourselves—it had come from the next apartment, Rosalie and Victor's apartment. I shouted, "That was gunfire!" We ran into the hall, where we were joined by other neighbors. A man was pounding on the door to the Appleby apartment, shouting something insane like "Open up in there!" The building superintendent, Mr. Janowski, arrived and used his passkey. We followed him into the apartment.

Rosalie was in the den. There was a bullet wound in her head. She was seated at the desk and, except for the blood, she was impeccably attired. On the floor at her feet lay a small handgun—the object, no doubt, that she had gone to Hackensack to purchase.

Abner phoned for the police. Other neighbors came in. A few shrieked with horror, others sobbed. We located Victor in Chicago.

And so that was the end of the woman I envied.

It was in all the newspapers. Victor was shattered by the tragedy. I made the funeral arrangements, though there were relatives and other friends who might have been accommodating.

At the funeral, Victor spoke a lovely eulogy I had ghosted for him. Rosalie's parents, who had flown up from Florida, stood at the graveside, he frail and somewhat tottering, she tall as a flagpole and just as imposing. Contrary to Victor's description, her face reflected strength and positive thinking. It was easier to figure out Rosalie now.

After the services, we returned to Victor's apartment, where caterers I had hired served a tasteful lunch complemented by several excellent wines.

Over the next few days, I supervised the removal of Rosalie's belongings, choosing several worthy charities for the donations.

Abner's new treatment wasn't doing him that much good. It gave him better color, but he was losing weight and energy rapidly. Victor and I no longer had to resort to grubby little motels. We could have our clandestine meetings in his own apartment right next door.

But I found my thoughts dwelling on Rosalie. "Victor," I said one evening. "About Rosalie—"

"What about her?"

"Her suicide. Was it anything I said?"

"No, cutie," answered Victor, snuggling me in his arms, "it's what you didn't say."

"What do you mean?"

"From the day we started our affair, you stopped telling her how much you envied her. The day before I went to Chicago, she said to me, 'Rebecca has changed. Have you noticed?' I asked her in what way she thought you had changed. She said, 'She's looking younger and younger every day. Her voice has new color in it and her skin seems to have taken on a fresh life. It's as though she and I have changed places. I don't think she envies me any longer. I think she's got what she's wanted.' "

"What did you say to that?"

"I didn't say anything. I went to Chicago."

Well, Abner did die. Although it was expected, it was unexpected. He was found dead sitting on a bench along Riverside Drive where he sometimes sat and fed the pigeons. Victor and I were married and for auld lang syne we spent our wedding night in one of the motels we used to frequent. I sold my business to a syndicate of lascivious Arabs. Now Victor goes to his office and I stay home writing and trying to look after his children. I've sold several short stories, there's my autobiography due next autumn, and at present I'm plotting a very overheated novel.

At first we talked of joining our two apartments into one huge apartment, but Victor decided his held too many memories of Rosalie, so we rented it to a very attractive writer named Miranda Braggiotti. I believe she's famous for several books on the occult and Victor thinks she dabbles in witchcraft.

It's too amusing what happened when I met her at the elevator this morning with Nicholas and Evangeline morosely in tow. She gave us a strange, mysterious look and said to me, "You know something, Mrs. Appleby?" I can hear her voice now—soft, insinuating, somewhat menacing. "I envy you very much."

ANTHONY ARMSTRONG
THE CASE OF MR. PELHAM

The very first intimation that Mr. Pelham received—the, as it were, tiny wind ripple that so lightly brushes a field of wheat but is nevertheless the unrecognized herald of a devastating storm—occurred at about six o'clock on Tuesday evening the twentieth of May, halfway along Cornhill. It was outside his City office and he was just hailing a taxi to take him home to his bachelor flat in Maida Vale. An acquaintance named Camberley-Smith, passing briskly by, gave him a brief squeeze at the back of the elbow and said: "How goes it, Pelham? Saw you at the Hippodrome last night, but you didn't see me. I was up in the Circle. Well, so long—can't stop!" A friendly pat with a folded newspaper and he was on his way before Mr. Pelham had time to tell him he had made a mistake.

For Mr. Pelham hadn't been inside the Hippodrome for months. Last night, in fact, he had got home at 6:30, had eaten two nice cutlets served by his man, had played a little bridge with neighbors, and had gone to bed at 11:00.

He shrugged his shoulders, climbed into his taxi, and promptly forgot the matter. Nine days later, however, it returned to his mind.

He was lunching, rather heavily, at Simpson's with an American businessman—though it was called "completing the deal"—when he saw a friend two tables away. Sociable with food and drink, he signaled the other to come over and be introduced.

They chatted a while. Then the friend said, laughing: "Thought I wasn't on speaking terms with you!"

"Why on earth not?"

"Last Monday you gave me the dirtiest cut I've ever seen. Walked right past me."

"Me?" Mr. Pelham, friendly and inoffensive by nature, was staggered—then was apologizing even before he knew the facts. "I'm extremely sorry. I suppose I can't have seen you."

"You saw me all right. Looked straight into my face. And when I said, 'Hullo, Pel,' you stared and walked on."

"It can't have been me."

The friend, who had known Mr. Pelham for twelve years, said simply and directly: "I couldn't mistake your mug anywhere, old man."

Mr. Pelham, quite worried, asked the question he should have asked before: "Where exactly was this?"

"About one o'clock, in Lombard Street. I guess you'd just left the office for lunch."

"Monday?" Mr. Pelham pondered a little. Then he brightened. "No, not guilty, old chap! I was down at Chislehurst all Monday, seeing a client. It wasn't me you saw."

The friend started to argue, seemed to realize that it would lead nowhere, and instead said banteringly: "Then you must have a double. Good God! Two Pels in one world!" He moved on, grinning.

"Say, does this sort of thing happen much in London?" asked the American, interested. Mr. Pelham was checking up the Chislehurst visit in his engagement book and didn't answer.

"Do you think I'm really likely to have a double?" he said at last, quite seriously.

His guest looked at him. He saw a small, rather precise man of about forty-five, with neatly brushed hair, small moustache, and a round, palish face. His general expression was earnest and faintly imploring, like a spaniel asking to be friends. To the American, he looked exactly like dozens of other English businessmen of the more inoffensive, humdrum type.

Not caring to say so—for the other was buying the lunch— he replied with a guarded: "Maybe." Then he suddenly added, "But I doubt it," for he had just noticed that his host had eyes of slightly different colors—one bluish-brown, one hazel. "Those eyes of yours are darned unusual, you know."

"I know. Well, it's a relief." It was then Mr. Pelham suddenly recollected the Camberley-Smith incident nine days previously. "Still, it's queer. Twice within a fortnight that's happened. Ah, well.—What about trying some real English port? Don't get *that* over your side."

"Not so's you'd notice it," agreed the American politely.

Actually, Mr. Pelham's "twice within a fortnight" turned out to be an understatement. For the very next morning he found himself puzzling over a letter. It was from a certain Tom Mason, a young stockbroker he knew, and it ran:

> Dear Pel,
>
> This is to confirm the sketchy appointment we made in the White Lion on Wednesday. I find I'm quite free to beat hell out of you at golf on Saturday. Shall I meet you at the golf club? Or at Baker Street Station and we'll go out together. Give us a tinkle!
>
> T.M.

Mr. Pelham left his breakfast at once and went to the phone. He returned with an extremely worried frown and poured himself a strong cup of coffee. According to Mason, they had met on Wednesday evening at the White Lion, a pub in Bishopsgate near their respective offices and occasionally visited for a short drink after the labors of the City day. A game of golf for that weekend had been suggested. Yes, it had definitely been Wednesday and they had parted at about a quarter to seven. Mason, a little surprised at the urgency of the immaterial questions, had been certain of those points. Yet Mr. Pelham had not the slightest recollection of anything of the sort having happened. As far as he knew, he hadn't been in the White Lion since the previous Monday, hadn't even seen Mason for a week. He passed his hand across his forehead, then rang for his manservant.

"A little mixup has occurred in my engagements, Peterson," he said as casually as he could. "I—er—do you happen to remember what time I got home last Wednesday?"

Peterson reflected a moment. "At your usual time, sir, I think. A little after six-thirty. Yes, I'm certain, because of the chicken casserole."

Mr. Pelham waved him away irritably. He found it all absolutely inexplicable, and for the next week took life rather

soberly. He read up all he could about "doubles," for he was
becoming convinced that somewhere in London was a man
who was, as the saying went, "the very spit and image of him"—
even to the different-colored eyes, a fact which he had cleverly
elicited from Mason during their afternoon's golf. For of course
he had kept the appointment, slightly curious indeed to see
whether the man who had actually made it would dare turn up.

He also realized the disturbing factor that the unknown was
now evidently fully aware of the resemblance. Instead of under-
standably cutting Mr. Pelham's acquaintances, he was now
willfully deceiving them. Or was it just a hoax, with Mason and
others implicated? If it were not that, it was obvious that the
unknown was becoming bolder.

How much bolder, Mr. Pelham did not wholly appreciate till
the following Thursday. He had dined at his club and was just
going home when the hall porter, with a pleased smile, handed
him a box of cigarettes. It was a hundred box, with a dozen or
so gone. They were of the brand he smoked.

"You left this in the billiard room when you were playing last
night, sir. Luckily the marker remembered your ordering them."

"I? Mine?" Pelham stammered, and for a moment swayed and
clutched at a table.

"No doubt it escaped your memory, sir," suggested the man
indulgently. Privately he thought Mr. Pelham lucky to get them
back, but he supposed the marker had considered it wasn't
worth risking. A wrong decision, too, it seemed, for Mr. Pelham
was staring at the cigarettes as if he'd never seen them before.
As indeed he hadn't, for if one thing was absolutely clear in his
mind it was that he hadn't been in the club last night. And that
meant that the unknown double was such an identical counterpart of himself in every way that he could impersonate him
successfully at his own club, not just briefly, but over a consid-
erable period of time—for any suggestion of the incident being
part of a leg-pull was now practically ruled out. No one would
go so far as to enlist the club servants' help in such a matter.

Mr. Pelham had recovered his spirits by next morning, and by
the afternoon had begun to feel angry. This sort of thing had to
be stopped, though he had no clear idea how to set about it. He

did not particularly want to call in the police—and, anyway, there had been no attempt so far by the Double, as he now called him, to profit from the resemblance. For he had naturally ascertained from the club secretary that no account had been run up in his name, or checks cashed.

He pondered the matter, and a few evenings later he visited the club again on his way home and skillfully questioned the marker. From him, he elicited that on the night in question he had played billiards with a very good friend of his, a Major Bellamy.

Bellamy! Everyone, thought Mr. Pelham furiously, was being deceived too easily. Something had to be done. He won the marker's confidence with a tip and then hesitatingly put it to him that he might have been impersonated.

The marker was almost affronted. "That's impossible, sir. Why, I know you as well as most members. And what about the Major? Better ask him." Mr. Pelham shrugged this aside. "Besides, sir"—the marker had searched his memory and now produced a bombshell—"you passed the funny remark to me, you remember, about that cannon of yours." Mr. Pelham had once made a spectacularly humorous cannon and it had developed into a time-honored hoke between him and the marker. How could an outsider have known about that?

He went straight to the bar and had a stiff drink. He decided to stay on at the club for dinner, settle down unobtrusively in the library afterward, and then go down to the billiard room. Maybe he could catch the double red-handed. He went to the phone to tell Peterson he wouldn't be back.

"Oh, Peterson," he said into the transmitter. "Mr. Pelham here. I shan't be—"

"Yes, sir. What name shall I say?"

"What d'you mean?"

"I said, what name shall I say?"

"I know you did," snapped Mr. Pelham. "I mean what the hell did you say that *for*?"

There was a pause. Then: "Perhaps you'd better state your business." Peterson's voice was suddenly icy. Mr. Pelham restrained with difficulty an angry rebuke.

"I don't think you've quite gathered, Peterson. This is Mr. Pelham speaking."

There was again a pause. When the man spoke, his voice was puzzled, but polite once more: "I'm afraid I don't hear you very well, sir. Did you wish to speak to Mr. Pelham? If so, would you give me your name?"

"My name is Pelham!" He almost danced in sudden temper. Was Peterson drunk? "This is your master speaking. I rang up to tell you—" He stopped suddenly. An explanation of Peterson's apparent denseness had occurred to him. He put the receiver down and leaned trembling against the side of the booth.

Then he burst suddenly out and, shouting "Taxi!" to the astounded hall porter, started struggling into his coat.

He was still trembling when he reached Montague Court and he could hardly fit his key into the door. "Peterson!" he called.

"Sir?" Peterson appeared. Beneath his trained exterior he looked a little surprised.

"When I— Did I—" He tried to pull himself together. "Ah, good evening. Has anyone—I mean, any messages for me?"

"A rather peculiar person rang up, sir. There was some confusion about the name. I was just going to consult you when he rang off."

"Just going to consult *me?*"

"Yes, sir. You were in your bedroom at the time. It was only a minute before you stepped out a short while ago."

"Stepped out? Why, I— But you didn't *see* me go, did you?"

"No, sir. But I heard you cross the hall and then I heard the door bang."

There was a silence. Then: "Bring me some whiskey," ordered Mr. Pelham hoarsely, and went into the sitting room.

Gulping down the spirit—he felt he was drinking more than usual these days, but really this thing was getting him down—he tried to face the facts. The extraordinary telephone conversation was explained: Peterson had imagined his master was in the bedroom at the time. Later he had thought he had gone out—even while in actual fact he was only leaving the club—and after a short while again returned. In other words, the

Double had now successfully impersonated him in his own home and to his own manservant of six years' service.

He rang the bell. Perhaps Peterson hadn't actually seen the Double come in, either—had, just as when he went out, only heard him, and assumed it was his master.

"You rang, sir?"

"Ah, Peterson. I'm ready for dinner. I want an early bed. Not feeling up to the mark. Don't you—that is, didn't you—think I looked a bit ill this evening when I first got back?" He was quite prepared for Peterson to say he hadn't actually seen him, when he would reply, "Oh, of course not—stupid of me! I was forgetting."

"Frankly, sir, it seemed to me the moment you came in that you appeared fitter than for some time. In good spirits, too, sir." A reminiscent smile touched his lips. "That little quip about what you said to the taxi-driver was most amusing, sir."

"Yes, yes, yes," muttered Mr. Pelham feverishly. There was something important he was trying to think of.

"But I must confess, sir," went on Peterson, "you *don't* seem quite as well now."

Muttering something about seeing a doctor tomorrow, Mr. Pelham abruptly pushed past him and went to his bedroom. He had just remembered what it was that was important. "The moment you came in," Peterson had said. The Double, therefore, had let himself in.

He looked in the little stud box where he kept his spare latchkey. It was there, all right. But of course it could have been put back there—once the fellow had got inside. And, anyway, how had he got possession of it in the first place?

He examined his dressing-table drawers. Nothing of value was gone—pearl links, a reserve five-pound note in a wallet, gold cigarette case for special occasions, all were present. *What* had he come for? Why, in God's name?

His eyes fell on something on the dressing table. It was a stiff collar with a crumpled tie still held in it—obviously only recently taken off. And the tie was the sedate dark striped tie he habitually wore to the office, the tie he had put on that morning, the tie that he would probably have changed at the same time as he put on a soft collar for the evening—*had he done so.* Which he had not, for this was the first time he'd entered the room. And his reflection in the glass confirmed that he was still wearing a stiff collar and his dark striped tie. He had similar collars, of course, but not another tie anything like it.

Yet an exact replica lay on the table before him.

He tottered to the bed and sat there a long time, his head in his hands. "What *is* all this?" he murmured. "Am I going mad?"

He felt for a sudden moment deathly afraid.

Next day, Mr. Pelham phoned his office that he was unwell and wouldn't be in that morning. Instead, at eleven o'clock, he visited a Harley Street mental specialist.

The specialist was definitely puzzled. He essayed, then discounted, hallucination theories—for, if so, it was plainly Mr. Pelham's associates who were having the hallucinations. He agreed that there could be no question of a stupendous hoax. Sounding out for paranoia, he gave him openings to state that he felt this Double, or imagined Double, was persecuting him deliberately, but got no reaction.

"Not willfully. Only by just being there at all," complained Mr. Pelham wretchedly, seeing that the other, for all his confident, competent air, was not going to be able to help him. "Besides, you used the word 'imagined.' How can anyone imagine that?" He pointed to the ties, which he had brought with him. "They are exactly the same—same marker, even the same amount of wear. Yet only *one* is mine. The other was left in my flat. *By someone.*"

"Hm! Well, if you want my opinion, your mental balance is all right, and it's really a matter for the police. Impersonation, you know. The tie might be a clue to work from."

"But what's he getting *out* of it? I haven't lost a thing."

"Not yet, perhaps. A clever criminal would wait for a big haul."

"I've thought of that. I—er—" he spoke a little shame-facedly—"I've even written my bank this morning and arranged to change my signature on my checks. But how can this fellow, whom I've never seen, know just what I do and wear?" He picked up the ties and looked at them.

"By watching you. And no doubt you are a man of regular habits."

Mr. Pelham nodded. "I do run in a bit of a groove."

"Try varying your movements and your dress a bit. Unexpectedly. And I should see the police. They may land him. I'm afraid there is frankly not much *I* can do for you."

Mr. Pelham left him, feeling like a child whose nurse has failed him at a crucial moment. He had not the slightest intention of going to the police, not after this new development. Not only did he feel they would fail him, too, but they would probably laugh at him. Besides, in his inmost soul, though he would not yet admit it, he knew that there was something about the whole business which the official mentality could never appreciate, that something which last night had momentarily filled him with a fear of a new and hitherto unexperienced kind.

After lunch he went to the office. Vaguely surprised that none of his staff asked after his indisposition, he did not appreciate the reason till his secretary brought him some papers to sign.

"The letters you dictated just before lunch, sir," she said with lifted eyebrows when he testily shoved them back at her, asking what the office thought it was up to. "I *was* glad you found yourself well enough to come down, after all. That Manson matter needed a proper clearing up."

Mr. Pelham sat very still for a moment, trying to get a grip of himself. Miss Clement had been with him longer even than Peterson had. "Of course, of course," he managed to get out, and motioned the woman from the room.

Then he began to study the letters—and grew more bewildered than ever. For they dealt efficiently with various details of his work—in particular the Manson matter, which he'd been putting off for days. He knew he had not dictated them, yet indisputably they were his. It was not that they employed his turns of phrase—conceivably his secretary could have been responsible for that—it was that in many cases they implied knowledge of his business activities she could hardly have possessed. Knowledge, too, that could not have been gleaned from the files without many hours' research, knowledge in fact that only Mr. Pelham personally could have had at his fingertips.

Moreover, they were good letters. With one exception, they took just the line he would have followed. The exception was a particularly bold decision, brilliant but a gamble. Mr. Pelham would have toyed wistfully with the idea, but in the end would probably not have acted on it, though even that was faintly possible. Otherwise, they were exactly the letters he would have written. He dropped his aching head on one hand. They *were* the letters he had written. Mechanically he began to sign them.

Nearing the bottom, a corner of pink suddenly showed itself. A check! He pounced on it. Had he caught the Double trying to—? No, it was pinned to a retyped letter he had yet to sign, and merely paid an overdue account. But the check was already signed—and signed with Mr. Pelham's altered signature, conceived only that morning!

He sat for a long while, trembling violently. What was happening? Who *was* this Double, this—his dry lips formed the words—*more*-than-Double, this veritable alter ego who somehow knew his inmost secrets? The uncanny, sickening fear swept over him with renewed force. When that check was signed, his letter to the bank must still have been in the post. By no possible manner of means could his new signature have then been seen or known by anyone except himself.

It was at that moment that Mr. Pelham realized for the first time that everything which had happened up to that afternoon might have had *some* normal explanation, impossible though it seemed to discover it. To this last incident, however, there was no explanation, unless—unless it was one that involved something more than purely human agency.

After some long while, he pulled himself together and went out. He walked a large part of the way home. Occasionally he muttered to himself. The phrase "more than purely human agency" stuck in his mind, and once or twice he frightened passers-by with it. The fear, however, had left him by the time he got back. He sat down and for a long while tried to face the situation.

Surely there was some way to fight this thing—this terror—that had come upon him? Tell Peterson to refuse admittance? But Peterson, he knew, would think it *was* his master. Confront the Double in the club? Or in the office? But he was never there when Mr. Pelham was. He always seemed to *know*. And why not—if something more than purely human agency *were* involved? Mr. Pelham shuddered again unaccountably, and swiftly looked up, half expecting to see the Double in the room with him.

He glimpsed Camberley-Smith next day, but avoided him, as a man shuns a place of once-happy memory which time has changed to bitterness and misery. For he had recalled that brief encounter three weeks before in Cornhill—the first intimation he had had of anything wrong—though everything then had seemed so simple. Just mistaken identity, or a possible innocent double by chance somewhere in London. Now it was the Double, an overwhelming terror lying in wait everywhere about his daily path. Growing bolder and bolder, too—seeping into his life like foul, wet mud sliding down a steep bank into a clear pool, till—till the pool was no longer clear, but all muddied and evil.

In the evening, he had a new idea. Rather shamefacedly, he looked up the address of a man he had greatly admired, but had lost touch with—an extremely broad-minded clergyman, who had left the neighborhood a year ago for a parish somewhere in Surrey. "The Reverend K. Fleming, The Vicarage, Littleshot," he turned up, and took pen and paper. But he did not write, after all. Somehow he didn't know what to say that wouldn't sound quite foolish. Anyway, the mere thought of Fleming being there, within call, had slightly restored his courage. He felt more inclined to fight back, and next morning he called in a locksmith and had the lock on his front door changed. Only one key was made and this he put on a ring with a stout chain attached to his suspenders.

Remembering the specialist's advice about varying his movements unexpectedly, he called up a friend just before he left the office and arranged to go to the six-thirty performance at a music hall instead of going home. He also phoned Peterson to leave some cold supper out for him. The two men had a drink or so afterward and it was quite late when he returned home.

There was no supper laid. Indignant and hungry, he knocked up Peterson, who had gone to bed.

Peterson, half-undressed, seemed staggered to see him, and even more taken aback when he asked about his food.

"But you—you've *had* some supper, sir."

"I've *what*?"

The man's manner changed to sudden solicitude. "Don't you remember, sir? Cold chicken. And you asked me for a half bottle of the Liebfraumilch and—you seemed all right then, sir," he gulped tactlessly.

Mr. Pelham saw what he meant. "You think I'm drunk?"

"No, sir," lied Peterson, thinking his master must have put in some good work on the whiskey since supper. "I—I—well, look here, sir." He led the way to the kitchen and eagerly showed Mr. Pelham dirty plates, explaining apologetically, "As it was late, I thought for once I'd leave them till tomorrow." Showed him, too, the empty hock bottle, even the chicken bones in the garbage pail. "Why, I served you with the wine, sir," he went on entreatingly. "And later you went to bed. At least I thought so—or I would have stayed up myself. I didn't hear you go out again."

Mr. Pelham was quickly at the bedroom door. For a moment he faltered, then abruptly opened it.

The room was empty, the bed untouched. His pajamas lay across the coverlet.

Peterson was frankly puzzled. "Well, I could have sworn I heard the basin running. And your wardrobe shutting. And then the springs as you got into bed. And only a short while ago, too, sir."

Mr. Pelham said nothing. He stood there, fingering the latch-key in his pocket. The only key, which had been on his person all day.

"All right," he got out at last. "That's all!" A little scared, the man backed out.

Mr. Pelham lay awake a long time. Fearfully, like a schoolboy starting to explore some dark, eerie cavern which he does not want to enter but by which he is as much fascinated as terrified, he tried to recall all he had heard or read about ghosts, about spirits who had taken human shape. It was unbelievable, impossible, but what then was it? Nothing made any sense to his tortured brain. Nothing was real—except the unknown terror steadily engulfing his life. Not till he had gotten up and written to Fleming that he wanted to meet him—that he was in great trouble and needed his help, though he could not explain in a letter—was he able to drop off into a troubled sleep with the lights still on.

He could hardly concentrate on his work the next morning and went out at twelve to get a drink. At least it was a change from his usual habits, though the specialist's advice had not proved very successful the previous night. The drink, however, and another, cheered him up and, recalling the advice further, he impulsively went into a shop and bought the most distinctive tie—within the limits of a certain taste—that he could find, a tie he would never otherwise have chosen. He even achieved a certain pleasure in this—having only worn quiet colors all his life. The clerk was vaguely amused, particularly when Mr. Pelham rejected several as being likely to be duplicated. "I want something unique," he kept saying. "Not loud—but unique!" He then chose a combination of dark-green and red with a small orange spot. He put it on and felt better.

Returning to the office after lunch, he was staggered to discover that, according to Miss Clement, he had apparently come back at a quarter past twelve and worked dynamically on all sorts of new and to-him-undreamed-of projects till a quarter to two. He called for the letters and papers and sat, half-terrified, half-fascinated, reading them as a child reads a story full of words it cannot understand.

In the middle of this, his club rang up to say he'd left his bag behind when he'd stayed there last night—would he be calling for it? At first he could hardly take in what was being said, then, "Keep it! Keep it!" he gasped and slammed the receiver down as if it were red hot. His bag was in his *flat*—it *must* be in his flat!

He sat staring into vacancy for a long time. This was too much for any man to face alone. The mud was seeping in—overwhelmingly, inexorably. He fought for breath as if suffocated. At intervals he tried to keep calm, found himself saying:

"*This* is I. *This* is old Pel. *This* is Mr. Pelham of Lake, Pelham & Company. I, and I alone, live at Flat 10, Montague Court." And even as he spoke, feeling for the key to the flat in his pocket, he knew that he did not live alone there, and the terror would engulf him again.

He jumped up. He could not wait for Fleming's reply. He could not face the flat that night. He would go down at once to Littleshot and stay there till the thing was thrashed out. Fleming would know what to do.

He rang his flat to tell Peterson to pack a suitcase and take it to Waterloo, and a man said, "Hullo." The voice was somehow familiar, but it wasn't Peterson. For a moment he could not place it.

"Who's that?" he said.

"This is Mr. Pelham speaking. Who is it, please?"

A sudden icy sweat broke out all over him. In an instant the instrument he held was slippery with it. No wonder the voice was familiar. *It was his own!* And the sweat on him was that of cold fear—the terror returned in overmastering waves.

"N-no," he croaked. "*This* is Mr. Pelham. I'm speaking from my office. Who are you really?"

"I've told you." The voice held just the slight superior amusement he would have experienced under similar circumstances. "I'm Mr. Pelham. There must be some mistake. Your name may be Pelham, too, of course. But I'm Mr. Pelham of Lake, Pelham & Company and Montague Court."

Mr. Pelham feverishly wiped his hands and forehead, tried to think clearly.

"Well, what can I do for you?" the other was asking.

"I want to speak to Peterson," was all Mr. Pelham could say. Surely Peterson would recognize him for the real Mr. Pelham.

"My man? Are you a friend of his? I've told him he's not supposed to be rung up on my phone, but if it's important—"

Why, thought Mr. Pelham feverishly, that's what he himself would have said—those *were* his instructions to Peterson. "It's not important," he got out. "It doesn't matter." How could Peterson believe a voice on the phone with his master obviously there beside him? He formed a sudden plan. "It was merely to say I'm going away for a few days," he said. "Sorry to have bothered you."

"I honestly don't know what you're talking about—" he heard the other begin in just his own puzzled accents as he put the receiver down and jumped from his chair. He had said that to put the other off the scent. He was going straight to Maida Vale.

He jumped from the taxi, ran up the stairs, and let himself into his flat. He had just shut the door when Peterson appeared. The man's jaw dropped. He stared at Mr. Pelham and then at the door of the sitting room. "I could have sworn—" he began, then suddenly his control snapped. "What *is* the matter with you these days, going out and coming in without my even hearing?" He pulled himself up. "I'm sorry, sir."

"Never mind that now," gabbled Mr. Pelham. "There's an impostor in there. It's not me at all. It's been going on for—" He noticed Peterson was backing away. "It's all right. This is me. And I want to see this fellow."

The door of the sitting room opened. A man came out.

Mr. Pelham stood transfixed. The other was an exact counterpart of himself. Moustache, round palish face, differently colored eyes, even the faintly appealing expression. Yet from him as he stood there, Mr. Pelham experienced a sudden wave of malignancy, of horrible power, of something that was not after all human for all its outward shape. And it carried the terror with it in wave after wave, a veritable physical presence, battering down his resolve.

There was a silence, broken only by Peterson. "Lord Almighty!" he ejaculated.

Mr. Pelham slowly fought back the terror. He had noticed with a sudden delight, and clung to the knowledge like a drowning man to a lifebelt, that the other was not wearing the new tie, but the usual dark striped one.

"Don't go, Peterson," said the stranger, as Peterson edged away. "You may have noticed I've been worried these last days. Well, this is the cause."

Would *he* have said that? Mr. Pelham found himself vaguely wondering. Yes, he believed, given the incredible circumstances, he would.

"You would," said the other surprisingly, though Mr. Pelham had not spoken, and went on before Peterson could grasp anything. "You've been pestering me for some time because of your likeness to me. And honestly I'm tired of it." He turned to Peterson again. "I didn't mention it to you before, but this man actually got into the flat here once. The night I rang up from the club, you remember?"

"But that's not true!" Mr. Pelham suddenly found he was almost shouting. Very unlike him to shout. He should have been quieter, more restrained—as indeed the other Mr. Pelham was now.

"You remember, Peterson, don't you?" the Double was saying calmly.

"Well, yes, sir, I do, and it struck me as strange at the time."

Mr. Pelham choked. That "sir" to—to the wrong one! "Peterson," he said almost imploringly. "Peterson, don't you know me? You've been with me six years, don't you know me?"

"Go on," said the other in Mr. Pelham's level tones. "Answer him, Peterson."

Peterson was almost too shattered to speak—and when he did, it was a man, not a servant.

"Well, it's Gawd's truth I've never seen a pair so alike before in my natural. No one'd believe me if I was to tell 'em. Those eyes of the both of you. If you was to put me on me oath, I couldn't swear. But I'd swear to each of you separate."

Mr. Pelham's heart sank. Till then he had thought Peterson would, must, could not help recognizing him instantly.

"But, Peterson," he cried, "think of the things we've done together—before this."

"Don't shout so loud," reproved the other. "No good can come of shouting." It was a stock phrase of Mr. Pelham's own, and he saw Peterson's recognition of it as he looked quickly at the speaker. "Look, here's a test. Tell Peterson what his master said to him last night when he poured the first glass of hock."

"I—I wasn't—" began Mr. Pelham and was silent. He couldn't say he wasn't there. "It was you who was here then," he said sullenly.

"That's the point I'm making," was the smiling retort. "Well, I said, 'It's almost a shame to drink it, there are only nine bottles left,' and Peterson said—what?"

Mr. Pelham was still stunned. He felt like a rat in a trap.

"Very well, then, Peterson said, 'Only eight now, sir. This one's as good as gone.' "

"That's right, sir," said Peterson, suddenly himself again. "You're Mr. Pelham, sir. But, good Lord, he's like you!"

"I'm not, I'm not! He's like *me!* He's sapping my life, my existence!"

"Keep calm, man, or get out. One last thing, Peterson. He's made one big mistake. Did you ever see me wearing a tie like that green-and-red thing?"

"No, sir. Never." Peterson was emphatic. "You haven't got one, and you'd never have bought one."

"Good! Remember all this, will you, in case of further trouble. All right. That'll do."

Peterson went. And with him it seemed to Mr. Pelham that all light and life and security went from the room. He turned to the other almost imploringly and saw the face had changed for him alone.

"That's nearly the end," said the Double. "You did make a mistake about that tie, didn't you? I could have been wearing it, but I didn't because it gave me a nice chance."

"But—but—" stammered Mr. Pelham, then he whimpered: "Why have you done all this to me?"

He was not answered. "At last," said the Double exultingly, "I am *here!* I have your business and what I shall make of that I alone know, as you may have noticed. I shall be free to do what I—but that won't interest you," he broke off. "You're mad, you know," he said suddenly, with an edge to his voice.

Tears were suddenly streaming down Mr. Pelham's face. "I don't believe this is real. It must be a dream. Why has this happened to me?"

"It just happened," said the other, and all the evil of the world was in his voice. Then abruptly, in Mr. Pelham's own tones: "Now I'm calling Peterson again and we're going to give you in for impersonation."

"No, no. Let me go away." Mr. Pelham advanced unintention-

ally to the other—and recoiled horribly from his presence.
"Who are you?" he cried. "Who are you?"

"Why, Mr. Pelham, of course."

It was then Mr. Pelham started screaming.

If you meet Mr. Pelham nowadays you find him much the same,
though his business is flourishing beyond expectation. And as
Tom Mason, who follows and trusts his stock-exchange flair,
says to him when they play golf together, "Pel, you must have
scooped a tidy pile by now. Heading for a millionaire, what?"

Mr. Pelham smiles his inoffensive little smile and says: "D'you
think I've changed much since I began to go ahead?"

"Not much, old boy," says Mason. "Still really the same old
Pel. But you just seem suddenly to have taken hold of yourself.
I believe that rather rotten experience—you remember, when
that fellow, that double, who tried to impersonate you and then
went off his rocker right in front of you—had something to do
with it. Made you face up to things."

"Maybe," says Mr. Pelham mildly. "Maybe. Poor chap! He's
been put away a long while now, hasn't he? I'm afraid he'll
never be right again."

HENRY SLESAR

THE KINDEST MAN IN THE WORLD

"Fifty-nine, uh-huh," Dennison said, giving the lock of his briefcase a firm, satisfying snap. "Well, it's not an age we write many policies for, Mr. Lewis, but that doesn't mean we don't *want* to. There's no such thing as being too old—or too young—for life insurance. So let's review what kind of protection you have, and how much more you might need to provide for your family."

Dennison took the fountain pen out of his pocket and gave the gold tip a delicate, adjusting twist. "Never used a ballpoint in my life," he smiled. Then he realized how insipid that sounded, and felt a flush of self-directed anger. He said, "Would the beneficiary be your wife?"

The man in the bathrobe, seated almost at the opposite wall of the hotel room, lifted his thin arms inside the tubular sleeves and yawned. In the dim light he resembled some kind of monstrous bird, a cormorant about to begin a slow deliberate flight across the grey carpet.

"No," he said, with a birdlike grin. "I don't have a wife. I don't have any family at all."

Dennison sighed, having expected nothing. The call had come in cold to the office on Las Palmas, and the caller had asked for Dennison by name. Dennison, in bondage to a sullen mood that resulted from a miserable sales month, hadn't bothered to wonder why, or what made a hotel transient interested in the permanency of life insurance.

"That's right," the man in the bathrobe said. "Neither chick nor child, nobody I give a hang about."

"I see," Dennison said, not seeing at all. "Then the purpose of this policy would be—?"

"I never said I *wanted* a policy, did I?"

"The message I received at the office—"

"Was that I wanted to see *you*. Joe Dennison. You."

A familiar, scratchy ball of irritation rose in Dennison's throat, and he squinted in search of comprehension.

"Why, you don't even remember me," Lewis chuckled. "That's salt in the wound, Joe. It's not even eight years, and you don't remember me."

"All right," Dennison said flatly, "I give up. Who the hell are you?"

"Joe, you may not believe this, but I'm the kindest man in the world. I've come three thousand miles just to do you a kindness. I thought I'd lost track of you for good when you left home— whatever made you do that, Joe?—but then a friend of mine, a private detective it so happens, found you right smack in the middle of Los Angeles, selling life insurance. Insurance! That's a good joke on me, isn't it? Maybe if Nettie had an insurance policy with your company, maybe you wouldn't have killed her. Is that possible, Joe?"

The man in the bathrobe interlocked his fingers, placed them on his lap, and waited.

Finally Dennison said, "You're Wilfred Covey."

"Yes, that's right. Sorry I had to fool you into coming here, Joe, but I didn't see any other way. I wanted things to be different between us now. You see, I'm not angry any more, not in the least." He rose slowly from the chair and shuffled across the carpet, his bony hand extended. "Will you shake my hand, Joe? Will you do that?"

Dennison looked at the hand in loathing. Then he grasped it firmly, almost belligerently, and pumped it once.

"There," Covey chuckled. "That wasn't so bad, was it? I told you I came to do you a kindness, Joe, and that's what I meant. I want to help you the way I helped the others."

"The others?"

"Yes. Fowler and Phil Hepplewhite and Wally Waldron. You see, I forgave them, too, a long time ago, and I went out of my way to make things up to them, to show them I didn't harbor any bad feelings for what they did. For killing Nettie, I mean."

Dennison's lips moved numbly. Fowler, Hepplewhite, Waldron. He hadn't heard their names in years, not since his family troubles had driven him from New York.

"All right," he said. "I'm glad you've forgiven us, Mr. Covey. Only now I really have to be—"

"Wait a minute, Joe, please. Don't you want to hear *how* I forgave them? It's very important, really. You see, I want to be equally kind to you, but you'll have to help me. You'll have to show me how."

Dennison frowned at the briefcase on his lap. "I can't stay long," he said . . .

"Of course, I was ten years younger," Covey said. "Funny what a difference ten years can make. I was nearly fifty, but I felt like a spring chicken most of the time. That was the effect Nettie had on me. She was thirty-one, thirty-two, I was never sure which—Nettie was always coy about birthdays. I wish you might have known her, Joe—alive, I mean. There was so much life in Nettie it spilled out of her eyes and mouth from morning to night. In any one day, Nettie could run up and down the emotional scale like Paderewski on a keyboard. She wasn't the easiest woman to live with. But she's a lot harder to live without.

"We were married only two years when I bought the lake house. Things were going better for me that year—my little company was getting to be a big company. Nettie wanted me to accept the offers I was getting, to sell the business and spend the rest of our life tramping around the world and finding things to laugh about. How that girl loved to laugh! I wasn't quite ready for retirement yet, but I did buy the lake house. That little sailboat of Nettie's, that was a birthday present. I don't know which birthday, exactly, because Nettie was always coy about— But I've already said that, haven't I?

"God knows what made her think she was a sailor. When we took the boat out together, she'd sit all huddled up with delighted terror and hardly move until we were back on shore. Only that day—*you* know which day I mean, Joe—she just got carried away by the beauty of the weather and the glassy stillness of the lake, and she went out all by herself. I guess she made a pretty picture, all right, that long blonde hair of hers streaming out behind her. I guess you fellows must have been drawn to that like moths.

"You know what I really think? I think Nettie most probably saw the four of you cruising along in that nifty little power boat of yours. I think the sight of four men in a lipstick-red Chris Craft must have stirred up the flirt in her. So you see, I don't entirely blame you for what happened.

"The trouble was, Nettie just couldn't handle that boat. When you came gunning toward her, laughing and yelling, full of the devil, and your wake started to make her little sailboat bob like a cork, Nettie just lost her head. Maybe you didn't even see when she fell overboard—that's what you said at the inquest, wasn't it? Even if you did see her fall overboard, you must have figured she was perfectly okay, that she could just hold onto the hull and climb back on. Only you didn't even come back to find out, did you, Joe? You and the others. You just left her there, in the water.

"Nobody knows for sure what happened, whether she bumped her head when she went over and became unconscious. God, I'd want to think it happened that way, quick, because Nettie hated pain of any kind—she broke dental appointments, cried over hangnails, ate aspirin like peanuts when she had a headache. I hate to think of her suffering, with water in her lungs, her mouth filling up, stopping her cries. I was sixty miles away in the noisy city, but you know I could swear I heard her calling for help.

"Well, I guess you know how bad I was, Joe. The things I said, the threats I made! When I think of your faces at the inquest, like four tombstones! I suppose you were mighty relieved at the verdict, even if I did carry on like a fool. You know I didn't mean what I said, Joe, You ask anybody—my associates, my customers, even my competitors—they'll tell you what a kindly person I really am.

"After a while I calmed down. I thought things over and realized how wrong I was to blame Nettie's death on you and the others. Eventually I even began feeling *guilty* about the way I had carried on. But I really didn't know what to do about it, to make things up, I mean, until the day I ran across Fowler at the River City Club.

"It was over a year since Nettie died, and it was odd how I had trouble remembering exactly what Nettie looked like, but I didn't have any trouble at all recognizing Fowler. There he was, wearing a nice linen jacket, pretty girl on his arm, looking prosperous, a little jowly, and full of life. Full of whiskey, too, I couldn't help noticing that. Guess you know about Fowler, the trouble he had with drink. I didn't know how bad it was, not until he passed out on the dance floor and had to be carted off by the waiters.

"I felt sorry for the poor girl he was with, so I went over to help. She was a nice girl, sweet little post-deb named Louise— not much on brains, but she had green eyes like Nettie's and that was enough of a recommendation for me.

"It was Louise who told me how serious Fowler's drink problem was. The poor guy considered himself a connoisseur of wines and liquors and maybe he was—he sure spent enough time and money on the stuff. The only trouble was, his income had taken a serious nose dive. The brokerage house he worked for didn't think drunks made the best account executives, not even connoisseur drunks. He'd been getting along on invitations to dinner parties and weekends, but his drinking was costing him friends, too. Pretty soon the jobs and the invitations and his health were all going to disappear—and what would happen to poor Fowler then?

"Well, I was sorry to hear all this, and the first question I asked myself was, How can I show him some kindness?

"About two weeks later, I found out where and how Fowler was living—that was my detective friend at work. It was rather sordid, I'm afraid—a cheap one-room flat in a rundown section of the city. But I was happy to learn that Louise was having a good influence on the man. They had become engaged to be married, and the prime condition she had imposed on him was total abstinence.

"Well, it's wonderful what the love of a good woman can do for us reprobates, eh? For over six weeks Fowler behaved admirably, soberly, and even industriously. He found himself another job and was well on the road to dull, middle-class respectability. What a pity!

"There seemed to be only one thing I could do to help him

under the circumstances, to spare him from the humdrum future that loomed ahead. I decided to become his secret benefactor, and I began with a gift worthy of any connoisseur— a bottle of Justerini & Brooks 1875 Cognac. Perhaps you don't know cognac? This was a great brandy bottled in honor of the coronation of some king or other. Unquestionably a collector's item, and I knew that a collector like Fowler would appreciate it, really appreciate it.

"I'm sorry to say that he appreciated it just a little too much. Louise was close to breaking their engagement when she found him in his unfortunate condition. But faced with the possibility of losing her, Fowler was repentant, and made staunch promises of sobriety.

"I then sent him a case of Chateau Mouton-Rothschild 1955, that fine vintage which becomes rarer and rarer. Surely there was nothing wrong with a good red wine? To be enjoyed at mealtimes? Sadly enough, Louise didn't understand this any better, and poor Fowler had the grim duty of disposing of the lot. Almost the lot—I have a sneaky feeling he managed to hide one or two bottles.

"At any rate, I thought he merited an award for his good conduct, so I sent him a fine Scotch whisky called the Glenlivet, and I believe he enjoyed that very much. Then, in quick order, I sent him a Marc Marquis d'Angerville, vintage 1924, an Armagnac Domaine Boingneres, a case of Chateau Cheval Blanc and another of Wehlener Sonnenuhr Auslese 1959, and then— Oh, yes. Louise. She finally left him, of course, and perhaps that was for the best. The girl was becoming an absolutely pernicious influence. I celebrated that event by sending Fowler a bottle of Louis Roederer Cristal Brut 1955.

"It was a pity that Fowler eventually lost even his meager quarters. It became hard to send him presents when he lost his permanent address and started wandering those filthy streets downtown. You can imagine how sad I was to learn of his illness—pneumonia, I'm told it was—and his subsequent death. His parents came all the way from Wisconsin for the funeral. It was a small, quiet affair, and I was sorry that business kept me away. However, I sent flowers.

"I didn't wait to stumble on Phil Hepplewhite now that I realized how much kindness could accomplish—I went out and found him.

"I knew from the very first report that Phil wasn't going to be an easy man to help. He seemed to have everything. He was a partner in a successful firm engaged in the manufacture of sunglasses. He was personable, even handsome, well educated and of good disposition. And wonder on wonder, he was also a very happily married man. I was certainly pleased to hear that, Joe—you know my views on marriage.

"Six months before, he had wed a charming creature named Linda Fisher. She had been a secretary at the Hepplewhite Company, a firm which employed many young women in its various departments. His marriage came as something of a surprise, because Phil, as you probably know, had a reputation for being a gay dog. Beautiful women had always been his weakness, and Linda was the loveliest he had met to date.

"In a way it was a shame he had rushed into marriage at the tender age of—what was he, twenty-five? I hadn't married until I was past forty, when a man is truly ready to devote himself to one woman alone. If physical beauty had been Phil's only standard, then he had simply underestimated the wealth of it available. I thought I would do him the kindness of showing him.

"The first young lady I sent to the Hepplewhite office was named Donna de Vrees, and, believe it or not, she had actually taken a secretarial course at one time and was equipped for the job. This was surprising, since Miss de Vrees had been gathering laurels for her pretty head since the age of fifteen. She was Miss Everything for a while, then a favorite of photographers hired to glorify undergarments, and, most recently, a striking addition to a musical revue which folded after three performances.

"She was hired for the job, and I'm afraid the inevitable happened. After two months, Phil became painfully aware of the contrast between Linda's hair-curlered, face-creamed, sallow morning appearance and Donna's fresh-blooming, well-groomed, perfumed loveliness. He began working late, and, naturally, so did Donna. The culmination was a domestic quarrel, and sobs, and packed luggage. Phil was repentant, and convincing enough to bring about a reconciliation. He discharged Donna, from both her job and his affection, and swore to be true forever.

"That was when I sent Tracey.

"Tracey was even more beautiful than Donna de Vrees. She had a face so exquisite that the only magazines in America able to resist her cover-girl charms were *National Geographic*, *Popular Mechanics*, and a handful more. The rest featured it over and over, so it had become too familiar for Tracey to pretend secretarial aspirations. I devised another form of introduction—simple but effective. Tracey went to see Mr. Hepplewhite on the pretext of wanting to model his sunglasses. He referred her to his advertising agency, but a lunch date resulted. The rest was—well, history is a good word. Don't they say that history repeats itself?

"It took two months before Linda became aware of Phil's new interest, and when she did nothing satisfied her except a legal separation—the lawyers prospered. A few months after, there was still another reconciliation. Tracey was retired to Palm Beach, where she lived for a year on Phil's generous parting gift, and Linda was once more queen bee of the Hepplewhite hive.

"So I sent Ilona.

"Ilona wasn't as chic as Donna de Vrees—her clothes weren't as smart and her hair wasn't done nearly as well. She wasn't as beautiful as Tracey. Her hair and her eyes were too black, her lips too full, her figure perhaps too voluptuous. But she walked into Phil Hepplewhite's life, and this time Linda's domestic felicity was ended but good. Linda carried on like all the Macbeth witches rolled into one. And when Phil finally moved out, bag and baggage, she went a bit further than most scorned wives do and shot him in the middle of the lower back.

"You mean you hadn't heard, Joe? Yes, poor Phil's marriage ended in tragedy. No, he wasn't killed, luckily. The bullets made a mess of his spine and cost him a kidney—he became a helpless paralytic, a permanent invalid, but he's alive. Isn't modern surgery wonderful? I understand Phil tried to undo the doctors' good work once or twice by slashing his wrists, but thank heaven he's still with us. I send him a Christmas card every year.

"Poor Wally Waldron. You knew *he* was dead, of course.

"Heart attack? Excuse me for laughing, Joe—I shouldn't laugh at something like that, I know. Yes, I suppose you could call it a heart stoppage—that's the way we all end, isn't it? But there's more to the story than that.

"You see, when I located Wally Waldron at last, I knew at once the direction my kindness should take. It was very much like the case of poor Fowler—the man put his weakness on public display.

"I found him in Las Vegas.

"You know what the psychologists say about compulsive gamblers, don't you? They say gamblers are rolling those dice and placing those chips all for the sake of love. Every time they place a bet, they're asking Fate to love them. It all sounds strange to me, but so they say.

"I guess Wally was badly in need of love, because he was a compulsive craps-shooter if ever there was one. By the time I caught up with him, he had used up every last drop of credit and goodwill he could find in the state of Nevada and was heading back East. All he had left in the world was that log cabin by the lake and his lipstick-red Chris Craft, both a legacy from a doting uncle.

"He sold the house and the boat to a man named Edwards for the sum of six thousand dollars. That was my first act of kindness to Wally, because Edwards was acting in my behalf. I haven't done anything about the log cabin, but I've burned and scuttled the boat. I suppose that was childish of me, but I wanted to do that.

"It was interesting to see how fast Wally went through that money. My private-detective friend had a hard time keeping up with his attempts to get rid of it. Half went to the parimutuels, the rest to private parties who held floating crap games in basements and garages around the city. It took about six weeks all in all, at the rate of a thousand a week, until there wasn't any left. Not a nickel.

"Then I knew how I could be kind to Wally. Not by giving

him large amounts of money to squander, but by small donations, to see him through these difficult days.

"I sent him a hundred dollars in cash, one day. My detective
friend reported his utter consternation when it arrived in the
mail. Wally's closest friend was named Webber, who ran a
bookshop—and a book—on Canal Street. Wally ran to Webber's
apartment to boast of his mysterious good fortune. Webber, a
sardonic young man with a serious spinal curvature and a bent
outlook on the world, probably warned him to beware of Trojan
horses, but Wally laughed and paid no heed. He lost the hundred
at the crap table that night, in less than half an hour of play.

"The next day, he found a fifty-dollar bill in the mail. It was
marvelous the way his spirits lifted. In fact, he was so exhila-
rated that he spent the fifty on groceries and liquor and brought
them all to Webber's apartment for a celebration. They ate and
drank and laughed like two college students on a dormitory
binge, and Wally even made the announcement that he was
giving up gambling and seeking steady employment. Or so I
surmise, for he went to an employment bureau the following
day and embarked on a round of job interviews.

"Then I sent him two hundred dollars, and he was back at
the garage. That night he won several hundred dollars more,
and he returned the following evening to double it. It was a hot
streak. Fate loved him. He was three or four thousand to the
good by the end of the week and ready for wider horizons. He
found one, finally—an invitation to Rich Eddie's green-velvet
private game in back of the kitchen at the Hotel Salud.

"My detective friend had many interesting stories to tell me
about Rich Eddie, a throwback to the days when Muscle was
king. I shudder to think of our friend Wally at the same table
with so violent a man. Nevertheless, he accepted the invitation
and brought his money with him. He also seemed to have
brought his luck, because he emerged big winner of the night,
with a total of about eight thousand dollars. Rich Eddie let him
go without regrets, but insisted, politely, on a return engagement.

"The next night Wally lost and lost badly. After six uninter-
rupted hours of play, he was physically, spiritually, and financially exhausted. Humbly, tearfully, he begged for a stake—for

a small loan to help him remain in action—and Rich Eddie was only too glad to oblige. "Wally left the Hotel Salud five hundred dollars in debt to the gambler, and a worried man.

"I sent him the five hundred. Rich Eddie was so gratified at Wally's prompt payment that he extended his credit once more. This time Wally left owing four thousand dollars.

"By the weekend he owed Rich Eddie twelve thousand.

"Of course, I couldn't go on sending Wally money. Not if he was merely going to gamble it all away. You understand.

"It was pitiful to observe Wally waiting for the mailman every morning, expecting further postpaid miracles to get him out of trouble. Eventually the idea began to dawn on him that the money had stopped coming, and that if he intended to repay Rich Eddie he would have to find another way. Because Rich Eddie was becoming grossly impatient, and was discussing reprisal measures with Wally that were unpleasant and even dangerous.

"Two weeks after incurring the debt, Wally realized that he would never be able to repay Rich Eddie. He left his apartment in the middle of the night. He went to Webber's place and asked the bookshop proprietor for sanctuary against Rich Eddie and his thugs. Webber agreed—he kept Wally sheltered, fed, and safe. But you know how it is with us good Samaritans, Joe. No matter how much kindness we offer people, they resent our benevolence more than they feel gratitude. Wally, penned up in Webber's tiny flat, became nervous, edgy, hostile toward everything and everyone. Then one day he called Webber the one name Webber despised and resented more than any other in the world. Coldly unforgiving, Webber stalked out of the apartment and went straight to Rich Eddie.

"Yes, you might say Wally died of a heart attack. A seizure, you might call it.

"I know what's on your mind, Joe. You're wondering about yourself. Well, it's this way. After Wally's death, I asked my detective friend if he could locate you, too. All he could learn was that you had left the city, your parents' home, and your job all very suddenly. And that was all he could find out. Your trail was as cold as a bloodhound's nose. If you'd been a professional

criminal, you couldn't have done a better job of making a clean
getaway. But I suppose that's why you did so well. There's
nobody so hard to find as an amateur who wants to drop out of
sight. You ask the Missing Persons Bureau if that isn't so.

"It was a long time before I finally caught up with you, Joe,
before I finally located you here in L.A. But, Joe, I've been here
a month now, and so has my detective friend, and neither one
of us knows any more about you now than we did when we
first arrived.

"Joe, will you tell me how I can help you? How can I be kind
to you—like I was to the others?"

Joe Dennison stood up, his fingers aching from making
clenched fists. "Like the others?" he said.

"Yes," Covey said. "To repay you for all those nasty things I
said at the inquest."

"You want to know my weakness, is that it?"

"If you want to put it that way—"

"That's exactly what you mean, isn't it?" Dennison said,
running short of breath. "Fowler was a drunkard—so you killed
him with your damn 'gifts.' Phil Hepplewhite had a weakness
for women, Wally for gambling—"

Covey gave him his cormorant's grin. "And yours, Joe? You
want to tell me your weakness?"

Dennison came to Covey's chair and stood over it. He
reached down and gathered handfuls of terrycloth, hauling the
birdlike figure to its feet. "You dirty murderer," he said, between
his teeth. He gave the bathrobe a shake and the thin body inside
it flopped loosely.

"I'm trying to be kind," Covey said shakily. "The way you
were kind to Nettie, Joe, you and the rest of them—"

"Killer," Joe Dennison said, and this time his hands found the
bony shoulders. He shook harder, until Covey's head, delicately
balanced on the thin reed of his neck, wobbled back and forth
in a blur of pink flesh and dark startled eyes. *"Killer!"* Dennison
shouted again, accelerating the movements of his hands like the
pistons of a machine gathering momentum.

Suddenly Covey's bones seemed to melt and his body became
soft, doll-like. Dennison didn't even hear the strange snapping
noises his joints were making—he was no more aware of the

exact moment of Covey's death than he was aware of the exact time of day.

"About ten minutes to six," Lieutenant Miner said to the Inspector. "That was when Dennison came downstairs and told the desk clerk what had happened. The clerk put in a call to the precinct, and Dennison waited for us in the lobby."

"Cause of death?" the Inspector said.

"The man's neck was broken. But we're not going to have a hard time with this guy Dennison, Inspector. He's dictating his statement right now." Miner paused, and then added, "I can't help feeling sorry for him."

"Sorry? What for?"

"He seems decent. Says he never meant to kill this Covey, that he lost his head. Said the same kind of thing happened to him a few years back, when he struck his own father during a quarrel. He felt so bad about it, he left home, quit his job, and came out West."

"Um," the Inspector said sourly. "Is that your idea of a decent guy?"

"So he's hot-tempered," Miner said. "We've all got our weaknesses, haven't we?"

GEORGES SIMENON

THE CASE OF THE THREE BICYCLISTS

The facts were so confused, the statements of witnesses so hesitant or contradictory, the line between truth and conjecture so hazily defined, that examining magistrate Froget was obliged to fall back on the classic procedure of setting down an objective resume of all the known data.

That resume, when the formal questioning of the Timmermans couple began in the magistrate's office, read as follows:

"On February 3, the Powell Circus opened in Nogent-sur-Marne, after a series of short jumps from Brussels. The tent was set up in the Place de Paris. Some of the performers lived in the caravans. Others stopped at the Hotel Gambetta. (Note: 3d-class hotel. Door closed at night, but tenants can open it from inside. To come in, they have to ring and call out their number as they pass the porter's wicket.)

"The Timmermans, man and wife, who have an acrobatic cycling act with their niece Henny, occupied rooms 15 and 16 on the third floor. They had been with the Powell Circus for five months. Engaged while the troupe was playing Antwerp. Had then just returned from a disastrous tour of South America.

"Jack Lieb, 32, bachelor, juggler with the circus on a one-month contract, had room 6 on the second floor. Good-looking boy, with designs on most of the women and particularly on Henny.

"The run lasted until February 17. No show on the 18th. On the 19th, the company was to leave for La Varenne. At eight o'clock, Jack Lieb and Henny were seen taking the streetcar for Paris. No baggage. Henny told someone they were going to the pictures.

"At twelve-thirty that night, the hotel porter opens the door from his bed and hears a lodger call out number six. He is

157

almost certain that this was Lieb's voice, but didn't know the man well and won't venture a positive statement. Neither is he sure whether one or two people came in.

"The Timmermans spent the evening at a cafe in Nogent and came home at ten.

"At three in the morning, the porter dimly hears the sound of people going out. Thinks there were several.

"He does not open the door again that night.

"At eight o'clock, the Timmermans raise a great hullaballoo and announce that their niece has run away. Claim they haven't seen her since seven the previous evening. Her bed, in room 16, hasn't been slept in. Her baggage has disappeared.

"They accuse Jack Lieb. They knock at his door. No answer. *Lieb has disappeared, along with his trunk.*

"The rest of the company receive the news cynically. The circus leaves Nogent. On the 19th, it opens at La Varenne. Lieb's act is replaced. The Timmermans, without Henny, have to cut most of theirs and insert an advertisement in the professional papers asking for a partner.

"On February 23, the canal boat *Deux Freres,* trying to land a hundred meters upstream from the bridge at Nogent, strikes bottom, although its draft exceeds the normal depth there. The pilot takes a sounding with a boat hook, strikes some obstacle, and informs the lock-keeper. They investigate and drag out of the water a trunk with the initials J.L.

"When they open the trunk, they find the corpse of Jack Lieb. The murderer had to bend the body double. Some sodden banknotes (three 100-franc notes and five tens) are floating around the body. Billfold intact in pocket.

"The autopsy shows that Jack Lieb was strangled, on about the 18th.

"The place where the trunk was found is 900 meters from the Hotel Gambetta. Trunk and body weigh (dry) 228 pounds.

"The authorities search vainly for Henny's corpse. She doesn't turn up living or dead; now, on February 25, there is still no sign of her existence.

"The performers of the Powell Circus accuse the Timmermans, but without any evidence. The couple has always had a bad reputation. Wherever they have gone, trinkets and billfolds and purses have disappeared, although they have never been caught *in flagrante.*

"Problem: to establish, if possible, their guilt, and to learn the whereabouts of Henny's body."

They sat facing M. Froget—a man of fifty-two and a woman of forty-eight.

Franz Timmerman was born at Workum, in the north of the Netherlands, but he had spent the greater part of his youth in Belgium. At twenty, he joined a German circus as stable boy. At thirty, he married Celina Vandeven of Gand, an acrobat.

Celina had in her care the daughter of her dead sister. They carried the child around with them over all Europe. Soon the Timmermans became a bicycling trio, but the act never went over well. After their debut, year followed year, always the same. They would go from one circus to another, play at foreign expositions, sometimes appear at provincial music halls.

Franz is short-legged. Everything about him is hard: his flesh, the lines of his face, the stubborn expression of his too sharply defined features. On M. Froget's desk is a photo of him in his act, half acrobatics, half-clowning. In the same photo, Celina Timmerman is standing on the shoulders of her husband, who is mounted on a bicycle.

"In short," M. Froget said, looking elsewhere, "for a good dozen years your act has had no success at all."

The woman's bosom rose. She was about to speak, but the magistrate paid no attention to her. His voice went on, dry and precise:

"In your former engagements, as in your contract with Powell, it has been stipulated that you, Franz, were to double all evening as one of the clowns that invade the ring between numbers. Madame, for her part, was to act as dresser for the equestrians."

Timmerman said nothing. There was a hard glint in his dark-grey eyes.

"For one reason or another, your own act was often omitted. At Nogent, you were booed."

Mme. Timmerman twisted and gesticulated, her mouth open.

"You had the poorest billing in the troupe. You complained

about it to anyone who'd listen. For ten years now you've been complaining."

Timmerman looked askance at the magistrate. The muscles of his jaw stood out.

"It is established beyond doubt that you have committed many pretty thefts among your colleagues."

"That isn't so! They're trying to frame us! They—" Mme. Timmerman was suddenly on her feet.

"Please be seated again, madame. And answer only when I ask a question." The precise voice clipped off the words as though she had never interrupted: "The finale of your act consisted, if I am correctly informed, of a tour around the ring on the bicycle with your husband carrying you on his shoulders while your niece stood on yours."

"Yes. And we're the only act in—"

"Henny is twenty-two at present, is she not?"

"She was," Mme. Timmerman corrected.

"As you please. It has been established that she has had many lovers, with your consent."

The man said nothing. The woman was indignant. "Consent? Could we help it if she was man-crazy?"

"Did you know that she was going to Paris with Lieb on the eighteenth?"

"We had our suspicions."

"You saw her as she was leaving. She had no suitcase. Therefore, she returned in the course of the night. Your room adjoins hers. You heard nothing?"

"Nothing. If we had—" Mme. Timmerman seemed afraid to let her husband speak and hurried to get her answer in first.

"Will you tell me exactly what baggage you carried?"

"First of all, our cycles and our props and costumes. Those stayed at the circus and went in the vans. Then we have a wicker trunk and a black wooden coffer for street clothes and the rest. And finally the two little suitcases, one for Henny and the other for us."

"The two trunks were in your room?"

"Yes."

"Your niece's suitcase was in her own room?"

"Yes. She took it away with her."

"With all her belongings?"

"All. Except her costumes for the act. They were at the circus."

"There was a communicating door between rooms 15 and 16?"

"Yes. We lived in one as much as the other. We did our own cooking to save money."

"You didn't know Lieb before he joined the Powell Circus?"

"No. He'd come straight from England, he said. We never played there."

"He talked of marrying Henny?"

"Him? Oh, no! He was a chaser. Any skirt was the same to him."

"He had the best billing in the circus, didn't he?"

"I guess so. Which just goes to show that it isn't talent that—"

"You were to leave the Hotel Gambetta early on the morning of the nineteenth. Was your baggage all ready?"

"Yes. We packed the trunks the afternoon of the eighteenth."

"And they were to be picked up early. Exactly."

Timmerman had been making such an effort to concentrate during this dialogue that his face was flushed.

"When you saw your niece for the last time, before she left for Paris with Lieb, what coat was she wearing? Her winter coat?"

"No, it was a nice day. For a couple of weeks she'd been wearing a green tailored coat she'd just had made. She liked to look smart; she'd spend as much to put on her back as we'd—"

"What was her winter coat like?"

"Brown, with real fur. She burned it down by the hem when she got too near a fire once, but that didn't show much and—"

"Could you bring me this coat?"

"How could I when Henny carried off all her belongings like I told you?"

"Of course. Your windows opened on the Place de Paris?"

"Yes."

"You really couldn't provide me with any clothing that your niece had worn? A dress, underwear—even shoes? How many pairs did she have?"

"Three. But we haven't anything left except her circus costumes. They're still with ours in Powell's vans."

"You don't know what picture Henny went to?"

"How should we know?"

"Of course you were never in Lieb's room. But do you happen to know where he kept his trunk?"

"No."

"Yours was at the head of the bed?"

"One of them. The other was in a corner."

"But at the head of the bed was the wicker one with the clothing?"

"Yes. All roped up."

"Mademoiselle Henny could swim?"

"A little."

"Have you any other relatives?"

"A cousin of my husband's. But we never see each other any more. Sometimes a postcard—"

"Professional?"

"He's a farmer. At Warns, not far from Workum."

"You weren't in any need of cash when the crime was committed?"

"Why should we be? We'd just been paid and we hardly spend a sou."

"On the nineteenth, you had only seventy-five francs on you."

"Which proves we're innocent! You don't go killing people for nothing."

Mme. Timmerman was animated, and looked at her husband with a certain pride as though to say, "You see? You've got to know how to talk back to them!"

M. Froget's last question pricked her bubble:

"How long did you stand at the window?"

And he closed his files.

Without so much as looking at the accused, M. Froget went on drily as though he were reciting a lesson:

"As circus and music-hall performers, you fall into that class of supernumeraries known to the profession as supers or stooges. And you were stooges, too, in your petty efforts at criminality. Without your niece, your bicycling act no longer holds up—and she was necessary to your other act as well.

"On the eighteenth, she goes off with Lieb, who has just received his very substantial salary. You have been paid off far more modestly. You are sure he will not be home before midnight. You enter his room. You take three hundred and some odd francs.

"Henny comes back with her lover. Lieb, noticing the theft, suspects you, bursts into your room, and threatens, no doubt, to be judge and jury himself and execute his sentence with his fists.

"You, Timmerman, overcome by panic, leap at his throat. Perhaps you did not intend to kill him. No matter. He is nonetheless dead, and behold the three of you trembling before his corpse.

"It is child's play to take the body downstairs noiselessly, shut it up in his trunk—*with the stolen money, so that no one will think of petty thievery and hence of you*—and carry it to the Marne.

"Henny disappears at the same time and goes off to hide somewhere in Holland, to give the impression of an elopement.

"You, Madame Timmerman, stand guard at the window to open the door from inside when your husband returns."

There was a scene. The man began to curse harshly in Dutch. The woman yelped in two languages. And meanwhile M. Froget went on writing in his ten-sous notebook:

"Proof: The Timmermans claim not to have seen Henny, who nevertheless carried off *all her belongings,* among them a large winter coat and several pairs of shoes. Now all she had of her own was a small suitcase. And the *family* trunks had been packed the day before and stood locked and roped.

"In other words, *she must inevitably have awakened her uncle and aunt to take her belongings out of the trunks.*

"They deny it. Then they have an important reason for wishing to seem ignorant of her *voluntary* departure.

"Presumptions: The murderer could not have worked alone since someone must have opened the door to him from the inside when he returned. The Timmermans' room looks out on the Place de Paris.

"Timmerman, who carries two women on his shoulders while riding a bicycle, is capable of carrying a 100-kilo trunk on those shoulders."

"Lieb had been robbed before the murder, as is proved by the notes scattered in the trunk. They were put there only after the crime, to avert the notion of theft. And the Timmermans were habitual petty thieves.

"The Timmermans, who had just received their week's salary, still had only 75 francs the day after the crime because they had had to give money to Henny for her trip."

The notebook has the later entry: "Timmerman tried to pass himself off as insane, received the benefit of the doubt, and at least saved his neck from the guillotine."

In the margin appears in red ink: "Crime of a frightened coward."

—Translated by Anthony Boucher

C. B. GILFORD

HEAVEN CAN WAIT

"**A**ge at time of death?" asked Michael, who was an archangel. "Fifty-two, correct?"

"Correct," said Alexander Arlington wearily. It seemed to him that he'd been answering questions ever since he arrived.

"Immediate Cause of Death?" continued the archangel.

"Heart attack. That is, I think so," Alexander replied, frowning slightly.

"Hmm." The archangel seemed embarrassed. "Now, this last blank. Contributing Circumstances, If Any. Check one, it says: Self-immolation, Foolhardiness, Stupidity, Murder, et cetera. There's a checkmark after Murder."

Alexander sat up. "Murder?"

"Yes," said Michael. "That's the information I have from my worksheet. Correct me if I'm wrong. You *were* murdered, weren't you, Mr. Arlington?"

"Well, I didn't think so. I—"

"Do you mean," asked Michael kindly, "that you didn't know you were murdered?"

"Why, I never dreamed it!"

Michael sighed. "That sometimes happens, of course. Most people know when they're being murdered, however. Not till the last minute, naturally, but they usually know. I never have learned how to break news like this gently."

"I can't believe it," Alexander repeated to himself several times.

"I regret that you're taking this so hard, Mr. Arlington. You must realize that such things make no difference whatsoever here."

"I was in my study. I think I must have been asleep. I seemed to awaken with a sort of bursting pain in my chest. I didn't have time really to think about it."

"There's a note added here," Michael said, consulting his

record. "It was your heart, all right, Mr. Arlington. You were stabbed with your own letter-opener—in the back."

"Why, that's positively fiendish!" exclaimed Alexander. "My letter-opener was really an ivory-handled dagger. Who did it?"

"I beg your pardon? Who did what?"

"Who murdered me?"

"Why, I don't know that."

"You don't know! I thought you had all the information on that infernal worksheet of yours."

"It's not an *infernal* worksheet!"

"All right, whatever it is. Who murdered me?"

"Mr. Arlington!" The archangel looked stern. "Ideas of revenge and recrimination are, as you should already know, forbidden here."

"Okay, okay. I just want to know."

"I don't know who murdered you, Mr. Arlington. I'm an archangel, but I don't know everything. We don't find out such things until the perpetrator of the deed has met his own demise. I'll have a worksheet on him then, and I'll let you know."

"How long will that take?"

"If the murderer is apprehended and hanged, let us say, it may be relatively soon. If the murderer has been smart and is not found out, it may be years."

"I can't wait! I want to know *now.*"

"Mr. Arlington, I'm sorry—"

"Is there anyone here who *would* know?"

"Well, of course, He would. He knows everything."

"Then ask Him."

"That's impossible. I can't bother Him with such trifles—Mr. Arlington, sit down!"

But instead of sitting down, Alexander continued his pacing. "You told me I should be happy and contented in this place," he complained.

"Absolutely," said Michael with great assurance.

"How can I be happy and contented if I don't know who murdered me?"

"I don't see how that makes any difference, Mr. Arlington!"

Alexander, making a distinct effort to compose himself, sat

down again in the golden chair. "Sir," he began more calmly, "what does it say about my profession on your worksheet?"

"You were a writer of mystery stories."

"Correct. Under the pen-name of Slade Saunders, I was the author of seventy-five mystery novels—more than a dozen of them purchased by the movies—assorted short stories, and articles too numerous to mention. Does that have any significance for you, sir?"

"Not exactly."

"Don't you understand?" Alexander almost lost his temper again. "Here I am, the famous mystery author, who for twenty years asked and answered the question, 'Who did it?' and now—now!—I myself have been murdered and I don't know who did it!"

The archangel smiled. "I see your point, Mr. Arlington," he said. "But the information you're after will come through in good time. Now, if you'll just be patient and compose yourself—"

"I must know the identity of my murderer," Alexander insisted. "I'll never be happy until I do. Stabbed in the back! Really!"

"Come now, Mr. Arlington," soothed the archangel. "Wait till you see our establishment here. The facilities for enjoyment are quite—"

"I don't want to see it." Alexander slumped in his chair, staring at the floor. "I don't want to see *any* of it."

"Mr. Arlington!"

"It's a fake. It's all a fake. Happy and contented! I'm not happy. I'm miserable."

"You *can't* be miserable up here," Michael said, something like panic rising in his voice. "It's utterly impossible for you to be anything but happy. You're in Heaven."

"I'm miserable."

The archangel rose and his large bare feet padded noiselessly on the beautiful marble floor. "This is ridiculous," he mumbled several times. "Preposterous! Mr. Arlington, won't you reconsider?"

"I'm miserable."

"Be reasonable, Mr. Arlington," the archangel pleaded. "You

simply can't imagine the embarrassment, the loss of prestige it would entail if you went about Heaven proclaiming you weren't happy."

"I'm miserable," Alexander insisted, and he looked it.

"I'd ask Him," said Michael—and he was beginning to look miserable, too—"really I would, but He has so many things on His mind these days. —On the other hand, if He knew there was somebody up here who wasn't happy, I'm sure He'd blame me. I'm a department head, Mr. Arlington, which puts the responsibility squarely on my shoulders."

"I'm miserable."

The archangel winced and resumed his pacing. Now and then through the open windows came the gentle sounds of laughter and music. But within the room, Alexander Arlington sat brooding.

Suddenly Michael's expression lightened. He strode back to his desk and sat down again. "Mr. Arlington, you're a writer of mystery stories," he said briskly. "You're reputed to be clever at devising clues, trapping murderers, and all that sort of thing?"

"Yes."

"What I have in mind," continued Michael, "is completely irregular, of course. But the situation demands swift action. Do you think, Mr. Arlington, that you could solve this mystery to your satisfaction if you were allowed to go back to Earth?"

"Well, I suppose—"

"It's as far as I can go," Michael said austerely.

"I could certainly try. But how—?"

"Simple," interrupted Michael. "You are now existing in Eternity, quite independent of the element of Time. So we repeat a certain period of Time as it were—let us say, one day. You would return to Earth and relive the last day of your mortal life. Let's see—Here! You died precisely at midnight. You would have from the moment you awakened on that last morning until midnight of the same day."

"One day?" frowned Alexander. "That wouldn't give me much time."

"If you'd rather not try—"

"I'll do it," Alexander said hastily. "When do I start?"

"Immediately. But first, Mr. Arlington, a reminder. That last day of your life is down on the records, so it's not technically subject to change. However, you *will* have to do a little investigating, some few things you didn't do the first time you lived that final day. I can make some minor erasures on the Books, but I should be extremely embarrassed if there had to be any major ones."

"But—"

"You will simply have to manage without important changes. It should present no difficulties. You will have, remember, a gift seldom granted to mortals."

"The gift of foresight," exclaimed Alexander.

"Yes. However, Mr. Arlington, I must remind you that you'll have to submit to being murdered all over again."

The gleam in Alexander's eye went out. "I suppose I'll have to be stabbed in the back again—"

The archangel nodded. "That's the way it is in the records," he said, and his voice was like the tolling of a bell. "Do you care to reconsider?"

"No—I'll go through with it. I've got to know who killed me."

"Very well, Mr. Arlington. I wish you luck. We do want all our souls to be happy."

"Thank you," said Alexander unhappily, and he walked out through the golden door . . .

And awoke in his own bed, in his own room, in the dark and drafty old mansion in which he had always thought it so fitting and proper for a mystery writer to reside. The ancient grandfather clock in the hallway was striking twelve. He counted the strokes, and for a horrible moment—before he could collect his wits—he imagined that it might be midnight already. But no, there was the sunshine just beyond his drawn blinds. Noon, the rising time of a successful author. But it gave him so little time.

There was an insistent knocking at his door.

"Come in," Alexander said.

The door opened and his secretary, Talbert, appeared. "The mail has arrived," Talbert announced.

"Well?"

"There's a letter from Fenton."

Talbert was a thin, scholarly man of thirty-five. He seldom

smiled, but at the moment the ghost of a smile played at the corners of his mouth. "I opened it, thinking it was routine. But you'd better read it yourself."

Alexander took the letter. "Dear Alex," it began, "I must be candid. It was with some hesitation that we decided to publish that last novel of yours, *Murder of a Mannequin.* Perhaps it will do all right, but if it does, it will only be because of your name and reputation. Frankly, it's the opinion here that you have been slipping. Each book has been a little weaker than the one before. Is the well running dry? Perhaps you should take a long rest. As we've still got a contract with you for your next five books, this is of great concern to us. So I'm coming out to talk things over with you. I'll arrive on the nine o'clock train Thursday morning. Yours, Walter Fenton."

Talbert was still standing there.

"I have a suggestion," he said.

"Oh, you have!" said Alexander savagely.

"Fenton suggests that you need a rest. I agree with him. But while you're resting, the public need not be deprived of the enjoyment of reading mystery novels by the famous Slade Saunders."

"Just what do you mean?" Alexander leaped out of bed.

"I," said Talbert calmly, "will continue to write the books under the pen-name of Slade Saunders. Fenton need never know. Or our public, either."

"*Our* public! Do you imagine for one moment that *you* could imitate my style?"

"I could do more than imitate your style, Alexander. I could improve on it."

"You insolent—you presumptuous—"

"Do I have to remind you, Alexander, how large a part of your last few books was mine, anyway? I worked on the plots, made corrections, did rewriting—"

"Get out of here!"

"It's your only chance to rescue the reputation of Slade Saunders. I'll split fifty-fifty with you."

"You're fired!"

"Alexander—"

"Fired!"

"You'll never be able to replace me. And what's more, you'll never be able to finish another book without me."

"Pack your things and leave, Talbert, or I'll have you thrown out!"

"You'll regret this." Talbert stalked out of the room.

Yes, that was the way Alexander's last day had started. The letter from Fenton and the quarrel with Talbert. What an odd feeling to be repeating one's actions precisely! Just as if the incident had occurred before, in a dream.

The thought shocked Alexander. A dream? What if his entire experience with the archangel had been a dream?

The ringing of the telephone interrupted this interesting line of thought. The bedroom extension was at his elbow. Alexander reached for it. "Hello?"

"This is Michael."

"*What?* Well-uh-where are you calling from?"

"That's a silly question, don't you think, Mr. Arlington?"

"What—do you want?"

"Just checking to find out if you made the trip safely. How are things coming?"

"Give me a chance, will you, sir? I haven't even got started!"

"Well, you'd better get to work, Mr. Arlington. You haven't much time, you know. Goodbye for now."

"Goodbye."

That settled that. It was no dream, so it was indeed time to get down to business. But to have to work with someone looking over one's shoulder, as it were—

For the next half hour Alexander occupied himself with shaving and dressing. He thought about Talbert—timid, shrinking Talbert, who chose today of all days to show his fangs. Yes, Talbert coveted the name and reputation of Slade Saunders, Alexander's most prized possession. Talbert had a motive for murder, all right.

What had happened next?

Alexander discovered that he didn't remember. He was to be murdered at midnight, in his study, stabbed with his own ivory-handled letter-opener. But he remembered nothing else. He should have picked up more information from that archangel.

On the other hand, it might be better this way. Foreseeing
every detail might be a little too eerie. And this way, too, he'd
have a freer hand.

Walking downstairs, Alexander realized that he was hungry.
In the dining room, Annie the cook was ready with his usual
afternoon breakfast. Alexander studied Annie's broad, empty
face as she served him. Besides Annie there was her daughter
Agnes, his wife's maid. But neither Annie nor Agnes had any
earthly reason to murder him. Anyway, they both went home
every night. Alexander decided that he could dismiss both of
them from his calculations.

"Better hurry with your breakfast, Mr. Arlington," Annie said
to him when she brought in his poached egg. "I've got to have
lunch ready on time, because there's going to be a guest."

"Who?"

"Mr. Armbruster."

Now he remembered! This, too, had happened the first time.
Armbruster, the big young man with the dark curly hair.

"Good morning, darling."

A quick cool kiss on his left cheek turned him around. The
thought shot through his mind—a kiss of betrayal. But he said,
quite pleasantly, "Good morning, Ariel."

Alexander abandoned the poached egg for a moment to
survey his wife. Twenty-eight, scarcely more than half his age.
She was beautiful because he had been able to afford a young,
beautiful wife. Blonde, slim, graceful, a creature of light and air.
His Ariel.

"So Armbruster's coming for lunch?"

"Do you mind, darling?"

"Yes, I do mind. I mind having that penniless young athlete
hanging around my house, devouring my wife with his eyes."

"What an imagination you have, darling!"

"Has he ever made love to you?"

"Of course not."

"That's a lie, my dear. I saw it all yesterday."

Alexander Arlington was amazing himself. Now that the
words were out of his mouth, he suddenly remembered what
he must have, in the excitement of being murdered, temporarily forgotten. This had all happened once before.

"I saw you, my dearest, out in the arbor. And I might add that I wasn't particularly stunned. Neither of you has been very discreet."

Ariel had paled, and sat down weakly.

"Surprised, my dearest one? Well, now, let me tell you something. It's perfectly all right with me, young Mr. Armbruster's coming here to lunch today. In fact, I think that after lunch you and he should have a long talk. You might tell him that I know everything. And then you can both decide what to do. You personally have two choices. The first is to leave me and go away with Armbruster. Of course, he doesn't have a cent and you can't expect me to subsidize a little love-nest for you. If you get tired of starving with Armbruster, however, you cannot return here. Your second choice is to stay. In that case, I would demand loyalty and fidelity from you, and Mr. Armbruster would have to look for his handouts elsewhere."

That, Alexander reflected, should settle Mr. Armbruster's hash. Ariel was not the sort who could live on love alone. She had been accustomed to the finer things for too long.

But then—and it hadn't, of course, been the first time he had delivered this ultimatum—another thought dawned.

Here was another motive for murder. Ariel was down in his will for half the tidy fortune he had accumulated in a lifetime of writing. If Armbruster knew that, he might prefer Ariel as a moneyed widow rather than as a dispossessed wife. Or if Ariel herself wanted the young man badly enough—

"Will you be lunching with us?" Ariel was asking.

"I think not," Alexander answered grandly. "I'd only be in the way. Besides, I'm just having breakfast. Also, I've more important things to do."

She went away then, and Alexander watched her trim figure as she departed. Then he returned to his egg, finished it quickly, and left the dining room to Annie's preparations for the luncheon guest.

He went to his study, the scene of the crime.

Alexander felt awe as he entered his own death-chamber. The blinds were drawn, making the room a shadowy place. Uneasily, Alexander let the sunlight in. Then he looked around.

There was his desk, of massive mahogany. He surely must have been sitting in his chair, at this desk. And he must have dozed off, as he often did, with his arms spread on the desk and his head on his arms. An inviting target. And there was the letter-opener. He picked it up gingerly, half expecting to find dried blood on its blade.

But of course there wouldn't be—yet.

The thing made a nasty murder weapon, Alexander reflected. Its handle was four inches long, of smooth and heavy old ivory. Would take fingerprints nicely, if the murderer were careless. The blade was even longer—neither razor-sharp nor needle-pointed. But quite adequate, if thrust with reasonable strength and accuracy, to impale a man's heart.

A knock interrupted his cogitations. The knocker entered without waiting to be invited. "Busy, Uncle Alex?"

"No, no. Come in, Andrew."

Andrew threw up one fat leg and hoisted himself to a perch on the desk. His weight caused the sturdy mahogany to creak. Andrew's small piggish eyes stared from behind thick-lensed glasses. "How's finances with you, Uncle?"

"How much this time?" asked Alexander.

"Five hundred."

Alexander leaned back in his swivel chair and considered the huge lump on his desk. "I told you last time, Andrew, there'd be no more squaring of your debts. At least not until you show some sign of helping yourself—which means getting a job. So my answer, Andrew, is no."

"My situation is pretty desperate, Uncle Alex."

"That's your affair."

"What am I going to do?"

"That's also your affair."

"I'll have to do something—drastic."

The remark startled Alexander. This conversation, as well as his argument with Talbert and his talk with Ariel, had also happened before. Andrew was heir to the other half of his estate—not because Alexander had ever liked Andrew, but simply because Andrew was his one and only blood-relative. And now the worthless nephew needed money.

Still another motive for murder.

"Just what would something—er—drastic be, Andrew?"

"I don't know. But if you won't help me, whatever happens will be your fault."

The great mass slid off the desk, walked to the door, and went out. Despite his size, there was a certain grace and quickness in nephew Andrew's movements. Strangely, Alexander had never noticed this before. But then he was discovering so many things of which he had once been oblivious.

The sunshine, filtering through the curtained windows, looked suddenly inviting. At the moment, Alexander wasn't feeling particularly fond of this room. He decided that he needed fresh air—and a chance to think.

In the garden, instead of solitude, he found Harry. Old Harry was gardener, caretaker, handyman, chauffeur, and, in the evenings when Annie and her daughter had gone home, he was the butler. Harry was also an admitted ex-convict. Here he had been especially useful to Alexander. Under the influence of alcohol supplied by his employer, Harry often reminisced of his past exploits in the world of crime for the benefit of Alexander's notebook. Some of these exploits, Alexander had gathered, had never been discovered or penalized. Doubtless there were at least a dozen cities in which Harry was wanted.

At the moment Alexander was in no mood for plot material. But Harry had something on his mind.

"I've been hearing things, Mr. Arlington."

"What things?"

"About your books."

"My books? What about my books?"

"Maybe there won't be any more."

Talbert had talked! The gist, if not the complete text, of Fenton's letter was probably known throughout the household by this time. Then Ariel and Armbruster knew, too. And Andrew.

"How does that concern you, Harry, even supposing it were true? Afraid of losing your job?"

The old man squinted up at him. Harry was remarkably ugly. "Not worried about my job," he answered. "But I've been thinking, Mr. Arlington, about all the things I've told you about myself. That was okay while you were writing your books. But now that there maybe won't be any more books, you might start talking to the cops."

"Why should I do a thing like that, Harry? What does it matter to me what your past is? You've reformed, and you're earning an honest living now."

"The cops don't care about that."

"Well, I'm not going to say anything to the cops. —Harry, don't you believe me?"

It was obvious he didn't. The old fellow turned away and started digging with the hoe again. The strokes were strong, swift, accurate. And his face was dark and grim.

This, too, Alexander remembered with the same strange feeling that it had all happened before. In his garden he had unearthed another potential murderer.

Back at the desk in his study, Alexander sat down heavily. Why, when he had first lived through this fateful last day of his life, hadn't any of these things occurred to him? Why hadn't he realized that he was literally surrounded by people who would profit by his death? Everyone in this house, except old Annie and her daughter Agnes, had a motive to kill him. And at least one of them must also have the nerve.

The telephone rang, and without thinking Alexander picked up the study extension.

"This is Michael."

"Oh. Good afternoon."

"Something wrong, Mr. Arlington? You don't sound very chipper."

"This has all been very disheartening, sir."

"Yes?"

"Except for two domestics who don't live in, everyone under my roof would like to see me dead."

"That's nothing to be downcast about, Mr. Arlington."

"No?"

"If you realize how much you're not wanted on Earth, you won't have the slightest regret about coming back up here."

"Hm. That's so, isn't it?"

"Anything else troubling you, Mr. Arlington?"

"As a matter of fact, sir, there is. I haven't found any clues."

"Look for some."

"That's just it. You see, in my books—and in real life, too—there are never any clues until *after* the murder. What am I going to do about that?"

"My dear Mr. Arlington, I'm sure I don't know. You should have considered that difficulty before you left."

"I wish I had."

"I'm afraid you'll have to sit tight and wait until midnight. See you then."

Alexander mixed himself a drink. It was four o'clock. One-third of his allotted time had already elapsed. He took his drink glumly to the window. Clouds had appeared in the sky, promising rain.

A good night for a murder.

It was thus by the merest accident, as he stood sipping his cocktail, that he saw his wife and Armbruster. The athletic young man was kissing her.

At that instant there was born in Alexander Arlington's heart a new determination.

He didn't smash his glass on the floor or crush it in his fist, as a more emotional man might have done. Instead, he stood there and slowly finished his drink while Armbruster slowly finished kissing his wife. For now, at last, Alexander had concocted a plan.

After he had drained his glass, he went to the kitchen. "Annie," he announced, "Mr. Armbruster will be staying to dinner, and so will Talbert and my nephew. And you may tell Harry to serve."

Up in Talbert's room he found his secretary packing. "You can put away that suitcase, Talbert."

"You told me I was fired," the secretary answered sulkily.

"You still are. But I'd like you to stay around till tomorrow. You may find it to your advantage, my boy."

Andrew was enjoying his afternoon nap when Alexander shook him awake. "If you have any plans for going out tonight, cancel them. I want to have a long talk with you. You may find it profitable."

Then Alexander went out to the garden.

"Sorry I couldn't have lunch with you, Armbruster," he told the man he had seen kissing his wife, "but I'd like you to stay for dinner with us."

Armbruster's handsome face registered surprise, but he mumbled that he would be delighted. Ariel was stricken dumb. Alexander smiled upon them with secret excitement. If his plan worked—

Dinner was at seven-thirty. It was already dark and it had started to rain when Annie and her daughter left the house. Harry served in grim silence.

Alexander was the only one who ate heartily. The others went through the motions, but they were preoccupied. Ariel looked at Armbruster frequently, and Armbruster looked back at her. Talbert's thin face was a mask through which only a glint of his sullenness showed. Andrew usually possessed an excellent appetite, but it was not evident tonight. All of them watched Alexander stealthily.

It was nine o'clock before the meal ended. Alexander rose, smiling down at them. "I'll see you all in my study in an hour. Having a little celebration—a sort of farewell party."

This cryptic remark left them staring blankly. Alexander went complacently upstairs to his bedroom and began to pack a suitcase. He had hardly stowed two pairs of socks in the bag when the telephone rang.

"This is Michael."

"I was rather expecting your call."

"Your mood has changed considerably in the last several hours."

"Yes, it has. Yes."

"Where do you think you're going with that suitcase?"

"I'm shortly to go on a long journey, am I not?"

"You don't need extra socks up here, Mr. Arlington. Everything is furnished."

"You've been spying on me."

"I don't have to spy on you."

"Sir, you're not worried about my doublecrossing you—are you?"

There was no answer. The line was dead. But that in itself

was answer enough. The archangel was worried. And if he was worried about a doublecross, a doublecross must be within the realm of possibility! Alexander went on packing and chuckling.

He put into the suitcase all he might need in the way of clothes for a few days. He packed his toothbrush and his razor. He went to the wall safe and took from it the several hundred dollars he always kept there. From his dresser he took his automatic, checked to make certain it was loaded. It was. The automatic, he had decided, was a little extra insurance.

But he did not return downstairs in an hour as he had promised. He wanted to keep his suspects on edge. He knew they would wait. Especially the murderer—he *had* to wait. Alexander spent some time in his easy chair, smoking his pipe and planning the future.

Not until a quarter to eleven did he carry his suitcase downstairs and rejoin his wife and guests. He found them satisfactorily upset. Talbert's face was flushed—he had evidently been at the liquor cabinet. Andrew was sulking in a dark corner, like a surly hog. Ariel and Armbruster sat together on the couch, defiantly close to each other. Old Harry was lurking in the hallway, and Alexander ushered him inside. Then Alexander locked the door from within and sat down behind his desk to face them.

"Has any of you," he began, "noticed anything queer about this day, which will end in exactly one hour and ten minutes?"

They obviously did not understand. For a few moments his only answer was the steady tattoo of the rain against the house and an occasional clap of increasingly loud thunder.

"I don't know what you're talking about, Alexander." That was from his wife. She had risen from the sofa and advanced a step toward him. He surveyed her coldly. She wore an evening gown which began very low on her torso and clung like skin the rest of the way. For Armbruster's benefit, no doubt.

"Sit down, my dear, and don't get excited." Something in his voice made her retreat. "I rather expected you to notice it, even if no one else did. You with your woman's intuition."

"Notice what, Alexander?"

"Haven't you sensed something strange about today? Haven't

you had the feeling that all the things you've been doing and saying are somehow familiar? That you did and said those very same things once before?"

It was clear they all thought he was drunk or playing a joke on them.

"Last night," Alexander continued with a smile, "I was—well, perhaps it really wasn't last night. In Eternity one can't be sure about the passage of Time. But I wasn't Up There very long, so I believe it must have been last night. Last night I was murdered."

Ariel stifled a scream.

"Ah, that jogs your memory, my dear?"

"My memory?"

Her ignorance of what he was talking about seemed genuine. Alexander looked around at the other faces, all staring at him without comprehension. So he told them. He told them about Michael, and he told them about why he was back. They listened, and occasionally they looked around at one another.

At the end of the recital, Andrew said, "Uncle Alex, you are completely out of your mind! You should see a doctor!"

"Fenton said you were slipping," Talbert said vindictively. "He didn't know how right he was."

"This is a madhouse!" said Armbruster, rising from the sofa. "I'm getting out of here."

"Sit down, all of you," said Alexander, producing the automatic.

They sat down. Just as the phone rang.

Alexander picked it up, and a voice began immediately, "What are you up to, Arlington?"

"It's an old gimmick, sir," Alexander answered glibly. "Used in lots of mystery novels. In the last chapter the detective herds all the suspects into one room. There he explains his deductions and the murderer usually confesses or gives himself away. Just some small erasures on your Books."

"Very well, I'll take your word for it, Arlington. But let me remind you that you have only half an hour left."

"That, I suppose," remarked Armbruster when Alexander had hung up, "was probably the archangel."

"Yes," said Alexander.

Armbruster subsided.

"I have been reminded," Alexander went on, "that my time is growing short. Consequently, I will proceed from my story, which none of you seems to believe, to the facts, which are indisputable. In this room there are five of you. All five have good reason to want to see me dead. One of you wants it so much that he—or she—will risk murder.

"There is my dear nephew, Andrew, who is up to his ears in debt. Andrew's only hope for enough money to make him solvent lies in my willing it to him, which, unfortunately, I have done. Andrew's needs are immediate, but if I were dead and the will being probated, his creditors would undoubtedly become patient.

"Then there is Talbert, my former secretary. Talbert thinks that if I were out of the picture, he might take over the career of Slade Saunders. My publisher arrives tomorrow, and that will be Talbert's big chance—if I happen to be dead.

"And there is Harry. Harry is afraid I'll give him away to the police when I've quit writing and have no more use for his inexhaustible past.

"Lastly, there are my dear wife and her dear friend, Mr. Armbruster. Ariel would have left me before this if Mr. Armbruster had any money. If she gets her half of my estate, they can afford to live in the style to which I have accustomed her. So either of them might find it worth the candle to murder me."

"What a morbid mood you're in, Uncle Alex," said Andrew placatingly.

"Morbid but accurate, my dear nephew. Now, here is my letter-opener. I am scheduled to go to sleep sitting at this desk. At precisely midnight the murderer—one of you five—will take this letter-opener and stab me in the back."

Talbert had grown very attentive. Despite himself, he had become fascinated with the problem. "Just supposing, Alexander," the ex-secretary began, "that all you have told us is true. Are you going to go to sleep there at the desk in time for the murderer to commit his crime?"

"Of course not, Talbert. Now that I know I'm going to be murdered, it would be pretty difficult, if not impossible, for me to go to sleep, don't you think?"

"Then that ruins the whole idea of the murder happening exactly as it did the first time."

"Precisely, Talbert. You've hit upon the very crux of the problem. It can't happen the same way. There will have to be some differences. But if you will recall, the archangel said he was prepared to make some few small erasures on the records."

All of them were now listening with the greatest interest, caught up by the spirit of the occasion.

"Alexander," Talbert continued, "I don't quite see how you're going to accomplish this feat of detection. Now in our books— rather, your books—the murder was committed, clues were left behind, and only then could the detective begin. But what clues are there in this case to begin on? To cite a crude example— that letter-opener would take fingerprints nicely, but the murderer wouldn't leave his prints until the moment of the murder, and by that time it would be too late for *you* to find them."

"A fascinating phase of the problem, Talbert. I have trained you well, I see. But that's exactly the difficulty which I confess I didn't foresee when I undertook this venture. How am I to solve the crime *before* it is committed?"

"And you've only fifteen minutes left, Uncle Alex," said Andrew with rising excitement.

"Are you expecting somebody to confess even before he pulls the job?" The question came from old Harry.

"It could happen," said Alexander equably, "but I certainly am not counting on it."

"Perhaps you're going to sit there and wait for the murderer to start for you. You'll see who it is and that will satisfy your curiosity." This suggestion was Armbruster's.

"Hardly that," Alexander retorted in a spirit of friendly debate. "That, I think, Mr. Armbruster, would take the kind of courage I don't possess—to sit calmly at my desk, watch the murderer over my shoulder, and offer my back to be stabbed."

"Then I can't see how it's going to happen," Ariel said peevishly.

"Of course you don't, my dear, so I will explain. You see, I have a plan. I'll keep my bargain with Michael—because he was so decent about the whole thing—to the extent of being right here at my desk at midnight. *But the murder will not occur!*"

They could not conceal their disappointment. Alexander smiled again.

"After twelve o'clock," he continued, "I shall be free of my obligation to the archangel. The murderer will have missed his date with destiny, and I shall live on—for years and years. But now that my eyes have been opened in respect to all of you, I shall of course not continue to live here. I have my suitcase packed, as you see. I am going away. Then I shall take steps to disinherit you, Ariel, and you, Andrew. As for my career, I have a new book in mind, dealing with this very case. I'm sure such an extraordinary plot will rescue Slade Saunders from the oblivion that threatens him. You'll be on your own, Talbert. As for you, Harry, you yourself have reminded me of my clear duty as a law-abiding citizen."

And Alexander smiled once more. The five suspects were silent. The clock above the fireplace fixed the time at seven minutes to twelve. It was old Harry who spoke first.

"So you're going to keep us all here at the point of a gun, Mr. Arlington. Of course nobody can stab you with that letter-opener if you've got a gun on us. Is that what you call keeping your agreement with the archangel?"

"It is not my intention," replied Alexander serenely, "to hold you at bay with a gun." And to prove his point he returned the automatic to his pocket. "My plan is really much simpler and far less violent."

"Are you going to tell us?" Talbert demanded.

"Why not? Here I am at the appointed hour and in the appointed place per agreement. And I have seen to it that all the suspects are here. What can be fairer than that?"

"There's a catch to it," his nephew said.

"Naturally, Andrew. One of you five is the murderer. Now, murderer, you have two choices. At twelve o'clock you can do the deed if you wish, here in the light before four witnesses, excluding myself. In that case you'll surely be apprehended by the police, for I can guarantee that these other scurvy characters will be most anxious to give evidence against you. But you have another choice: you can pass up your chance of murdering me. Since it will be your doing, not mine, that will put me square with Michael, and at one minute past twelve I will walk out of this house and out of your lives."

The phone rang violently. Alexander picked up the receiver and said cordially, "Hello, sir."

"Arlington, you're cheating!" said the archangel.

"But I'm not, sir. This is the only way I can find the murderer. There are simply no clues beforehand and I won't be alive after. If the murderer decides not to go through with it, you certainly can't blame me."

"That's very clever, Arlington—"

"Thank you, sir."

"But not clever enough. You forget that the murderer has a date with midnight, just as you have. So the murderer may have a counterplan, too."

Alexander returned the phone to its cradle, no longer smiling. He *had* forgotten that. His shaken confidence did not go unnoticed by his attentive audience.

"What time is it?" asked Andrew, whose vision was imperfect.

"Three minutes to twelve." Old Harry was nearest to the clock.

A heavy silence settled over the room. Ariel and Armbruster exchanged brief glances. The rest kept their eyes on Alexander. There were no unbelievers now. And somewhere among them, the murderer was making a decision.

Quite suddenly, Armbruster rose and walked across the room to the door. He walked with the grace of a cat, and his tread was silent on the carpet. Alexander watched him cautiously, feeling for his automatic. At the door Armbruster stopped and turned swiftly.

"Arlington is right in one thing," he said. "If the murderer kills in full view of the others, they'll be able to give evidence. It would insure their own safety. But suppose the murder could be done without the others witnessing it? Then none of us could be sure which one was the killer. It's true that each of us has a motive and we'd all be suspected—the police might even construe it was a conspiracy and we'd be tried for murder en masse. But suppose the police don't learn about this meeting? Then the rest of us are in the clear, the murderer does the job and takes the same chances of getting away with it that he took before. It all depends on the murderer being able to kill Arlington without being seen doing it."

It was one minute before twelve.

"And how is the murderer going to accomplish that?" Alexander inquired tartly, although he heard his voice quavering. "How am I to be killed without witnesses in a room full of people?"

Armbruster smiled. The smile of an enemy. "Why, that's simple," he answered. "How could you have overlooked it, Mr. Slade Saunders, famous writer of detective stories? *All I have to do is to turn out the lights!*"

Before Alexander could move, Armbruster's hand found the switch. Darkness came, and darkness remained. The lightning, which had been flashing almost continuously, perversely stopped flashing altogether. The rain slashed against the house, loud enough to snuffle any footsteps.

The murderer was free to move with perfect anonymity! If he had not been immobilized by surprise, Alexander might have done something. But he remained frozen in his chair.

There was somebody beside him. A hand pushed his head down upon the desk. Just as if he had fallen asleep. The other hand, Alexander knew, was seeking, finding, grasping the letter-opener.

The blow really didn't hurt very much.

Alexander dimly felt the hand which had pushed his head down exploring the left side-pocket of his jacket, removing his handkerchief. The murderer was wiping fingerprints off the knife.

There was a ringing in Alexander's head.

Or perhaps it was the telephone.

"Welcome back, Mr. Arlington! Right on schedule, too."

Alexander collapsed in the golden chair in front of Michael's desk.

"Have a nice time, Mr. Arlington?"

"I was murdered again."

"Of course."

"Who did it?"

The archangel laughed, a laugh that rang and echoed through

the high-vaulted marble room. "Why, that's what you went back to Earth to find out. And here you are, Mr. Arlington, asking the same old question. You're not proposing to go through all that a *third* time, are you?"

"No, thanks," said Alexander. "But I still won't be happy here—"

"Now let's not start that again," the archangel said hastily. "Let's think this problem over for a moment, shall we? Put yourself in the murderer's shoes, Mr. Arlington. When Armbruster turned the lights off, would *you* have gone over to the desk and committed the murder?"

Alexander thought with his head in his hands. "I might have suspected a doublecross. Somebody could have turned the lights back on while I was doing the stabbing, and I'd have been caught red-handed."

"Precisely, Mr. Arlington. Risky business. Now, another little problem. If you were the murderer, what reason could you possibly have for reaching into the *victim's* pocket and using the *victim's* handkerchief to wipe off your fingerprints?"

"I'd do that," answered Alexander, "only if I didn't have a handkerchief of my own."

"Right," nodded the archangel. "And which of your five suspects would be most likely to know that you carried your handkerchief in the left side-pocket of your jacket?"

"I see what you mean, sir!" Alexander perked up.

The archangel beamed. "Then maybe you'll be happy here after all, Mr. Arlington."

"Ariel's accomplice was at the light switch," muttered Alexander. "She could trust Armbruster not to turn the lights back on till she was finished with the murder. For confirmation— Ariel couldn't have been carrying a handkerchief, because there was just no place for one in that low-cut dress she was wearing. And my wife, I presume, would be the most likely to know where I'm accustomed to carrying my handkerchief!"

"Exactly the way I had it figured out, Mr. Arlington."

"Say, you're a pretty good detective yourself, sir."

The archangel looked modest. "I've picked up a few tricks here and there," he admitted. "It's the company I've been keeping."

"Company?"

"Didn't I mention that, Mr. Arlington? Dear, dear. If I had, you might never have been dissatisfied in the first place. Well, well, we won't delay any longer. You come in and meet the boys, Mr. Arlington. There's Edgar and Sir Arthur and G.K.C.—"

"Edgar and Sir Arthur and G.K.C.!"

"Certainly, Mr. Arlington. Didn't you know that all mystery writers go to Heaven?"

JAMES HILTON

THE PERFECT PLAN

Every public man has his enemies, but few of these enemies would wish to murder him, or are in a position to do so in any case. Sir George Winthrop-Dunster, however, was unfortunate in these respects. He had his enemies, and one of them, his secretary, both wished to murder him and did so.

Sir George, as chairman of the Anglo-Oceanic group of companies, was what is called "a well-known figure in the City." He belonged to the modern school of financiers who instead of being fat, heavy-jowled, gold-ringed, and white-spatted, look more like overgrown public-school prefects. He was fifty-five, played energetic squashrackets, wore neat lounge suits, and as often as not lunched in a pub off a glass of sherry and a ham sandwich.

Scarsdale, his private secretary, was not unlike him in physique, but nearly a quarter of a century younger. With a First in Greats at Oxford and a B. Sc. Econ. of London, he was well equipped to deal with the numerous complications of Sir George's affairs, and for five years he had given every satisfaction. Well, almost. Just one little rift had once appeared—in 1928, when Scarsdale had rashly bought Amal. Zincs in greater quantities than he had cash to pay for. He had not exactly pledged Sir George's credit in the transaction, but he had made use of Sir George's stockbroker, and when the account finished with Amal. Zincs well down, it was to Sir George that he had perforce to confess the little mishap. A hundred pounds more than covered everything, and Sir George wrote a check instantly. He did not lecture, or even rebuke—he merely specified arrangements by which the sum could be repaid out of Scarsdale's monthly salary.

This amounted to three hundred a year, and within two years the debt had been fully repaid, plus interest at five percent. No other unfortunate incident had occurred, and the relations between the two men seemed as good as ever. Then, in 1930, Scarsdale received a tentative offer of a better post. It was an important one, and his prospective employer, purely as a matter of routine, wished to effect a fidelity insurance for which a testimonial from Sir George would be necessary.

When Scarsdale approached Sir George about this, the financier talked to him with all the suavity he usually reserved for shareholders' meetings. "My dear Scarsdale," he replied in his curiously high-pitched voice, "I have no objection whatever to your leaving me, but I have, I admit, a certain reluctance to putting my name to any statement that is not absolutely correct. Take this question, for instance: 'Have you always found him to be strictly honest and reliable while in your service?' Now, my truthful reply to that would be: 'With one exception, yes.' Do you think that would help you?"

Obviously it would have been worse than no reply at all, and in default of the required testimonial the offer of the job fell through, and Scarsdale remained Sir George's secretary. Sir George, no doubt, congratulated himself on having secured a permanently good bargain. He was that kind of a man.

But had he known it, he was really much less to be congratulated. For just as Sir George was *that* kind of a man, so Scarsdale was another kind, equally rare perhaps.

It was not until a year had passed that Scarsdale decided that the time had come to murder Sir George. During the interval, he had come to regard the matter with something of the detachment of the chess player; indeed, the problem had rather comforted than worried him amid the botherations of a secretary's life. He had always, since his school days, been interested in the science of crime, and never for a moment did he doubt his own capacity to do the job; it was merely a question of waiting until the perfect moment offered itself.

That moment seemed to him to be arriving in February 1931, his choice being determined by two fortuitous circumstances— 1, that at 8:00 P.M. on Saturday the 22nd, Sir George was to deliver a broadcast talk on Postwar Monetary Policy, and 2, that immediately after the talk, which was to be given from the

London studio, he intended to travel to Banbury to spend the weekend with his brother Richard.

On the morning of the 22nd, Scarsdale awoke at his usual time at Bramstock Towers, Berkshire. It was a pleasant establishment, surrounded by a large and well-wooded estate, and Scarsdale, glancing through the window as he dressed, was glad to see that there had been no rain during the night and that the weather was fine and cold.

Sir George always breakfasted in his bedroom, and did not meet his secretary until ten o'clock, in the library. By this time, Scarsdale had, as usual, been at work for an hour or so opening letters and typing replies for Sir George's signature. After an exchange of good mornings, Sir George made a very customary announcement. "I'll just look through these letters, Scarsdale— then we'll take a turn round the garden while I tell you about my wireless talk tonight. I want you to prepare a few notes for me."

"Certainly, Sir George," replied Scarsdale. A great piece of luck, for the after-breakfast tour of the estate, though almost an institution in fine weather, might just, for one reason or another, have been foregone.

The men were soon dressed for outdoors and strolling briskly across the terrace toward the woods—the usual gambit, Scarsdale observed, with continuing satisfaction. Sir George meanwhile divided his attention between the garden and his impending radio talk. "You see, Scarsdale, I want those figures about the American Federal Reserve note issue—ah, that *cupressus macrocarpa* seems to be doing nicely—and a month-to-month table of Wall Street brokers' loans—" and so on, till they were deep in the woods, over half a mile from the house. The thickets, even in midwinter, were very dark. "I want your notes by three at the latest so that I can catch the three-fifty from Lincott and work up my talk on the train.—Ah, just look at that. Fanning really ought to notice these things. Confound the fellow!"

Fanning was the head gardener, and "that" was nothing more dreadful than an old kettle under a bush. But to Sir George it was serious enough, for if there was one thing that annoyed him more than another it was the suggestion of trespassers on his land.

"Why the devil don't Fanning and his men keep their eyes open?" he exclaimed crossly—but in that he did Fanning an injustice, since the kettle had not been there more than a few hours. Scarsdale, in fact, had placed it there himself the evening before.

Suddenly Scarsdale cried, "Why, look there, sir—the door of the hut's open! A tramp, I suppose. Wonder if he's still inside, by any chance."

At this point, Sir George began to behave precisely as Scarsdale had guessed and hoped he would. He left the path and strode vehemently amid the trees and undergrowth toward the small, square erection just visible in the near distance.

"By Jove, Scarsdale," he shouted, "if I do catch the fellow, I'll teach him a lesson!"

"Yes, rather," agreed Scarsdale.

Striding together through the less and less penetrable thickets, they reached the hut at last. It was built of grey stone, with a stout wooden door—the whole edifice intended originally as a sort of summerhouse but long disused. For years it had functioned at rare intervals as a storeplace for sawn-up logs, but now, as Scarsdale entered it, it proved empty even of them. Nor was there a tramp in it, either.

"He must have gone, sir," said Scarsdale, pulling wide open the half-gaping door. "Though it does look as if he's left a few relics.—I say, sir, what do you make of this?" He waited for Sir George to enter. "Damnation, that's my last match gone! Have you a match, Sir George?"

As Sir George began to fumble in his pocket in the almost complete darkness, Scarsdale added: "I say, sir, you've dropped something—your handkerchief, I think."

Sir George stooped, and at the same instant Scarsdale shot him neatly through the head with a small automatic pistol which he had that very morning abstracted from the drawer of the Boule cabinet in Sir George's private study.

Afterward, still wearing gloves, of course, he placed the weapon by the side of the dead man, closed the door carefully from the outside, and walked away.

All murders—all enterprises of any kind, in fact—carry with their accomplishment a certain minimum of risk, and at this point, as Scarsdale had all along recognized, the risks began. Fortunately, they were very small ones. The hut was isolated and only rarely visited. Fanning and his men were not interested in it at all, and the whole incident of the visiting tramp had been a mere invention to lure Sir George to the spot. Scarsdale felt reasonably sure that the body would remain undiscovered until a deliberate search was made.

Leaving the woods, he returned to the house by way of the garages. There he took out his two-seater car, drove it round to the front of the house, and had a friendly chat with Wilkes, the butler. "Oh, Wilkes, would you mind bringing down Sir George's suitcase? He's decided to go right on to town immediately, so he won't be in to lunch. He's walking over to Lincott through the fields. Oh, and you might label the bag for Banbury—I've got to get it sent off at the station."

"Will you be returning to lunch yourself, sir?"

"Oh, yes."

"Very good, sir . . ."

Lincott, which Scarsdale reached through winding lanes within a quarter of an hour, was a middle-sized village with a large and important railway junction. There were three facts about Lincott that were, from Scarsdale's point of view, fortunate—1, its railway station was large, frequented, and badly lit; 2, there were convenient expresses to London, as well as a late "down" train at night; and 3, Sir George's estate offered a pleasant shortcut to the village, a shortcut which Sir George was fond of traversing on foot and alone, even after dark.

Scarsdale drove direct to the junction and left the suitcase for dispatch to Banbury, whence it would be forwarded immediately to the house of Sir George's brother. Then he proceeded to a neighboring garage, arranged to leave his car until called for, and asked to use the telephone.

Ringing up the towers, he had a second amiable talk with the butler.

"Oh, hullo, Wilkes, this is Scarsdale speaking—from Lincott. Sir George has slightly changed his plans again—or rather my plans. He wants me to go along to town with him right away.

Yes. Yes. I'm leaving my car here. Yes, that's what I want to tell
you—I've decided that as I'm going to town I may as well spend
the weekend there at my club. I'll be back on Tuesday. Yes.
Goodbye."

Scarsdale then walked to the junction, booked a third-class
single ticket to Paddington, and caught the 1:00 P.M. train.

At Paddington, he did several things. First he went to the local
booking-office and purchased a third-class single ticket to Ealing. Then he took a snack at a nearby A.B.C. shop, and about
3:00 P.M. traveled by omnibus to the bank, whence he walked
to the Anglo-Oceanic offices in Bishopsgate.

There he met several people he knew very well, chatted with
them affably, and busied himself for some time in Sir George's
private office, saying, "Yes, Sir George *is* in town, but he's very
busy—I don't suppose you'll see him here today."

Williamson, one of the head-office people, grinned.

"Yes, he's busy," Scarsdale repeated, faintly returning the grin.
They both knew that there were aspects of Sir George's life that
had nothing to do with the Anglo-Oceanic companies.

"Taking her to the theater, eh?" queried Williamson.

"More likely to the cinema," returned Scarsdale. "He's not
free tonight, anyhow—he's got a date at the B.B.C.—and left me
the devil's own pile of work to finish, too."

It was quite natural, therefore, that Scarsdale should still be
at work in Sir George's private office when Williamson and the
rest of the staff left. At 6:00 P.M., by which time the huge office
building was tenantless, Scarsdale, having previously made fast
the door on the inside, turned to a little job that he had not
cared to tackle before.

Opening the safe by means of the combination, he carefully
abstracted certain documents—to be precise, South American
bearer bonds to the value of between thirty and forty thousand
pounds. How odd, he reflected, that Sir George, who would not
give him a simple testimonial of honesty, had never scrupled to
leave the keys and combination of his private safe in an unlocked bureau drawer at the Towers!

Leaving the Anglo-Oceanic offices about 6:30 P.M., Scarsdale
took an omnibus to Picadilly Circus and entered a cinema that

was showing a film so remarkably bad that in the five-and-ninepenny seats he had almost an entire row to himself at that early hour of the evening. There and then, in the surrounding gloom, he managed to transform himself into a fairly credible impersonation of Sir George Winthrop-Dunster. In build and dress they were rather similar: nothing else was required but a few touches of greasepaint, a false moustache, and the adjustment of Sir George's characteristic type of horn-rimmed spectacles. The disguise would have deceived anyone who did not know Sir George intimately.

Scarsdale left the cinema about seven-thirty, in the middle of the film. A few moments in a telephone booth enabled him, with the help of a pocket-mirror, to make good any small deficiencies in his quick change. It had all, so far, been delightfully easy. At 7:55 he took a taxi to the old B.B.C. headquarters in Savoy Hill.

Neither he nor Sir George had ever broadcast before, and Scarsdale was quite genuinely interested in the experience. In the reception room, he had an amiable chat with one of the studio officials and found no difficulty at all in keeping up the character and impersonation of Sir George. Indeed, he not only talked and behaved like Sir George but he found himself thinking as Sir George would have thought—which was rather horrible.

At eight o'clock, he took his place in the thick-carpeted studio and began to read from his typed manuscript. It was a cosy and completely restful business. With the little green-shaded lamp illuminating the script and the perfectly silent surroundings, it was a comfort to realize that, by such simple means, he was fabricating an alibi that could be vouched for afterward by hundreds of thousands of worthy folk all over the country. He read Sir George's views on monetary policy with a perfection of utterance that surprised even himself, especially the way he had got the high-pitched voice.

Leaving the studios half an hour later, he asked the commissionaire in the hall to get him a taxi, and in the man's hearing told the driver "Paddington." There he commenced another series of operations. First he put through a long-distance call to Richard Winthrop-Dunster, of Banbury.

"That you, Richard?" sang out the high-pitched voice, still functioning. "I'm extremely sorry, but I'm afraid I won't be able to spend the weekend at your place after all. Fact is, I've got a rather worrying piece of business on hand at the moment, and I can't spare the time. Yes, things *are* infernally worrying just now. Next week I might come—I'll try to, anyhow, so you might keep my bag, if it's arrived. Oh, it *has*, has it? Yes, I told young Scarsdale to send it. Yes, that's right—keep it till next week. I'm at Paddington, just about to catch the nine-fifteen home. Yes, I've just come from the studio—were you listening? Yes. Yes. Goodbye, then—next week, I hope."

Then Scarsdale went to the booking-office and purchased a first-class ticket to Lincott. Passing the barrier, he even risked a word or two with the man who snipped his ticket, and who knew Sir George very slightly. "Cold evening, Sir George," the man said.

Scarsdale found an empty first-class compartment and, as soon as the train moved out from the platform, opened the small nondescript attache-case he had carried with him all day. With the help of its contents, he began to make sundry changes in his personal appearance—then, taking from his pocket the single ticket to Ealing purchased earlier in the day, he cut out of it a triangular section similar to that snipped from his Lincott ticket. Finally, at Ealing, a slim, clean-shaven fellow in a cloth cap might have been seen to leave the train and climb the steps to the street. He carried a brown-paper parcel, which, if examined, would have been found to contain—rather oddly—an attache-case.

Scarsdale boarded a bus going east, and at Ealing Common changed to an Underground train. At 10:00 P.M.—long before the train from Paddington would have reached Lincott—Scarsdale, himself again, was entering a West End restaurant and exchanging a cordial good evening with a headwaiter who knew him well by sight.

Throughout the weekend, Scarsdale stayed in London, visiting numerous friends—indeed, there was scarcely an hour from morning to midnight which he did not spend in company. His nights at the club were conveniently preluded by friendly chats with the hall porter, and in the mornings at breakfast he was equally affable to the waiter.

On Tuesday afternoon, he returned to the Towers, collecting his car at Lincott on the way, and got to work immediately on Sir George's accumulated correspondence. "I know Sir George will expect to find everything finished," he explained to Wilkes.

But dinnertime came and Sir George did not arrive. It was peculiar, because he was usually back by the six o'clock train when he visited his brother.

At nine, Scarsdale decided to have dinner without further waiting—but when ten o'clock came and it was clear that Sir George had not caught the last train from Banbury, Scarsdale agreed with Wilkes that Richard Winthrop-Dunster had better be informed of the situation. "Maybe Sir George is staying there an extra night," said Scarsdale as the butler hurried to the telephone.

Five minutes later, Wilkes returned with a pale and troubled face. "Mr. Richard says that Sir George rang him up late on Saturday night from Paddington, canceling the visit and saying he was on his way back here."

"Extraordinary!" exclaimed Scarsdale. "Why isn't he here then? Where the devil can he be?"

They discussed the problem with an increasing degree of consternation until midnight and went to bed with mutually expressed hopes that some message might arrive by the morning's post.

But none came. At noon, after consultation with Scarsdale and further telephoning to Banbury, Wilkes notified the police. Inspector Deane of the local force arrived during the afternoon, and after acquainting himself with the known details of the situation motored over to Banbury to see Mr. Richard Winthrop-Dunster. All that was on Wednesday.

On Thursday morning, inquiries began at Paddington station, with immediate and gratifying result. As Inspector Deane put it: "Well, Mr. Scarsdale, we've traced Sir George as far as the Lincott train on Saturday night—there's a ticket inspector at Paddington who remembers him. We're not quite sure of him at Lincott, but no doubt he must have been seen there, too."

Everything, Scarsdale was glad to perceive, was still working out perfectly according to plan. From Paddington, the trail had already led to Lincott. Soon it would lead from Lincott to the Towers—and on the way, to be discovered inevitably when the constabulary intelligence had progressed so far, was that little hut in the woods.

But it was not part of Scarsdale's plan to anticipate this inevitability by any hint or suggestion. He merely said: "Perhaps you could advertise for information. The taxi-men in the station yard may have noticed him—or one of them may have driven him somewhere. Of course, if it was a fine night, he may have walked. He often walks. It was a fine night in London, I remember."

"Quite so, sir," agreed Inspector Deane. "I'm sure I'm greatly obliged to you for the idea."

It was queer how the two men took to each other; Scarsdale had a delightful knack of putting people at their ease. But for the mischance of working for Sir George, he would probably never have murdered anybody.

The plan remained perfect—indeed, he thought, as he settled for sleep that night, he could afford almost to be indifferent now. The dangerous interval was past, and it no longer greatly mattered when or how the body was discovered. Perhaps it would be tomorrow, or the next day, or next week even, if the police were exceptionally stupid. He had in mind exactly what would happen subsequently.

The medical evidence would, of course, be vague after such a lapse of time, but fully consistent with Sir George's death having taken place late on Saturday night, at an hour (if the matter were ever called into question) when he, Scarsdale, had several complete alibis sixty miles away.

Then would come the question: how had it happened? At such a juncture, the dead man's brother would probably recall that Sir George had stated over the telephone on the fatal night that he was worried about some business affair. Scarsdale would then, with a little reluctance to discuss the private affairs of his late employer, admit that Sir George had had certain financial troubles of late.

The next stage of revelation would doubtless be enacted at the Anglo-Oceanic office, when and where the disappearance of the bonds would be discovered. That would certainly cause a sensation, both in the City and beyond. Clearly it would suggest that Sir George, having monkeyed with the assets of his companies, had taken his life rather than face the music.

All this, of course, was according to Scarsdale's plan—and when, on Thursday morning, the police found the body of Sir George in the little hut in the woods, Scarsdale might have been excused for reckoning his plan ninety-nine percent infallible. Unfortunately for him, the remaining one percent took a hand, with the rather odd result that a man named Hansell was arrested a few hours later and charged with the murder of Sir George.

Hansell was an unemployed workman turned tramp, and had been arrested in a Lincott pub after trying to pawn a watch which an alert shopman recognized as Sir George's. At first Hansell gave the usual yarn about having found the watch, but after a severe questioning at the police station, he told a much more extraordinary story.

On the previous Saturday, he said, about a quarter past eight in the evening, he had been trespassing in the woods belonging to the Towers estate. Finding the little hut, he had pushed open the door and had there, to his great alarm and astonishment, come across the dead body of a man. At first he thought of going for help immediately, but as he felt that his own position might be thought rather questionable, he had contented himself in the end with rifling the pockets and decamping. He admitted having taken some papers and a wallet, which he had since destroyed, except for a few treasury notes it had contained. He had also taken the watch.

But at 8:15 P.M., as the police detectives did not fail to point out, Sir George had been broadcasting a talk from the B.B.C. studio in London. How, then, could he have been found sixty miles away, dead, at the same hour? Obviously Hansell must be a great liar.

He was brought before the local magistrates and speedily committed for trial at the assizes. Meanwhile, Scarsdale, in the

midst of well-simulated grief at the loss of a respected employer, was thinking hard. The arrest of Hansell had given him
a shock at first, but he was not long in finding a way of fitting it
into his plan. Indeed, now that the suicide theory was all out of
focus, Scarsdale himself thought fit to make the discovery about
the missing bonds, and was inclined to agree with the police
when they suggested that the bonds might have been among
the papers that Hansell had stolen from Sir George's pockets
and afterward destroyed.

The trial of Hansell came on in due course. He pleaded Not
Guilty, but his story sounded pretty thin and was not improved
by the fact that he still insisted that he had found the body at
8:15 P.M. He had heard the Lincott church clock chime the
quarter, he said, and no amount of cross-examination could
shake him.

Moreover, the prosecution was able to prove that his fingerprints were on the automatic pistol. Hansell explained this by
saying that he had found the weapon lying beside the body and
had picked it up, but the story was unconvincing. Was it not
more likely that Sir George had been taking the shortcut home
from Lincott station (as he often did), that he had been attacked
by Hansell and had drawn his automatic (which he often
carried) to defend himself, that Hansell had wrested it from
him and had shot him with it, and that Hansell had afterward
dragged the body into the shed and, in sheer panic, left the
telltale weapon behind?

Defending counsel could only offer the alternative theory of
suicide, which, in the case of so well respected a personage as
Sir George, seemed a breach of taste as well as a straining of
probability. As for Hansell, he must, whatever he said, have
mistaken the time of his visit to the hut. Neither of these
suggestions appealed to judge and jury, and it was not surprising that Hansell was found guilty and sentenced to death. This
was afterward commuted to penal servitude for life.

Scarsdale, with the trial over and everything settling down, had
now only the tail end of his plan to put into cautious execution.
He would wait, he had decided, for twelve months (to avoid
any semblance of flight) and then go abroad, probably to the

Argentine, taking with him the bonds. After a year or two in Buenos Aires, he would doubtless have formed a sufficiently intimate connection with some banker or stockbroker to enable him to begin disposing of the booty.

It has already been noted that the verdict of murder instead of suicide did not at first disturb the vast and almost terrifying equanimity of Scarsdale. What did trouble him, however, as time passed and the death of Sir George became history, was the gradually invading consciousness that the only thing that had saved him from the dock, and possibly from the gallows, was not his precious plan at all, but sheer luck! For if Hansell had reported the finding of the body without delay, the faked alibi of the broadcast would have been discovered. Scarsdale had been saved, then, not by the flawlessness of his own brainwork but by a casual circumstance entirely outside of his control!

It was an unwelcome conclusion to reach, partly because it robbed him of pride in achievement, but chiefly because it laid him open to disquieting thoughts of the future.

During the year of waiting in England, he lived at Kew, renting a house near the river and living on his savings while he devoted himself to writing a book on his favorite subject—criminology. It passed the time. Besides which, he had hopes that it would eventually establish his reputation.

He received several minor shocks during this period. One happened when an acquaintance named Lindsey accosted him suddenly at his club and apropos of nothing at all said: "You know, Scarsdale, you're awfully like old Dunster in appearance. Did you ever realize that? I'm sure you could easily have passed for him during his lifetime with the help of a false moustache and those goggles of his! Especially, too, if you could have managed that shrill way of talking he had. And you *are* a bit of an actor chap, aren't you? Didn't you once play in something at Oxford?"

Scarsdale wondered whether his face was turning fiery red or ashen pale. He managed to laugh, and an hour or so later reached the satisfying conclusion that it had all been pure chance—nothing but that. But it was upsetting all the same, and it was about this time that he began the habit of carrying a small automatic pistol about with him wherever he went. He would not be taken alive.

Just about a month before the year was up, Lindsey telephoned him with immense cheerfulness one morning.

"Oh, hello, Scarsdale. I'm in a job now, and you'll never guess where. It's at the B.B.C." They exchanged several minutes of excited chatter, then he said: "By the way, how would you like to do a short talk on crimes and criminals, or something of the sort? We're getting up a series here and your name occurred to me—you've always been keen on the subject. What about June eleventh, say?"

Scarsdale had hoped to be in Buenos Aires by that date, but he couldn't very well say so, and some kind of caution urged him not to make excuses. Besides, he couldn't help being slightly thrilled at the prospect of making the whole country listen to his views on crime and criminals. He told Lindsey that the date would suit him quite well.

During the eight weeks' interval, however, there came to him once or twice the faintest possible misgiving—soon banished, but leaving nevertheless a flavor of anxiety behind.

On the evening of June eleventh he didn't feel at his best as he set out for Savoy Hill. He was due to speak from 8:00 P.M. until 8:20, and he couldn't escape the recollection of the last time he had entered the building. It was odd, perhaps, that the very same announcer should be welcoming him again now, though it was quite natural, no doubt, that the announcer, knowing that Scarsdale had been Sir George's secretary, should begin to chat about the deceased gentleman.

"Awfully sad business that was," he commented in the familiar dulcet tones. "I talked to him that very evening just as I'm talking to you now. Amazing that he should have been so near his tragic end—indeed, I often wonder if he had any premonition of it himself, because he seemed just slightly uneasy in manner."

"Did he?" said Scarsdale.

"Of course it may have been my imagination. I was only comparing him with other times I'd heard him speak—at company meetings. Fortunately, I'd already sold all my Anglo-Oceanics. Queer he should have been carrying all those bonds about with him—forty thousand pounds' worth of them, wasn't it?"

"It was never absolutely proved."

"But bearer bonds, weren't they? Doesn't that mean that anybody who got hold of them could raise money on them?"

"More or less," answered Scarsdale absently. He had suddenly begun to feel troubled. He wished he hadn't arrived early enough for this chat.

By 7:55, the announcer had reached the stage of offering a few general tips about broadcasting. "This is your first experience of the microphone, I understand, Mr. Scarsdale?"

Scarsdale nodded.

"Curious—I thought I recognized your face. Or perhaps you're very like someone else. However, you'll soon get over mike fright, even if you do have a touch of it at first. The chief point to remember is never to speak too fast or in a very high-pitched voice. But then you don't, as a matter of fact, do you?"

Scarsdale was a trifle pale. "I don't think so," he murmured.

Five minutes later, he sat at the little desk before the microphone, with the green-shaded lamp before him. He was certainly nervous and, beyond his nervousness, strangely uneasy in a deeper sense. It was peculiar—he hadn't been like it before. As he sat down, his foot caught in the flex that connected the lamp with the wall plug. The lamp went out, but it didn't matter—the globes overhead were sufficient to see by. He waited for the red light to deliver the signal indicating he had been properly introduced to his unseen audience, then he began to read his manuscript.

But all the time he was reading, he was thinking and pondering subconsciously. He had been there before—the announcer had seen and heard Sir George in the flesh at company meetings. The announcer had told him he must avoid a high-pitched voice. Bearer bonds. This was the very same studio—and the same time, eight o'clock. And it was Lindsey who had fixed up his talk—Lindsey, who had once commented on his likeness to Sir George.

Suddenly the idea burst over him in full force, monstrous, all-conquering: this was all a plant—engineered jointly by Lindsey and the B.B.C., with perhaps Scotland Yard in the discreet background. They were testing him, and by the very latest psychological methods, as expounded by the great French criminologists. They guessed the truth and were probing subtly—it was *their* perfect plan seeking to undermine *his!*

At that moment, while Scarsdale's eyes and voice were reading automatically, the announcer stole into the room and silently replaced the lamp-plug in the wall socket. The green light blazed suddenly into Scarsdale's face as the intruder, in a whisper too soft to be audible to the microphone, murmured: "Pulled it off, didn't you? I thought that's what must have happened."

Scarsdale's broadcast talk on crimes and criminals will never, it is safe to say, be forgotten in the history of radio. Most listeners, as the talk progressed, must have been aware of a growing tension in the speaker's delivery—a tension ill-suited both to matter and theme. But it is certain that no listener remained unthrilled when, about sixteen minutes past eight, Scarsdale exclaimed, in a voice vibrating with excitement: "And here, if I may be permitted, I will interpose an example of what I consider to be the really perfect, undetectable crime—*I myself murdered Sir George Winthrop-Dunster.*"

At this point, the loudspeakers in some hundreds of thousands of homes delivered themselves of a mysterious crashing sound, followed by a long silence until 8:35, when a familiar Oxford accent expressed regret for the delay and gave out, without further comment, the continuation of the evening's program.

In the morning, however, the newspapers were less reticent. Scarsdale, it appeared, had made history by being the first person actually to commit suicide before the microphone. He had shot himself.

The inquest was held the following day and attracted great attention. The announcer was very gentle and soothing in giving evidence—almost as if he were reading an S.O.S.

"It seemed to me," he said, "that Mr. Scarsdale was rather upset about something when he arrived at the studio. He was a few minutes early and we chatted together. We talked a little about Sir George Winthrop-Dunster. I concluded that Mr. Scarsdale was probably nervous, as it was his first broadcast.

"Then, about halfway through the talk, I noticed that the lamp over his desk had gone out—he must have caught his foot in the flex and pulled the plug away. I went in to put it right for him and noticed then that he wasn't looking at all well. He was very pale, and he stared at me in a rather queer way when I mentioned something about the light. A few minutes later, I had to put up the signal warning him not to talk in such a high-pitched voice because the sound wasn't coming through properly. The next I heard was his extraordinary statement about Sir George Winthrop-Dunster. Of course I rushed to cut off the microphone immediately, but before I could, I heard the shot."

The verdict was naturally one of "Suicide during temporary insanity."

Even the last of Scarsdale's plans went astray. Instead of being acknowledged, however fearfully, as the perpetrator of the perfect murder, he was dismissed as that familiar and rather troublesome type—the neurotic person who confesses to a crime of which he is quite obviously innocent.

"Poor Scarsdale," said Inspector Deane in a special interview for one of the Sunday papers, "had been deeply distressed by the tragic death of his employer, and that, coupled with his interest in criminology—I understand he was writing a book on the subject—combined to unhinge his mind. We often get similar confessions during well-known murder trials and as a rule, as on this occasion, we can spot them at a glance."

Answering a further question, Inspector Deane remarked: "As a matter of fact, Scarsdale wasn't within fifty miles of Lincott during the whole of the time the crime could possibly have been committed. We know that because in the ordinary course of police routine we had to check up on his movements. Poor fellow, we all liked him. He helped us a good deal in our work, though it was clear all the time that he was feeling things badly."

Just one point remains—about those bonds. If ever it should
be discovered that Scarsdale had had in his possession a small
fortune in South American bearer certificates, a certain measure
of suspicion would inevitably be cast upon him—albeit post-
humously. But will such a discovery be made? Scarsdale had
put them in a tin box and buried the box three feet deep in the
back garden of the house he rented at Kew—and who, pray, is
ever likely to dig them up?

LEO TOLSTOY

THE MAN OF GOD

Once upon a time there lived in the city of Vladimir a young merchant named Aksenof. He had two shops and a house.

Aksenof himself had a ruddy complexion and curly hair; he was a very jolly fellow and a good singer. When he was young he used to drink too much, and when he was tipsy he was turbulent, but after his marriage he ceased drinking and only occasionally had a spree.

One time in summer Aksenof was going to Nizhni to the great Fair. As he was about to bid his family goodbye, his wife said to him, "Ivan Dmitrievitch, do not go today. I had a dream that some misfortune befell you."

Aksenof laughed at her, and said, "You are always afraid that I shall go on a spree at the Fair."

His wife said, "I myself know not what I am afraid of, but I had such a strange dream. You seemed to be coming home from town, and you took off your hat, and your head was all grey."

Aksenof laughed. "That means good luck. See, I am going now. I will bring you some rich remembrances."

And he bade his family farewell and set off.

When he had gone half his journey, he fell in with a merchant of his acquaintance, and the two stopped at the same tavern for the night. They took tea together, and went to sleep in adjoining rooms.

Aksenof didn't want to sleep long; he awoke in the middle of the night, and in order that he might get a good start while it was cool he aroused his driver and bade him harness up, went down into the smoky hut, settled his account with the landlord, and started on his way.

After he had driven forty versts, he stopped to get something to eat. He rested in the vestibule of the inn, and when it was noon he went to the doorstep and ordered the samovar got ready. Then he took out his guitar and began to play.

Suddenly a troika with a bell dashed up to the inn, and from the equipage leaped an official and two soldiers. He came directly up to Aksenof and asked, "Who are you? Where did you come from?"

Aksenof answered without hesitation and asked him if he would not have a glass of tea with him. But the official kept on with his questions. "Where did you spend last night? Were you alone or with a merchant? Have you seen the merchant this morning? Why did you leave so early this morning?"

Aksenof wondered why he was questioned so closely, but he told everything just as it was, and he asked, "Why do you ask me so many questions? I am not a thief or a murderer. I am on my own business—there is nothing to question me about."

Then the official called up the soldiers and said, "I am the police inspector and I have made these inquiries of you because the merchant with whom you spent last night has been stabbed. Show me your things—you men search him."

They went into the tavern, brought in Aksenof's trunk and bag, and began to open and search them. Suddenly the inspector pulled out from the bag a knife and demanded, "Whose knife is this?"

Aksenof looked and saw a knife covered with blood, and he was frightened.

"And whose blood is that on the knife?"

Aksenof tried to answer, but he could not articulate his words.

"I—I—don't know. I—That knife—it is not mine—"

Then the inspector said, "This morning the merchant was found stabbed to death in his bed. No one except you could have done it. The tavern was locked on the inside, and there was no one in the tavern except yourself. And here is the bloody knife in your bag, and your guilt is evident in your face. Tell me how you killed him and how much money you took from him."

Aksenof swore that he had not done it, that he had not seen the merchant after he had drunk tea with him, that the only money that he had with him—8,000 rubles—was his own, and that the knife was not his. But his voice trembled, his face was pale, and he was quivering with fright, like a guilty person.

The police inspector called the soldiers and commanded them to bind Aksenof and take him to the wagon. When they did so, with his feet tied, Aksenof crossed himself and burst into tears.

They confiscated Aksenof's possessions and his money, took him to the next city, and threw him into prison.

They sent to Vladimir to make inquiries about Aksenof's character, and all the merchants and citizens of Vladimir declared that Aksenof, when he was young, used to drink and was wild but that now he was a worthy man. Then he was brought up for judgment. He was sentenced for having killed the merchant and for having robbed him of 20,000 rubles.

Aksenof's wife was dumbfounded by the news and didn't know what to think. Her children were still small, and there was one at the breast. She took them all with her and journeyed to the city where her husband was imprisoned.

At first they would not grant her admittance, but afterward she got permission from the Chief of Police and was taken to her husband.

When she saw him in his prison garb, in chains together with murderers, she fell to the floor. It was a long time before she recovered from her swoon. Then she placed her children around her, sat down amid them, and began to tell him about their domestic affairs and to ask him about everything that had happened to him.

He told her the whole story.

She asked, "What is to be the result of it?"

He said, "We must petition the Czar. It is impossible that an innocent man should be condemned."

The wife said she already had sent a petition to the Czar, but the petition had not been granted. Aksenof said nothing, but was very much downcast.

Then his wife said, "You see, the dream I had—when I dreamed that you had become greyheaded—meant something, after all. Already your hair has begun to turn grey with trouble. You ought to have stayed at home." And she began to tear her hair and said, "Vanya, my dearest husband, tell me the truth: did you commit that crime or not?"

Aksenof said, "So you, too, have no faith in me!" And he wrung his hands and wept.

Then a soldier came and said it was time for the wife and children to go. And Aksenof for the last time bade farewell to his family.

When they were gone, Aksenof began to think over all that his wife had said. When he remembered that she had distrusted him and asked him if he had murdered the merchant, he said to himself, It is evident that no one but God can know the truth of the matter, and He is the only one to ask for mercy—and the only one from whom to expect it."

From that time on, Aksenof ceased to send in petitions, ceased to hope, and only prayed to God. He was sentenced to be knouted, and then to exile with hard labor.

He was flogged with the knout, and then, when the wounds were healed, he was sent with other exiles to Siberia.

He lived twenty-six years in the mines. The hair on his head had become white as snow, and his beard had grown long, thin, and grey. All his gaiety had vanished. He was bent, his gait was slow, he spoke little, he never laughed, and he spent much of his time in prayer.

Aksenof had learned while in prison to make boots, and with the money he earned he bought the *Book of Martyrs*, and read it when it was light enough in prison. On holidays he would go to the prison church, read the Gospels, and sing in the choir, for his voice was still strong and good.

The authorities liked Aksenof for his submissiveness, and his prison associates respected him and called him "Grandfather" and "the man of God." Whenever they had petitions to be presented, Aksenof was chosen to carry them to the authorities, and when quarrels arose among the prisoners they always came to Aksenof to be the judge. He never received any letters from home, so he didn't know whether his wife and children were alive.

One time some new convicts came to the prison. In the evening all the old convicts gathered around the newcomers and began to ply them with questions as to the cities or villages from which this one or that one had come, and what their crimes were.

Aksenof sat on his bunk near the strangers, and with bowed head listened to what was said.

One of the new convicts was a tall, healthy-looking man of sixty years, with a close-cropped grey beard. He was telling why he had been arrested.

"And so, brothers, I was sent here for nothing. I unharnessed a horse from a postboy's sledge, and they caught me in it and insisted I was stealing it. 'But,' says I, 'I only wanted to go a little faster, so I whipped up the horse. And besides, the driver is a friend of mine. It's all right.' 'No,' say they, 'you were stealing it.' I have done things which long ago would have sent me here, but I was not found out, and now they have sent me here without any justice in it. But what's the use of grumbling? I have been in Siberia before."

"Where did you come from?" asked one of the convicts.

"Well, we came from the city of Vladimir—we are citizens of that place. My name is Makar and my father's name was Semyon."

Aksenof raised his head and asked, "Tell me, Semyonitch, have you ever heard of the Aksenofs, merchants in Vladimir? Are they alive?"

"Indeed, I have heard of them! They are rich merchants, though their father is in Siberia. It seems he was just like the rest of us sinners. And now tell me, Grandfather, what were you sent here for?"

Aksenof did not like to speak of his misfortune. He sighed and said, "Twenty-six years ago I was condemned to hard labor on account of my sins."

Makar Semyonof said, "But what was your crime?"

Aksenof replied, "I must, therefore, have deserved this." But he would not tell or give any further particulars. The other convicts, however, related why Aksenof had been sent to Siberia. They told how on the road someone had killed a merchant and put the knife into Aksenof's luggage, and how he had been unjustly punished for this.

When Makar heard this, he glanced at Aksenof, clasped his

hands round his knees, and said, "Well, now, that's wonderful, Grandfather!"

They began to ask him what he thought was wonderful, but Makar did not answer. He only said, "A miracle! How wonderful that we should meet again!"

And when he said these words, it came over Aksenof that perhaps this man might know who it was that had killed the merchant. He said, "Did you ever hear of that crime, Semyon-itch, or did you ever see me before?"

"Of course I heard of it! The country was full of it. But it happened a long time ago, and I have forgotten what I heard," said Makar.

"Perhaps you heard who killed the merchant?" asked Aksenof.

Makar laughed, and said, "Why, of course—the man who had the knife in his bag killed him. If anyone put the knife in your things and was not caught doing it—that would have been impossible. For how could they have put the knife in your bag? Was it not standing close by your head? And you would have heard it, wouldn't you?"

As soon as Aksenof heard these words, he felt convinced that this was the very man who had killed the merchant. He stood up and walked away.

All that night he was unable to sleep. Deep melancholy came upon him, and he began to call back the past in his imagination.

He imagined his wife as she had been when for the last time she had come to see him in the prison. She seemed to stand before him exactly as though she were alive, and he saw her face and her eyes—he seemed to hear her words and her laugh. Then his imagination brought up his children before him—one a little boy in a little fur coat, and the other at his mother's breast.

He imagined himself as he was at that time, young and happy. He remembered how he had sat on the steps of the tavern when they arrested him, and how his soul was full of joy as he played his guitar.

And he remembered the place of execution, where they had knouted him, and the knoutsman, and the people standing around, and the chains and the convicts and all his twenty-six

years of prison life. He thought of his old age and such melancholy came upon Aksenof that he was tempted to put an end to
himself.

And all on account of this criminal! said Aksenof to himself.

And then he began to feel such anger against Makar Semyonof
that he almost fell upon him, and was crazy with desire for
vengeance. He repeated prayers all night, but could not cover
his calm. When day came, he did not look at Makar.

Thus passed two weeks. Aksenof wasn't able to sleep, and such
melancholy had come over him he didn't know what to do.

One time during the night as he happened to be passing
through the prison, he saw that the soil was disturbed under
one of the bunks. He stopped to examine it. Suddenly Makar
crept from under the bunk and looked at Aksenof with a startled
face.

Aksenof was about to pass on so as not to see him, but Makar
seized his arm, and told him how he had been digging a passage
under the wall—how every day he carried the dirt out in his
pockets and emptied it in the street when they were working.

"If you only keep quiet, old man, I will get you out, too. If
you tell on me, they will flog me—but afterward I will kill you."

When Askenof saw his enemy, he trembled with rage, pulled
away his arm, and said, "I have no reason to make my escape,
and to kill me would do no harm—you killed me long ago. As
for telling on you or not, I shall do as God sees fit to have me."

The next day, when they took the convicts out to work, the
soldiers discovered where Makar had been digging in the
ground; they began to make a search and found the hole. The
warden came and asked everyone, "Who was digging that
hole?"

All denied it. Those who knew did not name Makar, because
they were aware that he would be flogged half to death for such
an attempt.

Then the warden came to Aksenof and he said, "Old man,
you are truthful. Tell me before God who did this."

Makar was standing near, in great excitement, and did not
dare look at Aksenof.

Aksenof's hands and lips trembled, and it was some time before he could speak a word. He said to himself, If I shield him—But why should I forgive him when he has been my ruin? Let him suffer for my sufferings! But shall I tell on him? They will surely flog him. But what difference does it make what I think of him? Will it be any the easier for me?

Once more the warden demanded, "Well, old man, tell me the truth. Who dug the hole?"

Aksenof glanced at Makar, and then said, "I cannot tell, your Honor. God does not bid me tell. Do with me as you please. I am in your power."

In spite of the warden's efforts, Aksenof would say nothing more. And so they failed to find out who dug the hole.

On the next night as Aksenof was lying on his bunk, almost asleep, he heard someone come along and sit down at his feet. He peered through the darkness and saw that it was Makar. Aksenof asked, "What do you wish of me? What are you doing here?"

Makar remained silent.

Aksenof arose and said, "What do you want? Go away or I will call the guard."

Makar went up close to Aksenof and said in a whisper, "Ivan Dmitrievitch, forgive me!"

Aksenof said, "What have I to forgive you?"

"It was I who killed the merchant and put the knife in your bag. And I was going to kill you, too, but there was a noise in the yard. I thrust the knife in your bag and slipped out of the window."

Aksenof didn't know what to say. Makar knelt and said, "Ivan, forgive me, for Christ's sake. I will confess that I killed the merchant—they will pardon you. You will be able to go home."

Aksenof said, "It is easy for you to say that, but how could I endure it? Where should I go now? My wife is probably dead, my children have forgotten me. I have nowhere to go."

Makar did not rise. He beat his head on the ground and said, "Ivan Dmitrievitch, forgive me! When they flogged me with the knout, it was easier to bear than it is to look at you. And you had pity on me after all this—you did not tell on me. Forgive

me, for Christ's sake! Forgive me, though I am a cursed villain!"
And the man began to sob.

When Aksenof heard Makar Semyonof sobbing, he himself
burst into tears and said, "God will forgive you. Maybe I am a
hundred times worse than you are."

And suddenly he felt a wonderful peace in his soul. And he
ceased to mourn for his home, and had no desire to leave the
prison, but only thought of his last hour.

Makar would not listen to Aksenof and confessed his crime.

When they came to let Aksenof go home, he was dead.

R. L. STEVENS

THE GREAT AMERICAN NOVEL

She *was curled on the bed like a tired question mark awaiting the answer of his body.*

I read it over a second time but it didn't change. I flipped the pages till I reached the next chapter, but it was just as bad. "Lunchtime, Pete," someone called as he passed my cubicle. I nodded agreement and tossed the manuscript back on my desk. I needed some lunch to revive me.

We weren't top-echelon editors authorized to entertain authors on expense accounts, so we usually gravitated to the formica-countered coffee shops that lined the side streets of Fifth Avenue. They were good places for lunch—inexpensive, fast, and convenient. And they gave me a chance to meet and mingle with the slush readers from some of the other big publishing houses.

In fact, that was how I met Gilda—the only girl I ever knew who was named after a Rita Hayworth movie. Gilda was a slush reader at Associated Publishers, though she sported a classier title than that when signing rejection letters. She was just two years out of college and still had something of the cheerleader about her.

"Hi, Pete," she said as she slid onto the stool next to me. "How goes the slush at Ryder & Ryder?"

"Same old stuff. I keep hoping for another *Ulysses,* but at this point I'd settle for another *Carpetbaggers*—anything!"

She ordered a sandwich and Coke. "Is Brady still riding you?"

Sam Brady was a thirty-five-year-old managing editor trying hard to be the top man at Ryder & Ryder. Sometimes, when he couldn't take out his frustration on executive editor Carlos Winter, he settled for me instead. "He's been in Washington at the ABA convention," I said. "But he's due back this afternoon."

217

"All you need is to find one good manuscript, Pete, and you'll have Brady's job."

"It's not quite that easy. I wish it were."

Gilda took a bite of her sandwich and thought about it. "I wish I could write. I'd write you the biggest, sexiest bestseller you ever saw! And you'd get credit for it."

"I'm afraid Ryder & Ryder doesn't go for sexy bestsellers," I told her. "They're more interested in quote literature unquote."

"That's Carlos Winter's influence."

I had to agree. Winter was the grand old man of New York editorial circles. He'd been at Scribners in the early days of Hemingway and worked with Pascal Covici when Steinbeck was first beginning to write. Though well past normal retirement age, he showed no sign of surrendering the editorial reins at Ryder & Ryder.

"Winter has certainly been nice to me," I said. "Even when he's loading me down with over-the-transom manuscripts, he always has time for a kind word."

Gilda finished her sandwich and Coke, and we strolled down Fifth Avenue until it was time to get back to work. In the elevator, I ran into Winter himself, coming back early for a meeting. "How are you, Pete? Found any good manuscripts?"

"Not a thing, Mr. Winter. I keep hoping, though."

"That's the way."

Back at my desk, I found another batch of manuscripts from his secretary. They'd come in the morning mail, addressed to him personally, and I was to read and report on them. Her note told me to spread them around if I couldn't handle them all, but with Winter's slush I always made an effort to get through it myself. A writer who knew the name of Carlos Winter had at least that much going for him.

The first couple of manuscripts I glanced at seemed to be more of the same—a novel about a young man's awakening and an intensely written book about the Arab-Israeli conflict. I tossed them both aside for later consideration. The third one was different. It even looked different. Its 300-odd typewritten pages were spiralbound—something I'd never seen with a manuscript—and it had a stiff brown cover with the title and author's name neatly labeled: *Years of Earth* by Sumner Doud Chapin. I liked the title and I liked the author's name.

The book itself was a novel set in the mid-Twenties, which perked my interest right away. Sam Brady had told us only a few days earlier to be on the lookout for nostalgia items. It was well written for an unknown, and the earthy atmosphere of struggling farmers came through well. I settled down for a satisfying afternoon's reading.

"Is Pete Traven around?" Brady's voice interrupted my concentration after the first hour. I'd shifted to an empty cubicle to escape the phone.

"In here, Mr. Brady," I called out.

He poked his head in. "You hiding, Traven?"

"No, Mr. Brady. Just reading slush for Mr. Winter."

He glanced down at the manuscript. "I see. I wanted you to run an errand for me, but I'll get someone else." Running errands for Sam Brady was nothing unusual. He treated us all like office boys.

"I'll be glad to do it," I said.

"No, no, go on with your work." He turned to leave and then asked, "Is it any good?"

"It's the best manuscript I've read in a year."

"Good! You looked as if you were enjoying it."

"It might fit your nostalgia angle. It's about a farm family back in the Twenties. The sons that are supposed to carry on the farm all go off to war and don't return. They get a taste of the city and like it. The guy's quite a writer. It's just a bit slow in spots, but that can be fixed."

Brady nodded. "Maybe we've got something. Take it in to Carlos as soon as you finish."

It was after five when I finished the last page of *Years of Earth,* but I stayed on to write my report while the manuscript was still fresh in my mind. *Sumner Doud Chapin is a writer of the Twenties,* I wrote. *One might almost call him a rural Fitzgerald.*

My report ran three pages. I left it with the manuscript on Winter's secretary's desk, where she'd find it first thing in the morning. Then I went home, satisfied with my job for the first time in a long while.

It was a week before Carlos Winter summoned me to his office. That was something of a treat in itself, since I hadn't been there long enough to be invited to attend the weekly editorial meetings. In fact, the last time I'd sat opposite the cluttered oak desk with its ship model and lighthouse lamp was the day I was hired.

"I read *Years of Earth* last night," he began, busily tamping the tobacco into his pipe. "Your recommendation of it was sound. It's a fine book."

"Then we'll publish it?"

My voice must have betrayed my excitement because he smiled as he answered. "Now, now, we don't rush into these things. The novel is publishable, certainly—but it needs work. Parts of it are dull going, and I think it could use a bit more of the flavor of the period. Tell you what—this Chapin lives right here in Greenwich Village. His phone number's on the manuscript. Ring him up and arrange a meeting here. I'll sit in on it, but I want you to do most of the work with him."

"I've never done any real editing."

"Then it's time you got started, isn't it?"

I left his office walking on a cloud. Maybe I'd make it to being an editor, after all. I sat down in my cubicle and dialed the number on Sumner Chapin's manuscript.

"Hello?" a feminine voice answered after the fourth ring.

"Is this the residence of Sumner Doud Chapin?"

She hesitated, then answered, "Yes."

"Could I speak with him, please?"

"Well—he's not here now."

"When do you expect him?"

"He works during the day."

"Is there anyplace I could reach him?" I asked, and then added, "I'm calling from Ryder & Ryder about a manuscript he submitted."

"Oh! Could I have him call you back? Or could you call here this evening?"

"Yes," I said. "I'll do that."

I hung up the phone, a bit disappointed at not having made immediate contact with Chapin. I should have figured he'd be working. Unpublished authors have to live on something. I picked up his cover letter and read through it again. He didn't say where he worked—only that this was the first work he'd ever tried to publish.

I phoned again from my apartment a little before eight. The same young woman answered the phone, but this time she put Chapin on at once. "My name's Pete Traven," I said. "I'm in the editorial department at Ryder & Ryder."

"Yes." The voice was a low monotone, devoid of expression.

"We like your novel, *Years of Earth,* very much. If you'd consent to a few changes we'd like to publish it."

"No changes," the voice said.

"No changes? I don't think you understand, Mr. Chapin—"

"You wish to publish, send me contract."

"Would it be possible for you to come to our office, Mr. Chapin? We're on Fifth Avenue—"

"Impossible. I work every day."

"On your lunch hour, perhaps?"

"No."

"You don't seem to understand, Mr. Chapin. We want to publish your novel."

"Send me contract," he repeated. I thought I caught the trace of an accent, but I couldn't be certain.

"Our executive editor, Carlos Winter, would like to meet you personally," I said, playing my last card.

"I cannot meet. Send contract."

"I'll have to get back to you, Mr. Chapin," I said. I hung up and sat staring at the telephone, not knowing exactly what to do next. I hated to report failure to Carlos Winter on the first assignment he'd ever given me.

But by morning there seemed no alternative. I repeated the telephone conversation in Winter's office, with Sam Brady and the rest of the editorial board sitting in. It was just before their weekly meeting, at which they planned to discuss Chapin's manuscript.

"The hell with him," was Brady's immediate response. "He needs us more than we need him."

"Now, now," Winter cautioned. "Perhaps we have another Salinger or Pynchon here—a writer who craves anonymity. It might even be a pleasant change from these fellows who show up here once a month to be taken out to lunch."

"You going to go crawling to him?" Brady grumbled.

"There's no crawling involved. After all, we work with most writers by mail. I only suggested a personal meeting because the man lives here in New York."

"Then what do you suggest?"

Winter turned toward me. "Pete, could you go down to Chapin's apartment with the contract? Explain to him that the changes would be minimal—most of them could be done right here in the office and submitted for his approval."

"Sure," I agreed, anxious for a chance to redeem myself in Winter's eyes. "I could do that."

"Good. It's settled, then. We'll have the contract drawn up today."

When I called Chapin's number the following morning, the girl answered again. I announced that I would like to come down that evening if it was convenient. She said it would be. Chapin would be in.

After a quick sandwich at a coffee shop that evening, I took the subway down to West 4th Street, only a few blocks from Chapin's address. The evening was warm and the summer sun hadn't yet set. A few children were playing in the streets. At the corner of Chapin's street an artist was setting up paintings against the wire fence of a parking lot, in anticipation of the tourists who would surely come.

I found the address and climbed to the third-floor apartment. The name CHAPIN was on a card thumbtacked to the door. Beneath it another card read: ROSE. I knocked on the door.

A dark-haired girl in jeans and a sleeveless shirt answered the door. "Who are you?" she said. It had been her voice on the phone.

"Miss Rose? I'm Pete Traven from Ryder & Ryder."

"Come in." She tried a smile but it seemed forced. "Sumner will be with you in a minute."

The apartment was starkly furnished, with a half-finished abstract painting on an easel near the windows. "Is that yours?" I asked. "It's very good."

"Thank you."

Before I could say more, the bedroom door opened and a large bearded man came out. "You the guy from the publisher?" he asked in a deep angry voice. "Let's get on with it. I'm busy."

"You're Sumner Doud Chapin?"

"That's right."

"The author of *Years of Earth?*"

"Yes. Did you bring the contract?"

"How about some beer, Sumner?" the girl asked.

"Not now. How about you?" he asked me.

"No, thanks." I drew the manuscript and contract from my attache case. "There are just a few points we'd like you to think about changing."

"You handle all that. Just gimme the contract." He took the document and scanned it quickly. "Only $1,500 advance?"

"At Ryder & Ryder that's customary for first novels."

"Okay." He flipped through the rest of the pages with what seemed like mild interest. Finally he signed each copy and Miss Rose signed as a witness. I glanced at her signature and saw that her first name was Helen.

"We'll send you a copy of the edited manuscript," I said, "so you can approve the changes we make."

"Sure, sure." He turned to Helen. "I'll have that beer now."

After a few more minutes of conversation, I left the apartment and hurried downstairs. I didn't know what to do. The man who'd signed the contract was not Sumner Doud Chapin. He was not the author of the manuscript in my attache case. He was not the man I'd spoken to on the telephone.

I went no farther than the corner, where I crossed over to the other side and took up a position in the doorway of a record shop. From there I had a good view of the building I'd just left. If I was correct, the man I'd met would not be staying there

long. I couldn't imagine Helen Rose calling him Sumner any
longer than was necessary.

I didn't have long to wait. About fifteen minutes later, the
bearded man came down the front steps and headed west,
toward English Avenue. Though I had no immediate plan, I
followed him.

He walked about a block before disappearing into a dimly lit
bar in the basement of an old brick building. I paused a moment,
thought about it, and followed him inside. There were only
men along the bar, mostly young, and every one of them turned
to watch my entrance. I walked past them and joined the
bearded man at a table toward the rear.

"Hey! What are *you* doin' here?"

"I should ask you the same thing. Your girl wouldn't approve,
would she?"

"She's not my girl."

"And you're not Sumner Doud Chapin, right?"

He stared into his beer and didn't answer.

I slipped a bill from my wallet and slid it across the table.
"Right?"

The gesture seemed to embarrass him but he took the money.
"Ah, she gave me twenty bucks to say I was Chapin and sign
those papers. I don't even know her."

"Where's the real Chapin?"

"Who the hell knows? Who cares?"

I shook my head and left, climbing back up to the twilit
street. Well, I had a contract with a forged signature, and the
real Sumner Doud Chapin was as much a mystery as ever. And
the only way to find the real Chapin was through Helen Rose.

She opened the door, saw my face, and immediately tried to
close the door. But I had my foot in, and I pushed hard. "What
do you want?" she yelled at me.

"The real Sumner Chapin. Ryder & Ryder isn't paying out
fifteen hundred bucks just because you hire some bearded guy
to sign Chapin's name. Where is he?"

"Away."

"Away where? In prison?"

"Just away."

"I spoke to him on the phone, didn't I?"

"Yes."

"Then he can't be very far away."

Her eyes darted to the clock, then back to my face. It was an old banjo clock that hung on the wall near the door, and its hands were just one minute away from nine.

"Are you expecting?" I began, and my question was answered by the sound of a key in the lock.

"Sumner!" she cried. "Run! He's here!"

I yanked open the door in time to catch a glimpse of someone on the stairs. I started after him.

The stairs were in darkness, and I could see nothing below me. He was running, though, and the sound of his footsteps reached me clearly. When I got to the first floor, he was nowhere in sight, but I realized the front door hadn't opened. He had to be hiding somewhere close by.

"Chapin," I said. "I know you're here. I just want to talk with you." I stepped around the back of the staircase and heard a movement in the dark. Then there was a flash of pain as something struck me across the head and I went down hard.

"What happened to you?" Sam Brady asked the next morning when he saw the bandage on my head.

"I walked into a door," I mumbled. I was anxious to see Carlos Winter and didn't want to be sidetracked.

Winter listened to my story in sympathetic silence. When I'd finished he said, "I certainly didn't imagine for a moment I was getting you into anything like that. The man is obviously deranged."

"It would seem so," I agreed, placing a gentle hand to the bump on my head.

"Did you try to see the girl again when you regained consciousness?"

"No. I guess I was a little afraid at that point."

"The contract? The manuscript?"

"Both are safe in my case. He took nothing."

"Odd," Carlos Winter murmured. "The entire business is extremely odd."

"It sure is. What do we do now?"

Winter shrugged. "Return the manuscript, I suppose. We can't publish it without a valid contract."

I went back to my desk deep in gloom.

At lunch, I met Gilda and told her what had happened. "There'll be other manuscripts, Pete. I'm more concerned about your head. Did you report it to the police?"

"No. Nothing was stolen, and my story wouldn't have made much sense. They'd have listed it as an attempted mugging."

"But why should this Chapin attack you? It doesn't seem like the best way to get his novel published."

"There's something strange about the whole business. And it's a lot more than just a shy author I'm dealing with."

I went back to the office still depressed. The pile of unsolicited manuscripts in the day's mail held no promise for me. The chances of finding another novel as good as *Years of Earth* seemed remote.

When my telephone rang, I answered it automatically. For a second I thought it was Sam Brady complaining that I'd taken too long for lunch, but then the voice identified itself.

"This is Sumner Doud Chapin."

"Oh?" I couldn't think of anything else to say.

"I'm sorry about last night."

That angered me. "You sure as hell should be sorry!"

"I think I could discuss the book now with Carlos Winter."

"You do, huh? Well, let me tell you something, Mr. Chapin. I doubt very much whether Ryder & Ryder still wants to publish your book."

"Could I speak to Mr. Winter about it? I can explain my odd behavior."

I had to admit the voice sounded more friendly and rational than the first time we'd talked. There was still an odd muffled accent about it, but the tone was more relaxed. "Winter is out right now. I can speak with him and call you back."

"I'm phoning from work. I'd better call you. In an hour?"

I said that was agreeable and hung up.

When Carlos returned, I asked to see him. I relayed the telephone message and waited for his reaction. When it came, it surprised me. "All right, I suppose I can talk to him. There's no harm in that."

Back at my desk, while I waited for the call, I had a thought. I got out the Manhattan phone book and looked up Chapin's name. He wasn't listed. Then I looked up Helen Rose. She was listed, with the phone number I'd called that first time. As I'd suspected, the apartment was hers. Chapin might well be living there, or he might be living somewhere else.

Exactly on the hour, my telephone rang. But this time it wasn't Chapin. It was Helen Rose. "He couldn't call back," she explained. "He asked me to call for him."

I went to Winter's office and told him. "Put her on," he said, and took the call, motioning me to remain in the office.

I could tell from his end of the conversation that she was arranging a meeting between Winter and Chapin. He tried to schedule it for the office during working hours, but obviously she was resisting. Finally he agreed to come to the apartment that evening. When he hung up, he said to me: "I want you along, Pete. For protection, as much as anything."

I touched my bandaged head. "I'm afraid I'm not very good at that."

"You'll be good enough."

I had a sudden sense of danger, of walking into something I didn't fully understand. But with Carlos Winter I was willing to risk it.

A soft rain had started to fall by the time we reached the Village that evening. It made the narrow streets dimmer, the sidewalks almost deserted, the buildings somehow forbidding. "This is it," I said as the cab dropped us at the corner. "The second doorway."

We climbed the stairs and I knocked at Helen Rose's door. But one thing was different about the door tonight. The two name cards had been removed—the door was bare. "No answer," Winter said, and knocked again.

"Try the door," I suggested.

It swung open at his touch and we entered the apartment.

It was empty.

The banjo clock, the few chairs, the sparse furnishings, the easel, and the painting—all were gone.

"Strange," I said.

"Perhaps not so strange." Though the apartment seemed surely empty, Carlos Winter raised his voice. "We're here. You can come out now, Mr. Chapin."

I saw the bathroom door start to move and a chill ran down my spine. I felt a touch of fear—the fear of the unknown. Then the door swung wide and I saw that it wasn't Sumner Doud Chapin at all. It was Sam Brady from the office.

He was pointing a gun at us.

I glanced at Carlos Winter, but there was no surprise on his face. He nodded slightly, as if the presence of Sam Brady with a gun only confirmed what he'd been thinking all along.

"So it's finally come out in the open, has it, Sam?"

"It's out in the open, Carlos. You knew all along, didn't you? That's why you didn't come here alone."

Winter gestured toward me. "I felt this young man should be present. After all, he's the one who disrupted your scheme in the first place."

"Scheme?" I repeated, uncomprehending. "But where is Chapin?"

"Standing right here in front of us," Winter said. "And looking more like a thug than an author or an editor."

"What about *Years of Earth?*" I wanted to know. "Did he write it? Mr. Winter, that book could win the Pulitzer Prize."

"It already did," Carlos answered drily. "In fact, it won the Pulitzer under its real title more than forty years ago."

"So I wasn't able to fool you," Sam Brady said. He was still pointing the gun at us. "I thought I could."

"I'm sure." Winter carefully shifted position, but didn't try to get any closer to the weapon. "There must be half a dozen Pulitzer novels from the Twenties and early Thirties that are unknown today. Books like *The Able McLaughlins* and *Years of Grace* and *Lamb in His Bosom* are unread and unreprinted. Their authors are all but forgotten. By plagiarizing one of those books—having your girl friend type it up as a new work—you hoped to trick Ryder & Ryder into publishing it."

"Wait a minute," I argued. "That doesn't make any sense, Mr. Winter. A first novelist never gets much of an advance, and surely once the book was published someone would remember it. What could he hope to gain by stealing a novel that had won the Pulitzer Prize?"

Carlos Winter drew a deep breath. "Embarrassment," he answered. "Embarrassment so great it would force my retirement from the company. It would be the greatest literary hoax since the Clifford Irving affair, and I would be the goat because I bought and published the book." There was a faint smile on his lips as he spoke those words. "You wanted my job that badly, did you, Sam?"

"But where did I come in?" I asked.

"Brady knew you'd read the book first when it came in with the slush. He carefully prepared you by saying we were anxious to publish some nostalgia. Isn't that right?"

"Yes, and he checked on me while I was reading it. But you mean it was Mr. Brady's voice on the telephone?"

"It was his voice," Winter confirmed. "If we'd sent the contract by mail, his scheme might even have worked. But when we wanted to meet him in person, they had to bring in a substitute. You didn't fall for that, Pete, and you confronted the Rose woman with the truth. You even chased Sam down the stairs and got hit on the head. Of course I never would have countersigned the contract, anyway—I just wanted to bring them into the open. With your help, I did it."

"But why this meeting?" I asked. "And why an empty apartment?"

"Sam can't get me out through a hoax, so he's going to try murder. Right, Sam? Isn't that why your girl friend cleared out with all her possessions?"

Brady didn't answer.

"But now you'll have to kill two of us. Is my job worth that much, Sam?"

"I can't turn back now," Brady said, but his voice betrayed him. He was close to breaking.

"I left an envelope with my secretary, Sam. The whole story's in it."

The gun suddenly lowered till it pointed at the floor. "All

right, Carlos. You've won. Get yourself a new managing editor."
He turned and walked out of the empty apartment.

For a minute I stood frozen to the spot. "Was he really going to kill us?"

"I don't think so," Carlos Winter said.

I went to the window and looked down at the street. The rain had stopped and the evening's tourists were beginning to arrive. I could see Sam Brady crossing the street and mingling with them. "How did you know about the manuscript?" I asked. "Could you really remember the book from over forty years ago?"

Winter smiled. "I've been in publishing a long time, Pete. I started out reading slush, just like you. I read that very book when it was first submitted to the publisher I worked for all those years ago. I read it and sent it back. Believe me, when you've rejected a Pulitzer Prize winner, you always remember it."

JAMES HOLDING

THE PHOTOGRAPHER AND THE BUTCHER

When Manuel Andradas discovered that all five of The Butcher's victims were uniformly ugly, were wearing topazes when they died, and moved in the same social circles as Floriano Fonseca, he knew that he had found out who The Butcher was. The identity of the madman who had slit the throats of three women and two men in less than a month, and unleashed a reign of terror in Rio, was suddenly made clear to him.

He first felt surprise, then doubt, then a surging satisfaction as the bits of knowledge gleaned from his amateur researches pointed inexorably to the murderer. For he now knew something that neither the police nor The Big Ones, with all their resources, had been able to discover. And to Manuel Andradas, The Photographer, that knowledge was worth 100,000 cruzeiros.

It had begun yesterday in the usual way.

Rodolfo had arranged a meeting at the restaurant called A Cascatinha in the Forest of Tijuca. The restaurant was a mere barbecue stand, a cheap *churrascario*; yet being situated in a quiet wood in the middle of Rio, it was convenient and private. Rodolfo had ordered some barbecued ribs. The Photographer was content with a thimble-sized cup of coffee.

"You have an assignment for me?" he had asked Rodolfo.

Rodolfo chewed noisily; barbecue sauce stained his long rubbery lips. He nodded.

"A nullification?" That was Manuel's own word for his second profession. To him it was more dignified than the word "murder."

Rodolfo wiped his lips. "It is a common criminal this time," he said with a derisive grin, "so you should have no qualms."

"Qualms?" Manuel looked distastefully at his only contact

with The Big Ones. "Have you ever known me to have qualms? I don't let emotion interfere with business."

"If the price is big enough, true."

"Who is this criminal you want me to nullify?"

Rodolfo looked warily about him. He leaned toward Manuel and said softly, "The Butcher."

Manuel stared at him in surprise. "The Butcher? The man in the newspapers who has slit the throats of several Cariocas? And mutilated them afterward?"

"That is the one."

"I thought the police would handle that one."

"They cannot," said Rodolfo, "because they cannot discover his identity. They have tried desperately for three weeks now—ever since his first murder—without success. Hence, they have come to us." Rodolfo was complacent.

"The *police* have become a client of The Big Ones?" Manuel couldn't believe it.

"They have. Because of our wide underworld contacts, as they put it delicately."

Manuel laughed. "There is irony there somewhere, if I may say so."

"Undoubtedly." Rodolfo shrugged narrow shoulders. "But convincing proof, all the same, of the power of The Big Ones in Rio. Even the police must come to us to get their difficult jobs done, you see?"

"This Butcher is one of your own, then? A member of The Big Ones?"

Rodolfo shook his head vigorously. "No, he is not one of ours. God forbid."

"Then who is he?"

"We don't know."

Manuel snorted incredulously. "You mean you have accepted payment from the police to nullify The Butcher for them and you don't even know who he is?"

"No payment has been accepted. We will be paid only if we succeed in identifying and removing The Butcher from circulation. And can prove it, of course, to the satisfaction of the police."

"Then you don't need me yet," Manuel sipped his coffee.

"We need anyone who can help us. The word has gone out to every member of the brotherhood. To identify The Butcher for us—with proof—will be worth fifty thousand cruzeiros to whoever does it. To destroy The Butcher—with proof—will be worth another fifty thousand."

"A hundred thousand," murmured Manuel. Even by his standards, it was very liberal. "The police must have offered The Big Ones at least a quarter of a million, then."

"That is no concern of yours. The public outcry has brought such pressure on the police to capture The Butcher that quick success is essential to them—at any price. So we have informed all our people."

"I am not one of your people."

"True. But we offer you the same proposition."

"Why?" asked Manuel. "I am a nullifier, yes. But not a detective."

Rodolfo put his right hand into his jacket pocket. He said, "I am pointing a revolver at your belly at this moment, Photographer, under the table between us. It is a precaution only, please understand me."

Manuel froze. "A precaution against what?"

"In case you may feel insulted at my next words and attack me."

Manuel was amused. "Say your words, Rodolfo. It is hard to feel insulted when a gun points at one's belly."

"Very well, then. Here is the truth. The Big Ones believe you are better equipped to nullify The Butcher, when identified, than any of our own people. You have proved your ability in that respect to us many times."

"So?" Manuel preened himself a little. "This calls for a gun in my belly?"

"Not that. This. The Big Ones also believe you are better equipped than any of our own people to find out who The Butcher is, as well."

"Why so?"

"Because you yourself are so very much like him," said Rodolfo quietly.

"Oh," growled Manuel, his muddy brown eyes suddenly more

threatening than the gun in Rodolfo's pocket. "You think I am mad, then. For The Butcher is obviously mad. Is that it?"

"Wait! I said you might feel insulted. But let me finish. Remember, please, my gun—and the hundred thousand cruzeiros at stake in this matter. As I say, The Big Ones believe that you and The Butcher are two of a kind. Both—pardon me—heartless, merciless killers who seem to *enjoy* killing. Both, on your records, totally without remorse or pity. Both clever enough to make fools of the police at will. And as for madness, Photographer"—Rodolfo took a tighter grip on his gun—"you must admit that your obsession with money sometimes borders on madness." Rodolfo took a deep breath. "Am I not right?"

Manuel said nothing.

Rodolfo went on, "So it is at least a possibility, we think, that you might quickly discover The Butcher for us. Like calls to like—isn't that what they say? You may even know The Butcher's name at this moment, for all we can tell."

The Photographer grunted contemptuously.

"There, now," Rodolfo said. "I have delivered The Big Ones' message, anyhow." He watched The Photographer with a half smile on his lips, but his hand was still in his jacket pocket. "What do you say?"

Manuel's opaque gaze seemed to look beyond Rodolfo. After the space of five long breaths he shrugged and said, "No man likes to be called mad, Rodolfo. Yet for a hundred thousand cruzeiros I will even suffer that. Yes, tell The Big Ones that I shall do my best for them. To identify, as well as nullify, The Butcher. Meanwhile, I presume I get the usual one-third in advance?"

Rodolfo relaxed. "No, I regret it, you do not. This time our client, the police"—he snickered at the thought—"insists on performance before payment. We must supply them with proof of The Butcher's death before we get a single cruzeiro. So we naturally cannot give you an advance. You understand our position?"

"Not even a few cruzeiros for expenses?"

"Not even that," said Rodolfo, removing his hand from his pocket and picking up a barbecued rib. He knew he was in no danger now. When The Photographer began to haggle over money, which he loved better than anything else in the world, Rodolfo knew he was temporarily harmless.

Floriano Fonseca was an interior decorator—handsome, urbane, prosperous, well connected, and still single. He lived in an exquisitely appointed penthouse apartment behind Copacabana beach, an apartment which he had decorated himself as a showcase for his talents.

Manuel had photographed this apartment two years before, in color, to illustrate an article on the decorator that had appeared in Brazil's foremost society magazine, *Rio Illustrated.* It was therefore with a sense of familiarity that he stepped off the elevator and pushed the buzzer at Fonseca's door.

Manuel's camera case was slung over his left shoulder. A tiny derringer was concealed in the palm of his left hand. And a throwing knife, no larger than a bougainvillea petal and similarly shaped, was lightly bound to his right forearm under his jacket sleeve.

Floriano Fonseca opened the door. He was clad in a loose dressing gown of honey-yellow brocade picked out with gold thread, and was smoking a cigarette in an amber holder. When he recognized Manuel, his face wreathed into a welcoming smile and he exclaimed, "Senhor Andradas! How nice to see you again!" He stepped back invitingly. "What brings you to see me this time, with your clever cameras? Surely not another article for *Rio Illustrated?*"

"No," said Manuel, stepping into the foyer, "this time I have another assignment which I hoped I could discuss with you, since it is closely concerned with esthetics and good taste."

"I am flattered," said Fonseca, his smile widening. "Please come in and let me offer you some port while we have this discussion of yours."

Manuel followed him into the large living room he remembered—a serene haven high above the city and harbor, done in soft shades of yellow, tan, and brown, and breathtakingly beautiful in the mellow glow of the lamps.

Fonseca poured port for them both. Manuel settled himself in a straight chair, placing his camera case on the floor beside him but retaining the derringer in his palm.

He accepted his port with his right hand, and when Fonseca sat on a velvet sofa opposite him and lifted his glass in a polite gesture, Manuel returned the courtesy and sipped appreciatively.

"Now, then," said his host, putting out his cigarette in a marble ashtray, "what do you wish to discuss with me, Senhor Andradas?"

Manuel hesitated briefly. Should one be devious and subtle with a man almost certainly demented? Or was the blunt, straightforward attack to be preferred? The Photographer didn't know. So he settled for the direct approach, since that was more in keeping with his own nature. He said, "I need your advice, Senhor Fonseca, about this fellow the newspapers call The Butcher. Have you read of his crimes?"

"Certainly," said Fonseca easily. "Who in Rio has not?" He patted his lips delicately with a pale-yellow handkerchief that matched his blond hair. "But esthetics and good taste—weren't they the words you used?—what have they go to do with this Butcher person?" Fonseca made a moue of distaste but he seemed amused.

"Everything," Manuel replied. "They have everything to do with The Butcher. For it is my belief that his crimes have been committed in *defense* of esthetics and good taste. Out of a unique and profound devotion to beauty, you might say."

"Indeed?" said Fonseca with obviously deep interest. Had his eyes widened a trifle? Manuel could not be sure. "What a marvelous motive for murder! If I myself were ever to kill anyone, Senhor Andradas, I like to think that it would be for just such a reason as that."

"That was my conclusion also," Manuel said slowly. "That is how I discovered that you are The Butcher."

Manuel dropped his empty glass, as though by accident, so that his throwing hand would be unencumbered. His left hand tensed around the derringer.

Needlessly, it seemed. For Fonseca made no move toward violence. Instead, he threw back his handsome head and laughed. The laughter tinkled in the room with the brittle sharpness of glass fragments shattering on a pavement. Even to

Manuel, it had an eerie sound. Fonseca finally gasped through his laughter, "You're not joking?"

The Photographer shook his head solemnly. "I am not joking, *perdao*. I say that you, Floriano Fonseca, are The Butcher." Encouraged by the ambiguous expression of his host, he added persuasively, "Tell me the truth, Senhor Fonseca. You *are* The Butcher, aren't you?"

It was as easy as that. Fonseca showed his teeth in a delighted grin. "Of course I'm The Butcher," he said matter-of-factly. "How clever of you to ferret me out! The police couldn't do it. I've fooled them from the beginning." He sounded as proud of himself as the last child to be caught in a game of hide-and-seek.

"You fooled us all," said Manuel, trying to keep his breathing steady.

Fonseca sobered. "Except you, it seems, Senhor Andradas."

"Me, too. Until the police offered a large reward for your identity."

"A reward? Really?" He was pleased. "I have reduced the mighty Rio police to that? They *must* be desperate. How much was the reward?" he asked eagerly.

"Two hundred thousand cruzeiros."

Fonseca's face fell. "Minuscule!" he said. "A mere pittance for the identity of a truly outstanding criminal. Don't you think so?"

Manuel smiled for the first time during their interview. "Yes," he agreed, "you are right. You are worth much more than two hundred thousand. I realized that when I discovered who you are."

"Thank you," said Fonseca gravely. "You seem to appreciate my gifts, even if the police do not. How *did* you find me out, may I ask?" The decorator was as humble in his request as a child asking a favor of his father.

"Quite simply," Manuel replied, willing to oblige The Butcher now that his death was inevitable. "I read the newspaper accounts of your murders. From these I gathered some interesting evidence. First, that none of your victims seemed to *expect* death. There was never the smallest sign of a struggle at the murder scene, no expression of fear or terror on the dead faces, so the papers reported. So I assumed, for the sake of a starting point, that they were killed by someone they knew and trusted, someone whom they invited into their homes."

"*Bom.*" Fonseca was nodding. "Very good. I knew them all and have liked them all in years past." He drew a weighted leather blackjack from the pocket of his dressing gown. "That's why I struck them with this before I killed them, to spare them unnecessary pain. Death came as a surprise to them, just as you guessed."

Manuel said, "Then, the mutilations. They were revealing, too. Ears and fingers sliced off and carried away—with the earrings and rings still on them."

"The mutilations and slit throats were punishments, nothing more," said Fonseca in an oddly deprecatory voice, "for unforgivable lapses in good taste."

Manuel nodded as though he sympathized with Fonseca's point-of-view. "Then, Senhor Fonseca, it occurred to me, as I was searching the back issues of *Rio Illustrated* for color pictures of your victims, that all five of these people you punished so severely were quite sensationally ugly. Of the three women, one was grossly fat, with oily, big-pored skin. One was a mulatto whose mixed blood was at war with her dark features. And the third had been lovely at one time, until a liver complaint left her with a complexion like an overripe side of beef."

Fonseca's eyes were shining with admiration. "Go on, go on! What about the two men?"

"They were ugly, too. One was a stooped and swarthy ancient who had dyed his few remaining hairs bright gold in attempting to stay young. The other, a black-haired man-about-town, used women's makeup to try to conceal his yellow smallpox scars."

Fonseca clapped his hands as though at a play. "Good! You are a sharp observer! And what was the lapse in good taste deliberately committed by each of these ugly people? Did you deduce that, too?"

"That was what led me to you. Each of your victims was wearing jewelry on ears or fingers, leading the police to believe The Butcher's mutilations were merely a brutal form of robbery."

Fonseca said with dignity, "That was not my purpose, of

course. I am not a common thief. You guessed that robbery was not my motive? How?"

"I was struck by the *kind* of jewels that adorned the missing ears and fingers. The newspaper reports were quite specific."

The Butcher nodded his approval. "You *are* clever," he said, like a teacher complimenting a promising pupil.

"In every case," Manuel went on, "your ugly victims were wearing topazes. Either topazes alone, or topazes combined with diamonds or emeralds or other gems. But in each case topazes."

"Bravo!" said Fonseca. He laughed happily. "That was the master clue, was it not? The topaz jewelry?"

"It was. But only for me, you understand. For it led me to remember my former meeting with you when I photographed your apartment, and the conversations about the topaz we had while I worked here in this very room. And the article itself, in *Rio Illustrated,* which featured your almost violent preference for yellows, browns, tans, and golds in your decorating work because these were the matchless colors of the topaz. Your favorite gemstone, you told me then, was the topaz. And you told me so with a mystical religious fervor that puzzled me at the time. All this means nothing to the police, of course. They have never seen this room. They have never read the article in *Rio Illustrated.* Above all, they have never heard the strange awed reverence in your voice when you utter the word 'topaz.' "

Floriano Fonseca cut in as though on cue. "Yes, yes, the topaz!" Glaring amber shutters seemed all at once to slide down over his mild brown eyes. He spoke in a singsong monotone. "The topaz! It is beauty incarnate, I tell you. The divine gemstone that sanctifies Brazil, its blessed birthplace! Have you any idea what a topaz really is? It is precious gold, solidified yet translucent; it is liquid sunlight, poured foaming into a chalice of transparent rock; it is the gem fashioned by God especially for the adornment of beautiful people who are worthy to display its purity and magnificence!"

Saliva collected in the corners of his mouth and dribbled down his square chin. "The topaz is not for the ugly, Senhor Andradas. Not for unsightly people with sallow skins. Not for muddy-fleshed, slugbeige, repulsive travesties of human beauty. No, the topaz is for handsome brunettes whose skin is only slightly suntanned. It is for brown-eyed blonds with clear and glowing skin, like mine!"

The decorator cast a fond look at the ring finger of his left hand, which was encircled by a heavy gold band in which a single large honey-yellow topaz was set. "If any but the worthy dare display the topaz on their persons, I tell you, they must be punished—severely punished! As I have already punished five of the arrogant clods!"

Fonseca jumped up and hurried into an adjacent room. In a moment he was back with a small closed tin box which originally had contained pretzels. It did not contain pretzels now. He opened the lid to disclose six human ears and four human fingers, still wearing jewels and already reduced to a pale paste color by the putrefaction of the flesh. Manuel could smell them when Fonseca held the tin box out for inspection.

"I have punished them, you see! Here is proof of their blasphemy!"

Now at last Manuel could believe that this man was mad—an insane, ranting, psychopathic killer. To hear him rave was to hear the horrid vaporings of a deranged brain. To see his grisly trophies was final proof that Floriano Fonseca was indeed The Butcher.

To his surprise, Manuel found Fonseca somehow pathetic in this revealing moment. Yet he did not, for a single instant, forget the blackjack still dangling from Fonseca's hand. He said quietly, "So, then, I have won the police reward, it seems. You admit you are The Butcher."

"Why should I not?" Fonseca reseated himself on the sofa, placing the ghastly pretzel can on an end-table beside him. "I am doing good and noble work."

"Do you know the penalty for murder?"

"Certainly. But I am confident I shall escape it. I am not your ordinary murderer, Senhor Andradas, remember that—not merely a criminal who kills for revenge or profit. Oh, no, I shall not be executed. My uncle has assured me of that."

Manuel sat up in his chair. "Your uncle?"

"My own parents are dead, so I go to my uncle for advice and counsel."

"Who is this uncle?"

"He is my mother's brother, Santos Peixoto, a lawyer. You may have heard of him. He is prominent."

Manuel suddenly caught the faint odor of money in that topaz-colored room. He said, "I know of Senhor Peixoto. He is indeed prominent. You say he has assured you that you will escape the death penalty?"

"Not that *I* shall escape it. The Butcher. For my uncle, of course, does not suspect that it is I who am The Butcher. But when I asked him if a demented man, as The Butcher seems to be"—Fonseca smiled a secret, superior smile—"would be put to death if captured by the police and convicted of the murders, he told me that The Butcher could undoubtedly escape the death sentence by pleading insanity."

Fonseca laughed merrily. "Far from being executed, therefore, I shall be coddled in an asylum somewhere—a private one, I am sure, when my uncle learns who The Butcher is. And thus I shall live in ease and comfort for the last years of my life, as my mother did. *She* went insane after my father died, you know. So you see, everything will work out for the best. When I have finished my work." The expression on Fonseca's face as he mouthed these words could be described only as angelic.

"I am sure your uncle is right," said Manuel, rising, and taking a step toward his host. He put admiration into his voice. "It was a stroke of noble pity to render your victims unconscious before you killed them, Senhor Fonseca," he said. "You punished them properly, yet you spared them, mercifully, the pain of the punishment. May I see the admirable weapon you used so tenderly?" He held out his hand casually.

Fonseca gave him the blackjack. "I have always tried to temper justice with mercy," he simpered.

Manuel hefted the weighted leather in his hand. "It has a certain beauty of its own, has it not?" he murmured. With these words he swung the blackjack against Fonseca's temple.

The Butcher collapsed on the sofa like a bag of wet sand.

It was raining, with a heavy mist curling around the base of Sugar Loaf, when The Photographer left Fonseca's apartment at nine o'clock.

By ten, he was ringing the doorbell of Senhor Santos Peixoto, Floriano Fonseca's uncle. A party was in progress at the prominent attorney's luxurious house near Graves Golf Club. The sounds of gaiety came to Manuel through open windows.

He told the servant who answered his ring that he desired to see Senhor Peixoto on a matter of police business. He was shown into a richly furnished study, and there the lawyer came to him at once, a tall distinguished man with snow-white hair, craggy features, and ruddy coloring.

He invited Manuel to sit. Then, transparently anxious to get back to his guests, he inquired, "Is your matter pressing, Senhor? Can't it wait until tomorrow? I am engaged."

"It could wait until tomorrow," said Manuel, "but I think you would prefer to handle it tonight."

"Very well," said Peixoto. He seated himself. "Tell me."

"I have discovered the identity of The Butcher," Manuel said.

Peixoto's face lost a little of its high color. "What an astonishing announcement!" he exclaimed. "I fail to see why that fact, even if true, should interest me in the slightest." His tone was faintly defensive, Manuel thought. "Who are you, anyway? You told my butler you are from the police. Yet I do not recognize you."

"I said it was a police matter I came to discuss," Manuel replied, "which is an entirely different thing. I am not of the police. I have, however, earned a large reward from them for learning the identity of The Butcher."

"I know of no such reward. And I would know of it if it had been offered."

"It was offered secretly. To The Big Ones. You are familiar with that name?"

Peixoto nodded impatiently. "A collection of racketeers and extortionists, North American style. And you're telling me that the police offered *them* a reward to catch The Butcher? This all sounds extremely unlikely to me, Senhor."

"To me, also. Yet it is the case. And although I'm only an unimportant informer for The Corporation, I've been lucky enough to stumble on the identity of The Butcher. So I have earned the reward."

"Good for you," said Peixoto, striving to maintain a calm bearing. "But why come to me about it?"

"Because The Butcher is your nephew, Floriano Fonseca. Is that reason enough?"

The lawyer said with a faintly hectoring air, "Ridiculous! My nephew? My nephew Floriano is not only extremely talented and successful in his decorating business, but also a gentle, normal, well-adjusted man. If you think Floriano Fonseca is The Butcher, you must be mad!"

"No," said Manuel quietly, "I am not. But Floriano Fonseca is. And I think you suspect it."

Peixoto lit a cigar with a shaking hand. In his preoccupation he did not offer one to Manuel. He said, "Floriano—" and his voice trailed off. Then he rallied. "My nephew is *not* mad!" He said it loudly but without conviction.

"I beg you to be honest with me," said Manuel. "Have you ever noticed signs of dementia in him?"

Peixoto shook his head stubbornly and blew cigar smoke.

"Or noticed his strange obsession with certain colors, materials, decorations?"

No answer.

"Or been exposed, for example, to any of his odd ideas about topazes?"

Silence. The lawyer's countenance, wreathed in cigar smoke, mirrored growing agitation.

"Have you discussed The Butcher with him recently? When *he* brought up the subject? And perhaps showed an unhealthy interest in this psychopathic murderer?"

The lawyer remained silent.

With brutal directness Manuel asked him the key question. "Has anyone else in your family ever gone mad, Senhor Peixoto? A heritage of insanity might go far to explain The Butcher."

Peixoto groaned aloud. "Enough!" His face was now almost as white as his hair. "Enough, Senhor, I beg of you! I *have* sometimes suspected—How did you discover that my nephew—" He could not go on.

The Photographer explained in detail. When he was finished,

the lawyer said in a lost voice, "Poor Floriano!" He gave Manuel a look of despair. "What follows for him now will be, first, arrest, I suppose. Then imprisonment. Public trial. Commitment to an asylum. Pain. Scandal. Disgrace. Sickening publicity. Not only for him, but for me and my family as well." He sighed heavily. The sounds of party gaiety penetrating the study at that moment struck a macabre note.

Out of respect for the man's sorrow, Manuel remained silent. There were tears in Peixoto's eyes.

"However," the lawyer continued, "it is inevitable, I know that. There is no help for it."

Manuel held up a hand. "Wait. You asked me why I came to you. It was to offer you an alternative to all this misery you deplore—before I inform the police of The Butcher's identity."

Peixoto looked at him with distaste. "Blackmail, you mean?" he asked. "You think I shall pay you more to conceal The Butcher's identity than the police will pay you to undercover it? And leave a murderer, a madman, at large?"

"Not at all. You wrong me. Although money *is* a consideration, I will admit."

"Then what is this alternative you offer?"

"I can arrange for your nephew to escape the penalty for his deeds. I can prevent your family and your career from suffering as a result of your close kinship with The Butcher. I can even keep the world in ignorance of the fact that Floriano Fonseca, your nephew, is a raving homicidal maniac."

Peixoto stared at him as though Manuel, too, were mad. "How can you do that, in the name of God?" he demanded.

"By making Floriano Fonseca his own last victim."

"What?"

"By killing him in the exact manner in which he has been killing his victims. You see? He will never be exposed as The Butcher. Because to all appearances he will have been *killed* by The Butcher."

Peixoto's expression was a grotesque compound of horror, shock, and shrewd assessment. At length he whispered hoarsely, "You would slit his throat and mutilate him? Floriano?" His cigar had dropped to the floor unnoticed and was scorching the carpet.

"That would be more merciful than what the police have in store for him, don't you agree?"

"But to kill him deliberately—"

"Why not? He is a menace to society."

"You would do this yourself?"

"Certainly not. I can arrange it, though. The Big Ones handle such chores discreetly—if the fee is big enough."

At Santos Peixoto's next words, Manuel released an inaudible sigh of triumph. For the lawyer asked, "How much?"

Manuel replied, "I would have to forego my share of the police reward if we agree on my alternative. As would my employers, The Big Ones. And the police reward for identifying The Butcher is a hundred thousand cruzeiros, Senhor Peixoto," Manuel lied with an expressionless face. "So I fear I could not arrange the alternative for less than two hundred thousand."

The magnitude of that sum did not seem to shake the lawyer unduly. Perhaps I should have asked for more, thought Manuel. Then the lawyer said, "That is a great deal of money to pay an unknown man for a service which may never be performed."

"Think of it this way," The Photographer suggested. "Two hundred thousand is cheap compared with the cost of a private asylum for your nephew after his conviction. As for the service, I guarantee it. And only after you *know*—through the newspapers—that it has been performed properly do you need to pay for it. Satisfactory, Senhor?" Manuel arose from his chair and looked at Peixoto calmly.

The older man rose, too, and absent-mindedly stepped on the butt of his cigar, still smoldering on the carpet. "That will be satisfactory," he said evenly. "To whom shall I send my check? What is your name?"

Manuel hesitated. "You don't need to know my name. And no checks, if you please. Meet me at the main gate of the Botanical Gardens next Tuesday at three-fifteen in the morning and bring the cash with you. By then I promise you that you will be sure I have earned it."

"Very well." The lawyer saw Manuel to the door. "And thank you, whoever you are. We thank you from the heart. All of us. *Muito obrigado.*"

The Photographer waved a hand. *"Ate logo.* Until Tuesday."

A telephone call brought Rodolfo to the *churrascario* in Tijuca Forest at noon two days later. Manuel was already seated at an out-of-the-way table, awaiting him.

Rodolfo sat down, a puzzled expression on his face. "What do you want?" he asked Manuel abruptly.

"Merely to report that your mission is accomplished."

"What!" Rodolfo was angry. "What do you mean by that?"

"Only that I have discovered the identity of The Butcher and removed him from circulation. Wasn't that our phrase? So I want my money. A hundred thousand cruzeiros."

Rodolfo gave a barking laugh. Then he drew the morning paper from his pocket and thrust it before Manuel. "Look at that!" he said indignantly. Large black type said: THE BUTCHER STRIKES AGAIN—SOCIETY DECORATOR IS LATEST VICTIM. "Does *this* look as though The Butcher is dead, Photographer?"

Manuel smiled. "No. It does not. Nevertheless, he is." It amused him to irritate Rodolfo.

"When did you kill him, then? This morning? The decorator's mutilated body was found last night." Rodolfo spat into the dust beside his foot to express his monumental contempt for such a pitiful deception.

"The Butcher was as good as dead the moment you told me two days ago that his death was worth a hundred thousand cruzeiros to me," Manuel said. "Save for one last fling, of course." He nodded at the newspaper headline. "There is his last fling. The decorator, Floriano Fonseca."

"You are talking drivel, Photographer! What is this 'last fling' nonsense?"

"Consider," said Manuel patiently. "If I had not permitted The Butcher to butcher one last victim—*after* the police offered you the reward—you would never have got the reward. If no further murder had occurred, the police would have claimed that The Butcher had merely regained his sanity, perhaps, and ceased killing people, no thanks to The Big Ones. You see? Especially without a shred of proof that you'd ever made an effort to catch The Butcher. No, one last example of his work was needed, Rodolfo. That's why I waited for him to strike again. So that The Big Ones could get their reward. And I could get mine."

"Now it is riddles you talk in," said Rodolfo. However, he was listening very carefully to Manuel's riddles.

Manuel pulled two black-and-white photographic prints from an inner pocket. He offered one of them to Rodolfo. "Look," he said, "this picture I took of Floriano Fonseca after he was dead but before The Butcher mutilated him. His throat is not cut, his ring finger is not missing, you see?"

"Yes," said Rodolfo hoarsely. "And the other picture?"

"A picture I took of the victim *after* his mutilation." Manuel presented the second print. "His throat is now cut, you will notice, his ring finger hacked off." Manuel's gaze held steady on Rodolfo. "Does this constitute adequate proof that I knew who The Butcher was?"

Rodolfo tore his eyes away from the prints. "No! No, it does not! I know you too well, Photographer. To win a hundred thousand cruzeiros you would murder a dozen people, including the Devil himself, and mutilate them afterward—as you certainly did to this poor decorator!"

Manuel nodded placidly. "I feared you might reason like that," he said. "Will this, then, perhaps convince you?" He fumbled under the table and brought forth from the camera case in his lap the severed ring finger of Floriano Fonseca, the honey-yellow topaz ring still on the blood-smeared flesh.

Rodolfo recoiled. "Is it Fonseca's finger?" he asked.

"It is. You can identify it there in my picture by the particular topaz ring."

"It still proves nothing. It is part of the same trickery as these ridiculous pictures—" Suddenly Rodolfo's eyes widened. "Unless—" he stammered. "Unless—" and he looked at Manuel as people must have once looked at Medusa.

The Photographer nodded encouragingly. "Unless what, Rodolfo?"

Rodolfo whispered, "Is that what you're trying to tell me? That *you* are The Butcher?"

"Your Big Ones almost guessed it," beamed Manuel. "The Butcher and The Photographer, they said, were two of a kind.

We are not *two* of a kind, The Butcher and I. We are *one* of a kind. The same man, in fact."

Rodolfo took a gulp of his coffee and scalded his mouth. He did not notice the pain. "You are The Butcher," he said, almost as though talking to himself. He nodded vigorously. "By God, you *are!* That's what you meant jut now when you said The Butcher was as good as dead the moment I offered you a hundred thousand for his life! And that's why you accepted the commission without prior payment, a thing you had never done before. You knew you could earn the reward by merely ceasing your murders and mutilations."

"Now, at last, you are beginning to see the truth. That occurred to me at once," said Manuel in a modest tone.

"And yet you murdered another man, this decorator. Why?"

"I told you why. But also to get the proof. These photographs, and this finger, this topaz ring, easily identifiable. You yourself said the police must have proof."

Rodolfo fell silent after one explosive word. His eyes clung to the gruesome relic before him. His thoughts were in confusion. At last he said firmly, "The pictures and Fonseca's finger convince *me*, Photographer, because I know you. They are adequate proof for The Big Ones, therefore, that you have earned your reward. My own endorsement would make that proof stick. But, alas, that is not enough. We must have proof that will convince the *police* that The Butcher is dead. Otherwise you will not get your money, nor will we get ours. This finger and these photos could still be merely a trick, the police will argue, perpetrated by the unscrupulous Big Ones to win the reward under false pretenses. Just as I thought *you* were attempting to deceive *us*, don't you see?"

"I see," said Manuel comfortably. "I have already thought of that possibility—that the police might accuse The Big Ones of double-dealing. So I have brought you further proof which, properly used, should persuade even the police. And make them pay over the reward eagerly—yours and mine—to The Big Ones."

"Good," said Rodolfo. He glanced at Manuel out of the corners of his eyes as though reluctant to gaze directly on a madman. "What is this ultimate proof? Tell me."

Manuel nodded and brought out of his camera case underneath the table the small pretzel tin box that had belonged to Floriano Fonseca. He opened the lid with a casual gesture and offered the open tin for Rodolfo's inspection. "Do not get too close," he advised, "it smells of mortality. But it is absolute proof that you have found The Butcher."

Rodolfo, after one swift glance, withdrew as far as his chair would let him. "For God's sake!" he whispered. "What—what—?"

"Do my trophies sicken you?" The Photographer was smiling. "To me they are beautiful. Yet I perceive I must give them up if I am to earn my hundred thousand cruzeiros."

"Are these—are these the ears and fingers of The Butcher's victims?" Rodolfo inquired, recovering somewhat. "Truly the genuine mutilations?"

"Guaranteed," said Manuel. "Each can be identified by members of the victims' families, by friends, or whoever. For each, as you see, still wears its topaz earring or finger ring, described in detail to the police at the time of each murder, and in the newspapers also. These relics could only have been possessed by The Butcher. Agreed?"

"Photographer," said Rodolfo, pushing back his chair and putting his hand into the pocket where he carried his gun, *"you* nauseate me." He swallowed. "Not the relics."

"A pity," said Manuel, signaling to a distant waiter for another *cafezinho.* "Do I sicken you so much that you will fail to claim our money from the police?"

"This is still no proof that The Butcher is *dead,"* Rodolfo said. "Can't you understand that?" He frowned. "The police can say we recovered these relics, as you call them, without actually destroying The Butcher. It is all well and good for you to say you will cease your murders and mutilations, but to get our money we must show the police proof that The Butcher is *dead."*

"I understand that," said Manuel. "A moment ago I said these ears and severed fingers could provide that proof 'if properly used.' You remember?"

Rodolfo nodded.

"So nothing could be simpler. Show the police a dead body. Any body. Tell them this dead man, whoever he may be, was

The Butcher. And allow the police themselves to search his lodgings. They will find these two photographs of Senhor Fonseca, carefully placed in the pretzel tin with the ears and fingers of The Butcher's victims. Plant the pretzel tin, if I may suggest a refinement, in some odd place that will convince the police that The Butcher was indeed mad, a ghoul."

Manuel laughed. "Perhaps in the kitchen cupboard beside innocent tins of flour, sugar, or sweet cakes. Then, I promise you, you will have no trouble collecting our reward money. The police will be convinced. The newspapers will be convinced. Rio's citizenry will be convinced. And The Butcher will never be heard from again. I solemnly promise you that. Thus, the problem is resolved neatly and permanently. And I shall be a hundred thousand cruzeiros richer."

This was a long speech for The Photographer. Rodolfo listened to it in silence, occasionally nodding in agreement. When Manuel concluded, he said, "A very practical suggestion, Photographer." He paused, then asked sardonically, "And where do you suggest we find a dead body to show to the police?"

Manuel smiled. "I will be glad to supply you with one," he said promptly, "at my usual rates."

ELIZABETH BOWEN
TELLING

Terry looked up. Josephine lay still. He felt shy, embarrassed all
at once at the idea of anyone coming here.

His brain was ticking like a watch: he looked up warily.

But there was nobody. Outside the high cold walls, beyond
the ragged arch of the chapel, delphiniums crowded in sunshine—straining with brightness, burning each other up—bars
of color that, while one watched them, seemed to turn round
slowly. But there was nobody there.

The chapel was a ruin, roofed by daylight, floored with lawn.
In a corner the gardener had tipped out a heap of cut grass
from the lawn mower. The daisy-heads wilted, the cut grass
smelled stuffy and sweet. Everywhere, cigarette ends, scattered
last night by the couples who'd come here to kiss. First the
dance, thought Terry, then this: the servants will never get
straight. The cigarette ends would lie here for days, till after the
rain, and go brown and rotten.

Then he noticed a charred cigarette stump in Josephine's
hair. The short wavy ends in her hair fell back—still in lines of
perfection—from temples and ears. By her left ear, the charred
stump showed through. For that, he thought, she would never
forgive him—fastidiousness was her sensibility, always tor-
mented. ("If you must know," she had said, "well, you've got
dirty nails, haven't you? Look.") He bent down and picked the
cigarette end out of her hair. The fine ends fluttered under his
breath. As he threw it away, he noticed his nails were still dirty.
His hands were stained now—naturally—but his nails must
have been dirty before. Had she noticed again?

But had she, perhaps, for a moment been proud of him? Had
she had just a glimpse of the something he'd told her about? He
wanted to ask her: "What do you feel now? Do you believe in
me?" He felt sure of himself, certain, justified. For nobody else
would have done this to Josephine.

Himself they had all—always—deprecated. He felt a shrug in this attitude, a thinly disguised kind of hopelessness. "Oh, *Terry,*" they'd say, and break off. He was no good: he couldn't even put up a tennis net. He never could see properly (whisky helped that at first, then it didn't). His hands wouldn't serve him—things he wanted them to hold slipped away from them. He was no good. The younger ones laughed at him till they, like their brothers and sisters, grew up and were schooled into bitter kindliness. Again and again he'd been sent back to them all (and repetition never blunted the bleak edge of these homecomings) from school, from Cambridge, now—a month ago—from Ceylon. "The bad penny!" he would remark, very jocular. "If I could just think things out," he had tried to explain to his father, "I know I could do *something.*" And once he had said to Josephine: "I know there is *something* I could do."

"And they will know now," he said, looking round (for the strange new pleasure of clearly and sharply seeing) from Josephine's face to her stained breast (her heavy blue beads slipped sideways over her shoulder and coiled on the grass—touched, surrounded now, by the unhesitant trickle); from her breast up the walls to their top, the top crumbling, the tufts of valerian trembling against the sky. It was as though the dark-paned window through which he had so long looked out swung open suddenly. He saw (clear as the walls and the sky) right and wrong, the old childish fixities. I have done right, he thought (but his brain was still ticking). *She ought not to live* with this flaw in her. Josephine ought not to live, she had to die.

All night he had thought this out, walking alone in the shrubberies, helped by the dance music, dodging the others. His mind had been kindled, like a dull coal suddenly blazing. He was not angry. He kept saying: "I must not be angry, I must be just." He was in a blaze (it seemed to himself) of justice. (The couples who came face to face with him down the paths started away. Someone spoke of a minor prophet, someone breathed "Caliban.") He kept saying: "That flaw right through her. She damages truth. She kills souls; she's killed mine." So he had come to see, before morning, his purpose as God's purpose.

She had laughed, you see. She had been pretending. There

was a tender and lovely thing he kept hidden, a spark in him; she had touched it and made it the whole of him, made him a man. She had said: "Yes, I believe, Terry. I understand." That had been everything. He had thrown off the old dull armor. Then she had laughed.

Then he had understood what other men meant when they spoke of her. He had seen at once what he was meant to do. "This is for me," he said. "No one but I can do it."

All night he walked alone in the garden. Then he watched the French windows and when they were open again stepped in quickly and took down the African knife from the dining-room wall. He had always wanted that African knife. Then he had gone upstairs (remembering, on the way, all those meetings with Josephine, shaving, tying of ties), shaved, changed into flannels, put the knife into his blazer pocket (it was too long, more than an inch of the blade came out through the inside lining), and sat on his windowsill, watching sunlight brighten and broaden from a yellow agitation behind the trees into swathes of color across the lawn. He did not think; his mind was like somebody singing, somebody able to sing.

And, later, it had all been arranged for him. He fell into, had his part in, some kind of design. Josephine had come down in her pleated white dress (when she turned, the pleats whirled). He had said, "Come out!" and she gave that light, distant look, still with a laugh at the back of it, and said, "Oh—right-o, little Terry." And she had walked down the garden ahead of him, past the delphiniums into the chapel. Here, to make justice perfect, he had asked once more: *"Do* you believe in me?" She had laughed again.

She lay now with her feet and body in sunshine (the sun was just high enough), her arms flung out wide at him, desperately, generously; her head rolling sideways in shadow on the enclosed, silky grass. On her face was a dazzled look (eyes half-closed, lips drawn back), an expression almost of diffidence. Her blood quietly soaked through the grass, sinking through to the roots of it.

He crouched a moment and, touching her eyelids—still warm—tried to shut her eyes. But he didn't know how. Then he got up and wiped the blade of the African knife with a handful of grass, then scattered the handful away. All the time he was listening. He felt shy, embarrassed, at the thought of anyone finding him here. And his brain, like a watch, was still ticking.

On his way to the house, he stooped down and dipped his hands in the garden tank. Someone might scream—he felt embarrassed at the thought of somebody screaming. The red curled away through the water and melted.

He stepped in at the morning-room window. The blinds were half-down—he stooped his head to avoid them—and the room was in dark-yellow shadow. (He had waited here for them all to come in that afternoon he arrived back from Ceylon.) The smell of pinks came in, and two or three bluebottles bumbled and bounced on the ceiling. His sister Catherine sat with her back to him, playing the piano. (He had heard her as he came up the path.) He looked at her pink pointed elbows—she was playing a waltz and the music ran through them in jerky ripples.

"Hullo, Catherine," he said, and listened in admiration. So his new voice sounded like this!

"Hullo, Terry." She went on playing, worrying at the waltz. She had an anxious, methodical mind, but loved gossip. He thought: Here is a bit of gossip for you—Josephine's down in the chapel, covered with blood. Her dress is spoiled, but I think her blue beads are all right. I should go and see.

"I say, Catherine—"

"Oh, Terry, they're putting the furniture back in the drawing room. I wish you'd go and help. It's getting those big sofas through the door—and the cabinets." She laughed: "I'm just putting the music away," and went on playing.

He thought: I don't suppose she'll be able to marry now. No one will marry her. He said: "Do you know where Josephine is?"

"No, I haven't"—rum-tum-tum, rum-tum-*tum*—"the slightest idea. Go on, Terry."

He thought: She never liked Josephine. He went away.

He stood in the door of the drawing room. His brothers and Beatrice were punting the big armchairs, chintz-skirted, over the waxy floor. They all felt him there, and for as long as possible didn't notice him. Charles—fifteen, with his pink-scrubbed ears—considered a moment, shoving against the cabinet, thought it was rather a shame, turned with an honest, kindly look of distaste, and said, "Come on, Terry."

He can't go back to school now, thought Terry, can't go anywhere, really: I wonder what they'll do with him, send him out to the Colonies? Charles had perfect manners: square, bluff, perfect. He never thought about anybody, never felt anybody—just classified them. Josephine was "a girl staying in the house," "a friend of my sisters'." He would think at once (in a moment when Terry had told him), A girl staying in the house! It's well, I mean, if it hadn't been *a girl staying in the house*—

Terry went over to him and they pushed the cabinet. But Terry pushed too hard, crooked, and the farther corner grated against the wall. "Oh, I say, we've scratched the paint," said Charles. And indeed they had. On the wall was a grey scar. Charles went scarlet: he hated things to be done badly. It was nice of him to say: *"We've* scratched the paint." Would he say later: "We've killed Josephine?"

"I think perhaps you'd better help with the sofas," said Charles civilly.

"You should have seen the blood on my hands just now," said Terry.

"Bad luck!" Charles said quickly and went away.

Beatrice, Josephine's friend, stood with her elbows on the mantelpiece looking at herself in the glass above. Last night a man had kissed her down in the chapel (Terry had watched them). This must seem to Beatrice to be written all over her face—what else could she be looking at? Her eyes in the looking-glass were dark, beseeching. As she saw Terry come up behind her, she frowned angrily and turned away.

"I say, Beatrice, do you know what happened down in the chapel?"

"Does it interest you?" She stooped quickly and pulled down the sofa loose-cover where it had "runkled" up, as though the sofa legs were indecent.

"Beatrice, what would you do if I'd killed somebody?"

"Laugh," said she wearily.

"If I'd killed a woman?"

"Laugh harder. Do you know any women?"

She was a lovely thing, really; he'd ruined her, he supposed. He was all in a panic. "Beatrice, swear you won't go down to the chapel." Because she might. Well—of course she'd go down: as soon as she was alone and they didn't notice, she'd go creeping down to the chapel. It had been *that* kind of kiss.

"Oh, be quiet about that old chapel!" Already he'd spoiled last night for her. How she hated him! He looked around for John. John had gone away.

On the hall table were two letters, come by the second post, waiting for Josephine. No one, he thought, ought to read them— he must protect Josephine. He took them up and slipped them into his pocket.

"I say," called John from the stairs, "what are you doing with those letters?"

John didn't mean to be sharp, but they had taken each other unawares. They none of them wanted Terry to *feel* how his movements were sneaking movements. When they met him creeping about by himself, they would either ignore him or say, "Where are *you* off to?" jocosely and loudly, to hide the fact of their knowing he didn't know. John was Terry's elder brother, but hated to sound like one. But he couldn't help knowing those letters were for Josephine, and Josephine was "staying in the house."

"I'm taking them for Josephine."

"Know where she is?"

"Yes, in the chapel. I killed here there."

But John—hating this business with Terry—had turned away. Terry followed him upstairs, repeating: "I killed her there, John. John, I've killed Josephine in the chapel."

John hurried ahead, not listening, not turning round. "Oh, yes," he called over his shoulder. "Right you are, take them along." He disappeared into the smoking room, banging the door. It had been John's idea that, from the day after Terry's return from Ceylon, the sideboard cupboard in the dining room should be kept locked up. But he'd never said anything—oh, no. What interest could the sideboard cupboard have for a brother of his? he pretended to think.

Oh, yes, thought Terry. You're a fine man with a muscular back, but you couldn't have done what I've done. There had, after all, been something in Terry. He *was* abler than John (they'd soon know). John had never kissed Josephine.

Terry sat down on the stairs, saying: "Josephine, Josephine!" He sat there gripping a baluster, shaking with exaltation.

The study-door panels had always looked solemn—they bulged with solemnity. Terry had to get past to his father. He chose the top left-hand panel to tap on. The patient voice said: "Come in!"

Here and now, thought Terry.

He had a great audience. He looked at the books round the dark walls and thought of all those thinkers. His father jerked up a contracted, strained look at him. Terry felt that hacking with his news into this silence was like hacking into a great, grave chest. The desk was a havoc of papers.

"What exactly do you want?" said his father, rubbing the edge of the desk.

Terry stood there silently: everything ebbed. "I want," he said at last, "to talk about my future."

His father sighed and slid a hand forward, rumpling the papers. "I suppose, Terry," he said as gently as possible, "you really *have* got a future?" Then he reproached himself. "Well, sit down a minute. I'll just—"

Terry sat down. The clock on the mantelpiece echoed the ticking in his brain.

He waited.

"Yes?" said his father.

"Well, there must be some kind of future for me, mustn't there?"

"Oh, certainly."

"Look here, Father, I have something to show you. That African knife—"

"What about it?"

"That African knife. It's here. I've got it to show you."

"What about it?"

"Just wait a minute." He put a hand into either pocket. His father waited.

"It *was* here—I did have it. I brought it to show you. I must have it somewhere—that African knife."

But it wasn't there, he hadn't got it—he had lost it, left it, dropped it, on the grass, by the tank, anywhere. He remembered wiping it.—Then?

Now his support was all gone. He was terrified now; he wept.

"I've lost it," he quavered, "I've lost it."

"What do you mean?" said his father, sitting blankly there like a tombstone, with his white, square face. "What are you trying to tell me?"

"Nothing," said Terry, weeping and shaking. "Nothing, nothing, nothing."

JAMES M. ULLMAN

THE BOY WONDER OF REAL ESTATE

The little man with the intense blue eyes and the unruly shock of white hair said, "I gotta meet a guy in Denver for lunch, see. And another guy in L.A. tonight. So I can't talk long."

Michael Dane James, business- and industrial-espionage consultant, nodded. It was 9:24 A.M. in New York City. But time and distance meant nothing when you merged the efficiencies of jet air transport with the energies of Fritz Molloy, the Boy Wonder of Finance.

The Boy Wonder, of course, was no longer a boy. Like several other Boy Wonders James had encountered, this one was at least 35, probably older. But he still looked youthful enough to warrant the title in cafe-gossip columns, where many rumors of his active night life and of his fabulous real-estate ventures were chronicled almost daily.

The Boy Wonder was reclining on a chair in James's office, puffing strenuously on a cigar. He drawled, "I want you, Mr. James, to insure secrecy on a project that is so secret I haven't decided myself yet what it's going to be."

"I see," James said dubiously.

"And when I decide on the project," Molloy went on. "I'm *still* not going to tell you what it is. But I don't want any leaks."

James, a broad-shouldered, crewcut man of medium height, thoughtfully rubbed his pug nose. In his late forties, he wore hornrimmed glasses and dressed carefully to hide a growing hint of a potbelly.

"I think," James said slowly, "you'd better explain that."

Molloy glanced at his wristwatch. "I can't just now—I'm overdue at the airport. But you talk to my father-in-law, Ephraim Holt. He's also my bankroll—my biggest investor. He didn't like the idea of me hiring you, but he'll cooperate. Two more things:

259

first, I don't want anyone else in my employ to know I hired you, and, second, my father-in-law will give you a list of some people who work with me. Those are the *only* people connected with my organization you're to investigate. Nobody else, without my express permission. Understand?"

"Well," James said, "I'm a trifle confused, but I'll try to have some kind of report for you in a week. Where will you be?"

"I'm not sure. Miami, Dallas, or New Orleans," Molloy said, rising and starting for the door. "My father-in-law will tell you that, too. But wherever I am, have someone deliver the report to me in person."

A black-haired, black-eyed boy in blue jeans and a T-shirt perched on Ephraim Holt's desk. The boy grinned as James entered, jumped down, and said, "I'm Bobby Molloy. I was ten years old last week. Grandpa is gonna take me to lunch! And then to the ballgame!"

Holt, a bald, portly man, fondly patted the boy's head. "This man and I have business, Bobby. Go find Miss Nelson. She'll take you to the Stock Exchange, where you can watch all the crazy men yelling. I'll meet you in the gallery."

The boy ran off.

"Molloy's son?" James asked, shaking hands and then sitting down. "I'd never have guessed it."

"There's no resemblance," Holt said, "because he's adopted. I bet that's a side to Fritz Molloy you didn't know from reading the gossip columns. Fritz is a softie. He spoils Bobby something awful—almost as much as Fritz's father did, when he was alive. But I don't mind. I spoil Bobby something awful, too. You know grandpas."

"Somehow," James confessed, "I never thought of Molloy as a loving father."

"After you work for him a while," Holt said, "you will. Everyone does. He's got a big heart and is always making large donations that never get into the newspapers. He collects unfortunates and gives them sinecures—Eddie Green, a press agent who used to be a drunk; Burleigh Harris, a broken-down pilot who used to barnstorm with Fritz's dad; Mrs. Elliott, a private secretary who was caught embezzling in order to pay doctors' bills for a sick child; and plenty of others. That's why I was opposed to Fritz's hiring you. Innocent people might get hurt. Moreover, I don't cotton to the idea of one man in business spying on another."

"It's true," James grinned, "that I *did* engage in a little spying once, when I had a few pressing bills of my own to meet. But since becoming a member of several PTAs and the patron saint of a troop of cub scouts, I've confined my activities to helping men who are being spied *on.*"

"Even if you are a rascal," Holt grinned back, "at least you're personable. And I confess, I'm an old admirer of yours. I saw you in the Polo Grounds more than a quarter of a century ago, when you made that long run against the Giants. But Fritz engaged you, you know, only because he hasn't yet learned to control his emotions. He lost his temper."

"What about?"

"In nineteen fifty-seven he put together his first big New York deal. He had organized a motel chain and owned other interests, but no single enterprise as big as the one in 'fifty-seven. He assembled all the parcels on a block in Manhattan, tore the old structures down, and put up a hotel. That went fine. Then he assembled another block for a second hotel. No trouble there, either. But last February he tried to assemble a third block for the Molloy Building and he ran into trouble."

"I thought," James said, "he was going to break ground for the Molloy Building next month."

"Oh, we're going through with it. But we were delayed. And counting the mortgage interest, it may cost us up to a million more than we figured on. All because a chiseler found out about the project before we assembled the land. There are men like that, you know—legal wolves. They move in ahead of you, option as much land that you need as they can, and then try to sell it to you at an enormous profit to themselves. Do you know anything about land assemblage?"

"Not much."

"Well, when Fritz or any other big developer plans a multi-million-dollar project in a city like New York, he assembles the land with the utmost secrecy—he has to. He lets as few people as possible know what's going on, and even they might know only part of the deal. In our business, in fact, land assemblers are sometimes called 'land detectives.' Purchase money is deposited in different banks under different names, and purchases are made under dummy names. Fritz hires separate attorneys and title searchers for each purchase so that nobody can deduce what he's doing by studying the activities of his personal lawyers, or even analyzing the land-transfer records. The project itself, and all the parcels, are given code names.

"When we're actually assembling, the assemblers aren't even allowed to talk to their families—they work day and night. Secrecy and speed are essential, because once the rumor gets out that a developer is buying, every property owner involved will ask three or four times what his property is worth. What's more, the same thing happens to property all around where the developer is buying. A lot of people try to cash in, and get hurt when it turns out the developer doesn't want their land at all. Only the informed chiseler knows how to profit."

"I gather, then," James said, "that Molloy wants me to review his land-assemblage security procedures so that no chiselers can find out about his next big Manhattan development, whatever it's going to be. And particularly, to investigate the Molloy Building assemblage—to determine what went wrong."

"Exactly." Holt pulled an envelope from a drawer and handed it to James. "All the Molloy Building assemblers are listed inside, as well as an account of the security procedures we followed. The assemblers are practically the same team that handled the hotel projects. I've known those men for years and, if you ask me, I think you're wasting your time."

"I'd better check them out anyway. Who's the chiseler who held you up on the Molloy Building?"

"Jason Gard, an old pro. He'd never bothered us before. But the Molloy Building—he knew all about it, every detail."

"I'll look into Mr. Gard, too." James opened the envelope. Briefly he studied its contents.

"There aren't many names on the list," he observed, "and they're all real-estate men, brokers, or people working out of Molloy's New York office. What about the woman who was an embezzler? The old-time pilot? The publicity man, and the other people who follow Molloy around the country?"

"Fritz," Holt said, "never discusses an assemblage except with the men directly concerned. The people around him might guess something big is brewing, but Fritz is more security-conscious than anyone else. The publicity man isn't told any details until the assemblage is completed and Fritz is ready to give the story to the papers. And the others—they read about it in the papers."

Holt paused. Then he added, "Mr. James, although Fritz hired you, I'll warn you now. I'm still going to try to persuade him to forget his anger at what happened on the Molloy Building. If I succeed, don't be surprised if he fires you."

James blinked.

"He's angry," Holt went on, "not because someone chiseled him. Actually, the chiseler cost me more money than he cost Fritz, because I financed the assemblage. He's angry because the Molloy Building was conceived by his father and his father died before the assemblage could be finished."

"Then it's not just a business matter."

"Fritz," Holt said, "has had a lot of sorrow in his life. He doesn't know yet how to live with it. First, his wife—my youngest daughter. A few months after the marriage we learned she had an incurable disease. She did live five years, and the devotion between them was pathetic. Having little Bobby around gave her an extra year or two of life, I'm sure. She'd wanted a child so badly, and Fritz's father went out West and arranged for the adoption of an infant.

"And two years ago Fritz's father suffered his first heart attack. Before that he'd been a dynamic man, a big spender who loved life. He was an ace in the First World War—he barnstormed almost up to the second one. He managed an aircraft plant and then went into real estate, making a lot of money in Oklahoma and Texas. But the heart attack left him weak and frightened. Fritz turned the company plane over to him so that Burleigh could fly the old man wherever he wanted to go. Old Molloy still loved flying as much as he loved Bobby and his own son's success. But toward the end—Old Molloy died in April—he didn't even want to see Fritz. He was a proud man, perhaps ashamed of his infirmity. He traveled right up until a week before he passed away at his home in Tulsa. And that's why Fritz was furious—because he wasn't able to go to his father with a big clipping from a newspaper and say, 'Here it is, Pop. *Your* building. We're ready to put it up.' "

James pushed his chair back. Genially he said, "Well, I appreciate your frankness, Mr. Holt—about not liking my job. But I may need your help anyhow."

"Oh, I'll play square with you," Holt smiled. "Any information you want on Fritz's operations, I'll get it. If it's just routine office records, call my secretary direct. She's usually a sphinx, but I told her you're an efficiency expert."

"Where will I find Molloy a week from now? He asked me to send him my first report by agent."

"I'll see him for lunch in Chicago on Thursday. He'll know then and I'll let you know when I get back."

"Tell Molloy," James said, "that my agent's name is Ted Bennett. For security's sake, Ted will introduce himself as a potential real-estate investor from Spokane."

"Is Fritz to pretend Bennett is an old friend?"

"No. Bennett will manage an introduction. He's very good at insinuating himself into other people's company."

Ted Bennett, whose bank balance totaled less than $4,000, kept a straight face with difficulty as he said, "Burleigh, I might invest a few hundred thousand with this boss of yours. But no more."

"Don't apologize," Burleigh Harris replied. "With the mortgage leverage, it can do the work of a million." Harris—big, heavy-set, and balding—downed the rest of his drink, swiveled on his stool, and nodded to a group of people who had just entered the lounge, one of the most fashionable in Miami Beach. "There he is now. Greatest guy in the world. He put me in the air again, and flying is what I live for. Come on, I'll introduce you."

Bennett, a tall thin man in his late thirties, rose. Harris had already stepped away from the bar, so Bennett paid for the drinks. As a matter of fact, he had paid for the two previous drinks, and also for Burleigh's dinner. It was obvious that Burleigh was an expert at ducking checks. Michael Dane James wasn't going to like this expense account one bit.

Bennett followed Harris through the dim room. The Boy

Wonder, surrounded by his retinue, was slipping into a reserved booth. The retinue consisted of four other men and two women. One of the women was middle-aged, obviously the wife of one of the men. The other woman, an attractive, long-legged brunette in her late twenties and a few inches taller than the Boy Wonder, clutched Molloy's arm and snuggled against him. Harris pulled Bennett forward. "Fritz, this is Ted Bennett, from Spokane. He owns factories or something out there. Ted, this is Fritz Molloy."

Molloy looked up, cigar jutting from his mouth, and nodded. "Sit down and join us, Mr. Bennett. My associates—Mr. Green, Mr. Steelman, Mr. Earle, Mr. Rogers. And Mrs. Rogers and Miss Rogers."

Bennett shook hands and murmured the proper nothings. Miss Rogers winked and smiled at him, an action Mrs. Rogers noted with disapproval.

"You have business interests in Florida?" Molloy asked.

"Just looking around," Bennett said. "I was thinking of diversifying into real estate."

Green, a short pudgy man of about forty, howled. "Oh, brother! You came to the right guy!"

"Don't let Eddie scare you," Earle smiled. "Fritz isn't after your bankroll. He's already loaded with investors."

"Another never hurts," Molloy said cordially. A waiter came and took orders. Eddie Green, the ex-alcoholic, asked for tea.

"Seriously," Bennett said, "I *would* like to learn more about real estate."

"Then stick around," Molloy grinned. "That's all we talk." A band began to play and Molloy turned to Miss Rogers. "C'mon," he invited. "Let's twist."

Molloy and Miss Rogers climbed out of the booth, Mr. and Mrs. Rogers joined them, Mr. Rogers somewhat reluctantly.

"Bennett here," Harris said to the table in general, "touted me on some real wild stocks. I think I'll keep my serious money with my poor man's wildcat Oklahoma oil wells. But maybe he can make all you rich guys richer."

Bennett laughed. "If I could really beat the market, I wouldn't be thinking of buying land."

"You could do worse," Green said, nodding at Molloy, now

barely visible behind Miss Rogers, "than to tie up with him. He's a straight shooter. Just because I did him a favor once, he hired me as his public-relations man. Not that he needs one. He's sharp and tough, but he's more than fair with his investors."

"He likes to live it up, doesn't he," Bennett observed. "Not that I object."

"I'll tell you something," Steelman said. "No matter how late he stays out, he's dressed and through with breakfast by eight and going over a balance sheet. He's no loafer. And, confidentially, in his business you make as many deals in a nightclub as you do in an office."

"Sandra Rogers," Earle said, "sure has her eye on Fritz. She and her parents have been following him around for nearly a year."

"Ah, he'll never marry her," Eddie Green said. "He loved his wife too much. And don't think Sandra doesn't know it. She'd be glad to settle for any decent-looking guy with some dough." Green turned to Bennett. "Say, buddy," he ventured, "you married?"

"No," Bennett said.

"Then," Green advised happily, "watch out."

Bennett stepped into a Miami Beach pay booth at two in the morning. He broke open a roll of quarters, set them on the shelf, and placed a long-distance call to a suburban residence near New York City.

After four rings a man answered with a sleepy "Yah?"

"Hello—Mickey?"

"Lucky for you it is," James replied. "Anyone else might resent being hauled out of the sack before dawn. But me, I love it."

"Sorry," Bennett said. "I thought you ought to know. I've made personal contact with the Boy Wonder, but there were too many people around and I couldn't give him the report or discuss it with him. He invited me to fly to Dallas with his party a few hours from now for the grand opening of one of his motels, where supposedly he's going to tell me all about real-estate investments."

"How'd you meet him?"

"His pilot is a penny-ante plunger in the stock market. He was hanging around a brokerage office in the hotel lobby, so I struck up an acquaintance by giving him a few tips. The pilot steered me to Molloy."

James groaned. "Good grief. When those stocks go down, you'll be exposed. Who's with the Boy Wonder?"

"Eddie Green, his press agent; a lawyer named Steelman; an architect named Earle; and a substantial investor named Rogers. Rogers' wife and daughter are along. The daughter wants to marry the Boy Wonder. But late in the evening the Boy Wonder got to talking business with Steelman and Sandra started cuddling up to me. I told her some O.S.S. stories from the war."

"That's just great. You study our report again on the flight down there?"

"I did. And it still doesn't add up."

"This whole affair," James said, "is a puzzle. The men on the list of names the Boy Wonder provided are all clean—every single one of them. And except for a few minor flaws, his security procedures are excellent. But the Boy Wonder's father-in-law, who is also his biggest investor, doesn't want anyone nosing around the organization for one minute. And the Boy Wonder himself won't let us investigate anyone whose name *isn't* on his list—which includes everyone who travels around with him. The pilot, the press agent, the in-and-out investors like Rogers—the works. The only people on his list are New York real-estate men. It's as though the Boy Wonder was working against us, too. Screwy is the name for it, Ted. What did you learn about Molloy and his friends during your carousing?"

"To begin with," Bennett said, "Molloy is a softie."

"I've heard that before. But go on."

"He really is," Bennett persisted. "He pays his pilot ten grand a year, lets him eat and drink on the cuff all over the country, and gives him the run of Old Molloy's home in Tulsa whenever he isn't flying the plane—which is often, because Molloy prefers to go by jet. All because the pilot was once a barnstormer with Old Man Molloy, and the Old Man found Burleigh on the skids, dealing poker in El Paso in nineteen fifty-three. The old man persuaded Fritz to buy a company plane and make Burleigh the company pilot. Fritz pays his broken-down press agent fifteen

grand to follow him around and arrange interviews with reporters who want to interview him anyway. The press agent used
to be a real-estate reporter for a New York paper. He once held
back an exclusive story that would have hurt Molloy, when
Molloy was just starting. Molloy found Green in a drunk tank
years later, sobered him up, and put him on his payroll. And he
pays his secretary, the ex-embezzler, twelve grand so she can
take care of the sick child. The secretary isn't even with him
this trip. Molloy gave her a month off to visit the kid."

"Where'd you learn all those salaries?"

"From Miss Rogers. While we were twisting."

"Who's that girl's father?"

"A retired securities underwriter. Sandra says he's worth a
couple of million dollars."

"Now I understand," James said, "what you see in the girl.
Ted, I know Molloy didn't authorize it, but you start looking
into all those people as discreetly as you can. There's something
going on—some important fact being concealed from us."
James paused. "It occurs to me," he went on slowly, "that
Molloy was probably jumping all over the country last February,
just before the assemblage, just as he is now. Why don't I have
an agent get copies of this chiseler Gard's home and office
telephone bills for February? We'll see if Gard placed any long-
distance calls to cities where Molloy happened to be at the
same time. I'll compile an itinerary from his office files and mail
copies of the stuff to you. Show it to Molloy and see if it rings a
bell with him. I'll send it special delivery to the motel in Dallas.
You should get it the day after tomorrow. So long."

Bennett strolled out of the motel and down to the pool, the
latest report from Michael Dane James folded in his breast
pocket. Sandra Rogers, clad in a red bikini, cavorted in the
pool's shallow end, giggling and kicking her feet while holding
a rubber float. The Boy Wonder sat at a pink table shaded by a
pink umbrella. The Lieutenant-Governor, the Mayor, and two
Texas oil tycoons shared the table with him. Other freeloading
guests from Texas social and business circles, not to mention
opinion-molders from the Texas press, ringed the pool at other

pink tables. The motel was still closed to the public. Molloy was giving this all-day party for the publicity and good will.

Bennett glanced briefly at Molloy, who nodded. Then he sat at a table occupied solely by Mr. Earle, the architect. A girl wearing an abbreviated cowboy costume and carrying a tray laden with drinks walked by and Bennett grabbed a martini. He sipped.

"There's Sandra," he remarked, putting the glass down. "But where are our other friends from Miami?"

"Burleigh flew Steelman to Oklahoma City this morning—to settle some zoning problem," Earle said. "Then Burleigh said he was going to Tulsa, but I think he's really going to Little Rock. He's got a woman there. Eddie Green's in town, trying to line up some television interviews for Molloy. And the Rogers drove into town, too. Mrs. Rogers wants to shop at a certain department store."

"I think Eddie was right about Sandra," Bennett said. "Molloy doesn't really go for her much—except as a sort of shield maybe, to keep serious golddiggers away."

"You've hit it," Earle said. "How about you? When you and Fritz had that long talk yesterday, did Fritz sell you on a deal?"

"Not yet."

Molloy rose a few minutes later. He glanced at Bennett and then started toward the motel.

"Excuse me," Bennett said, getting up and following Molloy, who walked around the building and waited for Bennett.

"Well?" Molloy asked.

Bennett pulled the report from his pocket and handed it over. "Here it is. But Mickey already checked it against your itinerary. I'm afraid Gard didn't call a single city that you visited during February."

Molloy began unfolding the report. "Another bust, then. Like your first report. The one telling me that although three of my assemblers drink too much, and two of them bet on horses, and one maintains a mistress a block from his office, they're all honest men. And that my office manager consults a psychiatrist. And that my phones aren't tapped and my office isn't bugged. When will you tell me something I *don't* know?" He started to read.

"Gard did do a lot of out-of-town calling," Bennett observed. "Six to Chicago, five each to Boston and Philadelphia, three to Providence, and plenty of singles. As well as three collect ones—from San Diego, Las Vegas, and Tucson."

"Um," Molloy said. He went on reading. He shook his head. Then he folded the paper—rather abruptly, it seemed to Bennett—and handed it back. "Junk, Mr. Bennett. That's all you guys give me. I've just made a decision. You're fired. And so is Mr. James. Tell him I'll pay the full fee I promised, plus all expenses, and to forget everything."

Molloy turned and strode back toward the motel.

Bennett watched him go. He studied the report again. He then started toward the motel himself. As he reached the driveway, he saw the Boy Wonder pull away from the curb in a white Thunderbird. Bennett broke into a trot, heading for a line of parked rental cars. But two husky young men—the motel's recreation director and the lifeguard—intercepted him.

"Mr. Molloy," the lifeguard enunciated carefully, one hand on Bennett's shoulder and another on his arm, "said he wanted you to go on enjoying yourself here today. Everything is still on the house."

Bennett considered a maneuver that would have resulted in the lifeguard's suffering a broken arm. Then he realized he'd never catch up with the Boy Wonder anyway. He watched glumly as the Thunderbird turned toward Dallas.

The lifeguard took his hands away. Bennett shrugged and walked on into the motel. He handed a girl at the desk a five-dollar bill. "Change, please."

As the girl began counting silver, a bellboy said to an assistant manager, "You know what? Mr. Molloy just took that Colt .45 off the wall display and drove off with it. We got another one?"

"Was it a real gun," the assistant manager asked, "or one of those dummies?"

"A real one," the boy said.

Bennett pocketed his change and walked outside to a public telephone booth. He called Michael Dane James.

"This is Ted," he announced when the connection was completed. "We've been fired."

"Something tells me," James began, "you didn't handle the Boy Wonder properly. Me, I get along with him fine."

"There's more to it than that. This is serious, Mickey. He fired us after taking one look at Gard's February telephone bills. He said he'd pay full fee and all expenses. Then he walked into the hotel, lifted a gun off the wall, got into an automobile, and drove away. And he detailed two guys to keep me from following him."

"In that event," James said thoughtfully, "Molloy probably fired us because, as far as he's concerned, we solved his case. And now he's angry enough to shoot someone. I think we better go on working for Molloy. Got any ideas?"

"There's one key man," Bennett said, "who's *not* on Molloy's list—and who isn't working for Molloy, either."

"You're so right. I'll check him out and call back in thirty minutes. You in a booth?"

Bennett read off the telephone number.

"Stand by."

Bennett stepped out of the booth and glanced toward the pool. Sandra Rogers, standing poolside, spotted him and waved. She filched two martinis from a passing cowgirl and walked toward Bennett.

At least, Bennett reflected, the wait would be a pleasant one.

The cab pulled into the driveway and stopped behind the white Thunderbird. Bennett handed the driver some bills.

"Here," he said. "But hold it just a minute."

Bennett walked to the porch and rang the bell. A few moments later the Boy Wonder himself opened the door.

Molloy's eyes were ringed. His face was haggard, and he was in shirt sleeves, with his tie pulled loose. But he managed a weak smile.

"You guys," he said slowly. "I guess you *do* know your business. I thought I fired you, but if you got this far, you're hired again."

Bennett turned to the cab driver. "Okay, buddy, shove off."

Bennett followed Molloy into the house. The Colt Peacemaker lay on a coffee table, unloaded. Six cartridges lay beside it.

"Don't worry," Molloy said. "I've changed my mind. You don't have to prevent a murder. I've done a lot of thinking and I've decided not to shoot anyone."

"He's not in Tulsa, you know," Bennett said. "We checked some airports. Burleigh Harris flew your plane to Little Rock."

Molloy nodded. "I don't care about Burleigh any more." He sat down in a big chair and lit a cigar. "I'm sorry, by the way, that I asked those two fellas to stop you back in Dallas. They didn't hurt you, did they?"

Bennett flopped onto a sofa. "Not a bit."

The Boy Wonder looked up, eyes suddenly alert and cautious. "Exactly how much have you and Mr. James figured out? Since I just put you back on my payroll, I'd appreciate a complete answer."

"Well," Bennett said, "when you hightailed it from the motel after looking at the list of Gard's long-distance calls, I telephoned Mickey. We'd already deduced there was one person— *not* on the list you provided—who knew all about the Molloy Building and who wasn't in your employ. That would be your late father."

"That's right," the Boy Wonder said. "It was Dad's building and I told him everything."

"So Mickey checked your father's movements during February—a simple matter since all it involved was a check on the movements of the company plane. And sure enough, the company plane was in San Diego, Las Vegas, and Tucson on the same days that Gard got the long-distance collect calls. It was almost as obvious to us then as it was to you."

"But why did you peg Burleigh Harris? I never told Harris about my real-estate assemblages. And my father was a real-estate man himself—he knew the need for secrecy."

"Quite a few things. Minor item: Harris is tight-fisted. I can personally attest to that. I bought him a dinner and three drinks. Your late father was known to be a big spender. The three calls to Gard were collect. Another minor item: Harris invests in oil wells, an expensive hobby for a man on his salary who also keeps a woman in Little Rock. But biggest item of all: it hardly seemed likely that your father would betray you willingly. Someone must have blackmailed him into doing it. By arranging a few facts, we came up with a theory that would most certainly give Burleigh Harris a hold over your father."

"Go on," the Boy Wonder said.

"The theory involves Bobby," Bennett said, avoiding Molloy's eyes and staring at the table. "And it explains why your father-in-law—and even you, to an extent—had reservations about hiring James in the first place. Why you didn't want the people around you—that would include Harris—investigated. Bobby's adoption was supposedly arranged ten years ago by your father, who went 'out West' and came back with an infant. But what legitimate adoption agency would put a child out under those circumstances—to a mother afflicted with an incurable illness?

"More than likely, your father obtained the child through some illegal source. Arranged, let's say for the sake of theory, by his old flying buddy, Burleigh Harris, who was on the skids in El Paso in those days, and on the fringe of an underworld crowd that would know how to manage those things, since dealing poker is hardly legal there. Because what happened to Burleigh Harris in nineteen fifty-three, less than a year after the adoption? His old pal Molloy 'persuaded' his son—you—to buy a company plane and make Harris the pilot. Was it really persuasion? Or was Harris being rewarded for his role in the illegal adoption by being given the flying job he yearned for, and with it a sinecure for the rest of his life?

"Let's suppose the latter was the case. And that, as the years pass, Harris gradually gets over his gratitude for these favors and takes his new life for granted. Sure, he lives off the cuff wherever he goes. But he's forever rubbing elbows with people who have *real* money. He develops a greed for some himself. Who wouldn't? He's been hanging around you long enough to know that if a man can get inside information on a major land assemblage and act quickly, he can reap big profits. And long enough to hear of professional chiselers like Gard.

"Everyone in your organization knew you were going to put up a Molloy Building somewhere in New York. So Harris goes to Gard and they make some kind of deal. And then Harris puts the screws to your father, who by now loves Bobby only as much as a grandfather can, which is all the way. And whose confidence and strength have been shattered by illness. He forces your father to tell him about the Molloy Building assemblage on the threat of exposing the illegal adoption, perhaps even having Bobby taken away."

The Boy Wonder said, "That's the way it must have been. You're right about Bobby and the adoption. My dad, my father-in-law, Burleigh, and me—we were the only ones who knew. And that's the *only* threat that would have caused my father to tell Harris about the assemblage. Harris would never try to brace *me* with a blackmail scheme, or my father-in-law, either. We'd jail him and fight tooth and nail to keep Bobby. But my father—sick and scared, alone with Burleigh all the time—he'd give in."

"It also explains," Bennett said, "why your father didn't want to see you those last few weeks. He was afraid to face you. Undoubtedly, Harris threatened to expose the adoption anyway if your father ever told you the truth."

"And that," Molloy said, "is why I was sore enough to want to kill Harris after I saw Gard's list of calls. I knew where my father had been in February because I talked to him on the telephone every day. It was easy to guess the rest. I wanted to murder Burleigh Harris for what he did to my dad. And when I got there, to my dad's old house, I went through Burleigh's things upstairs and found an envelope in a drawer. From Gard's real-estate firm. The kind of envelope that checks come in. If Harris had walked in at that moment, I *would* have killed him."

Molloy stubbed his cigar out.

"I guess it's time," he went on slowly, "for the Boy Wonder to grow up. If I'd killed Burleigh Harris in a rage, I'd not only have ruined myself, I'd have pulled all the others down with me. Bobby, my father-in-law, the investors, the people who work for me—I'd have hurt everyone just because I personally hate a guy. I'll go on hating him. But I won't kill him. I'll just fire him and try to forget him."

He rose and went to a mirror, straightening his tie. "Get on the phone," he ordered. "Find a locksmith and order new locks for all the doors so Burleigh Harris can't get back in here. Then call the Little Rock airport and tell 'em to impound my airplane."

Bennett started for the telephone. "Are we going back to New York City?"

"Not immediately," the Boy Wonder said, reaching for another cigar. "While you're telephoning down here, I'm going upstairs and call my father-in-law and have him get some lawyers to setting that adoption business straight, publicity or no publicity. Then I'm going to dump all Burleigh's junk on the sidewalk. Then you and me, we'll drive to the airport and catch a plane to Phoenix. I may buy twenty percent of a desert out there. The Rogers will be waiting. Sandra likes you and it will be a relief getting someone to take her out nights so I can get some more sleep. If your Mr. James complains about the extra time you're taking, tell him I've given you a special new assignment for which he'll get his usual fee. Tell him the assignment is so confidential you can't even discuss it."

CORNELL WOOLRICH

JUST ENOUGH TO COVER A THUMBNAIL

I knew what it was like to wake up after being drunk the night before—everyone does, I guess—but that wasn't in it compared to what this was like. This had all the same symptoms of the other, and then some new ones of its own. My mouth felt just as dry and my head felt just as heavy and my stomach felt just as bad. And then, in addition, my eyes wouldn't focus right—everything I looked at seemed to have rings around it. And my hands were cold and clammy, and my teeth were on edge, as though I'd been chewing lemons.

But worse than anything else was the mental conditioning it had left behind. I was afraid—I was as afraid as a seven-year-old kid in an old dark house. And when you're afraid at one o'clock on a blazing bright afternoon, mister, you're afraid.

And at that, the aftereffects were nothing compared to what the symptoms had been like the night before, while I was still under it. I grabbed my eyes tight to shut out the recollection, and if I'd had an extra pair of hands I'd have stopped up my ears at the same time. But the images were inside, in my memory, where I couldn't get at them. Blurred, but there.

He was a fellow I'd known slightly—so slightly that I didn't even know his last name, just Joe. Joe said, "Aw, you need cheering up. Come on with me—I'm going somewhere that'll cheer you up." And then, probably an hour later, the parting hand on my shoulder. "Take it easy, be seeing you around, I'm blowing now."

I remember saying, "Well, just a sec, I'll go with you. I came here with you, after all."

I remember the knowing wink he'd given me. "Naw, you better hang around a while—I'm taking that girl in green home. You know how it is, two's company." Exit Joe, whoever he was.

So I stayed on there, like a fool, in a strange place with strangers.

The rest of it came crowding back on me, all mixed up like what they call montage in the movies. The man with the white scar on his jaw. I kept seeing that white scar, hearing disconnected things he'd said.

"Just enough to cover your thumbnail. Always remember that and you can never go wrong—just enough to cover your thumbnail. Then you bring it up the long way, like you were going to wipe your nose."

"Nice-looking place, isn't it? You want it, you can have it. Listen, I'd give away anything tonight. Make yourself at home, I'll be right back."

"What'd you do, have some trouble in here while I was gone? Look at that, look at the blood all over your shirt!"

"No, you can't get out that way! That's a dead window, you fool! It's nailed down fast, it's painted over! They built a house right up next to this and the brickwork sealed it up!"

"Aw, that's nothing—you want that to go away? I'll show you how to make that go away. Now hold steady. Just enough to cover your thumbnail. Watch and see how that makes it go away."

"Don't get excited, I'm not going anywhere. Just wait here for me, I'll be right back—"

And then it got worse and worse. At the end it was almost a frenzy, a delirium. Of fear and flight and pursuit. The very walls had seemed to whisper. "Look at him, sitting there waiting! They'll get him, they'll get him!"

They seemed to sing, too. Music kept oozing out of them. Ghost music. I could hear it so plain, I could even recognize some of the tunes—I could even remember them now! "Alice Blue Gown," "Out on a Limb," "Oh, Johnny," and "The Woodpecker Song."

And then the climactic madness, the straining, tugging trip to the closet along the floor, the frantic closing of the door, the locking of it on what it held, the secreting of the key in my pocket, the piling up and barricading of it with a table, a chair, anything and everything I could lay my hands on. Then flight through the labyrinth of the city, hiding in doorways, sidling around corners, hugging the shadows. Flight that went on forever. From—where? To—where? Then kindly oblivion at last.

All of it a junk dream, of course. But needles of cold sweat came out on my forehead even now, it was still so vivid, so haunting.

I didn't know what to do for a hangover of this kind. But I figured water, lots of cold water inside and out, was good for almost anything under the sun, so it ought to be good for this, too. At least it couldn't hurt it any.

I staggered rubber-kneed into the bathroom and filled the washbowl, sloshed my eyes and ducked my whole face in it, and slapped it across the back of my neck. After I got through, I felt a little better. Not a lot, though.

I went back to my room and combed my soaked hair and started to get dressed. If I'd had a job I would have been out of it by now, I'd overslept so long. But I didn't have one, so it didn't make any difference.

Just after I'd got my shoes and trousers on, Mildred knocked on the door. She'd heard me moving around, I guess. I told her to come in. I was ashamed to look at her, but only I knew the real reason why—she didn't. She looked in and said, "Hello, Tommy. I guess you had a drink or two too many last night."

I thought, I only wish it was that. I was sorrier than ever the thing had happened.

"I understand how it is—it helps to take your mind off your troubles once in a while." Then she rested a hand on my arm for a minute to show she didn't mean it for criticism. "But don't do too much of it, Tommy. It doesn't make it any easier to get a job. I'll fix you some coffee, that'll brace you up."

She was my older sister. She was swell. I was not only living with her, but she'd even been keeping me in pocket money since I'd been out of a job. She went out again, and I went ahead with my dressing.

First I was going to put on a clean shirt, but I thought I better not be too extravagant while I was out of work, so I decided I'd stick to the old one a day more. The way it was folded or rumpled must have hidden the stain. I only saw it after I had the shirt on and tucked into my belt, and was buttoning it down in front of the glass. It was brown, a sort of splashy stain in front.

I stared at it in a sort of paralyzed horror. I don't think I moved for about two minutes. Finally I touched it, and where it was brown it was stiff. Good and stiff. "What'd you do, have some trouble in here? Look at the blood all over your shirt!" It rang in my ears again. So that part of it was real at least, it hadn't been just a snow mirage.

All right, it was real. But it had to come from somewhere. It didn't just appear from nowhere, like a miraculous stigmata. I pulled the shirt up out of my belt, and hoisted my undershirt and scanned my body all around the lower ribs. There wasn't a scratch on me anywhere. I looked higher up, on my chest. I even rolled up my sleeves and looked at both arms. There wasn't a nick anywhere on my skin. And whatever had bled that much must have been a pretty good-sized gash.

So it had come from someone else.

I finished dressing. I kept talking it into myself that it meant nothing. Somebody you were with cut himself on something. You don't remember it, that's all. How'd it get on me, then? Well, maybe you were lurching around. You leaned up against someone, or someone did against you. You better quit thinking about it, you want to hang onto your self-control, don't you? Then quit thinking about it.

Which was a lot easier said than done, but I finished up my dressing, put on my coat. The last stage of all was what everyone's last stage usually is. To put my change, matches, keys, whatever loose accessories there were back into my pockets where they belonged.

Even in last night's befogged condition, habit had been strong enough to assert itself. The stuff was dumped out on top of the bureau, the way I always found it every morning. I started collecting it item by item, dropping each category into the particular pocket where it belonged. Three nickels and a dime. (I'd started out with thirty-five cents last night, I distinctly remembered that, so I must have spent a dime sometime during the course of the night, though I couldn't remember doing it.) A withered pack that contained a last cigarette—broken into two sections from pocket pressure. I put one into my mouth, threw the other away. And last of all, my keys—one that Mildred and Denny had given me to the apartment here, and the other a little jigger that opened my valise.

This time I didn't stand staring in frozen horror. The half cigarette fell from my relaxed lips to the floor and I lurched forward, steadying myself by gripping the front edge of the bureau. I stayed that way, sort of hunched over, goggling down at it.

There was one key too many there.

There were three keys staring me in the face, and up to last night I had only two. There was a strange key there mixed up with my own two, a key that didn't belong to me, a key I'd never seen before. Or at least only in a—snow flurry.

It wasn't one of these modern brass safety-lock keys, it was an old-fashioned iron thing, dun-colored, with an elongated stem and two teeth at the end of it shaped like a buzzsaw. The kind of a key used in an old-fashioned house, that has old-fashioned rooms with old-fashioned doors.

It was an interior key. I mean, you could see it wasn't for an outside door, a street door, but for some door on the inside of a house—a room door or a closet door.

That gave me a shot in the arm, that last word. I straightened up from my leapfrog position and did things around the room fast. First, I gave it the benefit of the doubt—although I knew as sure as I was born I'd never seen it before in my life, that it didn't belong around here. I went over to my own closet with it, to try it on that. It wouldn't go in, because the closet's own key was sticking out, blocking the keyhole. Then I went to my room door, but there wasn't anywhere on that to try it. It had no lock at all—it closed on a little horizontal bolt run into a hole. There wasn't anyplace else for me to match it up with.

It came from somewhere outside. Somewhere in a dope dream.

Then the panic came on again from last night, only now it was worse, because this was broad daylight and now I was in my right senses. I swung out my valise and kicked the lid up. I didn't have much to pack, so it didn't take long. But everything there was to pack I packed.

I'd gotten halfway down the short little hall with my bag in my hand when Mildred looked out and saw me. She gave a little moaning protest and ran after me. "No, Tommy—what're you doing?"

"I've got to go. Don't stop me, I've got to get out of here."

"No, Tommy—what is it?" She took the valise and set it down. I let her. I didn't want to go myself, that was why I stood there undecided. But yet I knew I couldn't stay—not now.

"I've got to, I tell you."

"But why? Where? You have no money." She took me by the arm and coaxed me into the kitchen. "At least drink a cup of coffee before you go, don't leave like this—I just made it fresh."

It was just a stall, she only wanted to gain time. I knew that, but I slumped into a chair anyway, staring down at the floor.

I heard her slip out to the phone when she thought I wasn't noticing, but I didn't try to interfere. I heard her saying in a guarded voice, "Denny, will you come home right away? See if you can get relieved from duty and come home right away—it's very important."

He was a detective. In one way, I wanted to talk to him very much. In another way, I didn't.

I guess I must have wanted to more than I didn't want to, because I was still sitting there when he showed up. He got there quickly, not more than ten or fifteen minutes after she'd phoned him.

He came striding in, looking worried, and tossed his hat onto the seat of a chair. He was a slow-moving, even-tempered guy as a rule, misleadingly genial on the surface, hard as nails inside. Mildred and I, of course, only saw him when he was off duty, we hadn't had much chance to see the latter quality in him. I only suspected it was there, without being sure. I had him sized up for the kind of man who would give you a break if you deserved one, or crack down on you like granite if you didn't.

He spoke to her first. "What's the matter?"

"It's Tommy," she said. "He packed his things and wants to leave. You better talk to him, Denny. I'll leave the two of you alone if you want me to."

"No," he said. "Come on, we'll go in your room, Tom." He

brought the bag in with him and closed the door after the two of us.

He sat down on the edge of my bed and looked at me, waiting. I stayed up. Nothing came, so finally he said patiently, "What's the matter, kid?"

I gave it to him right away. What was the good of paying it out slow? I said, "I think I killed a man last night."

He churned that around in his mind, without taking his eyes off me. Then he said, "You *think?* Listen, that's a thing you usually can be pretty sure of. You either did or didn't. Now which is it?"

"I was kind of fuzzy at the time."

"Well, who was he?"

"I don't know."

"Where did it happen?"

"I don't know that, either."

"You don't know *where or who or if—*" He gave me a half-rebuking, half-whimsical look. "I don't get it, Tom. You don't look yourself today. You look a little funny. And you sure sound a whole lot that way."

"Yes, that's it," I said bitterly. "I better start from the beginning and try to tell you as much as I can."

"You better," he agreed drily.

"There won't be very much. At eleven-thirty last night I was standing on a corner waiting to cross with the light when a guy I knew by sight happened along. I don't know who he is or where I knew him from—just that I'd seen his face someplace before—fellow named Joe. I told him I was down in the dumps and he said I needed cheering up. He asked me to come with him and like a sap I went.

"I can remember that much clearly. He took me to some apartment where there was a big party going on. I don't even know just where *that* was—down on one of the side streets off Kent Boulevard somewhere. I didn't know anyone there, and I can't remember that he bothered introducing me. They seemed a sort of free-and-easy bunch, no questions asked. It was almost like open house—new people kept showing up all the time and old ones leaving. He left, and when I tried to go with him he gave me some excuse and shoved off alone, leaving me there.

"From then on it gets all woozy. It was late and there were fewer people. The lights got dimmer and the place got quieter, people talking in whispers. There was some guy with a white scar along his jaw. I remember he seemed to be watching me for a long while. Finally he came over and offered me something—"

This was the part that was hardest to tell him, but I had to if he was to make any sense out of it.

"Offered you what?" he said.

"I thought it was a headache powder first. He told me to stick my thumb out, and he sifted it onto the nail from a little paper."

He just asked the question with his eyes this time. I looked down at the floor. "Coke," I murmured half audibly.

"You damn fool," he said. "You ought to have your head examined!"

"I was feeling low. I thought if it would make me forget my troubles for even half an hour it would be worth it. You don't know what it's like to be without a job for months, to mooch off your relatives—"

"Well, get drunk then, if you have to," he said scathingly. "Get so pie-eyed you fall down flat on your face—I'll pay your liquor bill myself! But if you ever go for that stuff again, I'll break your jaw!"

Again was good. There didn't have to be a next time—all the damage had been done the first time. I finished up the rest of it. It came easier once I'd gotten past that point. "—And I piled stuff up in front of it, and I beat it out of there. I don't remember getting home."

He hinged his palm up and down on his knee once or twice before he said anything. "Well, whaddaya expect if you go monkeying around like that," he growled finally. "To dream of honeysuckle and roses? It's a wonder you didn't imagine you stuffed six dead guys into a closet instead of just one."

"But do you think *that's* what got me rattled?" I held my head tight between both hands. "I found the key on the bureau when I got dressed a little while ago! And his blood on my shirt!" I hauled it out and waved it at him. I pitched the key down and it went *clunk!* and bounced once and then lay still.

His face showed me I'd made my point. He picked the key up

first and turned it over and over. You could tell he wasn't so much looking at it as thinking the whole thing over. Then he traced a fingernail back and forth across the stain once or twice, also absent-mindedly.

"A knife," he murmured. "A bullet wound wouldn't have bled that much—not on *you.* Can you remember a knife? Can you remember holding one? Have you looked—around here?"

I shuddered. "Don't tell me I brought *that* back here with me, too!"

He flipped up both thumbs out of his entwined hands. "After all, you brought the key, didn't you?"

He got up from the bed to look for it around the room. And then he didn't have to—it was there. His getting up had unearthed it.

The bedsprings he'd been pressing down twanged out, settled into place again. Something fell through to the floor with a small, soft thud. Something that had evidently been sheathed between them and the mattress all night.

He picked up a scabbard of tightly folded newspaper with a brown spot or two on it. He opened it—and there it was. With one of those trick blades that spring out of the hilt. Not even cleaned off.

All he said was, "This don't look so good, does it, Tom?"

I stared at it. "I don't even remember slipping it under there. It isn't mine, I never owned it or carried it—" I took a couple of crazy half-turns around the room without getting anywhere. "You haven't told me yet what I'm going to do."

"I'll tell you what you're *not* going to do—you're not going to lam out. You're going to stay right here until we find out just what this thing is." He rewrapped the knife, this time in a large handkerchief of his own. "Here's how it goes. There's a possibility, and a damn good one, that there's some guy stuffed in a closet in some room of some house somewhere in this city at this very minute—and that you killed him last night under the influence of cocaine. Now he's going to be found sooner or later. *But we've got to find him first*—do you get that? We've got to know ahead of time, before it breaks, whether you did kill him or not."

He stepped up and grabbed me hard by the shoulder. "Now

if you did, you're going to take the knock for it. I'm telling you
that here and now. That's the way I play. But if you didn't—"
He opened his hand and let my shoulder go. "We've got to get
to him first, otherwise I'll never be able to clear you."

"I think I did, Denny," I breathed low. "I think I did—but I'm
not sure."

"That's a chance we'll have to take. And I'm pulling for you—
for Mildred's sake, and yours—and even my own. I don't exactly
hate you, you know."

"Thanks, Denny." I gripped hands with him for a minute. "If
it turns out it was me, I'm game, I'm willing to—"

But he had no more time for loving cups. He was on a case
now. He took out an envelope and a pencil stub so worn down
that the lead point practically started right out of the eraser. He
sat down, turned over one foot, and began to use his shoe for a
writing board. He used the back of the envelope to jot on.

"What are you doing?" I asked, half-terrified in spite of myself
by these preliminaries to police activity, even though they were
still confined to my own bedroom.

"I always plot out my line of investigation ahead of time." He
showed me what he'd written.

1. "Joe"
2. Whereabouts of party flat
3. Man with white scar
4. Location of room with singing walls

"See the idea? One leads into the other consecutively. Inter-
locking steps. It'll save a lot of time and energy. 'Joe' gives us
the party flat, the party flat gives us the man with the scar, the
man with the scar gives us the room with the singing walls.
That gives us a closet with a dead man in it you either did or
didn't kill. A lot of dicks I know would try to jump straight from
the starting point to the closet with the body in it. And land
exactly in the middle of nowhere. My way may seem more
roundabout, but it's the surer and quicker way."

He put the envelope away. "Now we disregard everything
else and concentrate on 'Joe' first. Until we've isolated 'Joe,'
none of the other factors exist for us. Now sit down a minute

and just think about 'Joe,' to the exclusion of everything else. His whole connection with it occurred before you were stupefied by that damnable stuff, so it shouldn't be as hard as what comes later."

It shouldn't, but it was.

"You absolutely can't place him, don't know where you'd seen him before?"

"Absolutely not."

"Let me see if I can't build him up for myself, then. What'd he talk about on the way over to this place? You didn't just walk side by side in stony silence."

"No."

"Well gimme some of that. Maybe I can get a line on him from that."

I dredged my mind futilely. Disconnected snatches were all that would come back—it hadn't been an important conversation.

"He said, 'Aw, don't think you're the only one has troubles. Look at me, I'm working but I might just as well not be. A lot I get out of it! Caged up all day for a lousy fifty a week.'"

"And didn't you ask him what his job was?"

"No. He seemed to take it for granted I knew all about him, and I didn't want to hurt his feelings by letting him see I hardly remembered him from Adam. Besides, I didn't particularly care—I had my own worries on my mind."

"Well, is that all he said the whole way over?"

"That's all that amounted to anything. The rest were just irrelevant remarks that people make to one another strolling along the street, like 'Did you see that blonde just passed?' and 'Boy, there's a car I'd like to own!'"

"Let me decide whether they were irrelevant or not," he said impatiently. "I never throw anything away."

"I've given you about all there were. Then when we got to this place, I heard him say, 'Well, here we are,' and he turned in. So I went in after him without particularly noticing where it was. The flat turned out to be on the second floor; it was an elevator building, but the car was in use or something. I remember him saying, 'Come on, let's take the stairs for a change,' and he headed for them without waiting, like he was in a hurry to get up there, so I followed him."

Denny drove fingernails into his hair. "Not much there, is there? Fifty a week. Caged up all day. We'll have to try to figure him out from those two chance remarks. Caged up all day. Bank teller? They get more than that."

"I've never had enough money on me at one time to go near a bank."

"Cashier, maybe, in some cafeteria or diner where you've been going?" He answered that himself before I had a chance to. "No, you've been taking your meals home with us since you're out of work. Not a ticket seller in a movie house—they use girls for that. And you never go to stage shows, where they use men in the box office."

"No," I agreed.

"Caged up all day." He kept saying it over to himself, trying to make it click. "Change booth on the transportation system maybe, on the station you used to use going to work every day?"

"No, I know both the guys on shift there—Callahan and O'Donnell."

"Pawnbroker's clerk, maybe? You've been patronizing them pretty frequently of late, haven't you?"

"Yes, but that's Benny—I know him real well by now."

"I can see where this Joe's going to be a tough nut to crack." He mangled the pinfeathers at the back of his head. "It might have been just an idle expression—it don't have to mean he's actually in a cage, literally behind some sort of bars or wicket. But it's the only lead you've given me on him so far, and I'm blamed if I'm going to pass it up! Are you sure you can't dig up something else, Tommy?"

I couldn't have if my life depended on it. Well, it did in a way, and even so I couldn't. I just eyed him helplessly.

He got tough. Tough with himself, I mean. I guess he always did when something showed signs of getting the better of him. "Well, I'm gonna get it if I sit here in this room until cobwebs form all over me!" he snarled.

He raised his head alertly after a moment. "How'd they act at the door? What'd they say to him at the door?"

"Nothing. He thumped it, and I guess it was opened by whoever happened to be standing closest to it, a visitor there himself, just like we were. He didn't say a word to us, and we didn't say a word to him, just made our way in."

"Pretty free and easy," he grunted. He gnawed at it some more, like a dog with a bone. "You say he was kind of in a hurry to get up there?"

"No, not on the street he didn't seem to be. We just ambled along, the two of us. He took plenty of time. He stopped and looked at some shirts in a window. Then another time he went in a minute and bought a pack of cigarettes."

"But you said—"

"That was after we got in the entrance. Like I said, the elevator was in use, or at least on its way down to us. I remember the little red light over the shaft was lit up and the indicator showed it was already down past the second floor. It would only have taken a minute more for it to reach us, but he didn't seem to want to bother waiting. He said, 'Come on, we'll take the stairs for a change—' "

"That don't make sense. On the street he's not in a hurry, but once in the building he's in too much of a sweat to wait. Either a person's in a hurry to get someplace the *whole* time, or not at all."

Then he uncoiled so suddenly I jumped back from him. "I've got it!" he said. "I got something out of that! See, I told you it never pays to throw away anything." He stabbed his finger at me accusingly, "Your unknown friend Joe is an elevator operator! I'm sure of it. Fifty a week would be right for that. And he wasn't in a hurry when he took the stairs inside that building because he was sick of riding in elevators, glad for an excuse to walk up for a change."

He looked at me hopefully, waiting for my reaction. "Well, does it do anything to you, does it mean anything to you, does it click? *Now* do you place him?" He could tell by my face. "Still don't, eh?" He took a deep breath, settled down for some more digging. "Well, you've evidently ridden up and down in his car with him more than a few times, and he took that to be sufficient basis for an acquaintanceship. Some fellows are that way, without meaning any harm. Then again, some could be that way—meaning plenty of harm. Now, where have you gone more than once or twice where you've had occasion to use an elevator?"

I palmed my forehead hopelessly. "Gosh, I've been in so many office buildings all over town looking for a job, I don't think I've missed one."

Right away he made it seem less hopeless, at least trimmed it down. "But it would have to be a place where you were called back at least a second time, probably talked to him about it riding up to the interview. Were there any?"

"Plenty," I told him grimly.

"Well, here's your part of the assignment—and take it fast, we haven't got a hell of a lot of time, you know. You revisit every such place you can recall being in the past few months, where you *nearly* got a job, had to go back two or three times. Meanwhile, I'm going to get to work on this knife, slip it in at Fingerprints as a personal off-the-record favor, and see just what comes off it, how heavily it counts against you—"

He took out a fountain pen, splattered a couple of drops of ink onto a piece of paper, and made an improvised inkpad by having me stroke it with my fingertips. "Now press down hard on this clean piece, keep them steady. Homemade but effective. I'll make the comparison myself while I'm down there without letting anyone in on it—for the present. I'll probably be back here before you are—I'm going to get sick leave until we've broken this thing down. You call me back here at the house the minute you have any luck with this Joe. And don't take too long, Tom—it's almost midafternoon already. Any minute somebody's liable to step up to a certain closet in a certain house, and try to open it and do something about it when they find it's locked."

I flitted out on that parting warning. He stopped me a minute just as I got the door open and added, "Mildred's out of this, get that straight."

"I should hope so," I said almost resentfully. What did he think I was?

I could remember most of the places I'd been around to fairly recently looking for openings. I mean, the ones where I'd been told to come back, and then when I had somebody else had walked off with the job, anyway. I revisited them one by one.

Some of them were old-fashioned buildings with just one rickety elevator—they were easy to cover. Others were tall, modern structures serviced by triple and quadruple tiers of them, and a starter posted out front to give them the buzzer. In places like that, I had to stand where I could command all the car doors and wait until they'd all opened to reveal the operators' faces. And even then I wasn't satisfied. I'd ask each starter, "Is there anyone named Joe working the cars here?" He might be at home sick or he might be on a later shift.

I always got: "Joe who?"

"Just Joe," I'd have to say. "Joe anybody."

Once I got a Joe Marsala that way, but he turned out to be an undersized, Latin-looking youth, not what I wanted. No sign of the vague, phantom Joe who had, voluntarily or involuntarily, led me into murder.

At five to four, or nearly an hour after I'd left Denny, I finally ran out of places where I could remember having been job hunting. I knew there must have been others, so to make sure of getting them all I went back to the employment agency where I'd been registered for a time to see if a look at their files wouldn't help my memory. I figured they must keep a record of where they sent their applicants, even the unsuccessful ones.

I phoned Denny from there, from a little soft-drink parlor on the ground floor, all winded from excitement. "I got him! I got him! I came back here to the employment agency to get a record of more places where I was sent to—and he was here the whole time! He runs the car right in this building!"

"Has he seen you yet?" he asked briskly.

"No, I got a look at him first, and I figured I better tell you before I—"

"Wait where you are," he ordered. "Don't let him see you until I get down there." I gave him the address and he hung up.

I kept walking back and forth on the sidewalk in front of the entrance to make sure he didn't give me the slip before Denny got there. He couldn't see me from where he was—the elevator was set pretty far back in the lobby. I was plenty steamed up.

Kind of frightened, too. We were a step nearer to murder. A
murder it looked as if I'd done. A murder I was pledged to take
the rap for if it turned out I had.

Denny came fast. "In here?" he said briefly.

"Y-yeah," I stammered. "There's only one car and he's running it right now."

"Stay out here," he said curtly, "I'll go in and get him." I guess
he wanted to catch Joe off-guard, not tip his hand by letting
him see me with him right at the beginning. Then with a
comprehending look at my twitching face muscles, he threw at
me: "Buck up. Don't go all to pieces—too early in the game for
that yet." And went in.

They came out together in about five minutes, after he'd
asked the first few preliminary questions.

It was him, all right. He was in uniform now, and he looked
pretty white and shaky. I guess the shock of the badge hadn't
worn off yet. Denny said, "This your acquaintance?"

"Yeah," I said. I waited to see if he'd deny it. He didn't. He
turned and said to me querulously. "What'd you do, get me in
wrong? I didn't mean nothing by taking you there with me last
night. What happened after I left—was there something swiped
from the place?"

Which was a pretty good out for himself—I didn't have to be
a detective to recognize that. In other words, he was just an
innocent link in the chain of circumstances leading to murder.

If Denny felt that way about it, he didn't show it. He gave him
a shake that started at the shoulder and went rippling down
him like a shimmy. "Cut out the baby stuff, Fraser," he said.
"Now are you going to talk while we're waiting for the van?"
Which was just to throw a scare into him—I hadn't seen him
put in a call for a van since he'd gotten here.

Denny took out an envelope with his free hand and showed
me the back of it. "Sorrell—795—Alcazar, Apt. 2B," he'd pen-
ciled on it. He'd gotten the name and location of the party flat
out of Joe. I didn't know what more he wanted with him. It
seemed he just wanted to find out whether Joe'd been in on
anything or not. "How many times had you been up there
before last night?"

"Only once before."

"How'd you happen to go up there in the first place?"

"My job before this, I was deliveryman for a liquor store near there. I was sent over with a caseful one night, and they were having a big blowout and they invited me in. They're that kind of people—sort of goofy. They used to be in vaudeville. Now they follow the races around from track to track. Half the time they're broke, but every once in a while they make a big killing on some long shot and they go on a spree, hold sort of open house. People take advantage of them, word gets around, don't ask me how, and before they're through they've got people they don't even know crashing in on them."

"But how'd you happen to know there was going to be party last night, when you took this fellow up there with you?"

"I didn't for sure—I just took a chance on it. If there hadn't been anything doing, I would have gone away again. But it turned out they had a bigger mob than ever. They didn't even remember me from the time before, but that didn't make no difference, they told me to make myself at home anyway. They were both kind of stewed by that time."

"You make fifty a week chauffeuring that cracker box in there, right? How much did they charge you up there?"

"I don't get you," Fraser faltered. "They didn't charge me anything. It isn't a place where you pay admission—"

Denny gave him a twist of the arm. "Come on, you knew what they were passing around up there. How were you able to afford it? Did you get yours free for steering newcomers?"

"I don't know what you're talking about—honest I don't," he quavered.

"You didn't know that was a dope flat?"

Joe's consternation was too evident to be anything but genuine. I think even Denny felt that. I thought he was going to cave in for a minute. I never saw a guy get so frightened in my life before.

"Holy smoke!" he exhaled. "I never noticed nothing like that—I saw this girl in green and I took a shine to her, and the two of us blew the place after about fifteen minutes—"

Denny only asked him one more question. "Who was the guy with the white scar?"

"What guy with what white scar? I didn't see no guy with a scar. He musta come in after I left."

Denny took his hand off Joe's shoulder for the first time. He tapped his notebook meaningfully. "You may be telling the truth and you may not. You better pray you were. I know where you work and I've got your home address, and if you've been stringing me I'll know where to find you. Now get back in there and keep your mouth shut."

He turned and skulked into the building, looking back mesmerized over his shoulder at Denny the whole way.

Exit Joe.

We got in a cab. Denny said, "I think he's telling the truth, as far as you can be sure about those things. If he isn't, I can always pick him up fast enough. If I did now, I'd have to book him, and that would bring the whole thing out down at headquarters."

"How'd—how'd the knife come out?" I asked apprehensively.

"Not good for you," he let me know grimly. "Your mitts are all over it. And there's not a sign of anyone else on it. It must have been cleaned off good before it was handed to you. It's going to crack down on the back of your neck like a crowbar when I've finally got to turn it in."

The cab stopped and we were around the corner from the party flat. We got out and headed straight for the entrance without any preliminary casing or inquiring around. We had to. It was four-thirty by now, and the deadline was still on us— only it was shortening all the time. It was a kind of flashy-looking place, the kind that people who lived by horse-betting would pick to live in.

I couldn't help shuddering as we went in the entrance. We were now only two steps away from murder. There remained the man with the scar and the room with the musical walls. Getting closer all the time.

We didn't have any trouble getting in. They seemed to expect anyone at any time of the day and made no bones about opening up. An overripe blonde in a fluffy negligee, eyes still slitted from sleep and last night's rouge still on her face, was waiting for us at the door when we got out of the self-service car. She was shoddy and cheap, yes, but there was something good-natured and likable about her, even at first sight.

"I never know who to expect any more," she greeted us cheerfully. "Somebody parked their gum on the announcer a few weeks ago and you can't hear anything through it ever since. So I just take potluck—"

Denny flashed her the badge. She showed a peculiar sort of dismay at the sight of it. It was dismay, all right, but a resigned, fatalistic kind. She let her hands hang limply down like empty gloves. "Oh, I *knew* something like this was going to happen sooner or later!" she lamented. "I been telling Ed over and over we gotta cut out giving these parties and letting just anyone in. I already lost a valuable fur piece that way last year—"

"Okay if we come in and talk to you?" He had to ask that, I guess, because he had no search warrant.

She stood back readily enough to let us through. The place was a wreck—they hadn't gotten around to cleaning it up yet after the night before. "Is it pretty serious?" she asked nervously. "Who told you about us?"

Denny was trying to trap her, I could see. "Your friend with the scar on his jaw—know who I mean?"

She didn't know, and she seemed on the level about it—as on the level as Joe Fraser had been about not knowing there was dope peddled up here. "I can't place anyone with a scar on his jaw—"

"Are you denying there was a guy with a scar on his jaw up here last night?" Denny said truculently. He had my word for that, and I was sure of that part of it, if nothing else.

"No, there could have been ten guys with scars. All I'm saying is if there was I didn't see him. The excitement was a little too much for me, and I retired about midnight." She meant she'd passed out, I guess. "He may have come in after that. You'd better ask my husband."

She went through the next room and spoke into the one beyond. He was asleep, I guess, and she had to talk loud. "Ed, we're in trouble. You better come out here and answer this man's questions."

Ed came out after her, looking like a scarecrow in a dressing gown. Interest in the races had kept him thin around the middle, if it hadn't prevented his hair from falling out. Denny woke him up with the same question he'd just given her.

"No, I didn't notice anyone with a scar here last night. He might have been here and just happened to have that side of his face turned away from me each time I got a look at him. But even so, he wasn't anyone I know personally. I don't know anyone with a scar."

"Some guy got in here, and you not only didn't know him but didn't even *see* him the whole time he was in your place. What kind of people are you, anyway?"

"Well, that's the way we live, mister. We may be careless, but we have a helluva good time."

Denny scanned him for several uncomfortable minutes. Suddenly he said, "Mind if I look around?"

"No, go ahead." They were both frightened, but in the vague way of people who don't know what to expect next.

I didn't get what Denny was after for a minute. I trailed after him, and they trailed after me. In each room he went into, he only had eyes for the closet—when there was one. Or rather, the keyhole in the closet.

There was only one that didn't have a key sticking out of it.

We got to it finally. It was painted white. It was in a little room at the back, a sort of spare room. My heart started to pick up speed.

It seemed to stand out from the walls, as if it was coated with luminous paint. My eyes almost seemed to be able to pierce it, as though they were X-rays, and make out, huddled on the inside—I looked around in cold, sick fear in the split second that we all stood there grouped in the doorway.

That mission-type table over there—didn't it look like the very one I had upended against the locked closet? That window with the dark shade drawn all the way down to the bottom— "No, you can't get out that way, that's a dead window, blocked with bricks." I didn't have the nerve to step over to it and raise the shade.

Denny had tightened up, too, I could see. He didn't take out the key I'd found on my bureau. Instead he said, "D'you mind unlocking that?"

Right away they both got flustered. They looked at each other helplessly. She said to him, "Where'd we put it *this* time?"

He said, "I dunno, you were the one put it away. I *told* you to pick the same place each time. You keep changing the place, and then we can't find it ourselves."

They both started looking high and low. She explained to Denny, "We call that closet The Safe. When we feel one of these parties coming on, we gather up everything valuable and shove it all in there, and lock it up till it's over."

Denny didn't look convinced or relenting. I was leaning against the door frame—I needed support.

"It's all our own stuff," she said.

He gave her the stony eye.

The harder they looked, the more flustered they got. I kept wondering why he didn't take out the key and try to fit it in. Why did he have to torture me this way? My chest was pounding like a dynamo.

Was he in there, whoever he was? Would he topple out on us when it was opened finally? But if they'd known about it, they would have smuggled him out long ago, wouldn't they? Or else beat it away from here themselves? Or suppose they hadn't known about it themselves and still didn't? That wouldn't make me any less guilty.

The Sorrell woman suddenly gave a yelp of triumph from the direction of the bedroom, where the ever-widening search had led her. She came running in with it, holding it up between her fingers. You could hardly distinguish what it was—it was all clotted with some white substance. "I hid it in my cold-cream tin."

Denny wouldn't let her get over to the keyhole with it. He took the key, inserted it himself, gave it a twist, and the door swung out. Furs, silverware, luggage—everything that predatory guests might have made off with was piled up inside.

But no dead bodies.

I had to sit down for a minute—I felt weak all over.

"It's all our own stuff," the woman said for the third or fourth time. "Did somebody tell you we had something in there didn't belong to us?"

"No, just an idea of mine," Denny said quietly. He handed the key back and turned away.

It was dusk when we left the Sorrell apartment. All day someone had lain murdered in a closet and we were no nearer to knowing where. And now it was night again.

We stood down on the street outside the place not knowing where to go now. There was a gap. The first step had led into the second, but the second had led into a vacuum.

"Well, my way didn't pay off," Denny said glumly. "The thing's broken in two." He turned and looked up at the lighted windows behind us. "And I'm inclined to give the Sorrells the benefit of the doubt. I don't think they really know this man with the scar. I don't think they really noticed him in their place last night. I don't think they realized anyone had cocaine on him and passed some to you. I *have* to give them the benefit of the doubt—for the present. I can't go after it the way I would ordinarily—have them watched, check their movements, track down as many people as I can who were at the party in hope of getting a line on him. We haven't got time. We'll have to jump the gap blindfolded and try for the third foothold—the room with the singing walls."

We passed a cigar store and Denny went in, stepped inside the phone booth. I figured it was to headquarters, without his telling me so. It was. He came back and said, "Well, our margin of safety still holds—they haven't found him yet. I checked on all reported homicides and there's no one been turned up stabbed in a closet." He gave me a look. "But that don't mean there's no one in a closet still waiting to be turned up. We've got to hustle."

Sure we did—but where?

"Can you remember leaving here at all?"

"No, there's a complete blank. The next I knew was the room with the singing walls. Scarface reappeared in that sequence, so I must have left with him—he must have taken me there from here."

"But that don't tell us where it is."

It was strangely topsy-turvy, this thing. Ordinarily they get the murdered remains first, have to go out and look for the murderer. In this case, he had the murderer at hand from the beginning and couldn't find out where the remains were. Even the murderer couldn't help him.

"About those so-called singing walls. Was it a radio or television you heard through them?"

"No, I'm pretty sure it wasn't. There wasn't a scrap of human voice or of station announcement in between. If I was able to distinguish the tunes clearly enough to recognize them, I'd have been able to hear the announcer, too, wouldn't I? And there's at least a title given between numbers on any radio or television program."

"You can't remember how you got there? Not even the vaguest recollection? Whether it was on foot, or in a cab, or in a car with him, or by bus?"

"No—any more than I can remember how I got away after—wait!" I broke off suddenly.

"Which is it?" he pounced.

"I just remembered a little detail I didn't tell you before. I wonder if it's any good to you or not."

"I told you I never throw anything away. Let me have it."

"I either spent or lost ten cents sometime during the course of the night. When I met Fraser on the street, I had thirty-five cents in my pocket. I can remember standing there jingling it just before he came up to me. This morning there was only twenty-five cents on my bureau. I was out a dime. D'you think I spent it making my way home—from wherever this was?"

He liked that right away, I could see. "It could be a yardstick, to measure just how far out this place was, if nothing else. It don't give us the direction, but it might give us the approximate distance. Can you remember making your way back at all?"

"Yeah, partly—only the opening stages, though. I remember slinking along, hugging walls and doorways, scared stiff. I don't remember what part of town I was in, though. And then the curtain came down again, and I don't remember how I finally got back."

"What kind of coins was this thirty-five cents in, when you had it last night—can you remember that?"

"Easily—I counted it over enough times. Three nickels and

two dimes. And this morning there were only the three nickels and a dime left."

"That's important," he said. "That fact that the three nickels were carried over eliminates the possibility that you paid a fifteen-cent fare. If you paid any fare at all, you paid an exact ten cents. It's still possible you lost the dime, of course, but we can't let that stop us. If you spend a dime fare, that eliminates taxis. The bus system here runs on a mileage basis, you know that. Ten cents for a certain distance, then fifteen, and so on. This missing dime seems to show you boarded an inbound bus at some point within the ten-cent zone and rode in toward our place.

"D'you see what I'm driving at? We're looking for someplace in that ten-cent zone where there's music playing late at night, until two or three in the morning. And not a radio or television—either a real band or a phonograph that changes its own records by automatic control. Some roadhouse or resort or even just a hole-in-the-wall taproom. And then we're looking for a room right upstairs over it, or right next door to it, with a partition wall so thin it lets this music come whispering through. There's our problem."

"But it seemed to me I did a lot of this running away on foot first—my starting point might have been quite a distance off from this ten-cent bus zone."

"It seemed that way. I doubt you did in your condition. Narcotics distort your time sense, for one thing. Just down the block and around a couple of corners to you might have seemed like an endless flight that went on for hours. Then again, of course, you may be right about it—I wasn't on your feet. The only way we'll find out is to put it to the proof . . ."

There were two bus lines that passed the immediate neighborhood our own flat was in—the Fairview line and one that went out to the municipal beach at Duck Island. The routes were parallel this far in—they only diverged farther out. The double route was two blocks over from our place.

"We'll take whichever one comes along first," he said while we stood waiting.

A Fairview one drove into sight first—outward bound, of course. We got on and he said, "Two ten-cent fares." Then he stood behind the driver's back and, company regulations to the contrary, asked, "How many stops do you make in the ten-cent zone?" They ran on fixed stops.

"Only three." He gave us the intersection names. "After that, it jumps to fifteen."

"Well, offhand, could you mention any inns or dance joints out that way, where the music plays late?"

"Try Dixie Trixie's—that's just outside the city limits."

Denny cut him short. "No, I'm asking about the ten-cent zone, between Continental and Empire Road."

"Naw, I don't think you'll find many around there—one or two honkytonks maybe."

"We'll have to do our own scouting them," Denny said to me. He led the way back to a seat and swore bitterly under his breath, "We'll be at it all night."

We got out at Continental, the first ten-cent stop, and he did a little surveying before we moved off the bus route. The task before us wasn't as bad as it had threatened to be at first. It was no cinch by any means, but at least he was able to put physical limits to the terrain we had to finecomb.

The bus stops were eight blocks apart. A railroad embankment walled us off six blocks to the left and a large park with a lake in it dead-ended the streets four blocks over the other way. He divided the difference between the two bus stops, multiplied it by ten crosswise blocks, and that gave us forty square blocks to canvass for each bus stop.

Naturally, it wasn't a question of going into every doorway of every building along those forty blocks—that would have still been pretty much of a physical impossibility. A cop on the beat here, a storekeeper there was able to speed us through by listing the places in his immediate vicinity that provided music late at night. That way we sometimes only had to make one stop in five or six blocks. We investigated several bars that had coin phonographs, but none had all four of the selections that I'd remembered hearing in their repertoire.

We went back and boarded the bus, rode one stop ahead, and started the whole thing over. Same lack of results.

The closest we got to anything in this sector was when the harness cop told us there had been a lot of complaints about a

Polish family playing their phonograph late at nights with all the stops out. But they didn't play any of the records we were looking for.

We went back, caught another bus, got out at the third and last ten-cent stop, and finished the chore out. That fizzled, too. We limped aboard an in-bound bus and rode back to where the Duck Island line diverged from this one. The thought of going through the same routine all over again, on a new bus route, was more than we could face without a breathing spell.

We dragged ourselves into the nearest resting place we could find, which happened to be a diner, and just sat there slumped over the counter, too tired even to hold our backs up straight, chins nearly dunked in our coffee cups, talking it over in low voices so the counterman wouldn't overhear us.

"Even if I wanted to take you down with me and report it— and I don't, God knows—I couldn't until we've found out where it happened. They'd have to have that. And the longer it takes and the colder it gets, the harder it's going to be to clear you." He looked down at the wax-white, trembling hand I'd suddenly braked on his arm. "What is it?"

"Did you hear that, just then?"

He turned and looked over at the wire-mesh loudspeaker set on a low shelf near the coffee boiler.

"They just got through playing 'Alice Blue Gown' and now—"

He didn't get me for a minute. "But this diner's in the middle of a vacant plot—you saw that when we came in. There aren't any adjoining—"

"No, no, you haven't been paying attention to the program. I have. They got through 'Alice Blue Gown' a minute or two ago—now they've gone into 'Out on a Limb.' Listen—hear it? That's the same order I heard them in last night."

"That's just a coincidence. There must be a thousand bands all over the country playing those two pieces day and night."

"The third one'll tell. The third one was 'Oh, Johnny.'" I could hardly wait for it to end. It never seemed to—it seemed to go on forever. I balled a fist and beat it into the hollow of my hand to hurry it up. He sat there straining his ears, too. His back was held a little straighter now.

It wound up finally and there was a short pause. Then the

tune itself. I grabbed him with both hands this time, nearly toppled him off the tall stool he was perched on. " 'Oh, Johnny'! That's not a coincidence any more. That's the same sequence I heard them in last night! That's the same band!"

"But I thought you said it wasn't a broadcast, that you heard no station announcements. This is."

"But there are no station announcements on this, either—it's evidently a program that only makes one every five or six numbers. I still don't think it was a broadcast—this isn't the same hour I heard them, and they wouldn't broadcast twice in one night. Maybe they broadcast first, and then play in person somewhere later on—"

The "Woodpecker Song" had started in. I turned around to tell him that, not sure if he knew tunes by ear as well as I did, but he'd had enough—the stool next to me was empty and he was already over at the pay phone on the wall. His coin chimed in along with the opening notes.

"What station you tuned at?" he called out. The counterman read the dial, gave him some hick station I'd never heard of before. He got its studio number from Information.

"Who's that you got going out over the air now? Bobby Leonard's Band? Find out where they work from about one to three or four every night—hurry it up, it's important. No, I can't wait until they're through broadcasting, this is police business. Write the question on a slip of paper and hand it in right where they are now."

He had to wait until the answer was relayed back, evidently scribbled on the same piece of paper.

"The Silver Slipper, out on Brandon Drive." He hung up, bounced a coin on the counter, and ran out. We'd both stopped being tired, like magic.

"It's all the way over on the other side of town," he said to me in the cab. "God only knows how you found your way back to our place. It shows you what a wonderful thing the subconscious is, even under the influence of a drug."

We got to it in about twenty minutes, paid off the cab, and stood sizing it up. It was mostly glass, you could look in on three sides—it had a glass roof that could be pushed back in

fine weather so they could dance under the open sky. The
fourth wall was solid masonry. Only a scattered couple or two
were dancing. They evidently used a radio to provide the
incidental music until this Leonard and his band came over and
did a lick later on.

He snapped his head around to me. "Familiar?"

I shook mine. "Not a flicker of it comes back to me."

On the fourth side it backed against two buildings, which in
turn were set back to back, each one facing a different street.
We cased them both from their respective corners. One was a
trim two-story cement garage that looked as if it had only
recently been put up. The other was a sort of rundown lodging
house with a milky lighted globe shining down over its doorway. It was the obvious choice of the two—garages don't have
closets. Nor furniture to pile up in front of them, either.

We went in.

It couldn't have been dignified by the name hotel. The "desk"
was just a hinged flap across an alcove, within which sat a man
in shirtsleeves reading a paper under a light.

One good thing, there was no question of a bellboy showing
you up and looking on. You paid your fifty cents, you got a key,
and you found your own way up. We didn't want any witnesses—if it was in here.

He didn't even bother looking up at us, just heard the double
tread come in and asked: "Two-in-one or two singles?"

Denny said, "How many rooms you got here that back up
against that place next door? We like to fall asleep to music."

Even that didn't get a rise out of him—he expected anything
and everything.

"One on a floor. Three floors—that makes three altogether.
I've got someone in the one on the second, though."

So that was the one. My stomach gave a sort of half-turn to
the right, and then back again.

Denny said, "D'you have to sign in here?"

"You got to put down something when you pick up your
key—you can't just walk in." Meaning a place like this didn't
expect right names and didn't care if it got them.

"Let's see what was signed for that one you got taken on the
second."

"What's all this to you?" But he was still too indifferent to be properly resentful about it.

"We might know the guy."

We did. One of them, anyway. It was a double entry. The cocaine had vibrated my handwriting like an earthquake, but I could still recognize it. *Tom Cochrane, 2228 Foster Street.* For once they'd gotten a right name and a right address. It was probably the only one in the whole ledger—and it had signed for murder!

The second name, also in my handwriting, was *Ben Doyle.* No address given, just a wavy line. So I'd signed in for someone else, too.

We just looked at each other. Then at him. Or rather, Denny did. I was afraid to.

"Were you here when this was signed?"

This time he did get annoyed, because the question touched him personally. "Naw, I got off at twelve. Don'tcha think I gotta sleep sometime, too?" That explained, at least, why he didn't recognize me. But not why it hadn't been found out yet.

"D'you give any kind of service here? Don't you send someone in to clean these rooms in the daytime?"

He got more annoyed. "What d'ya think this is, the Ritz? When a room's vacated, the handyman goes in and straightens up the bed. Until it is we leave it alone, for as long as it's been paid for." I must have paid for this one for two days in advance, double occupancy—there was the entry "$2" after the two names. But I hadn't had two dollars on me—I'd only had thirty-five cents.

"What's all this talk about? Do you two guys want a room or don't you?" We did, but we wanted that second-floor room that already had "someone" in it. Denny obviously didn't want to use his badge to force him to open it up for us—that would have meant a witness to the revelation that was bound to follow immediately afterward, and automatic police notification before he had a chance to do anything for me, if there was anything he *could* do.

"Give us the third-floor one," he said, and put down a dollar bill. The man hitched down a key with a ponderous enamel tag from the rows where they hung. The one immediately below was missing. The "occupant" still had it. If I'd taken it away with me, I must have lost it in the course of that mad flight through the shadows. Only the closet key had turned up at our place this morning.

Denny, with unconscious humor, scrawled "Smith Bros." in the registry and we started up the narrow staircase. He turned aside when we got to the second floor, motioned me to keep on climbing. "Scuffle your feet to cover me—I'm going to try to force the other door open."

I shuffled my way up step by step, trying to sound like the two of us while I heard him faintly tinkering at the lock with some implement. I unlocked the one we'd hired on the floor above, put on the light, and looked in. Yes, there was something vaguely familiar about it—this was the end of the trail, all right. The closet in this one had a key in it and had been left slightly ajar by the last occupant.

I crept back to the stairs and listened. The tinkering had stopped, so he must have forced the door. A curt "Sst!" sounded, meant for me. I eased down one flight.

The light from inside was shining out across the grubby passage. A half section of his face showed past the door frame, waiting for me, then it withdrew. I made my way inside, moving slow, breathing fast.

It was the right room.

He'd already taken down the stuff I'd barricaded the closet door with—a table, a chair, even a mattress.

He sighed to me and I closed the door behind me. He gave the closet key I'd turned over to him a fatalistic flip-up in the hollow of his hand. "Here goes," he said. I got a grip on the back of a chair and hung on tight.

He fitted it into the lock. It went in like silk and turned the lock without a hitch. It couldn't have worked easier. It belonged here. I said a fast prayer—that was all there was time for. "Make it turn out it was somebody else who did it!"

Denny's body gave a hitch and there was no more time for praying. He'd caught it against him as it swayed out with the closet door.

It must have been semi-upright behind it the whole time. I

hadn't done a good job propping—it must have shifted over against the door instead of staying against the wall behind, and the way the knees were buckled kept it from toppling over sideways.

He let it down to the floor. It stayed in a cockeyed position from the way it had been jammed in. It was stiff as tree bark. He turned it over on its back, made me come over.

"Remember him? Take a good look now. Remember him?"

"Yeah," I said, dry-lipped.

"Remember him *alive*, that's what I mean."

"No. I only remember him lying there, only not so shriveled—" I backed away, nearly fell over a chair.

"Pull yourself together, kid," he said. "This is something they'd have put you through, anyway. It's a lot easier just with me in the room with you."

He disarranged the clothing, peered down. "Sure, a knife did it," he nodded. "Three bad gashes—one in the stomach, one between the ribs, and one that looks like it must have grazed the heart."

He looked at the belt buckle. "B.D.," he murmured. "What was that name down there—Ben Doyle?"

He started going through pockets. "No, he's been cleaned out. But the name checks with those initials, all right."

He drew back a little. I saw him scanning the corpse's upturned soles. "He did a lot of walking, didn't he?" The bottom layer of each was worn through in a round spot the size of a silver dollar. "But the heels are new, not worn down at all. What'd he do, walk around on tiptoes?"

He took something from his pocket and started to reverse a small screw that protruded like a nailhead. Then he pulled and the whole heel came off. It was hollow. Three or four folded paper packets lay inside.

He opened one into the shape of a little paper boat. I didn't have to be told. I'd seen that white stuff before.

"He was a peddler," he said. "But he wasn't the guy that contacted you at the party. Where does he come in it? I wonder if Narcotics have heard of this guy before, can give me anything on him. I'm going to check with headquarters."

Before he went out, he crossed to the window and raised the

dark shade that shrouded it. The pane behind it was also painted dark—a dark green. You could see the heads of heavy six-inch nails studded all along the frame, riveting it down. Even so, he took that same screwdriver from his pocket and scraped away a tiny gash on the dried-paint surface. Then he held a lighted match close up to it.

"Solid brick backed up to it," he commented. He started for the door. "You're down on their blotter for this room—and in your own handwriting—along with this dead guy. I want to find out if he was seen coming here with you. Or if it was the guy with the scar. Or both. Or neither. I gotta dig up that other slouch that was in charge of the key rack here from midnight to morning—he's the only one can answer all those things."

I started out after him. I couldn't help it. I couldn't have stayed in there alone for a million dollars.

"All right, go back and wait in the one over this, if it gets you," he consented. He closed the door on the grisly sight. "But keep your eyes and ears open—make sure no one gets in here until we're ready to break it ourselves." He went down and I went up.

I didn't know how long to give him, but pretty soon it seemed to be taking longer than it should have. Pretty soon the room up there started to get me just as bad as though I'd stayed down below. Try hanging around when you know there's a dead body under your feet in the room below, a body you're to blame for, and you'll know what I mean.

The band showed up for work next door while I was in there, and instead of making it better it made it worse. It nearly drove me nuts, that whispered music coming through the walls—it brought last night back too vividly again.

Finally I couldn't stand it another minute, I had to get out, wait for him down by the street entrance. I almost lunged for the door, a cold panic on me. I got it open, poked the bilious light out—

Then I saw something in the darkness behind me. Something that made me hold the door at half closing point and stand there on the threshold.

It should have been pitch-black behind me in there now—

the place only had a dead window—but it wasn't. A late moon must have come up since we'd been in here. Three phantom silvery lines stood out around the drawn shade like a faint tracing of phosphorous. There was moonlight backing it, only visible now that the room light was out.

My panic evaporated. I went back in again, leaving it dark. I crossed to the shade and shot it up. Moonlight flashed at me through the dust-filmed glass. There was no brickwork, no dark paint blanking out the windows on this floor. Denny hadn't been up here at all or we might have found that out sooner. The garage was only two stories high, the rooming house three—that was a detail that had escaped our attention until now.

The frame wasn't nailed. I lifted it and it went up. The garage roof was a bare four feet below me, plenty accessible enough to—But the fact remained that the body hadn't been in this room but in the one below, where the window *was* blocked.

I scanned the roof. It looked like an expanse of grey sand under me. In the middle of it, though, there was dim light peering up through some sort of skylight or ventilator.

I didn't have any theory—I didn't know what I thought I'd find out or what I hoped I'd find out. I just went ahead on instinct alone. I sidled across the sill and planted my legs on the graveled roof. I started to pick my way carefully over toward that skylight, trying not to sound the gravel.

I got to the perimeter of it, crouched down on hands and knees, peered over the edge and down. Nothing. Just the cement garage floor two stories below, and a mechanic in greasy overalls down there wiping off a car with a handful of waste. No way to get up, no way to get down—except head-first.

I straightened up, skirted it, eased on. I took a look down over the front edge of the roof. Just the unbroken cement front of the garage—a fly couldn't have managed it. I went around to the side, the one way from the Silver Slipper. There was a narrow chasm there, left between the garage and some taller warehouse next door. And midway down that there *was* something—a pale, watery yellow reflection cast on the warehouse wall by some opening in the garage wall directly under me, at second-floor level. And more to the point still, a sort of rickety iron Jacob's ladder leading down to it. I could only see this at its starting point up where I was—the darkness swallowed the rest of it.

I swung out on it, tested it with one foot. Narrow rungs. It seemed firm enough. I started down very slowly. It was like going down into a bottle of ink. The reflection of the lighted square came up and bathed my feet. The ladder didn't go any lower—it ended in a level "stage" of iron slats no wider than the window.

I tucked my feet in under the last downward rung so they wouldn't show in the light and leaned out above them, gripping a rung higher up backhand. It was a grotesque position. I slanted my head forward and peered into the lighted square.

It was an office connected with the garage. There were filing cabinets against the wall, a large flat-topped desk with a cone light over it. There was a man sitting there at it, talking to two others. Or rather going over some accounts with them. He was checking some sort of list on a sheet of paper he held.

There was money on the desk, lots of it—more money than any garage like this would take in in a month. It was separated into several stacks. As he finished checking one list, he'd riff through one stack, rapidly and deftly thumb-counting it, then snap an elastic around it and move it over to the other. Then he'd begin on a second list.

There was something vaguely familiar about the shape of his head, even seen from the back, and the cut of his shoulders. The other two I'd never seen before, I was sure of that. One was sitting negligently on an outside corner of the desk, the other standing up against it, hands deep in his pockets. They looked too well dressed to be hanging around the upstairs room of a garage.

I must have taken too much time to size them up. After all, a paring of a face is just as conspicuous against a blackout window as a full face would be. I didn't even see the signal passed, nor which of the two gave it. Suddenly the checkmaster had twirled around on his swivel chair and was staring out at me eye to eye.

That white scar along the underside of his jaw stood out as

visibly as a strip of court plaster. So there he was at last, the diabolus ex machina.

My position on the ladder was too complicated to make for a streamlined getaway, I had too many things to do simultaneously. I had to extricate my tucked-in feet and make a complete body-turn to face the ladder before I could start up. Even then, I missed a rung in my hurry, jolted down half a foot, and hit my chin on one of the upper ones. By that time the window had flashed up and a powerful grip had me around the ankle.

I was torn off the ladder, dragged in feet-first, and the only thing that saved my skull from cracking in the bounce from windowsill to floor was that it bedded against one of their bodies. I lay flat for a minute and their three faces glowered down at me. One of them backed a foot and found my ribs. The pain seemed to shoot all the way through to the other side.

Then I was dragged up again and stood on my own feet. One of them had a gun bared, brief as the onslaught had been.

The man with the scarred jaw rasped, "He's the patsy I used last night I toldje about!"

"There goes your whole setup, Graz!" the third one spat disgustedly.

The man with the scar they called Graz looked at me vengefully. His whole face was so livid with rage it now matched the weal. "What the hell, it still holds good! He was one of Doyle's customers. Doyle cut off his supply, so he knifed him!"

"Yeah, but he ain't up there in the room with him any more."

"All right, he come to, lammed out through a third-floor window. He'll be found dead by his own hand in Woodside Park when morning comes. What's the difference? It changes it a little, but not much. It's still him all the way through. Him and Doyle took the room together to make a deal. He was seen going in where Doyle'll be found. And you know how snow-birds act when they've got the crave on and are cut off. There's a lake there in Woodside. We're gonna dunk his head in it and hold it there until his troubles are over. Then throw the rest of him in. How they gonna tell the difference afterwards?"

"Suppose Doyle had already sang a note or two to the police, mentioning names, before you—"

"He didn't sing nothing—I stopped him before he had a

chance to. The minute I seen that narcotics dick beginning to
cultivate him, I cut out his tonsils. An operation like that in
time saves nine. Come on, let's get started." He gathered up the
money and lists from the desk. "And another thing," he added,
"we're giving this joint up—it's no good to us any more. We're
coming back as soon as we ditch this punk and move out all
them filing cabinets, tonight!"

His two subordinates wedged me up between them. He put
out the light behind us, and the four of us started down a
cement inner stair to the main floor of the garage. "Run out the
big black one, Joe," one of them said to the grease monkey I'd
seen through the skylight, "we're going out for a little air."

He brought out a big sedan, climbed down, and turned it
over to them. He must have been one of them, used for a front
on the main floor—they didn't try to conceal my captivity from
him.

They shoved me into it. It was like getting into a hearse. I
didn't say a word. Denny would come back to that room too
late. He wouldn't know what happened to me—he'd start
looking for me all over town and I'd be lying at the bottom of
the lake.

Graz and one of his two underlings got in with me and the
other one took the wheel. We glided down the cement ramp
toward the open street beyond. Just as our fenders cleared the
garage entrance, a taxi came to a dead stop at the curb directly
before us, effectively walling us in. The way it had crept forward
it seemed to have come from only a few yards away, as though
it had been poised waiting there. I saw the driver jump down
on the outside and run for his life across the street and around
the corner. The sedan's furious horntattoo failed to halt his
flight.

The big car they had me in was awkwardly stuck there, on
the slant, just short of the entrance. It couldn't go forward on
account of the abandoned cab, it couldn't detour around it on
account of its own length of chassis, and the mechanic had sent
down a sort of fireproof inner portcullis behind us, without
waiting, keeping us from backing up.

They weren't given much time for the implications of the
predicament to dawn on them. Denny suddenly straightened

up just outside the rear window on one side and balanced a gun over its rim. The precinct harness cop did the same on the opposite side. They had them between a threat of crossfire.

Denny said, "Touch the ceiling and swing out, one on each side."

But he and the cop couldn't control the man at the wheel—he was a little too far forward and they were wedged in too close. I saw his shoulder give a slight warning dip against the dashboard as he reached for something. I buckled one leg, knee to chin, and shot the flat of my shoe square against the back of his head. His face slammed down into the wheel. He didn't want to reach for any more guns after that.

It took a little while to marshal them back upstairs and send in word to headquarters and clean out the files and all the other evidence around the garage. They found traces of blood on the cement inner stairs, showing where Doyle had been knifed as he was trying to escape from the death interview with Scarjaw, kingpin of the dope ring.

Denny said to me while we were waiting: "A guy in Narcotics recognized this Doyle right away, even from the little I was able to give them over the phone. They'd picked him up several times already, and they were trying to dicker with him to get the names of the guys he worked for. When I got back to the room, that open window on the third tipped me off which way you'd gone.

"From what Officer Kelly here finished telling me a little while before, I figured there was something fishy about this garage. He'd seen people drive up at certain hours to try to have their cars serviced and they'd be turned away—and yet it was never particularly full of cars. I figured the smart thing to do was arrange a little reception committee at the street entrance, where they weren't expecting it."

The final word, however, wasn't said until several hours later. He came out of the back room at headquarters, near daylight, and came over to where I'd been waiting. "You didn't do it, Tom. It's official now, if that'll make you feel any better. We've been questioning them in relays ever since we brought them in and we just finished getting it all down."

He waved a set of typed sheets at me. "Here's how it goes. Graz and his two lieutenants killed Doyle in the garage about midnight last night just around the time you were arriving at the Sorrells' party with Frazer. That rooming house had already come in handy to them once or twice—it's got a vicious name on the police records—so they used it again, for a sort of dumping ground.

"Graz sent one of his stooges around and had him take a room on the third floor, within easy access of the garage roof. That was just to obtain a convenient back way in. They smuggled the body across the roof and passed it in to the stooge through the window. But this stooge wasn't supposed to take a murder rap, he was just acting as middleman. Graz himself went out looking for the real stooge, the stooge for murder—and that turned out to be you.

"Graz had been to those dizzy parties of the Sorrells before, so he knew all about them. He went there last night, picked you out, got you higher than a kite, brought you over to the rooming house in his car. He saw to it you were given a room on the second floor, directly under the one where the body lay waiting for transfer. Not only that, he had you sign for it, for yourself *and for Doyle*, who was already dead. Doyle was supposed to be along in a minute or two.

"He got rid of the fellow in charge of the keys by sending him next door to the Silver Slipper for some coffee to sober you up. By the time he got back with it, Doyle was already supposed to have shown up. The original stooge on the third floor spoke loudly to you to show there was somebody up there in the room with you. Graz said, "His friend's up there with him now—he'll be all right, so I'll shove off.'

"Doyle *had* shown up, but in a different way. They'd carried him down the stairs from the third-floor room to your room with the bricked-up window. They wiped off the knife handle and planted it on you. They smeared your shirt front with Doyle's blood. You were dazed, in no condition to notice anything that went on around you. Graz was careful to carry the coffee up only to the door, pass it in to you, come right down again, and leave. Doyle's 'voice' still sounded up there with you in the room, for the fellow at the key rack to hear.

"You were given another whiff of coke to hold you steady for a while. Then the original stooge came down, presumably from the third floor, handed in his key, and checked out.

"You were left there drugged, with a murdered man in your room, his blood on your shirt, the knife that had been used concealed on your person in newspaper. You even helped the scheme out up to a point—you got the horrors, hid the body in the closet, locked it, and piled everything movable you could lay your hands on up against the door. Then you fled for your life.

"You got a small break that wouldn't have helped out in the end. The guy at the key rack must have been either dozing or out of his alcove again. I spoke to him just now, and he never saw you leave. That postponed discovery, but wouldn't have altered anything.

"As I said, the subconscious is a great thing. In all your terror, and stupefied as you were, you somehow found your way back to where you lived. You didn't wake up in the same room with the dead man, the way they were counting on your doing, and raise an outcry, and thereby sew yourself up then and there. You had a chance to talk it over with me first. We had a chance to put our heads together without you being in the middle of it."

It was getting light when we got back to our own place. The last thing I said to him, outside the door, was: "Tell the truth, Denny—up to the time it broke, did you really figure I did it?"

His answer surprised me more than anything else about the whole thing. "Hell, yes!" he said. "I would have eaten my hat that you did!"

"I did, too," I had to admit. "In fact, I was sure of it."